STERLING

A Mageri Series Novel
Book 1

DANNIKA DARK

Also By Dannika Dark:

THE MAGERI SERIES
Sterling
Twist
Impulse
Gravity
Shine

NOVELLAS
Closer

THE SEVEN SERIES
Seven Years
Six Months

"Courage is the power to let go of the familiar."
—Raymond Lindquist

PREFACE

D YING ISN'T THE HARDEST THING you'll ever do—living is. There are many choices that determine the direction of your life, but death only has one outcome. At least, that's what I used to believe.

Fate changes with every single decision made: right turn instead of left, yes instead of no, chocolate instead of vanilla, or taking the shortcut.

I can't admit to doing anything remarkable on the last day of my life.

But then, can anyone?

They say (whoever "they" are) that you should live each day like it's your last. In my former life, I would have thought that was a true statement. Go out swinging, throw caution to the wind, and break all the rules.

I've learned something far more valuable since I was given a second life, a second chance, and a new beginning—live each day of your life like it is your first.

I was born Zoë Winter Merrick.

If names hold meaning then perhaps my fate was sealed from the beginning. Zoë means life, Winter represents death, and my surname means fame and power.

Fate is not without a sense of humor after all.

Merrick was my surname, but not my last name. Rebirth has a funny way of starting things anew.

CHAPTER 1

A BLACK PANTHER LAPPED HIS ROUGH tongue across my cheek. Max wasn't actually a panther, just a house cat with a massive ego. When the only tongue you're getting is from your cat… it's time to get out more.

"Someone's hungry," I observed. "Do you want some tuna?"

Did I spoil my cat every night with a can of tuna on top of his food? Guilty.

Max extended his front claws and I flinched when they poked through my grey shirt. A quick shove to the floor solved that problem.

Six years ago when I was between jobs and going through a rough patch, I adopted Max. He was abused and needed special care, as did I. There was a grim chance that Max would be blind, but that didn't stop the affection I felt for him. He needed me, and in a strange way, I needed him too. When the bandages were removed, it was a miracle—Max could see. But what I didn't know was that my little panther had what the guys in spiffy white jackets like to call heterochromia. Mismatched eyes are what they really meant to say. I never understood the significance of medical jargon. Call it a bum liver, bad ticker, even the evil little bump—but for god's sake, make it *understandable.*

My friends were put off with that stare—one green eye and one yellow—but I loved him for being unique.

Eventually, Max grew into a seventeen-pound badass, but he also deserved recognition for his services as an alarm clock and a foot warmer. Not that I needed much foot warming in a southern climate, but his efforts were appreciated.

The room was eerily silent, the kind of quiet that makes you wonder if the rest of the world existed anymore. The tips of the leaves on my bamboo plant glowed from the light creeping through the wood shutters. My apartment was small, but it surrounded me like a warm security blanket. A stream of rainbows slanted across the coffee table from a crystal hanging on the window, telling me it was late afternoon.

When the cordless phone went off I jumped, giving the flashing blue light on the coffee table a nasty scowl.

"Hello?" I answered, rubbing my eyes.

"Zoë, girl! Rise and shine," a female voice giggled.

"Sunny, friend of my loins, what can I do for you?" I was irritable and needed to shower after spending all day attached to my sofa.

Sunny was my best friend and partner in crime. I could tell she was in better than usual spirits—the kind that meant I was going to be ass-deep in Saturday-night mischief.

"Uh, I don't think I want to be that friendly with your loins. I know you aren't asleep on that couch because I'm coming by in an hour. My car is finally out of the shop, *thank God*. That chucklehead robbed me blind after holding it hostage for three weeks. Seriously, Zoë, I'm going to have to sell my firstborn to pay him and I don't even want kids."

I craned my neck and squinted at the clock. Jesus, I slept for *five* hours. My afternoon nap had turned into a full-on coma.

"Sunny, I don't know about tonight. I worked late last night and I'm not the best company at the moment," I protested.

Which was true. Sunny was a flirtaholic and after watching a depressing romance movie that day, I was not in the mood to be charming.

"No four-letter words allowed on a Saturday, not unless they involve acts beneath the sheets."

The one thing we never discussed when we went out—or tried not to—was work. Nothing kills an evening like a fifteen-minute recap on how the toner cartridge from the printer exploded on your hand. Those stories were reserved for our phone conversations.

"Unless you have a man over there—which I'm sure you don't—I'm coming to get you. And on second thought, if you do have man over there, then I'm *still* coming over. Some miracles are worth seeing. I know you've heard me say it a million times but you need to put yourself out there. Brandon was a royal ass, but you deserve someone who can appreciate your finely sharpened wit."

"I wouldn't want to put out anyone's eye with my wit." Not wanting to discuss that particular subject, I switched gears. "I take it I'm paying?"

"That, my dear girl, is the most fabulous part of all. Tonight it's on the house."

"Whose house?"

"Finnegan's. Anything we want. That means food and drink, free of charge."

"How did you swing that, Sunshine?"

I dragged my stubborn feet to the floor, praying she had not slipped into the dark and lurid world of prostituting for rib eye.

"I have my sources. In fact," she said in a voice edged with secrets, "I want you to meet my source. You met him once before—remember Marco?"

"Marco…"

I had to give it some thought. Sunny tried men like flavors of ice cream. I heard a short stubborn sigh on the other line and smiled.

"At Finnegan's—he came over and I introduced you. Italian, tall, sexy accent?" She paused in irritation. "Mother of God, you spilled your beer on his lap."

"Oh, Marco! Sure, I remember. Just how are his pants these days? I'm assuming you've been in them."

"Ha ha."

"So why the reintroduction?" Sunny was never evasive; this was a girl who could talk nonstop about her trip to the nail salon in *bleeding-ear* detail.

"No time. Get ready because I'll be there in an hour. Put a hustle in it!"

To be honest, I had no qualms about slumming it on my sofa for the evening, but Sunny would give me no choice in the matter. That girl was always on the prowl for men. I didn't get the kind of attention she did, nor did I want it after my last relationship with Brandon.

The ex.

The one I tried to push away like a terrible nightmare.

After I turned twenty-nine, Sunny's personal goal was to make sure that I had a good time. I loved her to the moon for it. I could tell her anything—she was the vault that held all my secrets. Plus no one else could make me laugh so hard I would spit my drink out. I felt more comfortable with Sunny than anyone else in my life—especially my mother, who was about as affectionate as a Brillo Pad.

Sunny approached life with a reckless abandon that I adored. The truth is, she and Max were all I had in the world.

"Hold down the fort, panther boy."

Max glanced over his shoulder indifferently and proceeded to polish the windowpane with his tongue.

Fifty-six minutes later, I stepped off the curb as Sunny's bright red mustang prowled around the corner. A glittery disco ball swung from the rearview mirror as she flung her arm out in a pageant wave. That girl was a walking cliché without a clue.

"Hey, Sunshine," I greeted her, slipping into the passenger seat. As I buckled my seat belt, I was blasted by the air conditioner that sent strands of coppery hair all over the place. I smoothed the ends and frowned; all that time wasted on straightening and gloss cream.

"I hope this is something you won in a radio contest and not one of the perks for dating a waiter."

Sunny's eyes flashed at me as she blew past a stop sign.

"*Owner.* Not waiter."

"Ah, moving up the food chain are we? Nice." I shocked her with a snap of static electricity.

"Cut it out!" she squeaked.

My friend gave a brilliant performance at hiding her amusement, but failed miserably. It was one of my few quirks. I could build up a static charge that was unparalleled. So naturally, I used it to my absolute advantage. It kept Max off the dining table and Sunny in check.

I felt the hostility behind those icy blue eyes and guilt crept up on me… until I became distracted by the glitter shadow on her lower lids.

"You know you're a freak of nature, Zoë."

"But you love me, admit it."

"Can you please move out of BFE? These half-hour drives are killing me." A topic she launched into almost every conversation in her futile attempts to get me to move in with her.

The girl lived downtown where the crime was as high as her rent (and her neighbor for that matter). Personally, I preferred to live as far away from prostitution and drunks as possible. I guess everyone has their thing.

The city invested in a public rail system after job expansion increased to accommodate the commuters. I loved the rail and rode it daily; after a while you start wondering why you need a car.

Forty minutes and two obscene gestures later, we arrived at Finnegan's.

They had a huge bar that curved around two walls, and it was filling up fast. Mosaic candleholders brightened the tables and if I had a big enough purse I might be tempted to take one home. A busy game room was nestled behind closed doors, but we never went in there. Sunny insisted a quality man would never be found lingering over a musty pool table. Winding stairs spilled into the dining room on the lower level—showy with its bright colors and metal art sculptures on the walls. The food was delicious, even if it was served on triangular plates.

"Follow me to the bar," she called out over her shoulder.

Sunny floated across the room with the finesse of a cat and I followed her trail of perfume to a high table. She slid into the tall wooden chair, crossing her sun-kissed legs as predatory eyes watched her from all angles. The formfitting black skirt and sparkling blue eyes were a deadly combination. Sunny had the kind of hair most girls would kill for—thick, wavy, honey-blond and styled fashionably above her shoulders. She could have been a model, but instead she was just adorable.

I, on the other hand, didn't spend much time with primping. I was a few inches shorter than her five-foot-eight stature, but in heels no one noticed. She was always trying to drag me to the gym to tone up, but I liked my soft figure. I was slim, but by no means perfect. My hair was like a chameleon—sometimes brown and other times a rich auburn. Overall, I may have been considered average, but I had a confident swing in my step that got noticed.

Touching the footrest with my heels, I studied my slim khakis and plain shirt. I was grossly overdressed for a Saturday—every woman in that bar wore nothing less than sex appeal.

After the waitress took our order, Sunny dropped her red sparkly clutch on the table. I admired her new manicure of silver nails with diamond flecks on the corners as I rubbed my thumb over my own chipped polish.

"I've been keeping a secret," she said, grinning like a fox.

"This should be good." I gave a casual smile so as not to reveal my curiosity.

"Marco and I have been dating for almost two months now and it's gotten... *exclusive.*" She lifted her plucked brows, anticipating my reaction. "He's loaded, but that isn't why I'm with him, Zoë— contrary to my past liaisons." She snorted.

"Exclusive," I said, tasting the word and all it implied. "This means you aren't dating *anyone* else, just him?"

Sunny was a boat on the sea that never wanted to be anchored. Never once did she lead her lovers on; I was always astounded at her candor when she told them her expectations up front.

"You're serious?"

"As a heart attack. I never keep secrets from you, but I didn't want to jinx it since I didn't know where it was going. Trust me, I'm just as shocked as you are. But I really like him; he's *nothing* like the guys I usually go for. He's sophisticated. And he stands up to me... doesn't just do whatever I say."

Sunny beamed.

I curled my fingers around the bottle that appeared in front of me. "So you finally decided to date a real man who has a pair?"

The guys she dated were beautifully packaged, but men of substance they were not. Most of them followed her around with puppy-dog eyes and a neutered expression.

"Don't give me your sass. You just wish you had snatched him up first because he's delish."

She stirred the cherry in her vodka drink and pulled it out by the stem. It lingered on her bottom lip, glossing it up while her eyes scanned the room. When her tongue swept out and circled around the stem, I released a lengthy sigh.

"You're telling me that you are in a serious relationship with one man, yet here you sit, molesting a cherry in public. Really, Sunshine? You do realize that's an open invitation for every guy here. What would Marco say if he found you seducing other men?"

Her teeth bit down and those blue eyes narrowed. Sunny was so easy to bait. She flicked the stem at me in silent retaliation.

"Flirting," she corrected in her usual bright tone. "I have to say that he's very yummy in bed, too. Well, we've only had sex twice. He's got this kinky thing about not touching me with his hands, but dang… he touches me with *everything else*. It's so damn sexy." She paused. "He even asks about you."

I came close to sucking my drink down the wrong pipe.

"Me?" I was nonplussed, given I only met the man once and it was brief.

"Sure, I've told him *all* about you."

"Lovely, so glad to amuse. Did you tell him all of the embarrassing stories or just the highlights?"

"That's why I like him, Zoë. He's interested in what's important to me and *you* are one of those things."

Several hours later, Marco texted Sunny with a "sorry I can't make it something came up" message that kept her eyes glued to the phone all night. While she acted nonchalant about it, I could see an ugly layer of pissed off brewing below the surface.

In the middle of her story about the mechanic who screwed her out of $2400.00, the tiny hairs on my arms stood on end. Just like before, a terrible feeling moved through me like a swarm of bees. A quick scan around the room revealed nothing out of the ordinary. Still, I had the distinct feeling I was being watched.

I was distracted by a floating tray of nachos that settled on a table to our left. I crinkled my nose in disgust at all the finger-licking and double-dipping between the three men who had made obvious efforts to gawk at Sunny's gazelle legs.

"Zoë, did you hear me? Are you feeling okay? You look pale."

"I always look pale, I'm part Irish, remember?"

She smiled and twirled her hair between two fingers. "What's the other part?"

"Tired." I thinned my lips, hating to be the one to ruin the party. "It's time for me to head out. I promise that I'll have dinner with you and Marco another time. I need to meet the man who might put my best friend in a wedding gown."

Her wide eyes protested and I gave her a teasing wink. Sunny was not the marrying kind, thanks to her screwed-up parents.

"I'm so glad you came, Zoë girl, we need to do this more often. All my other girlfriends are a snore," she said, waving a hand.

Sunny bounced out of her chair with a radiant grin and threw an arm around me, making sure that I knew how much I was loved.

Just then, one of guys at the nacho table wolf whistled, causing a few other patrons to turn in our direction. When I felt Sunny's hand slide down to my ass, I laughed out loud.

"Are you trying to torture them?"

"No," she said with a subtle purr in her voice. "I'm just giving them something to dream about later, no harm in that." When her neck curved in their direction, I shoved her off.

Suddenly a shiver skated across my skin. My stomach knotted as if I had swallowed a nightmare and it was growing within me— prowling and trying to claw its way out. I needed to get out of here.

"Hey, what's wrong? Are you okay?" Sunny touched my arm with concern and the corners of her mouth turned down.

"I'm fine; I slept too much earlier and now I just feel… off."

She looked concerned and brushed a hand through my hair in a motherly fashion. "Let's get you home."

Sunny's car roared into the train station with an attitude. The drive to my apartment was too far, so I didn't see the point in wearing her out playing cab driver. Besides, it was pretty obvious she had undisclosed intentions of dropping in on Marco. I pitied the bastard; if he was really up to no good then hell hath no fury like what he was about to receive.

I stepped out of the car and signaled her to roll down the window as I cupped my elbows. "Call me when you get home so I know you're safe."

"Will do, Zoë *dahling*," she said in her snobby accent. "Stay away from the weirdos on the train!"

I nibbled on that thought with a smile. At night, there was almost nobody on the train except a few late-shift hospital workers.

"Hey, I *am* the weirdo on the train."

"You got that right!"

The car eased away. "Next Friday let's do this again, but no pants allowed. Skirts only. Love you, sis!"

Sunny—always the fashion bully.

I lost track of time during the short ride home thinking about her new... boyfriend? I guess that was the word. I just hoped he was a good guy.

When the train reached my stop, I leapt off and began my walk home, listening to the click of my heels on the uneven pavement. 15th Street was filled with small shops—now closed—where I spent my Sundays shopping and eating.

I passed the last streetlamp on the right, facing a dark, open field. Just on the other side I could make out the subtle glow of my apartment lights, and it was the only feasible shortcut. It took twice as long to take the road, which did a complete U-turn and it was three times as scary. The creek was shadowed with trees, and living things scurried from beneath the bridge. No thanks—not a fan of getting eaten by shadow monsters.

The one risk was that summer rain often brought colonies of fire ants. They could turn an otherwise innocent stretch of land into a minefield, unleashing an assault like never imagined. It was a hard lesson learned when I first moved in and decided to grab a sandwich in my flip-flops. Since then, I always brought an extra pair of sneakers if I went anywhere.

I also kept a bottle of Calamine in the medicine cabinet.

Taking my time, I walked across the fragrant field of wildflowers. I loved the heady scent in the evening.

Not that I could see a damn thing.

My hair twisted about my face when a sudden gust of wind came up from behind.

At least, I thought it was wind.

A blanket of darkness circled around, tilting me off balance so that I landed flat on my back. The wind was knocked out of me like I had taken a fist to my lungs and I grunted like an animal.

Staring up at the stars, it took a moment to get over the initial shock of the fall.

Except, those weren't stars.

Brilliant green eyes, lit by more than the moonlight, stared watchfully at me. They were jewels whose colors shifted from the glowing embers behind them. My body stung with an electrical charge that intensified the more the dark-haired man leaned in, but I was too stunned to do anything… to say anything. Fear overwhelmed me and felt as palpable as a million dull spikes pressing against my skin.

"Hello, little girl."

His voice was thick, accented, and colossal in power. A short-bearded cheek brushed against mine and I recoiled. *Too close.*

Cruel fingers squeezed my arms forcefully until my hands were pinned over my head. His eager palm pressed against mine.

"So glad we can finally be acquainted. You must lie very still so we can get this over with. The last one died in the process and this requires careful timing."

When I was ten, I put a 9-volt battery to my tongue on a dare. Needless to say, after I felt the surprising sting of pain on my tongue, it didn't last more than two seconds. It doesn't mean it was the last time I ever did it—strange how you challenge yourself with pain tolerance. The sharp metal flavor was as close to that sensation as I could describe.

Energy buzzed in my fingertips and a feathery bluish light drifted between our hands like delicate cobwebs. A scream was surfacing from my lungs, but before it escaped, I snapped my head forward and struck him in the face.

There was a crack and as soon as I felt the pain, a stream of warm blood poured all over my neck from his broken nose. Tears welled, but I refused to let them free. That clever little idea came courtesy of countless action films, but something they never went into detail about was that a headbutt hurts on both ends.

Lesson learned.

He roared so loud that I stiffened like a dog about to be spanked for shitting on the rug.

"Get off of me! Let me go, *get off.*" Words that meant nothing to an attacker.

"You worthless female whore, I will not make this as easy on you as the rest," he promised. His hands fell over my eyes, and in a flash of pain, I was temporarily blinded.

My hand sought the one place I knew I could gain the advantage. I wasn't going to be the only one who saw blinding light, so I reached down and twisted his balls with a punishing grip.

That was enough to make him jump back, so I flipped over like a coin and ran aimlessly in the dark.

I managed twelve long strides before slamming into a wall, which not only immobilized me but also wrapped itself around me like a midnight tornado.

I sat straight down, slipping through his grasp and onto my knees. Salty sweat tickled my brow and within seconds, he fell on top of my back and locked his arms around my neck in a vise-like grip. I clawed at his steel arm, but he didn't loosen his hold by even a fraction. There was no more air.

This was the moment that every mortal feared.

"Let's finish this," he said.

Nausea erupted as slick blood poured from his nose and smeared across my face. "We can play games later."

When his grip tightened to an excruciating degree, tiny flashes twinkled in my view. Seconds before I lost consciousness, he pushed me back down and pulled my arms over my head once more. I had never felt so helpless, so afraid… so pissed off as I lay there gasping for air.

"Mmm, I enjoy this part," he muttered, pressing his body against mine. "Going to give you a little extra for the trouble you've caused."

A current flowed between our hands and crawled through me like a living thing. The thick metallic taste of adrenaline was heavy on my tongue and I writhed beneath him—my bare heels dug in the dirt.

"Let me go! What are you doing to me?"

He ran his tongue over his bottom teeth. "Marinating."

Life was flowing away. I was no longer able to speak, to move, and it felt as if there was no me or him, no grass below, no summer breeze.

I was becoming reacquainted with the universe as if we had been separated at birth. Death was imminent, and my soul knew it.

"Not quite, little girl," I heard from my detached state of mind. "It's the giving that makes the taking so much *sweeter*. And I have perfected the taking to the nth degree."

Motion sickness overtook me and all I could do was look into that bastard's eyes—those green, glowing eyes that looked like traffic signals.

"I can taste your fear. Want to know what it tastes like?" His tongue ran across my cheek and my body revolted; I jerked my head as far away from him as I could get. I didn't want to look at him anymore, so I squeezed my eyes shut, blocking out that hardened face and midnight hair.

"*Delicious.*"

I barely listened, but he kept going. "Humans are such ignorant things. All that struggling will only make it harder on you. Had you complied, you would have been put under like the rest. But now I think I should give you an extra something for the trouble. Call it a tip."

I snapped out of my trance, focusing on the gleam of a knife held just inches away. Something dark and frightening dripped off the edge of the blade.

Blood. *My* blood.

The dark-haired man straddled me and observed with detached curiosity.

My hands went to the source of pain on my neck and my life poured out in a frantic, pulsing rhythm. I gasped, pressing my palms tightly against the gaping wound. The jugular was severed and I knew what that meant.

In the last fleeting moment of my life, I did not have enough time to make peace with it. A fire burned within me, not ready to be extinguished—especially not while being watched by a man who wiped his blade on the sleeve of his shirt without a hint of remorse.

God and the devil took a vacation that night, leaving me alone with the shadow of death. My eyes widened in a last attempt to hold me to the waking world. The universe silenced and I felt a million light years of elegance shining on me. A tear spilled out; one that held the entire contents of my life as the last heartbeat stilled my mortal remains.

My body quaked to an explosion that became the very last sound I heard. I prayed for rain; I wanted to feel it one last time. Instead, all I felt was the world slipping away.

That was the last thing I remembered when I died.

CHAPTER 2

"PULL OVER. I HAVEN'T EATEN since five and I'm craving a monster burger like a motherfucker. Don't give me your look."

"We're not supposed to. You know we could get written up," a voice replied, seasoned with age and cigars.

"Fuckin' A, it's not like she's got someplace to be." I heard a tongue click. "Live a little."

"Fine, but you're paying, and I want extra fries."

Brakes in need of repair squealed as the vehicle rolled to a stop. Two doors slammed and I waited until the voices grew distant.

Darkness enveloped me; I was covered in some kind of smooth plastic. Straps secured me in three places and my fingers explored the material. A bag?

Before I went into full-blown panic, I pulled my right arm up near my face to feel for a way out. It was hot and stuffy, and while I was never claustrophobic before, it was a sensation that was rearing its ugly head. Two words came to mind when I pieced together the last few hours: *body bag*.

That's when the ugly head of Medusa reared and something raw and primal took over. Using my teeth, fingers, and a shitload of determination, I tore my way free.

I sat up so fast that I almost fainted. White cabinets, a long bench, medical equipment—I was inside of an ambulance. Sickness rolled in my stomach and tightened like a hard fist.

I shuffled out of the bag and stumbled to the rear door so I could look out of the dirty glass window.

There wasn't a single car in the parking lot except a beat-up VW. Straight ahead, two men stood in line at the counter of a twenty-four-hour burger joint. The older one with the gunmetal-grey hair and potbelly arched his stiff back.

These weren't familiar surroundings, and I wasn't planning on hanging around in the back of an ambulance to ask questions. Drawing in a deep breath, I lifted the handle and the door swung wide. The second my bare feet touched the ground, all the tension sprang out like a released coil and everything that tethered me to the world dissipated.

I ran so fast that it felt as if someone was chasing me. My throat ached for water, my lips were cracked, and I struggled for air with each leap I took. Each time I stepped on a rock or stick I winced but kept going.

I'm not sure what kept me moving—fear, anger, or an absence of clarity?

The woods thinned out and my feet hit hard pavement, still warm from the afternoon sun. I was fast approaching a figure up ahead. A man with a slow and steady gait, but no trench coat, so I knew it wasn't the man who attacked me.

I shot right past him like a streak of lightning.

"Hey!" the voice called out from behind.

I cut across an open field when I heard his quickened footsteps from behind. My knees finally buckled and I collapsed on the dry, brittle grass.

Who was he and why did he do this? I drove my hands into the ground, so pissed off at myself for not having fought him hard enough. I let out a primal scream, but that didn't make me feel any better. Something else was wrong.

The energy within me was reversing itself like a black hole and I wrapped my arms tightly around my body. It wanted to leave… it wanted to escape. It was fire burning in my veins, life throbbing at my fingertips, and power. I felt it just as sure as I felt a tiny ant crawling on my ankle. That man did something to me—changed me.

The footsteps slid right up behind me.

"Are you all right? You shouldn't be out in this part of the woods, are you lost?" an out-of-breath voice questioned.

"Stay away." My voice cracked.

But he didn't. The demanding tone softened. "I won't hurt you; do you need help? Look, I don't have a phone but my house is up the road."

My knuckles must have been white from the tight little fists I made as I turned to face him.

"*Je-sus Christ*," he exhaled.

A beam of light from a flashlight stung my eyes and I flinched.

"Take that off of me," I croaked. With each hard breath my throat burned, so I tried to swallow.

His arm dropped and the light bounced off the grass, illuminating the man from bottom to top. He was tall and dressed in black, but I felt no threat from him. He wasn't a cop either, like I initially thought by his questioning. His dark hair was as lovely as those big brown eyes—serious eyes—that were frozen on me. While I saw his mouth moving, the words were drowned out by a steady hum in my head. Stars burned my shoulders as the world became a disappearing speck of light.

"You need help, you need a doctor," he started but never finished.

The flashlight tumbled to the ground as he surged forward to collect me in his arms when my body gave out.

I looked at him with fading eyes. "Just leave me here. I don't need you; I don't need anyone."

"I'm not leaving you." He glowered. "Who did this to you?"

He asked because I was covered in blood.

"I don't know."

Images spiraled out of control and my head lost gravity. The last words that fell from my lips were "You need a shave."

Adam was about fifteen minutes from hitting the front door and turning in for the night. But those fifteen minutes changed his life.

He pulled out his pocket flashlight and looked at his watch—just a couple hours left before dawn. Occasionally when he got a little lonely, he paid a visit to Nina. She was single, independent and always willing to let Adam into her bed. Not one of those girls who wanted him to stay the night either. They worked out a quiet arrangement and neither one of them had ever mentioned taking it any further than the bedroom, or the kitchen counter for that matter. Adam wasn't a complete bastard, but Nina wasn't the girl he saw himself settling with.

A rock tumbled into the darkness and he slapped a mosquito on his arm. It took only seconds to realize that someone was coming up fast and hard behind him. Twisting his back, he saw a woman running as if she were a gale-force wind.

At least, he thought it was a woman. The figure was cloaked in blood with torn scraps of clothing fluttering behind her. But what made him uneasy as she flew right by him was the panic in those eyes. He looked on, but saw no one chasing her.

Before he knew it, that fierce compulsion to protect overtook him and his legs were pumping right behind her and closing in fast.

She stumbled in the grass and even from behind he could almost smell death and fear on her—a scent he knew too well. Nothing ever happened in this small town, that's why Adam came here—to get away from all that. Except for a few local kids shooting off fireworks and setting the grass on fire, it was a quiet place to live.

Adam stared at the young woman in his arms just after she fell unconscious, now able to see the full extent of her condition. Her shirt was cut open all the way down the front, blood was smeared across her neck, and her hair was matted with it.

He knelt to the ground and gently put her down, cradling her neck so that he could scan her body for injuries with the flashlight. A quick check revealed a steady, strong pulse—not typical for someone who lost a large quantity of blood.

His brow furrowed when he brushed her hair aside. Blood everywhere, but no cuts or puncture wounds. Was this the face of a killer or a victim?

She moaned. Adam went still as he looked at her face again.

A lovely face. His pulse raced.

Light freckles were splashed over her cheekbones, and her lips had a pronounced Cupid's bow. She wasn't the kind of beauty splashed all over fashion magazines, but the kind of girl who could have made a man blush with a compliment because if she said it… she would mean it.

Intelligence carved her features, not at all dolled up with jewelry and expensive makeup.

Poor girl, what kind of sick motherfucker would do something like this? But then, Adam had seen everything.

I should call the cops, he thought.

He glanced over his shoulder; if someone was after her then they weren't safe out here. He couldn't shake the imploring look in her eyes before she fainted, the ones that searched for meaning.

Adam wiped his brow with his bicep and knelt on one knee. This wasn't the kind of attention he wanted to draw to himself, not the kind of trouble he needed. She would be better off if he called the cops and left her here.

He scratched his chin and watched her face—worried brows pinched together and left a tiny little line in the center.

She looked scared.

That triggered something hardwired and primal in him—he needed to protect her. Didn't know who she was, where she came from, or what kind of trouble she was in.

Adam pulled the fragile body into his arms, into his life, and walked into the unknown.

Fuck it.

CHAPTER 3

THERE ARE FEW THINGS IN life that are worth waking up to: sex, the dark spices of freshly brewed coffee, and bacon. Sex didn't wake me up.

I smacked my lips, rousing from my sleep with an eager stretch. The bacon smelled delicious and I couldn't wait. I was starving.

Maybe it was the feel of the mattress, or the one hundred thread count on those sheets that tipped me off, but at some point in that dreamy state, I jolted awake. The sheets were battleship grey, but not my sheets.

Not *my* bed.

The décor gave off a very masculine feeling with its light grey walls—empty of decorative items except for a single photograph of two children standing in front of a cabin in the snow. The sun bled into the room, leaving a heavy veil of light across the bed.

I touched the long white T-shirt I was wearing that smelled like sunshine. *Where the hell was I?*

Pulling myself out of the bed, I went into the adjacent bathroom and felt for the light switch. When it flipped on—I couldn't believe it.

I didn't recognize my own reflection. Inky hair spilled past my broad shoulders; green eyes the color of polished glass swallowed me up with their gaze.

So there I stood, for I couldn't count how many minutes—staring, waiting—as if by some magical spell I would reappear or wake up.

But nothing happened.

I don't know how long a person can hold their breath, but I couldn't remember in that moment ever taking one. Sure enough, the hair was real—smooth and silky like a newborn. Was it possible I was dead and this was the afterlife? Maybe when I was running down that road I was a ghost escaping from my body.

Yet, how could I be a ghost? I could touch things, feel things, I even slipped on a red baseball cap I found on a hook by the wall and tucked in my hair. Ghosts can't wear baseball caps.

Can they?

I continued staring at my eyes, waving my hand as if I would catch the figure in the mirror as an imposter. They were vibrant and intoxicating... yet strangely familiar.

"You're awake."

I jumped and gripped the sink with my left hand.

A male figure framed the door, flushed in the cheek. He was strikingly handsome; a strong, charismatic face lurked behind some of the unshaven stubble that shadowed the lines of his square jaw. His dark brown hair was a thick and luscious length, the kind you wanted to curl your fingers in. A heavy brow lowered with concern over his earthy brown eyes. I never saw a man who looked equally boyish and stern.

I looked down the length of his weathered jeans to his bare feet and his posture relaxed with a near hint of a smile.

Grabbing a pair of scissors, I held them out defensively. "Who are you?"

"Adam," he politely replied.

I was three seconds from going batshit after catching my reflection again.

"You don't have anything to be afraid of."

It was the kind of thing you would idly say to someone. But it was the way he said it—the conviction in his tone told me that his words were a fact that no one should doubt.

"Take all the time you need. I have food ready when you're hungry. This is my home and I brought you here, remember?"

"How come I'm not at a hospital?"

It was a stupid question because there was no trace of a wound on my neck.

"If you want me to take you, I will." He closed the door without another word and left me to spend more quality time questioning my sanity.

The sound of my hands brushing along my arms caught the

attention of the man standing in the kitchen by the sink. He shut the water off and turned around, wiping his large hands on a tiny white dishtowel.

"Sit. I'll bring you a plate of food."

He gestured to the oval table surrounded by flimsy chairs with metal legs. It reminded me of something I saw in an Ikea magazine once. The chairs were curiously small for a man of his size and stature. I wrapped my fingers around the back of one as I watched him set down a plate of sausages and toast.

"How long have I been here?"

"Three days."

"What? That can't be," I whispered in disbelief.

A heavy finger wagged at my chair as he went back to pull something from the fridge. "Maybe you need to sit down and eat first."

I eased into the chair, looking around at the small home. The kitchen was closed off with a row of cabinets that served as a divider between rooms. I faced the sink and stove, the fridge was farther to my left.

His approach was slow and calculated as he leaned forward to set a cold glass of juice on the table before taking the chair across from me. Our proximity was closer than I cared for, so I scooted back. The sausages captivated my attention, taunting me to take a bite, and he reached out, nudging them forward.

"Take all you want."

"I bet you say that to all the girls," I mumbled.

One sausage was devoured in roughly five ravenous chews and one giant swallow. He leaned forward on the table with his fingers laced together loosely and his head tilted. I didn't feel threatened by his demeanor, but I was still on edge. While he took me in and fed me, I still knew nothing about this man named Adam. Our eyes met and he lowered his gaze to allow me privacy to eat. But I could see a smile play across his features as he considered what I said.

After three swallows of juice and another two sausage patties, I eased off when my stomach did a somersault. It was delicious going down, but I didn't want it to come back up for an encore.

"How did I get clean?"

He bit the inside of his cheek. "I waited a day but you didn't wake up; it wasn't right to leave you like that." He ruffled his fingers through his hair with a look of embarrassment before his eyes hardened. "Who were you running from?"

Before I could think of what to say, he continued with the interrogation.

"Whose blood was it?"

I touched my unscarred neck. "What do you mean whose was it?" I didn't like the accusation, or the fact I couldn't appropriately explain how it was mine and yet I had no injuries. "Why don't we start with introductions before inquisitions? I'm Zoë Merrick."

"Adam Razor."

"I've been here the whole time?"

Adam scratched his chin and looked like he was considering whether or not it was a good idea. "I carried you here."

Which as it happens was a fifteen-minute walk. I didn't say anything about it, but that's a long walk to have to carry someone in your arms.

"I assumed you slept because you were in shock. I didn't find any injuries, so I didn't call a doctor."

Adam waited three days for me to wake up. On the second day he washed off the blood when something peculiar caught his eye. Adam described waves of movement beneath my skin and to the touch it burned, so he rushed to get a wet cloth from the bathroom. He admitted that he was very close to taking me to the hospital and I didn't blame him. But after hearing the full story, I was relieved he hadn't or else I might be in some government lab in Virginia being studied like a science monkey.

Adam had stepped out of the room for no more than twenty seconds. When he returned, my hair had changed from fire to coal. Over the course of twenty-four hours, he observed my body undergoing a gradual transformation.

Now of course, this was a little game of share and tell. Adam gave information in hopes that I would shed some light on where I came from and what happened. Honestly? How the hell do you explain to someone you were murdered and yet you aren't dead? I couldn't even explain it to myself. So instead, I said nothing. Adam was no idiot and while he wanted the full story, he saw my unease at discussing it, so he didn't press. I went into the living room and sat down on the leather sofa.

"Do you want to call anyone?"

"Who?" I frowned. "My voice isn't even the same." I pushed up a brow in thought before tucking a strand of hair behind my ear. "You don't decorate much," I observed.

Outside of a chair, which Adam sat in on my right, the only other things in the room were a television, coffee table, and a bag of birdseed in the adjacent sunroom.

"You know what I think? That you're avoiding the topic."

I straightened my back and peered at him through my lashes.

"Do you live alone?" I asked, ignoring his statement.

"Mmhmm."

"How long have you been out here? It's kind of… country." My eyes focused on the woods only a few feet from outside of the windows.

"Two years. And there's nothing wrong with country."

I snapped my head around. By the looks of things, I would have thought he moved in a few months ago. *Talk about the basic necessities.*

"I don't need much. Do you want me to drive you home?" His eyes narrowed a fraction, waiting for my answer.

I couldn't go home. *He* might be there. Whoever he was. I didn't have my keys and I couldn't even go to Sunny for help because she would think I was some crazy lunatic pretending to be her friend.

A friend she thought was missing or dead. I scratched my wrist nervously and bit my lip.

Adam disappeared into the bedroom for a few seconds before returning. "I'm afraid that's all I've got that'll fit." A pair of sweats landed on my lap and Adam ran a distracted finger over the top of the leather chair. "What I'll do is go pick up a few things for you and you'll stay with me. I can't have you wandering around in my trousers; people will talk."

I smiled with gratitude at his humor.

"You would do that?"

"I'll be back," he said, twirling a set of keys in his fingers as he went toward the door. I didn't feel like going on a shopping spree, but I also didn't feel like being left alone.

"Wait, I'll go too!"

I shot up out of my seat and rushed forward when my legs wobbled. Adam cleared five feet of space between us in a heartbeat as he reached out and caught my fall. When I stood upright and backed away from him, something didn't make sense. My legs felt strange and clumsy.

"How tall are you?"

"What?" Adam's face crinkled.

"How tall are you?" I repeated.

"Six foot two."

"Can't be," I whispered to myself. I remembered in the field how much taller than me he seemed; I might have measured up to his shoulders.

Adam stood motionless as I moved closer; our bodies were just fingertips apart. A smile crept across my face as I leaned forward and bumped his chin with my nose.

"You need a shave." I smiled. I moved in closer to be sure of the height, sliding the edge of my foot against his.

There's no way I'd measure up against a guy over six feet tall. I just couldn't believe something like this was possible; wouldn't my bones hurt from growing? On the upside, I didn't need to worry about wearing heels anymore. My eyes centered on his parted mouth and I wondered what my transformation looked like.

His hand slipped around my waist, barely touching—but it was there.

Adam's breath grazed my cheek with an unsteady rhythm. Our bodies didn't touch, but it was as if I could feel his energy in the unmistakable friction of heat that was swelling between us. I became dizzy from it. His fingers brushed through that soft, short brown hair that had a slight wave, and he blew out a breath, stepping back.

"I'm sorry."

"Okay, so we got our first awkward moment out of the way." *To say the least.*

"I'm not so sure that was our first." His fingers worked at tucking his shirt into his jeans and I noticed that men shouldn't look that good in something so casual.

"It seems like it's not just my looks, but I'm also taller than I was before."

His gaze dropped to the pile of sweats on the floor. "Get dressed if you want to go." He turned around and I slid my legs one at a time into the sweats, pulling the string tight.

I snorted as I grabbed the sides of the pants, pulling them wide.

"I've got a pair of Bermuda shorts in there somewhere, if you'd rather." His beguiling eyebrows rose as he peered over his shoulder.

"I think these will strip enough dignity from me, don't you think?"

"Spandex?"

"Okay, this conversation is officially straying into the 'things I really don't want to know about Adam' territory."

Adam's grin was broad and handsome with a subtle tilt of the chin, and I felt a prick of heat flush my cheeks. Adam didn't smile with teeth; he gave a sexy pressed-lip smile that crinkled his eyes in a provocative and yet charming way.

I walked past him toward the door. "Let's go, Razor."

"Adam," he corrected.

Adam may have had smoldering good looks, but he gave me the impression he was normally a very serious guy. Too serious, if you ask me.

"I'm calling you Razor."

"Why's that?" I heard the sound of his hand rubbing against the back of his neck before I noticed he was doing it.

"You're sharp, you can figure it out." He groaned at my pun and despite how bad it was I delighted in every bit of it. I needed a moment to feel normal again.

We bobbled down the dark road in Adam's beat-up Land Rover, circa 1980, that looked like it had been driven straight to Egypt and back—without a car wash, at that. Strange noises rattled from the engine whenever the car rolled to a stop.

"Are you sure there's not a squirrel in there?"

"I might say the same about your hair," he teased in the dark interior. My smile faded as I touched my tangled strands and his hand fell across my shoulder.

"Sorry, I can be a mean bastard."

After a minute, he cleared his throat and turned into the parking lot. "I only use the car for long trips; otherwise I foot it out here. Everything a man needs is within walking distance and I prefer the exercise."

The engine shut off and a tapping noise from beneath the hood filled the silence.

"You see? Her heart still beats for only me."

I smiled and shifted my gaze out the window. Just as my fingertips touched the handle of the door, something in the darkness just beyond the parking lot moved. The hairs on my arms rose and it felt like waves of electricity were caressing me. I had never felt anything quite like it before. But just as quick as I felt it, the feeling suddenly disappeared.

"Something's wrong," Adam noticed. Not a question, but a statement.

"No, I just got a chill."

Adam shifted in my direction with his left hand pressed against the dash. "Bullshit. Tell me what's wrong." His eyes flicked out toward the bus stop. "Did you see something?"

Shaking my head, I pushed him back and relaxed my voice. "I changed my mind about going inside. I just wanted to… well I didn't want to be left alone in your house. I'm not fit to be seen in public. All I need is a toothbrush and—"

"I'm on it. Keep the doors locked."

Before I could finish, he was breezing through the automatic doors.

I didn't know Adam, but I liked the feeling that he wanted to protect me. I never had siblings and always wished that I had an older brother. I wanted someone to look after me and approve of my boyfriends, beating them up if they were jerks. I used to hear Sunny roll her eyes when she spoke of the car trips she took with her brother, Kane. How he would pinch her relentlessly until she'd cry out and then she would get the spanking. She called childhood "survival of the fittest." Sunny would say I was lucky that I didn't have to grow up with a sibling.

But was I? I didn't feel lucky. I wanted to have someone I could always count on to look out for me. Maybe if I did, I wouldn't have gotten in so much trouble with Brandon. I only had my mom and she wasn't the most loving woman. Sometimes I wondered if she just feared losing me and being left all alone.

Ten minutes later, Adam reappeared with bags in tow. I couldn't help but notice the odd way in which he looked around the parking lot, as if he were constantly on patrol.

"Here," he said, handing me a smaller bag.

My hands pulled the edges apart to reveal a large chocolate bar in colorful wrapping.

"Oh… you didn't have to."

The key slid in the ignition, but he paused before turning it. "You don't like chocolate?"

I loved chocolate—but his thoughtfulness caught me off guard. "Thanks. I promise I'm going to pay you back for everything."

"The only payment I'll accept are answers. Let me know when you're ready to close out that tab."

I bit my lip and remained quiet for the trip back. I wasn't ready to give answers and Adam felt that he was owed them. Maybe he was right.

He had bought a couple of T-shirts, shorts, tank tops, razors, and other odds and ends that I needed. But the price of truth was high. That truth could get me wrapped up in a snug straightjacket.

I claimed the sofa, tossing the bags beside me and crossing my ankles. I felt pitiful, like a lost dog.

Adam eased into his armchair with a bottle of Heineken. "So, what's your plan?"

He lifted the bottle and took a long sip as my eyes watched the slow movement of his Adam's apple. The light reflected on the green bottle, imitating the hue of my new eye color. Adam's lips hovered on the mouth of the bottle as he noticed me noticing him. A tongue swept across and licked them, snapping me out of my haze.

"I've thought about it and I don't have a clue what to do."

His finger tapped on the bottle as he wedged it between his thighs. "Is there anyone you could call, someone you trust who would believe you?"

"I don't even believe me."

"You need money. Without access to your apartment or family, what do you think you can do?"

"Why don't I just strip for a living, I bet I could wrap these legs around one of those poles pretty good. I doubt they'd ask for my Social Security number."

"Is that what you want to do, prostitute yourself?" he snapped. I looked up and there was no humor in his face, but a fire lit behind those eyes.

"Kidding, only kidding. I can't go back to my life anymore. I can't risk talking about what happened because they'd lock me up in the funny farm."

"I don't think you need to worry about that," he said. "You have to be funny in order to get in." He took another swig and I realized that Adam had a funny bone after all.

"I just wish I could see Max again."

"Max?" Adam's thumbnail scraped the glass bottle as he shifted in his seat. There was an edge in his tone, and a muscle in his jaw ticked. "Your boyfriend?"

"I don't have a boyfriend." Nodding at his bottle I asked, "Can I get one of those?"

Perhaps there was none left or he was too tired to get up, so he leaned forward and handed me his.

I took a swig, hoping to drown some of the depression that was settling in my bones. How do you start from square fucking one? Another swallow sent an army of happy bubbles sailing down my throat and I felt miles better.

Relaxed.

"Zoë?"

"What? Sorry, I didn't hear you."

Adam rose to his feet, hiking up his jeans a little. I admired his arms as his fingers locked over his head. It wasn't until they were on display that I could appreciate how beautifully toned they were. And he lived out here alone? It just didn't make sense. Adam had the kind of body and seductive casualness about him that was extremely attractive. Guys like him I'd met before, and they were always married. I tried to put my finger on what it was—he didn't have model beauty—but it was charisma. Yeah, that's the word.

"You want to go to bed?"

I blinked and my heart did a quick ricochet.

Adam chuckled in a deep voice and dropped his arms as if he knew where my mind went. "Christ, Zoë, that's not what I meant. It's too late for planning; we'll talk about visiting your apartment another night. Until we have some answers, you need to lay low. Tell me, who is after you?"

I looked away sheepishly because not telling felt very close to lying. I didn't like to lie.

"I won't be able to help you until I know the truth of it."

Adam had no intention of letting me crash here for a couple of days. He wasn't even inviting me to stay longer… he was planning on it.

I set the beer on the table and curled up on my side, tucking my arms beneath my head.

"What do you think you're doing?" Adam's voice boomed.

Being it was the first time I ever heard him raise his voice that way, I was startled. He intimidated me in a way that propelled me right to my feet as I ran toward the back door.

"Whoa," he said, holding his arms wide and moving in my direction. "Hey now, I didn't mean to yell, I'm not… shit, you know I'm not going to hurt you."

Still didn't leave me with warm fuzzies, even if I knew I could trust him. He corralled me in against the door and stroked my arms softly. I was shocked by his sudden affection and froze. When I didn't meet his glance, he lifted my chin with his knuckle.

When he spoke, there was poison on his tongue. "I don't

like men who hurt women." His fingers weaved through my hair, cradling my head. "What I meant was that I'm not letting you sleep on the sofa." Emphasis on "sofa," as if it was a dirty word.

"I don't care; I'm fine with it." I gulped, swallowing down that last bit of panic that was doing a crazy dance on my nerves.

He snapped his fingers and pointed at the bedroom. "You bed, me sofa." That simple phrase snapped the tension in the room and put me at ease. The smile helped, too.

"Nice to know you're not entirely a caveman," I said, staring at his bare feet.

"I'm not that prehistoric."

"Fred Flintstone called and he wants his car back."

I meant to be funny but it occurred to me I was being rude. Adam broke the awkward moment when he burst out laughing, and it was a rich, deep, and enjoyable laugh that had me smiling again.

"Don't encourage me," I said, pushing on his chest. "I know I haven't gone about this the right way, but thanks—for everything." My words were weighted and sincere.

Adam scratched the back of his neck, looking as if the gratitude embarrassed him.

"Let's call it a night."

CHAPTER 4

TWO WEEKS LATER.

"I think you'll want to read that."

Adam tossed a newspaper on the table as he carried a giant bag of birdseed out the back door.

I held a cup of coffee to my nose and inhaled deeply. Adam brewed the best coffee, and he always had a pot ready when I woke up, even if he was out and about. I had lived with a man once before, but I was never treated this good with just the simple things. I didn't have to ask for a drink when he got up to get himself one—he just brought it. Adam was kind, and that kind of thing just can't be taught.

I took a careful sip and turned the page. My eyes skimmed over an article on page four.

The blurb read no more than ten sentences, stating the police had no leads on a stolen body. Stolen—as if someone would rip through a body bag versus take the whole thing. It sounded to me like they were incompetent law enforcement at its finest, since I now officially moved to a cold-case file.

Adam was whistling to himself as he came back inside and chucked the bag over by the door. I watched in amusement as he peered out the window to watch the feasting. I think that's what I liked the most about Adam—how pleased he was as he admired the end result of his putting out that seed; he liked taking care of things. He never killed bugs in the house either, but scooped them up, showed them to me so he could watch me scream, and released them on the porch.

"I think it's time we had a talk." Adam placed his hands impatiently on his waist. I pressed my nose back into the paper, licking my finger and turning a few pages.

Everything stopped when I landed on the last page.

Zoë Winter Merrick, age 29, died September 5. Survived by mother, Abigail, and sister Sunny. Funeral 10 am Monday at Morgan Funeral Chapel.

It was so brief; no accomplishments, no surviving children, not even a respectable age to have lived to. What really got me was that Sunny put herself down as my sister. My fingers were devouring the paper like angry claws.

I felt Adam's hand on my back, stroking in small circles. He was great on the punch lines, but he knew when to give that needed space and quiet. Sometimes I just didn't want to say anything. He squeezed my neck in two quick pinches… the "you'll be okay" kind.

"It's time we go to your apartment and get your things. Time to close out that life."

By late afternoon, I had slipped my long legs into a pair of knee-length grey shorts, black tank top, and flip-flops. Sadly, it was becoming my signature ensemble and I normally was a long skirt kind of girl.

I found Adam in the kitchen, so I took a lazy posture at the end of the table. Noticing my need to talk, he set down a glass in the sink and lifted a chair, turning it around so he could straddle it in front of me with his arms crossed over the back.

"What's on your mind?"

I shrugged.

Adam knew when I was battling a sense of not belonging, an empty feeling I couldn't explain that never existed before. But there it was, poking at me in quiet moments like a hot branding iron.

"Tell me where you're from," he said.

"I came out of thin air."

Adam squinted as if trying to read me and I chuckled as it was always an inside joke with Sunny. I decided to end the suspense. "I was born on a transatlantic flight somewhere over the ocean. My mom was coming back from Germany and went into premature labor. Flight attendants delivered me during an electrical storm."

His brown eyes were momentarily suspended on me. Reaching out, he gripped the seat of my chair and dragged it forward so we were even closer. "Go on."

"We landed in Boston, so I'm American, but I also have Canadian citizenship."

Adam laughed, shaking his head. "Now that's a story."

My mood was already brightening.

"What was your mom doing in Europe?"

"I don't know; she said she lived there but she never talked about her past. I wish I had asked her more about it."

Not that I would have gotten answers. When my mom didn't want to talk about something, that subject was closed and buried. I guessed maybe that part of her life was too painful to remember.

I was a little tickled because it was the first time that we sat down and talked about ourselves. "So what about you, what's your story?"

"That picture in my room? That's me and my twin sister."

I never made the connection. I had looked at it a few times but thought it was a purchased photograph.

"My mother was a career woman who decided to give it all up to become a mother. She met my dad and had us. He was older, didn't have kids of his own, but he was a respectable man. I knew they had a relationship of convenience, but say what you want, that man did right by her."

"People have married for less," I agreed. "Where do they live now?"

"He was a smoker—died of lung cancer when we were kids. The medical bills didn't leave us with much, so my mother had to get a job up north, and our bohemian life ended."

I hadn't even noticed Adam's fingers were pinching the edge of my shorts as he was lost in his thoughts.

"We were really tight after that, the three of us. I was the man of the family, even as a kid, so I did what I could to help out. I worked all through high school and when our mother died—"

"Your mom died?"

I felt awful. To have lost both parents when you weren't even out of school was unimaginable.

"It was a reaction to anesthesia. Bell took it hard." He lifted his eyes to mine. "Annabell, my sister."

"Did someone take care of you?"

"No, we had no other family. It was senior year when she died so I quit school and we moved into a loft where I worked two jobs to put her through college."

I felt the need to connect to Adam for his selflessness and touched his hand. "I know she appreciates what you did for her."

She better have or I'd rightfully kick her ass. The man quit school and by that time, she was old enough to take care of herself. But there he was, looking out for his sister.

"I've moved around a lot since then."

I crossed my legs and leaned an arm on the table. "And you ended up moving here?"

"Yep." He leaned over my arm and snatched a green toothpick from the holder on the table, rolling it on his tongue.

"Witness protection program?" I sniffed a quiet laugh.

Adam took out the toothpick and held each end between his thumb and index finger. He studied it as if he were looking at the molecular structure of an atom bomb.

Now who was being evasive?

I palmed his forehead and gave it a slow push as I got up from my chair and paced over to the fridge. There were strange meats and cheeses on the shelves that I wasn't quite sure of, so I dug a little deeper.

Reaching in, I picked up a bowl of what looked like thick, red blood. Adam's bare feet made sticky noises as he crossed the floor.

"What the hell is this?"

"Dragonfruit." He snatched it and frowned. "Or at least, it used to be." He tilted the bowl, giving it a skeptical appraisal.

"Looks like dragon's blood."

Adam slid the contents into the trash and I pulled out the jar of pickles from the fridge. When I turned back around, all the color drained from my face.

Adam spun around, holding a knife.

The pickles slid free, crashing to the floor as my hands covered my throat. His eyes flashed back and forth between me and the knife before he tossed it into the sink.

When I stepped sideways, my foot rolled on a pickle and I lost my balance. Everything tilted as I made a hard landing on my side. Adam dove forward, but it was too late. I hit the floor on my hip and came pretty close to smacking my head on the cabinet.

"Goddammit!" he scolded. But I was already in his arms as he lifted me off of the floor and set me on the kitchen counter. "Are you okay?"

I cringed.

He placed a hand over my chest and I looked down at the odd gesture. He felt my heart racing and knew it was more than a clumsy fall. "I'm not yelling at you, I'm yelling at me," he said.

"I'll clean it."

Ignoring me, he bent over and turned my legs in his hands. "No cuts." Then he checked my arms and lowered his eyes to my hip. "You'll live."

"That's a relief." So was his concern. It was a strange reaction, but I thought about the men in my past and he just didn't fall in the same category.

Adam cared.

"What do you do for a living?" I wondered aloud. Something was off about Adam; he wasn't like anyone I had ever met. High school dropout or not, he had intelligence in addition to agility. Strength combined with such a gentle spirit and warrior eyes that were haunted.

Leaning in with a hard posture, he closed the space between us. "Do you want me to show you?"

Goosebumps scattered across my arms when his hand slid up my leg over the pickle juice and he suddenly lifted me off the counter, carrying me through the house until we came to a door in the living room.

"Open it."

"The closet?" I stared at the doorknob.

He snorted. "That's no closet."

I liked him holding me, so I stalled. "If there are jars full of heads in there, I don't want to know."

A frown pushed through his humored expression, carving a few small lines around his eyes. "Do you want to see or not? Be nice or I won't cook my world-famous enchiladas."

I clamped my mouth shut.

In the past couple of weeks I learned one hard fact—Adam had a gift with food. I simply had a gift of putting it in my mouth. Eating it was only half the pleasure, watching him prepare it, cook it, and serve it was like foreplay.

"That's better," he said, in a voice rich with honey and purr. "How did you get a name like Zoë Winter?"

"My cold, cold heart."

He squeezed me ever so slightly in protest.

"My father donated his sperm and my middle name."

"Come again?"

"I don't have anything nice to say about a man I never met. Like most men, he didn't stick around."

Adam dipped down and opened the door; it swung slow and heavy, revealing a completely black room. No windows.

"Flip the switch, my hands are full."

"You could always put me down."

The door kicked shut behind him and we stood in the dark. "Where's the fun in that?"

"I'd rather not know if this is any insight to your vast spandex collection, so if you could just warn me now?"

I heard the smile in his voice. "Then consider yourself forewarned, woman."

Adam brushed the switch with his shoulder. A red glow illuminated from a series of red lamps that hung from the ceiling over a workbench filled with trays, bottles, and equipment.

"Put me down," I breathed.

Adam let me go and stood by the door as I walked to the center of the room. The back wall was lined with built-in cabinets and drawers. On the left was a smooth white table with a magnifying glass on it. To my right was a weathered chair with a projector on a table.

"You're a photographer."

I walked over to several photographs hanging on a line: an old barn, a lazy cat stretched over a tractor wheel, a man on the street swinging a little boy over his head who looked three shades of tickled. I was peering into the mind of Adam and how he saw the world around him.

"These are so good."

I turned to look at him and he leaned against the door with his arms folded.

"It's my life and salt, the only thing that has kept me going. I needed to be able to look through the lens and see something good in the world."

Leaning against the cabinet on my elbows, I raked my fingers through my hair with a little frustration building up. "You know, sometimes I think that I'm not the only one keeping secrets."

I dropped my head down and gasped.

A photograph was peering out from behind another and I pulled it out. It was me, lying on the bed with my fists curled up on my chest like a feral thing about to fight. My body was smeared in blood, my shirt was ripped—how could I have survived?

The picture vanished with a snap of a wrist when Adam saw what I found.

"I'm sorry, Zoë. I forgot I had it." He turned around and cursed under his breath. "I wanted to get evidence of what happened. I never meant for you to see it." His fingers let go and it flew in an angle across the floor.

I stepped up behind him and hugged my body against his back. "I'm sorry you were dragged into this."

That's when he shifted around. "Sorry?"

"Say the word and I'll go."

Adam startled me when he pulled me into a hug. "You're not going anywhere, Z."

"Z?" I snorted into his shirt. "Since when did we get on such friendly terms?"

"Ready for some chow?" Adam planted a soft kiss on my nose before opening the door.

I reached over to flip out the light.

"I'm starving, so it better be world famous."

"Zoë?"

"Yes?"

A finger brushed along the curve of my jaw. "Some men do stick around."

CHAPTER 5

BITING WIND SLAPPED MY FACE as the ground beneath my feet hurtled by. There was no sense of feeling to it. I was on the run.

I wanted to slow down but he was right on my heels. I couldn't see him, but I could feel him closing the distance with every perilous step. A tree branch tore my cheek as the brush became thicker.

So dark, I can't see.

The forest snapped beneath his stride and when sudden explosions lit up the path, I realized it was from lightning bolts that ripped through the sky moving horizontally on either side of me. Euphoria and danger mixed into a dangerous poison.

"You can't run from me little girl. I'm going to find you and when I do, I'm going to crack your skull."

Bile rose in my stomach; I had no sense of where he was anymore. Risking another glance, I slammed against something hard and unmoving.

My head flew up, staring at two pools of green light—his unholy gaze terrified me with every flicker. I cried out when his fingers bruised my arm, shaking me harder with his impossible iron grip.

"Let's finish this, progeny. Show me where you are!" he demanded.

"No! Let me go!"

Gasping for breath, I opened my eyes, staring into Adam's panic-stricken face. *His* arms were the ones gripping mine—*he* was the one shaking me.

"Wake up! Wake the fuck up, Zoë," he demanded.

Adrenaline surged in my veins and leaked out of every pore. I had a violent reaction and thrashed about.

"Don't touch me!" I yelled, and his hands went comically up as if the cops had him under arrest.

The leather sofa, I'm on the sofa. Just a dream, wasn't it? His voice was so real.

"Christ, I heard you screaming." Adam wiped his face against his bicep and blew out a breath. "I thought someone was in here; you were shouting." He lowered his arms and I glanced up at a vein protruding from his neck with an unbelievably hard rhythm.

"I wasn't shouting," I said in a soft voice.

Suddenly, Adam leaned down and gave me a cold stare. "Tell me everything that motherfucker did to you."

My senses returned; I was only caught between dream world and real world for a few fractions of a second.

"I didn't mean to…"

What—flip out on him? Smack him? Mooch off him or intrude on his life?

"Scare you."

He smoothed my hair away from my eyes with his hand and my self-doubts drained. I felt safe with Adam. Yet, the dream stuck to me like tree sap and while I could wash it all I liked, there would still be residual stickiness.

"You have no idea how close I was to coming in here and putting holes in someone."

"Adam, don't be ridiculous."

It was then that I glanced to the floor and saw a black gun. That scared me a little because Adam didn't strike me as the type who carried weapons. This was a far cry from a country redneck's shotgun collection—that piece looked like something a cop would carry.

It wasn't until I noticed his wolfish grin that I broke the silence.

"What's so funny?" I pulled myself to a sitting position; that'll teach me to take an early-evening nap.

"You called me Adam."

"Well don't get all warm and gushy. It was a slipup; it won't happen again, *Raze*." I teasingly shocked him in the bicep with a snap of static, but he didn't jump.

"You're no fun."

"How's that?"

"Sunny always jumps when I shock her. Maybe you aren't quick enough on your reflexes."

"My reflexes are just fine where it counts."

I posed a questioning glance at the double entendre.

"I didn't know cavemen came to the rescue of a damsel in distress. I thought they just clonked them over the head with a big stick and—"

That's when he cut me off and playtime was over. My shoulders hunched up as I looked into those eyes, burning with restrained anger. He leaned in so we were nose to nose and I held my breath.

"*Never* do that again."

I hit a raw nerve. Pieces of a puzzle began falling together from earlier conversations.

"How did she die?" *Meaning his sister.*

Adam sucked in his bottom lip and released it slowly. It caught my attention as it glistened and for a brief moment, for whatever reason, my blood heated for him. I lifted my gaze to his rich brown eyes and noticed that they were fixed on *my* mouth. I became self-conscious of every movement they made.

And my lips were dry—damn if I didn't need to lick them, but I made every effort not to go that route.

"She was killed in an alley when we were twenty-one," he said, leaning back.

"I'm so sorry. Can I ask what happened?"

I didn't care for that look of guilt.

"We were barhopping, the kind of thing you do when you get legal. I started talking shit to these guys in an alley when they were catcalling the girls, and they jumped us. One girl was taken out right away and I was too busy beating the shit out of one of the guys to even notice that it had been my sister to go next. That fucking animal tossed her over like a pile of garbage." It seemed to take all the strength he had to draw in another breath. "I was looking for a fight when I should have been protecting her. He took everything from me."

"Were they arrested?"

"No, they got away. I could have chased them down, but they took off fast and… I couldn't leave Bell lying next to a dumpster." This was something that took place years ago, but for him, it was yesterday. Adam didn't just lose a sibling, he lost the other half of him.

"She was so young, but *so were you*. You can't protect someone all the time—it wasn't your fault. You did what you could but you are not responsible for her death. I hope you realize that."

He looked like a man who had been punishing himself and running away his entire life.

"Sunny was the closest person to me, and I hope she isn't blaming herself for leaving me at that train station. Things happen, it wasn't her fault." I stopped because that was the most detail I had given Adam on that night and his eyes rose to meet mine. "I know your sister would tell you that if she could." I placed my warm hand over his. "Adam…"

Hearing his name triggered something in Adam, and his body leaned in slow like a predator. His lips brushed over mine and Adam hesitated, savoring the first touch and perhaps waiting for me to reciprocate. The moment I did—he ignited.

A raw need was behind every hungry stroke of his tongue, and he was a hell of a kisser. No aftershave or cologne, just the natural spice of how a man should smell. The whiskers I could have done without, as they scratched against my chin.

A perfect kiss blindsided me—there was something in his touch and the lean of his body that was overpowering. Did Adam really care for me the way his body told me he did? His hand slipped around the nape of my neck, cradling it, as his kiss slowed to a torturous linger.

When he moaned unexpectedly, deep and pleasured, a spark lit in me. It tingled in the center of my chest, becoming a surge that pushed through to my fingertips; I felt like a sponge dripping with power.

My right leg slid down his side, but he was busy nipping at my bottom lip with his teeth.

"I'm going to touch you," he whispered.

Adam announcing his intent was so unexpected that I stopped kissing him. His mouth moved across my neck and when his fingers ran over my shirt, I arched my back.

"Zoë, you're so soft," he breathed, tracing his skillful fingers down to my stomach, where they slipped beneath the shirt and stroked my bare skin.

His tongue lapped across my neck and my hand reached out to stroke his cheek, circling my fingers around the rough stubble. I heard a low-decibel hum, increasing with frequency—that's when Adam catapulted off the sofa and yelled out.

I could still feel his lips on mine and my hand was suspended where only seconds ago it had traced along his jaw and hairline. I was horrified by my willingness to yield to him.

Sex always ruins friendship, and I didn't know that I was ready to give that up. I needed a friend and couldn't afford to lose him. Although sex would have been nice.

"What was that?" he hissed, pushing the skin of his cheek around with his hand.

"I guess a mistake?" I threw my feet on the floor and glared at his disheveled shirt. Adam ran his hand through his hair and stared down at me like I were a freak of nature.

"Do you know what you just did to me?"

I didn't like his accusation or his tone. "Don't turn this around on me; you're the one who kissed me first. Why are you looking at me that way?"

Adam sat down and lifted my hand by the wrist, like he might have picked up a dirty dishtowel that had been soaking in urine. There was no warmth in his touch as he flipped it over, stroking his finger down my palm.

I shivered and pulled it away.

"Something weird just happened with your hand. You didn't feel that?"

I didn't want to admit to the fact that there was something fundamentally wrong with me. I'd felt it since the night of my attack.

But I sure as hell didn't want to be called out on it.

"You haven't noticed anything odd about yourself?" he added.

"Odd," I said defensively. "Weird. Thanks for all the compliments."

"You're hiding something from me, and I want to know what it is."

I was already in his debt and I didn't like that feeling of entitlement he had over me.

Moving briskly toward the front door I pulled at the handle when Adam muscled it with his strong arm.

"Where do you think you're going?"

"None of your business," I spat.

When I pulled again he leaned harder, and that pissed me off.

"Let go; you can't make me stay here. You don't own me, so quit treating me like property. I have a life I need to figure out and I can't keep hiding."

He shouldered the door and wrapped his fingers around my wrist, pulling it away from the knob. I jerked free and scowled.

"Look, you aren't the boss of me."

Adam didn't budge.

"Fine," I said, backing away from the door. "Whatever."

I locked eyes with the back door and took off in a dead run. I was halfway out on the porch when he caught my arm.

"Get back in the fucking house! I'm not letting you leave."

I struggled to pull free, but he reeled me in like a fish until I was inside. I looked at him with defiant eyes and he locked his arm around my hips.

"You're not a prisoner, that's not what this is about. I want to help you, but you have to let me, you have to trust me." When his voice softened, I considered his sincerity.

"Did I hurt you?" I asked.

"Not exactly."

I swallowed down my relief. "Then what was it you felt?"

"So you know what I'm talking about?"

I nodded. "I'm not really sure how to answer that. I haven't been right since my attack, and that was…" I shook my head. "I'm protecting myself because I don't want you to think I'm crazy. I don't want you to judge me. I don't want you to leave me."

And there it was, in a neat little nutshell. Adam using words like *weird* or *strange* to describe me felt like I had an affliction. He was all I had in the world and I didn't want to lose that.

I shivered as the northern wind snuck up from behind and curled around my legs like icy fingers.

Adam leaned on the door with one hand until it closed.

"I won't judge you, and I won't leave you." He remained in that position, with one arm resting over my head and the other around my waist. "When your hand was on my face it was as if you were charging me up, like an electric shock. How is it that you can do that?" His eyes narrowed almost suspiciously. "It was energy. I can still feel it." He let go of me and flexed his fingers open and closed.

"It's not just my looks that changed, Razor, there's something else different inside of me. I don't know what it is, how to control it, or why it even comes out—but it's there."

"I don't want you to leave," he sighed. "I want you here, feel me? You need someone to look after you until we figure this out."

We.

That was Adam—always wanting to look out for someone. Perhaps it was that lost opportunity with his sister. I gave him a chance to walk away, but he planted his feet firmly on the ground and folded his arms, ready to go wherever this little journey led him.

"No more physical contact, it's too risky and I have a feeling that I could have done more damage than curled your hair. Strictly platonic, okay?"

His mouth crooked up in a grin and he stuck out his hand. "Deal. Shake on it?"

I stuck out my tongue at him and sauntered off.

"Don't tempt me, woman," he growled.

While his voice was laced with humor, I looked back and saw his sexy eyes hung on me heavily. Residual from our kiss no doubt, but something lingered in that expression.

"Put on your shoes and pack the ladder, Romeo. We're going to do Spidey work."

CHAPTER 6

"**A**RE YOU SURE THAT YOUR window is open?"

I looked over my shoulder at the dark, empty street. "I usually keep it unlocked in the late summer. I like a cool breeze. Are you *sure* no one is watching?"

Adam glanced around my apartment complex. The cops would be one thing, but the last thing I needed was my neighbor, Mr. Harvey, pointing a shotgun at our asses.

I nervously gripped the edges of the ladder and took a deep breath. "You're good. Hurry up and don't fall."

I'm not sure whose idea it was that I was the one to go up, but Adam was stronger and could steady the ladder better than I could. I bit my lip, looking up at where the ladder rested against the window.

"Hold it tight, okay? I don't have nine lives."

"No, you have eight." A grin distracted me a moment while his hands worked to steady the ladder.

Halfway up, I realized two things. One: climbing was not a silent feat. Two: flip-flops are not recommended. My toes grappled onto those shoes like grim death. I shot a worried look when Adam's eyes gave me a reply: *you can do this, and hurry your ass up.*

I pushed the window up and threw myself inside as fast as I could, my legs still dangling over the ledge.

Jesus, I will never do anything like that again. Just then, one of my flip-flops slid free.

The first thing I noticed was some of my things were gone.

"Max?" I frowned at where his food dish once was.

After a couple of minutes, there was a light tap in the living room and I flipped the lock and pulled the door open.

"Lose this?" he said, dangling my shoe between his fingers. I snatched it and victoriously displayed my ATM card.

"Sweet, now you can buy your own panties."

"Try to be quiet, I have thin walls."

Adam was on it. Without a word, he slipped out of his shoes and turned off the light. I watched with amused curiosity as he closed the curtain in the bedroom as if he had done this kind of thing before. The man was a photographer by day and a ninja by night.

"Hey, I'm not Helen Keller—I need some light."

A soft glow beamed from the connecting bathroom. Adam stopped short in the doorway. "That should give you enough. Hurry up, get whatever you need, and let's get the hell out of here."

I brushed past him and as I did, he yanked a stick out of his pocket and cracked it. After a few shakes it released a soft green glow.

"Who are you, an international spy?" I giggled to myself out of earshot range.

I stuffed a few personal things into a small bag and rejoined him in the living room.

"Can you help me get this down the stairs?" I whispered, dragging my white flokati rug behind me.

"Christ, Zoë," he scolded. "If you take anything personal let it mean something to you. Hurry up; we need to clear outta here."

I stared at the rug, disappointed. "I took my first steps on this rug." I sighed, dragging it back into the bedroom. I guess it seemed a silly thing to him but you can't help what you form attachments to.

When I finished, I followed the glow of green light in my hall that was lingering over one of my picture frames. I stepped beside Adam, who was looking at my former life.

"That's my mom." I pointed to an old Polaroid of my mother when she was young, standing behind me as I clutched an orange teddy bear. "And that's Max, my baby." My finger brushed over the glass, scratching his imaginary head.

"That's a big baby," he said, looking at the picture of Max lounged out in my bathroom sink with his massive jackrabbit legs spilling over the edges.

"And that's—"

"You", he whispered.

My ex had taken the picture; I was sitting on my white rug gazing out the window. To anyone else it looked like I was daydreaming, but that was the day I was thinking about getting away from him.

"Yeah. Was." I cleared my throat.

When memory lane turned into an HOV lane, I made a quick break for the exit, not wanting to get lost in sentimental bullshit when I had a job to do. Adam went into my bedroom while I moved toward the front door.

"I'm heading down; I'll be in the car."

I glanced down. "Don't forget your shoes, they're by the door." I could feel his *no shit* look through two inches of door.

Once in the Rover, I slouched down in my seat and mentally collapsed. The remnants of my life were zipped up in a bag and I knew I was never going back. That chapter was closed, and yet I wasn't as upset as I should have been. I had a clean slate. My life wasn't much, but I was still grateful that I *had* it.

A few minutes later, the rear hatch lifted for a few seconds and then Adam slammed it shut. He hopped in and punched the key in the ignition.

"Anywhere else?"

I opened my eyes and turned to face him. A laugh escaped that reverberated off the walls of the truck and spiraled out of control.

Adam had shoved the glow stick in his pocket, causing his entire crotch to radiate like a nuclear meltdown. I was hysterical for a minute or two before I could breathe again.

"My stomach hurts," I said, wiping a tear. "That's money." I groaned, letting out a few stray laughs. It was the first time I really let down my guard with Adam and he was thoroughly enjoying every minute of it. His eyes squinted from a broad grin and he winked at me.

"Kryptonite, sweetheart." He tossed the stick in the back and the engine growled as the car pulled out.

"Wait!" I hissed.

Adam reacted, slamming the brakes as I flew forward. He threw his arm out protectively, despite the fact I was buckled up.

Between two buildings, someone was watching us, and this time I *saw* him. He stepped into the dark shadows and that prickly feeling surfaced. Somehow—I *felt* him. Now I knew that he was not just a phantom memory chasing me in my dreams and that terrified me.

When I lost consciousness during the attack, I never knew what happened to the man. With that uncertainty there was always an underlying fear that he was behind every door, every dark shadow, and in my head. He became my boogeyman. What if he found me? He couldn't possibly know what I look like now, but what if…

Adam threw the car in park and sprang into action, hitting the pavement in a full run.

"Adam, wait!" But it was too late.

My hands started shaking as he charged between the buildings and vanished from sight. The car was quiet except for the sound of my stampeding heartbeat. Minutes passed.

I popped open the door and I took a few cautious steps toward the corridor, but as I neared the curb I had second thoughts.

Just as I turned on my heel, I was grabbed by an arm. I spun around to face Adam.

"What are you doing out of the ca—"

I slapped him. The sound cut through the air and marked him with my anger in red splotches that formed on his cheek.

"Don't you *ever* leave me alone like that again! You can't just run off; what if something happened?"

Adam paled. It didn't occur to me how those words might affect him, but I wasn't thinking rationally. He attempted to pull me against him but I recoiled, trembling all over. It wasn't just me, but what if something happened to *him*?

"Adam Razor… if I don't live and fucking breathe."

We simultaneously turned to the right and emerging from a black Jeep Commander was a brute of a man—thick and stocky in build, wearing a black beanie hat and a tight, white, long-sleeved shirt that looked like buttercream icing over his body-builder frame. His inquisitive eyes glowed from the illumination of the cigarette burning at the end. He pulled in a long drag, eating up the time as the paper crackled.

"Knox… you're a little off the map, aren't you?"

"Likewise, brother." The cigarette was tossed to the asphalt and crushed beneath sizable laced-up boots as he blew out the smoke. I didn't like the way he glared at me, so I stepped closer to Adam. Knox folded his arms, pushing out those boulders he called muscles.

"Go wait in the car."

Adam didn't wait for an argument but escorted me to the car and slammed the door. I watched the two men lock arms and I cracked the manual window just a little so I could eavesdrop.

"I told you I'm out," Adam stated factually.

"Which brings me back to my previous question—what brings you out here? It's a pretty big *mother of a fucking* coincidence." His muscled arm stretched out over the car door and I didn't see him blink once. Intimidation oozed out of his pores as if it were part of his DNA makeup.

"This is my life, Knox. Deal."

"Sure you don't want to tell me something? Last chance, because I'll find out."

Adam's stance widened. "I'm squeaky clean, as you'll see. No one sent you to find me?"

"Hell no, we got bigger fish in the frying pan." Knox lowered the tip of his hat so his eyes were hidden. I remained quiet, knowing any sound I made would alert them that I could hear what they were saying.

"Pretty girl." His eyes skated to the car and Adam turned to check on me. "She yours?"

"She's a friend; I'm helping her out."

Knox rubbed his hand against his chin, pulling in his lower lip. "Do me a favor and cook up that big juicy steak you're going to put over your cheek when you get home, brother. I like it well-done. Looks like you're the one that needs the help."

Adam softly chuckled and his hand touched the back of his neck. It was his thing, one of those gestures that was intrinsically Adam. "Sounds to me like you haven't found that someone special."

Knox sounded like a distant motor when he laughed and he tilted his wide chin up with a smirk. "I like my women naked with their legs wrapped around my neck—now that's special." I almost shuddered at the visual. His smile spread tight across those steel jaws. "Relationships are for pussies, I think we've established that."

"Still the same old whore you always were, Knox." Adam's tone warmed and despite their banter, I could see they were friends.

"It isn't the same. You should see the mindfuck they paired me up with."

I turned in irritation as a small Chevy sputtered out of its parking space. The engine drowned out the conversation at the most critical point. Once the car narrowly missed losing its transmission turning the corner, their voices drifted back.

"Got to fucking love it." They laughed in unison and I turned my mouth, thinking that this wasn't the type of friend I imagined Adam pairing up with. But then, there was a lot about Adam I didn't understand.

"Is this a job, anything I need a heads-up on?"

"Sorry, brother, you know the rules. Let's just say this is my R&R. It's never too late to come back."

"You know where I stand on this, Knox. There's no going back. I already got them on my ass. I've worked hard to make a life here and stay under the radar. You need to open your eyes to what's going on."

"My eyes are wide fucking open. The elusive Trinity files were hacked. Yeah, that's right. My partner is a royal dick but his skills are impeccable. What I saw would pop your cork, and it sheds a little light on some of the jobs we did."

"Are you out of your fucking mind hacking into that database? I hope your twisted buddy knows how to cover his tracks, or you'll end up out here with me."

Knox looked around, unimpressed. "Yeah, this blows."

"This doesn't seem like standard—" When the voices abruptly cut off, my eyes lifted from the floor of the car. Busted. I cringed as their gaze splintered me.

Knox reached into the Jeep and pulled out a cigarette, cupping his hand around the end as a flame poked out of a polished silver lighter. The metal clinked and it was tucked safely in his back pocket. The cigarette, on the other hand, stood no chance against his long, life-sucking drags. Knox threw a heavy hand over Adam's shoulder and gave it a firm shake.

"You're a jackass for not calling. My proctologist keeps in better touch than you do."

"You know me, never been one for postcards."

Knox threw another glance in my direction. "To be continued."

"Knox." Adam inclined his head. "I was wrong; *we* were wrong." He glanced over his shoulder at me but this time I didn't break eye contact.

On the drive back, I was running on empty and Adam gave me a look as if he were daring me to ask who that was. So I decided to rest my eyes and think about Max for a little while.

I stirred when I felt someone hooking their arms beneath my legs; I wanted to open my eyes but I drifted back to sleep.

That is until I was thumped in the head by something solid. My cheek was pressed against a cold wooden door.

Adam was struggling to turn the key in the lock while carrying me.

I stiffened my back so that he would drop me. Honestly, I wasn't used to being carried around like that.

"Wait, put me down."

"Shhh, go back to sleep, hon."

The key turned and Adam cradled me tighter.

Through tangled lashes I saw his handsome face, that soft ruffled hair and brows that dipped low like a shadow. It felt good to be held. Adam made me feel safe, something no man had ever done.

There was a glimmer of fire in those bottomless eyes. "Woman, don't you move a single muscle."

"What about my hands?" I mumbled as my eyes closed.

"I guess you'll have to keep your hands to yourself. Think you can manage?"

Versus the alternative of electrocuting my best friend? You bet.

My head lolled back on his broad shoulder until I felt the cool press of the comforter beneath my body. I was floating on a cloud. The flip-flops were removed from my feet one at a time and something exquisitely soft brushed across my legs.

Warm breath tickled my face and the bed depressed in two spots. But it wasn't breath, it was the wind. I was standing on the shore on a moonlit night. The wind called so very close to my ear, but the water was warm and inviting as I moved forward.

"You awake?"

"Mmhmm."

"I'm going to let you sleep tonight."

"Mmm."

"You hear me?"

I grunted. The wind was noisy and needed to put a sock in it. I just wanted the silent waters.

"Tomorrow you're telling me everything. All of this secrecy ends. It's time that you learn to trust me, Zoë. Can you do that?"

My body slipped deeper into the dark and inviting waters, feeling the warmth run up my legs and smother me.

"Zoë?"

Waves were lapping over my mouth, brushing my lips with promises. I could feel Adam all around me.

"Did you hear me? Tomorrow."

"Okay," I promised and completely submersed into the darkness.

CHAPTER 7

THE NEXT MORNING I STRETCHED my muscles into consciousness. My bones, however, creaked in protest.

Adam stood over me: legs apart, arms folded (shirtless I might add), with the most self-satisfied smile I'd ever seen. Yep, this was definitely going to be the day we had the talk.

His body was kept in exquisite shape—toned and strong, but not muscular. He acquired strength from the pull-up bar on the back porch and endurance from his morning runs. And when I say runs, I don't mean jogs. I once caught Adam on the trail and that man was hauling ass, giving those sneakers a run for their money.

Without a shirt, I could see the V-cut in his lower belly. A jagged scar on his side caught my eye where one of his hands rested.

"Get dressed," he said, scratching one of his pecs. He was freshly showered and still flushed from his run.

I pulled the sheet over my head and grumbled, "You first."

While Adam was anxious to know the details of my attack, blood and gore would have to wait until after bacon and eggs.

Adam ripped the sheet down. "Get up out of that bed or I'll drag you out."

"I want to sleep in."

My body nearly catapulted off the edge when Adam sailed over and collapsed beside me.

"Sounds like a plan. What shall we talk about?"

I ripped the sheet over him and stormed into the bathroom where I showered up and dug through my bag of clothes. He could be a real pain in the ass when he wanted.

Unfortunately, my old clothes no longer fit my taller frame. I slid into a pair of distressed jeans and a red, sleeveless blouse, applying a thin layer of peach-scented lotion to my skin. I combed out the tangles of my long, dark hair and gathered it up, neatly pinning it back. My hips were narrow and less hourglass, but there was enough there to keep my jeans from slipping too low. My shoulders were broader than before and my arms slender and toned, even though I never worked out. What stood out the most were my green eyes framed against midnight lashes.

"Five minutes, almost done," Adam called out from the kitchen as I sat down to a very lovely table setting.

The silverware rested on cloth napkins beside the colored plates. He even scooped out the apricot preserve and put it in a pretty crystal dish. Nice touch.

"What's the occasion?" I called out, staring at the handpicked wildflowers in the vase with an arched brow.

He ignored me, whistling a made-up tune.

Adam strolled in barefoot with a black shirt neatly tucked in a pair of tan slacks.

"I like the pants," I said as he set a glass of juice on the table. "I was beginning to think you were having a love affair with Calvin Klein."

He looked nice—very put together. Even jazzed it up with a smart leather belt.

"We agreed to see other people."

Adam set down a bowl of strawberries and slid an omelet on my plate.

"Many women would see you as the holy grail if you didn't hide yourself in a wilderness retreat. Good looks, good food, so-so sense of humor."

Adam turned back to the stove, clearing his throat.

I didn't bother to wait before diving in. "This is so delicious," I said with a full mouth.

"It's nice to have someone to cook for."

A ladybug crawled across the table from the flowers and spread her wings, threatening to leave. When Adam took his seat, I figured she was enchanted and decided to sit for a spell.

I turned my neck at the sound of birds stirring up a frenzy outside by the feeder. "You were up early."

But Adam didn't want to talk. Not yet, perhaps not wanting to spoil the breakfast he put so much effort in preparing.

When we finished, a half strip of bacon sat on a plate between us. I reached for it when the plate disappeared, hovering out of reach.

"Don't make me put the hurt on you, *give*."

"I don't think I've ever seen a girl eat as much as you. I don't know where you put it."

True. I hadn't gained a single ounce since the day we met, and he fed me very well.

"You trying to tell me I'm a pig?"

"Just observing your overzealous appetite." He grinned.

I waved my fork in the air and narrowed my eyes. "I've got a fork and I'm not afraid to use it."

"Well then, I've got a glow stick and I'm not afraid to use it."

"You need to keep that stick in your pants." I laughed as Adam cleared the table. "You really should quit your day job," I yelled out. "Open up your own bistro. I could waitress and flirt with the customers, if I'm flirt-worthy."

"You're definitely flirt-worthy. I bet you had to beat the men off with a stick."

I carried the remaining plates to the sink and stood beside him. He washed, I dried.

"You saw what a ravishing delight I used to be." Sarcasm dripped off my tongue. "Sunny was the flirt, I just hung back and observed the master."

"Some men prefer beer over a fine wine. That doesn't mean much."

"So what am I in this scenario—the beer or the wine?"

Adam dropped his chin and frowned. "The wine, of course."

"Sunny would kick your ass for calling her beer."

"It's not a put-down. Some girls are the kind that every man appreciates, and there's nothing wrong with that."

He ran the plate under the faucet, scrubbed it with the bristle sponge, and passed it over to me.

Part of our perception of our looks is shaped from a lifetime of comments, opinions, and reactions to it. I always knew where I stood before. But now, I had none of that to go on outside of what I saw in the mirror—was I still wine, or was I beer? Hell, maybe now I was moonshine.

"I'm sorry I slapped you and said what I did," I said guiltily.

"Don't apologize, you were right. I shouldn't have left you alone like that; you could have been hurt." There was a delicate stretch of silence. "So who was I chasing?"

I tensed. Here it was, the moment Adam would decide how farfetched this whole thing really was. He knew what he found and he knew what the paper said, but he didn't know the whole truth of it.

"I was crossing a field that night on my way home when someone jumped me."

Adam played statue, holding a bowl under the running water but not looking up. Perhaps afraid if he startled me, I might quit talking.

I continued to dry the plate, every square inch of it.

Three times.

As I told him the details of what happened to me, my pulse quickened and I was out of breath. While I had replayed the events in my head a million times, I didn't realize how much it would still affect me when I actually verbalized it. When I finished, I recapped.

"I didn't even hear him come up on me; he just knocked me over and was doing something with our hands."

"Doing what?"

"I don't know, it was like he was sucking the life out of me, and then it was back. It was electric, like you described. He tried choking me after I kicked him in the groin, but then…"

"Zoë." Adam's expression tightened. The water was no longer on. My name was a single request to keep going.

"He said he had done the same thing to others and that he was going to make mine so much worse. It hurt, Adam, it hurt so much when he cut my throat with that knife."

An angry curse sliced through the conversation.

It wasn't mine.

"You feel it when you die. You just know. My heart stopped and I had this weightless, disconnected sensation." Remembering Adam's sister, I didn't want to give him nightmares. "Once it was done, it was okay. Your soul wants to go… somewhere. I wanted to hold on, too. But there was a familiarity to it. That's all I remember until I woke up in the body bag."

My arms wrapped around my waist. "I don't know how or why I'm still here. He wasn't normal; and somehow whatever he did changed me. I don't think he meant to kill me; that's the strange part. Do you think he made me this way on purpose?"

I stood there, trying to remain stoic. I wanted to shut it off like a faucet and just not feel anything.

Adam captured my hands and wrapped them around his body, pulling me against him. He cradled me and even with the uncertainty of knowing I could hurt him again, he held me with such devotion. I fell against his chest and closed my eyes.

Adam wiped strands of my hair away from my forehead.

"Zoë, you can stop being a tough bitch now. Cry if you need to."

"I don't cry in front of people."

I was not a crier, especially in front of someone else, because that was showing too much vulnerability, which I wasn't willing to give anyone.

"Would it make you feel better to know that I'm going to kill him?"

The threat hung at the end of the conversation like a stinger on a bee. No more words were spoken, and we remained like that until I felt ready to let go.

CHAPTER 8

I T WAS JUST AFTER DUSK and Adam left the house to run some errands. Earning my keep became an important role, so after polishing the floor to a solid shine, I tucked the mop back into its corner in the hall closet and looked up. There were three rows of high shelves. Adam put the stupid cleaners on the top shelf. Because I wanted to scrub out some of the grime that dripped to the bottom of the fridge, I dragged one of the small kitchen chairs over and climbed up.

Just as my fingers reached for the lemon-scented cleaner, the metal legs slid across the wet floor and away from my feet.

I grabbed one of the shelves and it snapped away from the wall, sending all the contents spilling to the floor. Luckily, the metal toolkit broke my fall and I cringed as the top-shelf items of batteries, nails, and screws showered over me like shrapnel.

When the last screw rolled to a stop, I looked around. *What a mess.*

There was an unexpected knock at the front door.

"Hold on!" I called out, thinking Adam forgot the keys to the house. I flicked a few nails that had stuck to my arm and cursed at the board on the floor that used to be a shelf. *He's going to kill me.*

More impatient knocking.

"Okay, I'm coming," I said in annoyance. I winced when I stood up—my shoulder cried out and I kicked a few of the screws in the closet.

When I swung the door open to apologize to Adam—before he even saw the catastrophe—my jaw hung silent.

The gun show was in town and I was getting the private tour. Two giant biceps were swallowed up a sleeveless white shirt. I looked up at a steel expression, as if his skin had been pulled taut over a thick jaw and broad cheekbones. Knox gave his greeting with a thin-lipped grin. He wore the same black cap snug to his head, and black hair peeked out around the edges.

"I don't think we were properly introduced," he said without moving those folded arms. There was no attempt to shake my hand.

Blocking the doorway with my body, I blew out an agitated, "Can I help you?"

He dropped his arms but his smile remained fixed. "I'm Knox. I'm an old friend of Raz—Adam. And you are?"

My eyes arrowed to the shadow of a weapon beneath his shirt. "Is he expecting you?"

"Is he around? I need to talk to him."

"He's busy," I lied. When I shouldered the door closed, his oversized boot wedged inside of the open space.

Knox shook his head. "Adam isn't here."

"How do you know? Because the only balls I see on you aren't crystal."

Knox snorted and actually shifted his balls. I averted my eyes at the gesture. "Adam would never let anyone else answer his own door. I didn't get your name.

"Then wait outside; he didn't tell me you were coming, so you're not invited."

"He's not expecting me, true. I know I'm intimidating, but fuck, I'm as harmless as—" Knox quieted as he leaned over my shoulder, craning his head around the door to look behind me. "What the *fff*—"

I was brushed to the side and stumbled over my feet when the door swung open. Knox signed, sealed, and delivered his own invitation as he marched into the kitchen and loomed in front of the closet. His combat-style boots stopped short of the fallen chair, broken shelf, and scattered tools. Knox twisted his large body around, gripping something beneath his shirt.

"Are you alone?" Not waiting for an answer, his eyes scoped the house.

"Not anymore."

Well, the invitation situation was now a moot point. I closed the door behind me and walked into the kitchen, glaring at the new visitor.

"The chair slid out from under me when I was rehearsing for my strip routine."

Knox wasn't listening; he slanted his eyes, staring out the back window. "You sure about that?"

The legs of the chair slammed on the floor as my best fake smile played across my face. "Can I offer you some tasty refreshments?"

That broke the tension. Knox huffed out a laugh and strolled back into the kitchen, pulling his shirt down. "You aren't exactly the kind of woman I pictured Adam falling for."

I laughed back and pulled a couple of beers out of the fridge. "I'm not his woman."

"Damn shame to hear that," he said as he slid his wide frame into the tiny chair. It quivered beneath his weight and looked about as frightened as an inanimate object could.

"Let's go into the living room before you give that chair a heart attack."

I set his beer down on the coffee table, easing back against the sofa while picking at the label on my bottle. "So how do you two know each other?"

The beer let out a sigh of relief, as did the chair he collapsed in—Adam's black leather, ass-pampering seductress of comfort. Knox didn't just sit in the chair, he eclipsed it.

I waited while he knocked back half the bottle. "We served together."

"Military?" *That would explain a lot about Adam's behavior.*

"He didn't tell you, huh? How long you guys been… *not dating*?" He smirked. Yet it was not a casual question.

I could see why Adam would click with Knox; he was an extremely likable guy once you got past all of the bulk and attitude. What particularly interested me is that most people automatically assume a guy of his size is all brawn and no brain, but there was intellect behind his eyes, and he was analyzing every answer I gave, making me more self-conscious. With the mention of military I might have assumed front lines—Marine. But intelligence was more like it.

"He's just helping me out. I'm between jobs right now and he's letting me stay here for a while." I tried to twist off my cap but a sharp pain sliced through my shoulder. I grimaced as my muscles gave a silent warning not to try that again.

Knox leaned over and snatched my beer, popping off the lid as easily as a six-hundred-pound gorilla would crack a peanut. "If you don't have a home, what were you doing at those apartments?"

"You first."

"Visiting a friend."

"Likewise."

That answer didn't satisfy him, but he looked as if he were expecting it.

"Where did you meet?" He pressed on.

I shrugged and considered a little rephrasing. "I was out for a run."

"From who?"

I leaned back to take a long, very long, slow sip of that beer.

Knox leaned forward. "I think we're both bullshitting here—you ever play that card game?"

"With my grandma, every Sunday after church."

He laughed and that's when Adam burst through the front door. If he had just seen us sitting in the living room there might not have been such concern on his face. But his features were marred by the state of disarray the kitchen closet was in.

"In here. Ignore the mess, everything's fine."

Adam came in, not surprised to see Knox, as his Jeep would have tipped him off. The keys were tossed on the bar and Knox stood up to give him a handshake when Adam shoved his hand against his chest. "Did you touch her?"

"*As if,*" Knox choked out.

I interrupted the birth of a fight. "I'm sorry I broke your closet shelf, but you don't put cleaners out of reach unless you have kids. They go under the sink."

"You should listen to the woman," Knox said as he patted Adam on the back. "Or should I say… *your* woman?"

"Sit the fuck down." Adam laughed.

"Quite the little smut-mouth, isn't he?" Knox winked and I smiled, scooting over to make room for Adam. Beer splashed on my legs when he pushed me forward.

"What are you doing?" I protested.

"Jesus, what the hell did you do to yourself?"

He was staring at my back. *Oh yeah, that.*

"I fell out of my chair." I could almost hear the snare of a drum at the poor choice of words that sounded like a bad joke. My curtain closed and I took another swig of beer.

"Wanna kiss it and make it better, or can I sit back now?"

"You're bleeding."

Shit, all over his sofa. I turned around and saw the smear on the black leather. I cursed under my breath. Adam loved his leather and even hated the fact that I ate on it. "I'm sorry... I didn't realize. I'll get something to clean it."

"Fuck the sofa, woman—stay here."

He disappeared in the bedroom and I watched Knox's eyebrows slowly rise up as he polished off his beer. "Friends, huh?" He examined the last drops swirling at the bottom.

Knox shared my sense of humor, or sarcasm. I rolled my eyes and paced into the kitchen to retrieve a case of beer. I was glad Adam was here as a buffer, since I didn't know what questions I could and couldn't answer.

The beer disappeared from my hand when Adam set it on the cabinet and pressed a cold, wet cloth to my shoulder. "You're a pocketful of trouble."

I felt a sting and jumped. "You could eat off this floor, you should thank me."

The second sting made me shut up.

"Tomorrow I'm going to show you how to build a shelf. Hold still, almost done."

"Nice place you got here, brother," Knox said as he strolled to the sunroom. "If you like woods and shit."

I smiled as Adam pressed an adhesive patch on my shoulder. His fingers ran along the edges and I involuntarily shivered. Knox was beginning to grow on me, but Adam didn't seem too thrilled he was here.

"All done."

The mammoth was standing quietly in the sunroom with an unreadable expression that reflected on the glass. "Sorry to have barged in on Annie; I thought you would be here."

"It's Zoë," I called out.

"Is that so?" he mumbled.

"Do me a favor and wait outside, I need to talk to him alone. It won't be long." Adam sounded upset. Now if that wasn't the disappointment of the evening. I was really looking forward to getting tipsy and arm wrestling with our guest. But this was Adam's turf and it was hardly my place to complain.

I snuck around the side of the house near the back door to listen in.

"Don't fucking lie to me, your prints are all over that goddamn apartment. You've gotten sloppy, Razor."

"What game are you playing?"

"Where's the girl?" I heard Knox ask.

There was a short silence and Adam sounded off, "What the hell are you up to, Knox? Speak truth."

"Her name came up in a database. I thought you were out but now I'm not so sure; this thing reeks. That isn't Zoë Merrick, not from the pictures I've seen, but it's too much of a coincidence you were at her complex. Quid pro quo, brother."

"I don't know how much I can tell you, Knox. I don't know much myself."

Adam's voice cut off when my dumb ass stepped on a twig. The door creaked open and I strolled off into the yard, glaring at Adam, who was frowning. When the door shut I continued my pace, there was no point in trying to figure out what they were arguing about. But what piqued my interest was the fact that my name was in some kind of a database. I didn't think to ask if Knox was still in the military—if that were the case it brought a whole new spin on things. I didn't know a thing about the man who attacked me or what he might be a part of.

I had never felt more isolated. Not just because we were out in the middle of nowhere, but there was this emptiness I carried, a longing I couldn't explain. Even the welcomed visit with Knox made that knot in my stomach even more pronounced.

The house vanished from sight, and I hugged the chill off my arms as I strolled down the trail.

That's when it hit me. It was too quiet—I didn't hear a single cricket chirping. Someone whispered, and while I couldn't make out the words, it made my blood run cold. The sound wasn't in my head, wasn't part of the dreams, but it was right here, just beyond the thick of trees. Shaking like a leaf in winter, I strained to look at all the shadows in the deep woods that surrounded me. My breath thinned out into a sheet of frosty panic and I sucked in a sharp breath when a slow crunch of leaves sounded on my right.

A macabre laugh rolled through the darkness and wrapped itself around me like a vise.

It was him—I knew that laugh.

Without a moment to reason, Adam's name poured from my lungs in a scream as I ran up the trail toward the house.

The back door crashed open and within seconds, Knox and Adam were eating up the distance between us in a desperate run. Knox looked more like a bull that couldn't be stopped as he charged past me with his gun in hand. I flew into Adam's arms, pulling him tight.

"What's wrong?"

"He's out there, Adam," I said, out of breath. I looked back and Knox was gone, but I could hear his heavy footsteps as he continued to move.

"Are you sure?"

"I'm sure, please don't let him—"

"Don't worry, Knox will secure the area. Let's get you inside."

CHAPTER 9

TWO DAYS LATER, ADAM WAS called on a photo shoot in Memphis. While he primarily freelanced, he had a friend who pimped him out for bigger jobs that paid more. There was no question about it—I was going with him. Not that it was an option, but I was anxious to get out of town and maybe have some fun.

We arrived late in the afternoon; our reservations were at a modest hotel, nothing fancy in the least. Adam had some prep work to do and because he was methodical about his job, I agreed to stay in and watch movies.

A lie.

The bandage was beginning to itch, so I went into the bathroom to peel it off and clean the wound.

"Let me," he said, pulling the edges slowly. "You heal... remarkably well." He wiped down my shoulder with a towel. "Doesn't look like you need to tape it up again." Adam slapped my skin three times and buried his back against the wall.

"I should be back before nine. They have room service, so order whatever you want."

I always shared a meal with Adam. "I'll wait until you get back; we can order then. I'm not hungry right now." I was too excited about the idea of having an afternoon to myself in a new city to think about food.

"Then I'll bring back some Chinese. I know how you like those little sugar donuts." He grabbed his keys with a single swipe and took off.

I felt a little guilty, I admit it. Adam left without a clue that I had intentions to explore the city like Columbus. My patience was also tried by the fact he kept watch of me like a babysitter. I was a girl who thrived on my independence.

We were right on the heels of fall, which was gracing us with cooler weather and chilly evenings. I changed into a long, sage-colored skirt, white blouse, and flats. I had stopped wearing perfume years ago, so I applied some peach-scented lotion and tucked a cheap digital camera in my purse.

My feet hit the pavement and the thick aroma of barbeque filled the air from a nearby barbeque pit. It was a short walk to the station and I made mental snapshots so that I wouldn't get lost later.

"Is this where the trolley comes?" I asked a woman close to my age, also alone.

"Yes." She gave me that "you must be from out of town" once-over.

Ten minutes later, I was all aboard, enjoying the view from the window. It was a short ride and I stepped onto a busy street with my camera in hand. After walking around and taking the usual tourist photographs, I started people watching. Adam said he connected to his humanity through a lens, yet strangely, I never felt more distant from it.

Time slipped by and before I knew it, the horizon drank in the last sip of light. I licked my dry lips and decided to duck into a bar for a beverage before heading back.

I was seated at a small wooden table by a large window trimmed in tiny yellow lights. Waving off the menu, I ordered a glass of sweet tea and the waitress smiled, turning her nose up. Women like her worked for tips and I had all the red flags of a cheap tipper. Couldn't blame her, I always felt guilty ordering just a drink.

There was a flavor to the ambiance of the room. The glasses sparkled under the amber glow of track lighting behind the bar, and there was a small stage in the back for entertainment. On the downside, the walls were atrocious—license plates, old signs, photographs, a wagon wheel, and rusty pieces of metal. It was as if a junkyard exploded inside of a charming little pub.

A congregation of women lingered at the bar, fueled with laughter and flirtatious behavior. One lovely blonde stroked her silky hair, while another arched her back in a way that accentuated the curves behind her outdated jeans. A third was straddling a barstool in a way that made my lip turn up in repulsion. After a quick scan of the room, it dawned on me that every available woman in that establishment circled around something—someone—behaving like cats in heat.

I stretched my neck to see what the action was all about. My waitress flew out of the kitchen and cocked her hip to the side, setting my drink on the bar. *What the holy hell is going on?*

When a brunette stepped aside to grab her purse, I was able to see what the fuss was all about. It was a man, propped against the bar on his elbows, gazing at his concubines.

And what a man.

With an easy change of position, he shifted over to lean on one arm—a well-calculated move as it emphasized his toned biceps straining against the weight. A seductive smile drew their attention, and the swarm responded with eager giggles and hair tosses as they admired his assets. My waitress leaned over so that he could whisper in her ear.

When she turned to approach my table, she swung her hips like a pendulum. He narrowed his gaze and watched her like a predator.

No wonder the bees were busy; he was what Sunny would have called a primo. The grey form-fitting shirt was made of material so thin it looked like sheer frost on a windowpane—making every cut of his abs visible like a wearable washboard. Those thick arms beckoned to be stroked, but they were not as huge and obscene as the ones Knox displayed. *Then again, no one was quite like Knox.*

His legs, on the other hand, were a powerhouse. He had the upper thighs of a thoroughbred, which was something to be appreciated against his tall frame. His mouth lifted in a sexy sideways smirk as he admired her, and then those eyes fell on me.

While this man was built like a Navy SEAL, looks alone couldn't have drawn such a crowd. His blood was pumping with one hundred percent pure sexuality and it oozed from his pores.

Women were gravitating toward him from all directions like a planetary orbit.

I always considered the biggest turnoff to be arrogance, and this man wore it as cologne. I shook my head and redirected my attention out the window.

"Here you go, honey. Anything else?"

"No, this is going to be it."

She swirled around and disappeared.

The frosty glass dripped with condensation after taking the scenic route to my table. I pressed the cold glass against my cheek, closing my eyes as I enjoyed the delicious feel of it along my neck. The ice clinked and I sighed.

"Will you be drinking that or wearing it?"

Startled, I jumped. The icy tea splashed my neck, dribbling down my shirt. I looked at the new stain forming on my white blouse and frowned.

The latter, it seemed.

I arrowed a hostile glance in the direction of the voice sitting at a table next to mine.

It was him. The man who, only moments ago, was giving every woman in that bar an eye-orgasm. His body melted over the chair as he leaned back, legs stretched forward and crossed at the ankles. All the women at the bar were giving me a sour expression of jealousy.

"I did not intend to startle you," he said as his eyes fell over the stain spreading on my collar.

"Waitress, seltzer please," he ordered with a crook of his finger.

I set the glass down and lifted a napkin, blotting the liquid on my neck and arm.

"You shouldn't sneak up on people like that."

"You aren't from around here."

I twisted my mouth, wondering how he had guessed. I had no recollection of waking up that morning and writing "tourist" on my forehead.

"The tea, it's not a Long Island." His laugh was as rich and deep as his baritone voice. He stretched back, giving the chair a good solid creak, but never removed his eyes from me. "Locals don't come in here for the tea."

The waitress zipped back around, handing him the seltzer, but he didn't so much as look at the woman who, moments ago, had his utmost attention out of all the women in here. I didn't think I was especially that attractive, so maybe I was nothing but a challenge.

Perhaps his ego was shot when I didn't swoon from his playful smile that made soccer moms give up their firstborn.

"Would you allow me?" he offered.

I considered the gesture as I sized him up to see if he could be the wrong kind of company. He was probably an inch shy of Adam, but there was an air of authority about him that I couldn't put my finger on. Up close, I could see that his shaved hair was dark blond, and winding around his right bicep was an intimidating tribal tattoo that disappeared beneath the fabric of his shirt. I had the strangest mental picture of him on a bloody battlefield, but as he stood at the edge of my table with a bottle of seltzer and a napkin delicately held between his fingers, I found nothing but honorable intentions.

He made a gesture toward my collar and I shrugged at the invitation. It was an oddly intimate position to be in when he suddenly went down on one knee and began to work on the stain. His large hands carefully dabbed at my white blouse while I tried to look elsewhere. Difficult to do when every inch of his body was hovering so close to mine.

I sniffed discreetly. *Curious, no cologne.* What kind of man goes out to pick up women without wearing any cologne? I reached for the tea and killed a little time rubbing off water droplets from the glass.

"You're a quiet thing; do you come with a name?"

"Zoë."

"Zoë." He spoke my name in that deep voice, tasting the word on his tongue. "Not a very common name."

"Not a very common girl," I replied.

"Indeed." He watched me with serious eyes.

I wondered what exactly he meant by that. Perhaps it wasn't common for a girl to not fall at the feet of the Adonis. Heaven forbid. Ye gods.

He pressed his lips together and pulled back, studying his work. It wasn't just the handsome features that drew you in—it was an intangible power. Even when he wasn't looking at me, I found his gaze riveting. It was as if a handful of Caribbean sky was crushed into a million tiny shards and fashioned into polished glass to color his eyes.

When his cobalt gaze rose to meet mine, I was the first one to break eye contact.

They say that the eyes are the windows to the soul, but I guess I never wanted any Peeping Toms looking in my windows.

"I think that should do?" He looked at me, seeking my approval.

Sure enough, the stain was gone, leaving only a patch of water. I was a little embarrassed when I could see how cheap the fabric looked up close. Fashion was nothing I had ever concerned myself over, but those were also the days when my clothes were not secondhand and off-brand. A few times I'd settled for a shirt that had a hole or rip in it. I refused to take money from Adam, and my ATM card only stretched so far before my account was closed.

"Thanks, but no big deal. It's not expensive or anything."

"But it's yours," he said.

His attire, on the other hand, was casual: dark denim jeans, a shirt, and combat boots. Yet, there was nothing casual about it. The jeans were a high-end brand, secured with an expensive leather belt. The shirt was a soft material that, up close, looked cut in all the right places, and the boots gleamed as if right off the shelf, and the laces were perfectly tied. He was a man who took pride in how he presented himself, even if he was dressed down. I bit my bottom lip as he remained in that position a few seconds longer than needed before standing up.

"Would you allow me to join you?"

Near the bar, one girl shot me a sour "rot in hell" look, while another whispered something in her ear. Both glanced back and they laughed in unison like a couple of jackals. *Bitches.* I twirled a finger in my hair as I decided to win the unspoken showdown.

"Why?"

"You intrigue me."

"I don't know you well enough to intrigue you." I chuckled softly.

"I am Justus De Gradi," he said, giving a slight bow but never looking away. "Now you know me." He sought approval to take a seat.

I couldn't help but smirk at the girls at the bar who were having a conniption. I was imagining how Sunny would love every juicy bit of this. He was exactly the type of man she cozied up to, from his smug confidence to the size of the bulge in his pants. His *wallet*, that is.

"It's a free country."

Justus eased into the chair across the table, stretching his left arm over the back of the chair. By his body language, I would have been willing to bet his legs were wide open. I had a theory that men who sat that way were the alpha males. But despite his cockiness, he was quiet and serious, not the sort of guy I usually had a drink with. I had to mentally argue with myself, because if anything—the evening was becoming interesting.

An enigmatic smile lurked, but beneath it lurked something else: frustration.

"Are you a photographer?"

"No, why do you ask?" My camera had never come out of my purse the entire time I was in here.

"You were taking pictures on the street earlier; you seem to have a fascination with people. Unless you are a private investigator." He studied me, waiting for a response while tapping a gold ring he wore on the table. Not a wedding ring, I noted, as it was on his right hand. Was he kidding?

"I don't stalk people for money, no." I removed the lemon wedge from the rim and set it on the table. "My friend is the photographer; I thought I would impress him with my lack of skills. The atmosphere is different here than where I'm from. The people are interesting."

"Some more than others."

I wondered how he noticed me outside when it seemed he had plenty of other distractions in this fine establishment that reeked of onion rings and whore perfume. Not to say that I wasn't flattered, but I had no intention of hooking up with a stalker… no thank you.

"Are you from around here?" I asked.

He closed his eyes slowly and when they opened, they sparkled—pleased that I was asking him a question. Justus shook his head. "No, just passing through."

"So you're a wanted felon on the run?"

His eyes narrowed a fraction before we were interrupted.

"Can I get you anything, honey?" The waitress leaned over

Justus, making sure he had a criminal view of her open blouse.

Justus leaned to his left to keep his eyes locked on mine. "No, that will be all," he answered.

Stacy (according to her nametag) ran a manicured hand down her tight, black pants and I could tell that rejection stung. This guy was a real piece of work with how quickly he could turn off his interest in these women. She glared at me the way a woman does when she's become the consolation prize and walked off.

"I do hope you are meeting with someone, Peaches. This isn't the place for a female without an escort, and it is now evening."

"So you're saying I should have a male escort?" I snorted as I tapped my glass.

Justus leaned forward with his elbows on the table, letting his left hand fall across his tattooed bicep. He stroked it like a pet—rough and slow—so that I could hear the hiss of skin on skin. It was an obvious attempt at directing attention toward his body. With every methodical stroke, he watched. I grabbed a saltshaker and began mentally counting the holes on the lid. One, two, three, four, five...

"Are you not pleased by my body?"

The shaker slipped out of my hand, spilling salt across the wooden table. An army of tiny granules scattered to the far corners. Dumbfounded, I laughed at the question.

"Not as pleased as you are." I scooped up the salt and piled it on a napkin. Part of me thought he was visually handsome and wanted to flirt back, yet another part was still hung up on the fact that he completely expected it. "I'm sorry, I didn't know debauchery was on the menu this evening."

Through my peripheral vision, I watched his face contort as a man provoked.

"What brings you here, Zoë?"

"A friend of mine is on a job assignment, so I'm the tagalong. I've never been here, so I wanted to see what it was like."

"The photographer?"

"He's working; I'm just sightseeing."

"How do you find this city?"

My, wasn't he proper with conversation? He gave off an air of refinement and superiority that just annoyed me. Did he think he was royalty? I had to wonder what it was about him that made every woman go into heat. He was hot, but he also wasn't the only male on the premises. In fact, there was a pretty one sitting near the front door that I sent my eyes over to investigate.

Before I could answer, Justus peered over his shoulder, following my gaze. Just then, he leaned enough to his right so that my view was obstructed.

Oh, right. Conversation.

"It's not bad here—I think the trees are beautiful and the culture is interesting, but it's not Paris. Not that I would know what Paris looks like—of course, I guess I can travel now if I wanted to."

"So you are financially taken care of," he thought aloud, silently drawing a conclusion.

I laughed, nearly spitting out my drink. I considered how I should answer while setting down my glass on the square napkin of salt. "If you're asking if I'm a kept woman, then no."

"What are you looking at?" I could see he was growing apprehensive.

"Nothing, just that thing over your eye." He knew what I meant—Justus had a silver bar that ran through the top of his brow straight to the bottom. I didn't particularly care for this type of piercing on a man.

His hand lightly touched it and I caught a flash of insecurity in that massive ego. If I didn't know better, I'd say Justus wasn't used to anyone being honest with him, or for that matter, disagreeing with him. This was a man who was used to getting his way and hearing what he wanted.

"You don't like it?"

I scratched at my earlobe, pondering how to broach this with a little tact, something I wasn't entirely good at. "It's just that you would look better without it. I mean, you might as well get one of those bone things and put it in your nose. No offense, it's just that for some reason I don't get the piercing vibe from you. I'm not sure what kind of image you're trying to project, but you don't need it."

"Can I buy you dinner?"

I blinked.

I practically insulted the man and now he wanted to feed me. *What the hell just happened?*

Of course I *was* hungry; I hadn't eaten since we arrived. My face suddenly paled when I remembered Adam. He was going to call around nine—the thing about distractions is they always seem to come at the most inopportune time. If I wasn't in the hotel when Adam returned, there was no telling what he would do. I didn't know our hotel number, let alone Adam's cell number.

"What time is it?" I grabbed my purse and looked around the bar. The clock on the wall was screaming nine thirty with its hands.

"I'm sorry, but I have to go!" I reached in my purse and snatched a dollar, placing it under my glass as I stood up.

"Wait." Justus held an arm out without touching me to get my attention. "I'll walk you to your car."

"I don't have a car; I took the trolley."

He frowned and dropped a twenty on top of my dollar bill.

"Is it still running? I need to get back right away!"

"You'll be fine, white rabbit. I am escorting you to the station."

I guess I got my male escort after all.

I thought I overheard one of the girls at the bar spit up a hairball when they caught wind of what was going on.

"Umm… I'm not so sure that this is a good idea. I don't—"

"You will accept my company," he stated as fact, walking beside me as we approached the door.

"And how do I know you aren't some kind of serial killer?"

Those serious brows lifted a fraction, bemused. "I should be offended. Why would you imply that?"

I stopped near the door. "Oh, I don't know, your *prey* over there?" My arm swung theatrically toward the bar. Mascara-lined eyes bored into the back of my skull, but I didn't turn around.

"I don't think I'd qualify, as they are the ones stalking me." He winked.

"I bet."

"And what of this one?"

When I watched Justus set his hand on the shoulder of a man

seated at the table, I blushed from head to toe. It was the dark-haired man I was admiring earlier. He rose from his seat and looked as strangely confused as I was.

Justus pushed him back down, giving me a wolfish grin that sent me running out the doorway—mortified.

CHAPTER 10

THE STREETS WERE FILLED WITH a young crowd after dark—mostly drunk—and looking for fun. My eyes occasionally looked away from the tips of my shoes to the signs we passed. While I had adjusted to my new legs, I still didn't trust that I wouldn't go sailing across the uneven concrete.

Justus tucked his hands in his pockets. For every two steps I made, he only took one. There was a comfort walking with him; I felt like I had a personal guard, even despite the fact he was a stranger I just met in a bar.

Another strange thing I noticed was how I didn't have that empty feeling when I was with him.

"Why did you do that in there," I asked combatively.

"Do?"

"Embarrass me?" *As if he didn't know.*

There was a deep chuckle. "Apologies."

Yet, no regret. I muffled a grunt and took a deep breath of the clean evening air.

"So, Miss Zoë, where are you visiting from?"

"We're from Texas."

He lowered his head and followed the swing of my hand, perhaps looking for a ring. When he got the answer he needed he continued. "Boyfriend?"

I played with that idea for a minute before I responded.

"Ah, no. Just a friend."

That filled a little corner of my heart, knowing that I had a friend. Although once I got back to the hotel, that remained to be seen.

Justus looked up when a car blew past us and muttered to himself, "Friends with benefits."

I fell back just a pace. "Now that really stung. Do you think I just sleep around? You think just because a woman has a male friend she's automatically sleeping with him? Don't go around making blind assumptions, because you're probably wrong."

He sighed, and I *almost* felt bad for snapping at him—except that he had *almost* called me a whore. It wasn't really what he said, but the way he said it that irked me. Otherwise, a comment like that I might have brushed off with a laugh.

"Don't you have a car, Justus?"

"I do," he replied. He caught the look I was throwing. "It would not be suitable for me to offer. A woman should be watchful of her safety; never ride in a strange man's car."

"Strange man, indeed," I mumbled.

Wow, this guy I would have never expected to get the safety lecture from. I suspected if Justus caught Smokey the Bear lighting a match, he would probably beat him down with a cane.

We sank into the shadows of the dark road as the street lamps became fewer and dimmer. A long brick wall stretched out on our right, and across the street were dark shops—closed for business. Up ahead, I heard voices and saw two men leaning up against the wall talking.

"It's cooler here than I thought it would be." I brushed the chill off my shoulders. "I should have worn something else."

The heavyset man nodded at his friend in the red shirt, who hopped off the curb with an extra skip in his step. There was no reason to be concerned until the guy against the wall pushed off and began stalking toward us with dark eyes scoping my purse.

Before I could react, Justus flung his arm out in front of me so swiftly that I ran into it and gasped. He guided me protectively behind him while he positioned himself in a fighting stance. I couldn't see anything but T-shirt.

A thick voice as sharp as a knife challenged him. "What's up?"

Justus didn't respond. I looked down and saw that my hands were trembling.

A cheap purse with fifteen dollars in single bills was not worth my life. I already lost it once and I had no intention of losing it again. At least, not this soon.

I stepped left for a better view. They were toe-to-toe, and Justus bested him by at least four inches.

"Here," I said, holding my purse out. "I don't have anything worth taking, but you can have it."

"Is that so, honey pie?"

I snapped my head to the left and saw the second man in the red shirt closing in. He came out of nowhere and I grabbed Justus by the back of the shirt, twisting it nervously in my hands as my heart thundered.

We were in the worst possible area and completely alone. I thought about turning back and running in the opposite direction, but the man in the red shirt was too close. He also had flashy white sneakers, the kind that you couldn't outrun in a pair of flats. I tossed my purse to his feet and the contents spilled out.

"Check out the honey," he said, edging closer. "She's sweet—look at her blushing. She knows what's waiting for her." He took a wide step over my purse and smiled wolfishly.

"Tell your pawn to back off," Justus growled.

The man in front of him lifted his chin. "Do we have a problem here, *motherfucker*?"

"Back. The. Fuck. Off. And we won't."

Tension: sharp as a blade, thin as a hair, and acidic on the tongue. That's when I let go and stepped back. Heat flared off Justus like a fever and the moment I heard metal click, I jumped.

Someone had a knife.

Justus stood like a powder keg—legs in an open stance, arms hovering inches from his body, as if he were ready to combust with some ass kicking. Alarm ran up my spine, latched on, gripped tightly, and clawed with dull nails.

"Leave us alone," I said meekly. "Just let us go."

Red-shirt guy snatched my skirt in a tight fist—leaning forward as if he were bowing to me. The tip of his tongue swept against the corner of his mouth. He looked like a wolf on the hunt with his crooked teeth—I his prey.

"Justus," I started to whisper.

I cried out when my skirt was yanked hard and I flew out, stumbling over my feet.

That's when all hell broke loose.

I heard grunts from behind, shoes sliding on concrete, flesh and knuckles hitting bone—but I didn't see a thing. I landed in his arms and when he pushed his nose in my hair, drawing in a deep breath, I shuddered. Without a thought, I punched his jaw upward and there was an audible click of his teeth cracking together.

He flashed those canines at me and scowled. "Goddammit, you stupid bitch!"

I didn't even see his arm swing out, but he hit me in the face with a solid fist.

The concrete broke my fall, but I was by no means defeated. Livid might be a better word.

While he distracted himself by flexing his jaw, I kicked him in the shin with everything I had. At the same time there was a shout from behind and something heavy hit the ground.

I pushed myself up, ready for a fight, when he rushed at me but never made it. Justus launched himself between us and cracked the man's nose so hard I involuntarily cringed at the deformity.

He roared out in pain, pivoting around and nearly falling over as he took off running. Justus hauled ass after him and got in a few good punches. His friend was splayed out on the ground, unconscious. There was no trace of blood.

The attacker sprinted off as if his life depended on it, becoming nothing more than a vanishing silhouette. Justus lingered in the center of the road as if he had a mind to chase him, but instead he turned back, stalking toward me with a control and confidence that was distinctly territorial.

He said nothing when he knelt down before me.

"Are you okay?" My voice was husky and out of breath.

"You first," he mumbled, focusing in on my face with an intimate stare. His expression tightened when it settled on my throbbing cheek. The next sentence was spoken slowly, through clenched teeth.

"Had I known he hit you I would have hunted him down and snapped a few more bones."

One minute I felt flattered by his statement, and when he spoke the next, I only felt the sting of annoyance. "You have a fearless heart; shame that you are weakened by your words."

"Sorry if begging for my life seemed like a good idea."

A strange sensation came over me, like poison was pumping through my veins—hot, numbing, and full of adrenaline. I licked my parched lips and searched for a calming breath. Justus reached around, touching the back of my neck, and that's when it happened.

His touch. That touch was pulling something from me as if I had an internal magnet that was rising to the surface to meet its match. It was that power I had, that unexplainable thing living inside of me, buzzing in my fingertips. Leaning in—as close as two people could get without an exchange of lips and tongue—he tilted his head and searched my eyes.

"Look at me, Zoë."

The smooth command of his voice lifted my eyes. A current of energy was bubbling in every nerve, snapping at the ends like a hungry dragon. Realizing that I was coming very close to that same sensation that threw a volt of electricity into Adam, I pushed him away. Justus leveled me with his eyes, pulled me close, and put his thumb on my forehead.

"*Mage*," he breathed. There was nothing sensual in his tone. In fact, his lips curled as if he were staring at the enemy.

My lips parted, confused by his statement. Mage? Maybe this guy was crazy, after all.

Justus gripped my arm and shook it—he was angry. Angry? I just got clocked in the face in the middle of the street by a man wearing hubcaps on his teeth, and he had the nerve to be angry with me?

"Why did you conceal from me?"

"What are you talking about? I didn't have a weapon." I huffed, pulling from his grip, but he did not let go.

"Tell me why you concealed, Mage!"

"Don't touch me, let *go* of me!" I pushed my hand against his chest, but it merely absorbed my efforts.

Tires screeching in the street pulled my attention away. A door swung open from a beat-up Land Rover and I was so relieved to see Adam. That is until I saw the violence in his eyes.

Adam didn't just walk over, he charged. With alarming speed

he ran at Justus, armed to the teeth with fists and fury and a big knuckle sandwich.

"Wait! Razor, no!" I leapt up and crashed into him—but he was an unstoppable force and I wasn't strong enough. I never really tried to control a hurricane, but hell, it was worth a shot.

Justus was still crouched over when he pivoted his head around to look at Adam. His eyes were blazing with anticipation as he rose to his feet. "You must be the *friend*." He didn't have to say it like that—teasingly—but it was laced with all kinds of insinuations.

"Razor, it's not what you think. Look at me!" My legs anchored to the concrete, pushing him with all the strength I had.

"So you're the kind who hides behind a woman?"

"Shut up!" I screamed at Justus, putting more of my shoulder against Adam.

Adam looked past me as if I weren't even there. "Who the fuck are you? No one puts their hands on Zoë, feel me?"

"No, I'm not feeling you. And neither is she, from what I understand."

Adam lunged and spit out a profanity when I fell off balance and hurtled toward the cement. I squeezed my eyes shut and held my arm out when I was caught.

It was Justus.

"How the hell did you just do that?" Adam said with his jaw nearly unhinged. I looked up and knew exactly what he meant. Justus was at least ten feet from where we were standing; there was no way he could have caught me that fast.

Shock wore off Adam long enough for him to pull me into his arms and give Justus a hard shove. "You okay?"

"Too late for a hero, Adam. Can you calm down?" I wriggled free, deciding not to be anyone's claim.

Justus looked between us. "We need to talk."

CHAPTER 11

SOMEHOW, WE MADE IT BACK to the hotel without Justus and Adam killing each other. After Justus made a player's catch, he divulged a little information that was convincing enough for us to talk with him privately. I was pretty surprised that Adam was agreeable to this, but maybe Justus had some answers I was looking for.

"Get out," Justus barked at Adam. "This does not involve humans."

"He stays or you go," I said. Justus narrowed his eyes and tried to burn a hole in my head with them. I drew the line at excluding Adam.

Reluctantly, Justus found a chair, took a seat, and changed my life with a single word—Mage.

The very first thing he explained was that the word Mage did not have the same definition among Breed as the one I associated with it. Breed—meaning there were actually other species out there that were nonhuman.

According to Mr. De Gradi, a Mage was a type of Breed that could harness and manipulate energy in various ways. They didn't work magic or spells, nor were they sorcerers. The simple truth was that a Mage was created from a human upon special selection. The reason he caught me so fast is that a Mage could ride a current of energy and move at impossible speeds across short distances. Some called them lightwalkers, but the common term was Mage and it was an honor to be made.

Some honor. I got the short end of the honor stick or got beat by it.

"We live among humans, but we are not bound by human laws. Each Breed has its own social order, and we must abide by it. There are consequences for breaking laws, and the one universal rule we never break is to reveal ourselves to humans." A deliberate glare fell on Adam.

"Why?" I asked. Seemed like a reasonable question, after all—we were civilized now.

"Humans fear what they cannot have, and that is not a cliché. It has become much easier in today's world to not be noticed. Despite their obsession with the paranormal—Vampire bars, animal-pattern tattoos, or altering their eyes with special contacts—humans want to feel safe. They want to be tucked in each night and know that there are really no monsters under the bed. It is safer to remain as we do and you'll find there are many cities that are thick with Breed."

"Like the middle of nowhere, Tennessee?" I asked, mocking him.

"I travel."

"Whatever."

Adam stayed quiet on the sidelines, listening as his fingers worried his chin.

"There are rogues who live among Mage, they live outside the laws and most of them are juicers." He gave me a pensive stare. "Juicing is stealing someone's light—stealing their energy. They do it as a high, it becomes addictive. They prefer other Mage because our light is so strong, but finding an unprotected Learner is not easy. But they're out there... looking for them. The rogues usually attack humans and kill them in the process; their energy is too weak to satisfy a Mage who would take it all. We hunt them, track them down, and bring them to justice."

"No pun intended, huh?"

"You've got quite a mouth on you."

Adam lifted a finger. "And you better watch yours."

I held my hand out before Adam started up again. "So what tipped you off that I was like you... a Mage?

Adam scraped his teeth over his bottom lip and I could tell despite the drive, he was still pissed off. "Was it when you grabbed her?"

"No," Justus replied. "I saw it in her eyes. The light was there and it is unmistakable. Do not question my intentions, human. You do not play by the same set of rules we do."

"I've never seen anything with her eyes. When she was emotionally charged there was an incident, but that's all." Adam shifted in his chair and worked his jaw to the side.

The only thing I gave him was a sour look. Now was seriously not the time.

Justus examined our body language and a smirk lit up his eyes. "Perhaps…" he let the word slide off his tongue, "she wasn't charged enough by your encounters."

Ouch.

Adam looked at me almost accusingly. "What were you two doing?"

But it was Justus who replied back. "Nothing I would recommend her ever doing with you, human." There was a verbal warning stretching across the room like invisible daggers. "You should not touch her, and she definitely cannot touch you."

Adam exploded onto his feet and Justus rose simultaneously. "Are you challenging me? Step outside and we'll settle this like men. I only brought you here for information. You keep your insults in check or I'll knock you on your face."

I just sat back ringside, half-amused by the level of testosterone but equally unsure of how to handle the situation or even whose side to take. Justus was out of line for playing instigator, but I wasn't ready to kick him out just yet. He knew more about me than even I did.

"Our kind does not mix with yours for a reason. I will say no more in the presence of the human. I must speak with you alone."

"Adam," I begged, searching for some kind of understanding. It was then that I saw the look in his eyes—as if I had betrayed him. When he left the room without a word, I sank in the red chair, miserable with guilt.

"Were you not approached to become one of us?"

"Attacked would be a better word."

He pressed his lips and looked away. "The one who made you is a Creator. There are only a small few who possess the ability to create another Mage. It is regulated by the Mageri—the higher order of Mage law—and the Creator presents them officially. They do not abandon their progeny. There are regulations. If a Creator wants to make the blonde at Starbucks a Mage, that's his decision. But everything must follow by the book."

My chin rested against my knee as I idly picked at my toenail.

Did he think I understood anything he was talking about? I was still trying to get over the fact that he referred to Adam as a human. Sparkler fingers or not, I still thought of myself as human. Justus suddenly grabbed both sides of the chair and shook it.

"Pay attention; you repeatedly try my patience."

"Get out of my face," I yelled. I wasn't a fan of space violation, and his car was parked over the line.

"Who is your Creator?" When he stepped back, I looked at him with a measured degree of restraint.

"I don't know."

"Learner, you would be attended by your Creator through your first years. You appear in a human bar and pretend to not know the custom of introduction; did someone put you up to this to gain information? Who is your Creator?"

"I. Don't. Know."

"*Liar,*" he roared as his body swayed forward like a dog on a tether. "How can you *not* know?"

"Because maybe he's a rogue, a criminal, ever think of that? Don't you think it's possible there are Creators who break your laws? I don't know why I am what I am, or even how. All I can tell you is that this man sliced my throat and left me for dead in the middle of an open field. I'm sorry if I didn't have a chance to exchange fucking names," I screamed back. "So you can take your self-righteous ass to the bank and deposit that. And by the way, you approached me in that bar, not vice versa. So don't play off like I'm trying to come after you for something."

Justus swayed with a blank expression. "He hurt you, your Creator?"

Tapping my head in annoyance, I said, "Are you listening? He killed me. Dead, as in my heart stopped." I threw my head back and closed my eyes. "Doesn't matter, you won't find him anyhow. He's probably dead."

"First of all, you didn't die. Second of all, how is it possible he would be dead?" Justus stared down his nose at me as if I were a child making up a story so they wouldn't get in trouble.

"Before we take this conversation any further, you need to know one thing—*I fucking died*. I'm not going to play ring-around-the-rosy about it either—accept it or don't, but quit challenging me on it. If that's not how a Mage is made then I guess he broke some rules. He's probably in the cemetery because in the end I heard a loud noise, like a shotgun."

He dropped his arms and turned away. "This is unprecedented."

"Yeah, tell me about it."

Justus finally took a seat by the window.

"After my body changed I started to notice something was off. I shocked Adam with my hands as if they were a pair of CPR paddles."

"New body?"

I gave my hands a magical wave over myself. "And you said there was no magic involved."

"You woke up changed… physically?"

"No, I woke up as myself in a body bag full of my own blood." He cringed when I brought up that juicy little tidbit. "I changed later. I was still unconscious, but Adam saw every mesmerizing detail of it."

Justus flew out the door, which thumped against the wall on his exit. A couple of minutes later he returned with Adam tracing his steps.

"Please, sit," Justus said as the door clicked shut. He motioned Adam toward the table, who gave me an inquisitive glance before obliging him.

"I would not involve a human in Breed matters as this is not within the law, but you already know more than you should. I need you to tell me what happened to this Learner; she says that you witnessed her body change and I want to know every scrap of fact."

Thirty minutes later, Adam divulged every detail of my transformation—some of which he had never mentioned to me. Hearing it out loud, knowing it was fact, made me question the sanity in that room. It didn't seem possible in a world of science that magic really did exist.

Adam wasn't without his own questions. "You said juicers steal from humans?"

"Only the strung-out ones will attack humans—they're just a

sampler. A human doesn't hold as much energy and they will die when used up. The high you get from juicing a human is not as gratifying, and it requires more to get their fix, which is why there are often multiple attacks. It makes them easy to find; they get sloppy. That's why most hunt for unprotected Learners. A Mage can be used repeatedly as an infinite source of power, and that is very desirable for a juicer."

"What did you mean by conceal?" I asked.

"It is custom that we do not conceal entirely in a human establishment. We flare, it's our call mark. Once a Mage picks up the flare of another, you either introduce yourself or face the consequences. I can't pick it up on one so young since you don't know how to flare. Until you are properly learned, you must be escorted in public. I'm not interested in learning you. Right now, I need to learn *from* you. Who is your maker?"

Only this time when he asked the question it was indirect, as if he were asking himself.

"If you say you were killed, then no one has ever created a Mage under these circumstances. It is transference of power, a consensual act. Progeny belong to their Creators until they are fit to become independent. You may not realize what that means now, but your life is no longer your own."

"I don't belong to anyone. The man who made me has no rights, none whatsoever, after leaving me to die. That, my friend, is what I consider disownment. He relinquished his rights to me the minute that blade touched my neck."

"Define *belong*." Our heads turned simultaneously to Adam.

"He can claim her whenever he wants. A Creator is responsible for those that they make, because a Learner must know how to wield their power. They are a child. They are… dangerous to humans. If left abandoned, they would be corrupted with power and abused. Abandonment is not taken lightly and no Learner is left to wander. I've never seen one abandoned upon their making. A Mage literally owns their progeny, with full entitlement to them as a parent would have over a child."

His eyes fell on me, weighted with concern. "You will be free of him only upon his death or official disownment of you. And the latter would be more likely. That can only be made official in front of the Council, otherwise he has fair claim whenever he chooses to take it."

"Like an unclaimed lottery ticket." Adam sighed. "You mention a Council, so I'm assuming you have your own laws. If what he did was—"

Justus waved his hand up. "We have no laws for what he has done to create her. So with that, I do not know how much of the law applies. No one dies during the exchange. I do not know how that is even possible. It is a great honor and privilege to be made. I cannot explain the transformation—only the Creator knows the magic; perhaps he has a special gift."

Justus turned his attention to me. "And that was no gunshot; it was the first spark of your life as a Mage." His eyebrows pressed down, shrinking the color from his eyes, and I saw something in there I didn't like—pity.

"I don't want to belong to anyone." I looked to Adam for support.

Adam ruffled his wavy hair, now a good three inches long, and made a decision.

"Zoë stays with me as long as she needs, but she is her own. She didn't consent to any of this and does not belong to your... *kind*."

I should have liked to hear those words, but for some reason I was bothered by them. Adam still saw me as different and wanted to keep me from what I was. I didn't mind the security of his protection, but if his intentions were to shelter me, I was going to have a problem with that.

Justus, on the other hand, was infuriated, and it showed in the accusatory finger-pointing. "If she does not comply with our laws, she will be considered a rogue! Her maker will know her; he can sense his own. Let me put a fright in you—that he may already have watch on her and is deciding this very moment her fate."

Adam's face was worried as he rubbed his hand across his frown. We both knew that to be true.

"A human could never offer the protection she requires," Justus began. "Eventually, she'll run into another Mage and will be taken—

used. You carry his mark; for better or worse you are his." Something flashed across his face. "I will speak to the Council to be placed as your Ghuardian. I will deal with him if he comes to claim you; if the Council learns the conditions of your making, they may be lenient and force him to relinquish his rights."

"I am not marked, and who are you to speak to anyone about me, you don't even know me." I bit my quivering lip in a feeble attempt to contain my emotions of panic and anger. The adrenaline was wearing off and I had never felt so empty, so exposed for what I was. I occasionally stole a glance at Adam, but I was never quite able to read his face.

"You are marked. We are all marked." Justus rose to his feet and lifted his shirt above the belly button, revealing with pride what could have easily resembled a small tattoo. It was an inch long on his stomach, in the shape of an unfamiliar symbol. "Upon your making you take the mark of your Creator."

"Nice tattoo."

His eyes shrank into tiny slivers that set those golden lashes aflame. "Why don't you show me yours? I showed you mine."

"I just bet you'd like that."

"Your mark will reveal who your maker is; it is unique to only him and all his progeny carry it."

"Are you bleeding?" While I had noticed the tear in his shirt, I hadn't been paying attention to the dark stain around it. I guess I thought it was dirt or mud, but when I finally saw the smear of red against his skin, it became evident he was hurt.

"Yes, but I'll heal."

"You're saying that a Mage heals differently?" Adam asked.

The shirt fell loose and Justus tucked his hands over his waist. "I'm saying we are immortal, human. If the mark is known by the Council, it will identify her Creator."

"Again, I'm not marked. I think I've taken enough showers in the past few weeks to do the whole getting to know me bit." Anger was flaring.

Primarily the reason I was angry was the way Adam was looking at me. I couldn't tell if it was fear or repulsion, but it struck a chord deep inside.

"I saw your shoulder, Zoë, it shouldn't have healed that fast."

I placed my feet on the cheap carpet and stood up. "You need to leave."

"Are you refusing my offer?" His nostrils flared. "Think carefully before you answer."

"I know it's hard to believe a girl would turn you down, but yeah, I'm refusing you." I shot him a defiant look, my fingers digging into my palms, anger bubbling up like a bad case of indigestion.

"You need to be measured."

"Measured?" Okay, at that point I was yelling a little bit. "Maybe you're a rogue, what makes you think I could trust you? I have a life to get back to that doesn't involve playing with your magical wand."

He widened his stance and folded his arms. "You have no respect."

"Don't you dare talk to me about respect," I fumed, going over each syllable. "You think I owe you respect after what your kind did to me, what I was turned into against my will?"

I walked right up to this man who had turned my entire world upside down and pushed him.

"Get. Out."

Adam went rigid, but he did not interfere. That's what made me even angrier—because Adam always came to my defense. Now I was alone.

I felt a strong pull where my hand was placed on his chest, as if we were connected by some intangible force. Justus covered my hand with his and spread a devilish grin across his face. From fingertips to toes, a numbing sensation covered me as if Novocain were pouring out of him. There was a vibration, a culminating heat, and my eyes widened at the unfamiliarity of it all, and yet how strangely right it felt. Adam stepped forward to break the contact… but after his face looked into mine, he paused and actually stepped back.

"Holy shit, Z, your eyes," he breathed.

Electrical impulses generated in every fiber of my being. My eyes were locked on Justus, and I was pissed. Justus rested his thumb on my temple and in the flecks of his eyes were tiny flashes of light. He looked surprised and suddenly broke contact, dropping his hand.

I could barely stand. I was spinning.

"What did you do to her?" Adam moved to grab me, but Justus knocked him to the ground, sending one of the chairs flying against the wall. Adam looked ready to knuckle up, but Justus held him firm with his forearm.

"Back off, human! She is a conduit; you shouldn't touch her when she's charged. If you do," he growled in Adam's face, "you will know what it feels like to be a bug in a zapper should she touch you back."

"Make it stop," I gasped. It was moving within me like an animal in a cage—growling, thrashing, and snapping.

Justus appeared in my line of vision. "Look at me, Learner. You must level down."

My hand was pulled over his wound and I drew in a deep breath. Spider webs of thin, bluish light, barely visible to the naked eye, threaded between us. There was a connection forming, like a rush of wind down my neck and through my hair. Justus stepped closer—our bodies nearly pressed.

"Release it into me." His voice was soft, yet demanding. "You know what to do, listen to what your body wants to do. It's leading you."

His breath touched my face as his lips whispered into my ear. I wasn't sure what he meant, but my body reacted in a way that felt shockingly natural. A pulse of energy left through my fingers so quickly that once it was released, my knees gave. Justus caught me with his right arm and set me on the bed.

I was freezing and my teeth chattered.

Adam was perched against the wall, looking at us through his peripheral.

My confusion rose when I looked at Justus. His head was tilted back, eyes hooded and mouth parted as if he were being serviced.

Suddenly, his hand came down over my face and caressed my neck. A thumb settled over my throbbing cheek and a flash of white heat penetrated from his touch. Within seconds the pain simply vanished. He traced the outline of my jaw with his fingers as a lover might.

"I want you to leave." My head jerked away.

"As you wish, Learner."

I stood in the bathroom, pulling a tank top over my head. It was as if all the warm energy had been expelled when I released into Justus, and even after a hot shower, I still felt like ice was running in my veins. Adam was unresponsive. After Justus left, he avoided me.

Completely.

I went downstairs and heated up the Chinese food before deciding to give up the aversion game. I had a lot running through my head as well. Adam might hate me now, he didn't sign up for this. But what really had me concerned was the danger I could be putting him in—if my Creator was after me, then he wouldn't hesitate for a moment to hurt Adam.

When the door cracked open, Adam was lying on the bed in his black, cozy sweats, shirtless with his arms behind his head. He didn't really have much chest hair; most of it was dark and fine against his tan.

"Hmmm," he chuckled. "Shorts?"

I glanced down at my boy shorts panties. "You do the laundry; you should know." There was an awkward pause.

The air-conditioning was cranked to level Siberia. I shivered, tiptoeing to the other side of the bed. Adam stretched out as if he were a cat basking in the sun, watching every move I made from the corner of his eye. A gust blew my hair forward and I captured it.

"So how are we going to do this?" I asked.

"I prefer to be on top, if you don't mind." A subtle wink.

"Excuse me?"

When he caught my expression, his body shook, muscles tightening as he laughed out loud. Snatching the pillow from beneath his head, he covered his face. I'm the girl with all the lines, so when the table was turned and I was caught off guard, it only peeved me off. I folded my arms and gave him an evil eye powerful enough to reduce the pillowcase to ash.

When he uncovered his face, he peered up at me, fluffing the pillow behind his head.

"Covers, I mean. I'm a perfect gentleman, so don't give me your look." His eyebrows wiggled mischievously. "Baby doll, I can't sleep on that hard floor and be functional tomorrow. The bed is large enough, so I think you should be able to keep your hands off of me, being that I'm so irresistible to you," he said wistfully, turning his back to me.

He *was* irresistible—he just didn't have a clue.

Tugging the end of the comforter off the bed, I curled up on the floor. The sheets rustled and a voice hung over the bed.

"What are you doing?" he spoke softly. "I swear I won't lay a finger on you; if you won't trust me then you can have the bed."

"No."

"Then come up. I'm not letting you sleep on the floor," he said as his anger began to surface. "Are you mad at me?"

"It's not too late to back out, Adam." I looked over my shoulder. "You don't have any obligations to me and I won't judge you, I won't even blame you, so it's not something you have to carry on your conscience."

Adam threw his legs over the bed and scooped me up in his arms.

"I meant what I said—some men stick around. I'm one of those men. You think I'm going to turn my back on you just because of a little static?"

That set me to laughing, a welcomed distraction from the press of his bare chest.

Adam dropped me on the bed. I bounced twice before he threw the sheet over me and switched out the light. As promised, he took the other side, lying on top of the covers.

"I like you, Zoë. I'm going to be straight with you and I think you know it. I know how you feel and I'm not pushing you into anything. You need to figure things out—I get it. But I'm still here, I'm not going to bullshit you and tell you that if I didn't mean it."

I made a short groan and rolled over.

"What's wrong?"

"If you hand me a book I could read to you in this light." I laughed, staring at the window. The streetlight was right outside the window and streaming in.

A minute later Adam got up and went into the bathroom. After

I heard a few noises, the light switched off and he moved quietly back into bed. I pretended to be asleep.

A shadow went across my face and I felt something brush over my eyes. I reached up and saw Adam with a strip of material that looked like a long, carefully cut… blindfold? It was one of his T-shirts.

"And what is this for?"

He spoke very softly. "You said you couldn't sleep. I want you to trust me, Zoë."

That's what it was all about; I'm not sure why it was so important that Adam gain my trust, but it was what he had always been seeking. He said it as if he were the kind of man who couldn't be trusted, and he was trying to redeem himself. There was no need.

"I trust you."

Adam reached around and secured the tie in the back, his thick fingers fumbling with the edges until they were pulled over my eyes comfortably.

"We're going to take this one day at a time and figure it out, maybe there's a way to undo what was done. I don't want you to worry about anything."

"If I didn't know better I'd say you've done this before."

His fingers hesitated as they adjusted the last bit. "All good?" he asked. "Not too tight?"

"Yeah, just lead me to the barrel of apples." I chuckled.

"Zoë, what did you think of what Justus said?"

A thought twisted in me like a root and it was the way Adam looked at me when he saw what I truly was. "I wouldn't have believed him before this happened to me, but I am different, and I know what I am now—a freak."

"You're not a freak. And if anyone ever says anything like that to you I will personally beat the shit out of them."

The bed shifted and while I couldn't see anything, I felt Adam turn his back on me. But in reality, I knew he never would.

CHAPTER 12

I DID A CAT STRETCH, ARCHED my back, and let all the muscle tension drift away. It was morning, judging by the unmistakable sound of a distant lawnmower. I had a feeling Adam took off without me to get an early start, but I was okay with that. My stomach let out a bobcat growl in the silence of the room and I rubbed my itchy nose and pulled away the blindfold. My pupils went into shock from the light and I shut my eyes.

I hated the smell of musty hotels; it was depressing because they were an in-between place for travelers. Mid-yawn, I flinched when I opened my eyes and Adam came into focus. He was lying on his side, fully dressed.

"How long have you been doing that? I thought you were gone." I pulled my pillow over my head, hiding.

"Long enough to know you need to run a bristle over those pearlies."

I groaned in the oversized pillow.

"Zoë, I'd like you to come with me. I think you'd find it interesting to see what I do." He was all serious this morning, as if last night never happened. "I could use an assistant; I need help with some of the equipment and changing out the lenses."

"You've been on a million photo shoots and never needed help before. You just don't want to leave me alone."

"True that. You seem to get yourself in all kinds of trouble when I'm not around."

I lifted a middle finger slowly and before he could grab it, I shoved my fingers through his hair. "You need a haircut. Do you want me to do it?"

"Have you ever cut hair before?"

I shrugged. "Sure. I shaved a poodle once."

"And this gives you experience?"

"As long as I don't have to shave anywhere near your butt it might come out pretty good."

"Well that shouldn't be a problem." He pinched my nose and I snickered. I really, truly adored the relationship we had going at times—it was so effortless.

"Do I have time for room service?"

"*At* your service." Adam reached behind his back and brought a large white paper bag around, setting it down between us. I unrolled the top skeptically and peeked inside. "Donuts!"

"They're cinnamon sugar; hope you like them. If not, we can pick up something on the way."

I was already shoving one in my mouth, dusting the granules off my fingers. He tried to take the donut from me and I tilted back.

"Now, Zoë, you're getting crumbs all over the bed," he said sternly. Adam hated crumbs on the furniture and it drove him absolutely mad that I liked to eat crackers on his leather sofa. So I obligingly took a donut from the bag and shoved it in his mouth, scattering tiny flecks of sugar all over the sheets.

"That's what maid service is for."

Once I showered, I slid on a pair of cotton shorts and a yellow shirt that tied around the neck. The weather was warmer than back home as summer was extending itself.

The first location was in front of a beautiful historic home. During the setup, Adam smuggled a pair of jeans from the wardrobe lady and gave them to me. It was the first time I ever changed in a car and most definitely the last when one of his crew walked by the window and whistled.

The last location brought us back to town, and it was closing in on sunset. A pretty model sat by Adam, touching his wrist whenever he spoke, and I had a slight pang of jealousy to see him give attention to someone else, but it was actually nice to see someone flirting with him. Adam needed some normalcy, and he was a handsome guy. He deserved to have someone throwing affection his way.

I walked to a sandwich shop up the street for a bite to eat. When the door swung open, a small bell jingled, announcing my entry, an old-fashioned touch I rather liked. Leaning over the counter, the scent of lemon cake had me inhaling deeply, but I stuck with a ham and avocado sandwich with a tall lemonade. I still couldn't take my eyes off that cake, but I pried myself away to a small table by the window.

After I finished my meal in what seemed like five bites, I dusted the crumbs from my fingers.

"Are you planning to eat that?"

I looked up without surprise to see Justus eyeing my pickle.

"Help yourself."

He slid in the chair across from me, setting a small plate with a slice of lemon cake in front as he grabbed the pickle.

"You can't be with him, you know."

"Who says I'm going to?" My finger swiped at the icing and brought a taste to my lips.

"Well, you can't."

Today Justus looked a little less like the playboy I had seen the night before as he was dressed in a button-up shirt and slacks. His demeanor was still smug, just toned down. There was one other woman in the shop and she couldn't take her eyes off him.

"Knowing what you are, how long do you think it would be before you hurt him? You can do some serious damage, you know. You *could* kill him. If you accept me as your Ghuardian, you can learn to control it enough that, should you want," he said and nodded at the window, "you could be with a human."

"You say 'human' like we are some kind of alien," I said flatly.

"Have you ever seen *Invasion of the Body Snatchers*?"

I pursed my lips.

"I'm giving you a chance to live a worthy life. You must know about the world you belong in—the world of Breed. You must feel this. Being among humans is no longer your place. You cannot run from what you are; you will not be able to protect yourself when another Mage finds you. And they *will* find you."

I sighed and watched a passing car. I didn't want to live my life on the run, in hiding.

"Yes, you should be afraid. God help you without a Ghuardian who could protect you. You would be used in the worst kind of way. You need to be taught."

"So I can wield the power as you do? Sending out your energy to the nearest pair of panties is such a great example of the power you have. I'm not stupid, you know. You're good-looking," I reluctantly pointed out, "but you aren't *that* good-looking. That was quite a show you put on last night."

He leaned back and laced his fingers behind his head. "Power has its perks."

"Power also corrupts," I added.

Justus's eyes fell to his lap and his brow formed a single, vertical crease on his forehead. Completely switching gears, his voice suddenly thundered, "Turn around. *Now!*"

I blanched as I whipped my neck around and hunched my shoulders, thinking that someone was coming up from behind to attack. But all I saw was a man at a nearby table whose eyes sank low and turned away. When my heart came out of my throat, I realized he wasn't yelling at me, but the guy behind us.

Justus gazed over my body. "You really should dress more appropriately; too much skin draws attention and you do not have enough fabric in the back." He swirled a finger in the air.

"I'm wearing a sleeveless shirt, not a thong."

"I can't force you, but I can promise you one certainty."

I raised my head and looked directly at him as he rose to his feet.

"You cannot control it on your own. I tapped your energy and there's a lot of it. You are not tempered enough to protect yourself. The wrong kind of Mage will find you and make you their pet." His lip curled when he said that and I was surprised at how much it angered him. "And I'm not about to go into the many details of why you don't want that to happen. Time is ticking and you can't hide from who you are. Leave this life behind, Zoë, while you still have the freedom to do so."

He took my wrist and pressed a card into it, making a crisp snap from his finger pulling off the edge.

"Keep it, should you change your mind. My offer still stands. Goodbye, Zoë."

When he left the shop, I studied the card. It was charcoal grey with the name Justus De Gradi in white raised print and a phone number below. I ran my finger over the finely embossed gold ring before tucking the card in my jean pocket.

The trip to Memphis ended soon enough, and we were back at Adam's house, but there was tension beneath the surface. Things had changed, and he didn't look at me quite the same. His look was sad and distant. I didn't like who I had become either and it had nothing to do with being a Mage. Living off his generosity only proved that I had become nothing less than a mooch.

There was a light knock on the bedroom door.

"Come in."

Adam stepped over my legs and took a seat on the floor across from me, leaning against the wall with one leg propped up and his arm casually draped over his knee.

"There's something you should know."

My attention focused away from the blank ceiling overhead and fell to Adam. I didn't like the look on his face at all. "Now you're scaring me."

He knocked his head against the wall. "You have a mark. I didn't say anything before, I guess I was hoping—"

"What mark? I don't have a mark; I've seen my body, Raze."

"I've seen your body, too." His face became splotchy as it heated with embarrassment.

"Care to elaborate?"

"When I cleaned you I didn't dress you right away; I put you in the bed and covered you up. It wasn't until later, after you transformed, that I put clothes on you." His hand scratched the back of his neck. "I had some underwear, and I didn't want you waking up naked. Suffice it to say that putting underwear on an unconscious woman is something I've never done before, and it's no easy feat."

My bottom jaw stuck out. *Underwear.* I never really thought about where those mystery panties had come from, let alone how they got on me. I had other things on my mind at the time, but now it was sparkling clear.

"Let me just save myself the embarrassment." *As if he could.* "You have a mark on your right cheek."

And I knew he didn't mean the cheek on my face.

I propelled into the bathroom—the mirror was too high so I lowered my sweats on the right, exposing part of my bare ass as I strained to get a glimpse from over my shoulder. Adam tapped my arm with a handheld mirror, which I snatched away.

"Lower," he said.

There it was—a mark low on my cheek, nearly where it met my leg on the inner side. It was smaller than Justus's and different. It looked like a wavy line with two curved patterns intersecting it at one end.

I set the mirror on the sink and pulled my pants back up. There was only one option.

"This—whatever we're doing here—I can't do it anymore. I need to know what I am." My eyes fell on him imploringly.

"I know." His finger swept a lock of hair from my face.

"Why did you just decide to tell me all of a sudden? You could have kept it to yourself."

"I had no right to, and there's something else that concerns me. It's been on my mind since Justus brought it up that night. On more than one occasion, someone has been following you. I don't like that someone wants to hurt you and I may not be able to protect you. Maybe you're safer... with him."

So I made the call.

CHAPTER 13

I T WAS DAWN ON A Thursday when Justus arrived. I sat on the edge of the bed with my bag packed. Adam walked in and sat down beside me; his shirt smelled like clean laundry and sunshine. We were on the heels of winter and I didn't have a single scrap of warm clothing, so Adam lent me his sweatshirt. The sleeves were rolled up since they were far too long for my arms. I dipped my nose into his heavy scent, deciding I would not wash it.

Adam was my home.

"You call me if you change your mind. I'll come get you, no questions asked."

So much had happened in a short period of time and I was forever indebted to him. It was my decision but I didn't realize how much it was going to hurt to leave Adam, and I was staving off tears.

"If he treats you bad I want to know, I don't put up with that shit and neither will you. Anyone who raises a hand to you will bleed."

The softness of his hand stroking over mine swelled a sadness in me something awful.

"I've been pretty annoying to live with."

"Not true."

"You mean to tell me you'll miss the cracker crumbs on your sofa, the fact I peel off all the labels from your beer bottles and leave the water running the entire time I'm brushing my teeth? I guess now is the time to confess I've also been drinking straight out of the orange juice carton *and* I ruined two rolls of your film. They're in the fern pot on the back patio, in case you're wondering."

His eyes widened.

"See? Things are already looking up."

"You brought life into my home, Zoë, you make me laugh. That's something that I hadn't done in a long time."

My arms fell over his shoulders, pulling him close. "Promise you'll see me again?"

There was a loud pounding at the front door. Adam pulled from my reach and went to answer.

"Is she ready? I don't have time to linger." Justus sounded annoyed.

"I want you to listen to what I'm putting down. For whatever reason, Zoë trusts you, and I trust her decision. But I don't know you, so I don't fucking trust you. You treat her with respect, and if you lay one goddamned finger on her I'll break your neck in five places, feel me?"

"I'm ready." The two men were standing toe-to-toe as I dragged my heavy bag.

Justus tucked his hands indifferently in his fitted leather jacket. He greeted me with a restrained smile. "I'm glad you came to your senses."

Completely irritated with that greeting, I bumped my shoulder against his arm as I walked past him through the door. Without warning, Justus lifted my bag and strolled toward a gunmetal sports car parked in the driveway. One that hollered "this driver has a big cock." Not that I wanted to test that theory.

"Nice wheels," I said, unimpressed.

"This, my dear lady, is an Aston Martin." He slid his fingers along her polished side as if it were the upper thigh of a woman.

I kicked a rock, dreading the inevitable goodbye. Thoughts plagued my mind. *Will I see him again? Will he forget about me? Am I completely crazy for deciding to live with a stranger?*

Justus cleared his throat. "Let's go, Learner."

Adam's arm slipped around my waist and Justus gave him a puzzled look. I took a moment to collect my thoughts and turned around. A leaf dropped from one of the taller trees and twirled between us. "Just call me sometime and don't—"

Adam's lips pressed against mine unexpectedly. He gathered my hair in a tight fist and held me close. The kiss was slow, lingering, and bittersweet. I was intoxicated by the passion behind it, every slow sweep of the tongue weakening my knees a little more. It wasn't until I peeked through my lashes that I saw he wasn't into the kiss as much as I was. Those sultry brown eyes were venomous and locked on something behind me.

A horn blasted, breaking the kiss. Adam grumbled as I curved my neck around to see Justus laughing in the car. His eyes were low and there was a lot of head shaking.

"That wasn't for me, was it?" I narrowed my eyes at him when he finally severed his gaze. That kiss—which could have single-handedly changed my mind about leaving—was nothing more than territorial pissing. "Don't ever kiss me again if you don't mean it."

He took my wrist and rolled down the sleeves one at a time. "Remember what I said, Z—call me if you need me. He so much as talks down to you and I'll come. You don't have any warm clothes, so I packed some extra money in your bag. I want you to buy a jacket and take care of yourself, you hear?"

I nodded and quickly turned away before I had second thoughts.

The bucket seats were tall and I looked around at the fancy interior. Justus slid a clip into the dash, which started the ignition. The car roared like a caged lion and he was about to let it out.

"Your friend is forward with his overzealous invitations."

"He's confused," I grumbled.

"That isn't confusion, it's desperation."

The car rolled back and some warm air drifted through the vents.

"So, where are we going?"

"Sorry, Peaches—no specifics. But it will be a long journey. In fact…" he said, dangling a long strip of fabric, "at some point I will need to blindfold you."

While his eyes were serious with direction, I caught a slight curve of his mouth. "And that will be an order."

"Exactly how long is this drive, Mr. I Carry A Blindfold In My Car For Emergencies?"

"Twenty-six hours, roughly."

"What?!"

"Human time. In Mage time I can shave that in half."

"Mage time—that translates to: you were too cheap to buy plane tickets?"

He laughed. "We don't work magic, Learner, not like that. But we do have a talent for disabling police radar. And my car can go very fast." To emphasize his point, he slammed the gas pedal down and my head was introduced to the headrest.

By late afternoon, we arrived at a modest-sized gas station. I took a quick break and ran inside for a cherry slushee.

When I returned, he had gassed up the car and bought a bag of junk food. "Resources," he said. *Everything a girl needed to gain five pounds.*

"You do realize that I eat real food, right?" I glanced at the trail mix, beef jerky, and potato chips.

"I did not think you would have an appetite after this morning. Are you hungry? We can stop if you want to eat."

After a half hour of his erratic driving that morning, we had to pull over while I got sick on the side of the road.

"I'm not that hungry, but we can pull over if you want."

"Not necessary."

I cleared my throat and looked at him. "You aren't hungry?"

"No, I am hungry."

I laughed in disbelief. "So then why don't you eat?"

"It would not be polite."

"You know, Justus, you may be hard around the edges, but you're soft in the middle." I had a sense about him, something you picked up in the little gestures people made, or comments. Somewhere inside of that rough and tough exterior was a human being. If I was going to live with this man I needed to know there was a human in there, even if he wasn't.

I sipped my icy drink and the brain freeze hit so fast I palmed my forehead, waiting for it to pass. There was a low, ominous laugh that sounded like the intro to a classic horror movie.

"I hear those are most uncomfortable. So tell me, why would you drink more—glutton for punishment?"

"Haven't you ever tried one?" He shook his head and I smiled. "You've got to be kidding me. *Try it.* Go on." I waved the cup in a dare at his face. "I don't have cooties."

Justus snatched the cup from my hand and frowned, looking at the sugary concoction undecidedly. Fingers slowly wrapped around the purple straw and his lips pulled in the first taste. I waited eagerly and saw approval on his stony expression. His smile was becoming— not the arrogant one perfected—but a genuine smile.

"What did I tell you? Good, right?"

"You are not dressed appropriate for this climate," he observed while savoring a little of the juice in his mouth.

"Last trip to the thrift store and they were pushing out the summer clothing. Adam lent me the sweatshirt."

He grumbled as I tore open a bag of trail mix, fishing for a raisin.

"Where's your piercing?"

A thick hand rubbed across his jaw and his answer was silence. I had a feeling my comment in the bar had gotten to him. He never wore that piercing again after that night.

"Hmm. Mind if I change the music?"

"Do as you wish, Peaches."

The annoyance in my gaze was flashing. "Quit calling me Peaches."

"Yes, on second thought, you aren't as sweet."

"Why don't you just call me Zoë?"

"You are no longer of the human world; that is past. You are Breed, and every Mage born is bestowed a name by their Creator— that is our custom. Until such time you go by Learner, your title."

"You mean the only one who gets to name me is that monster? And what if he never does, I go the rest of my life being called Learner? Nameless… no identity?" I wrung my hands together angrily.

"Calm yourself, Learner, before you overload the circuits in my car. I knew I should have brought the Honda."

"What *is* a Learner?"

"It's the name for a newly made Mage who requires learning on their abilities—a novice. It is the basic definition for any Mage who is not yet ready for independence. Your independence is largely determined by your knowledge, strength, and ability to acclimate."

"If we don't work magic, why are we called a Mage? Isn't that supposed to be a sorcerer?"

He scoffed at the comparison. "We do not practice alchemy, Learner. Mage is an old name—humans never understood the magic, so through stories they fabricated our gifts. In ancient times we were not so hidden from the human world; we have learned since then the value of secrecy. There are some we trust with truth, but betrayal is not taken lightly."

The way Justus spoke of humans was odd; it was as if they were aliens he didn't understand, although he was more than willing to take those aliens to his bed for some probing.

"If the name isn't correct, why keep it?"

"The word has always been ours," he said matter-of-factly. "Human definition holds no meaning in our world; you will soon discover that you belong to the Breed. You probably already noticed a difference in how you feel around humans; deep down you know that you do not belong. Over the years we have been called many things: lightwalkers, channelers, even years ago some tried to change it to conductors, but that never quite caught on."

"I don't ever want him to claim me, Justus. That means I'll always be called Learner.

"If he refuses his claim or dies, the Council will name you. If he dies, I will remain your Ghuardian."

"Like a stepfather?"

He laughed. "Something like that."

"How much longer?"

Justus shifted in his seat trying to stretch out his thick legs. "Tonight. We'll be there tonight."

I twirled the straw of my drink and focused on my feet, trying to keep my attention anywhere but the road. I cocked my head to the side to find him staring at me hopefully.

"What?"

"May I have another taste of your cherry?"

CHAPTER 14

NIGHT FELL. AS THE CAR rolled to a stop, I strained my ears but heard nothing.

"You may remove the blindfold."

"Where are we?" I inquired, pulling it free.

"I'm presenting you to the Council for right of Ghuardianship."

"Now? Tonight? Thanks for the heads-up," I said sarcastically. If he had at least told me we weren't going straight to his house I might have run a comb through my hair.

Justus slicked back his brow with his thumb and scraped his fingers through his short hair a few times, a nervous gesture that wasn't exactly putting me at ease.

The car lights illuminated the woods in front of us; tall trees stood like dark soldiers guarding a fortress. To the right was a broken wall made of stones that looked a million years old, covered with dying vines. Justus walked around to open my door and the second I got out, he immediately pinned me against the car.

I choked out, "What are you doing?"

His eyes narrowed and scanned through the darkness all around as if he were looking for someone. I trembled, uncertain if we were in danger. His searching eyes—rich and deep with moonlight—slid down to meet my gaze.

"If you're with me then you will be looked after. It will be my duty to ensure your safety, but you must never let your guard down for even a moment."

While Adam's sweatshirt was snug and warm, my bare legs sure felt the sting of northern air and I lengthened the sleeves. Justus shifted out of his jacket, placing it around my shoulders, and when I slipped my arms through the lining of his coat, I actually got a heat flash.

"Damn, you really run on hot," I muttered.

The only response he gave was: "Follow me."

I shadowed behind him closely. "What city are we going to live in?"

"Cognito."

"Really?" I laughed. "I've always wanted to go there."

"You'll find more Breed in Cognito than any other city in the States."

Cognito was a metropolis that boasted itself as the center of the universe for artists. Supposedly, it had a very diverse crowd, not to mention it was a twenty-four hour city like Vegas. The cost of living was higher and from what I heard the crime rate was pretty bad, so not many people actually wanted to live there.

"Tonight I will present you to the Council. Each territory has a Council of members who work directly under the Mageri. This will make you official. It is not just customary, but it is *law*. To house a Learner who has not been documented is illegal and they have agreed to consider your case."

"My case? Am I on trial?"

He sucked at his teeth and replied in a low baritone voice, "In a matter of speaking, you are. You have a unique set of circumstances for coming into the Breed that may not meet their approval. The Council has dominion over all—they will decide your fate."

"Wait a minute." A slice of moonlight filtered through a tree and softly outlined his jaw. "What if they don't approve of my circumstances, do they have the authority to… to kill me?"

He showed no sign of emotion and I began to see the complexity that was Justus. "Yes, Learner, they have all authority. Because our power is within you, they have the right to decide what to do with it. This is serious business, so put your childish jokes aside and speak to them with respect. It is not likely they will put you to death; we do not so hastily discard the life of one of our own. Remember, anything you say could hold weight on the decision they make. Do not speak unless spoken to. Do you understand?"

I nodded and we continued our walk. I thought about how it was like going into a pit of lions while holding a juicy steak. I had fascinating information about my creation that could very well be the nail in my coffin.

In a small clearing, two women and three men were dressed in white robes. Didn't these people realize what century we lived in? All that ceremonial-looking garb—this wasn't a séance. I refrained from smiling and let Justus take the lead, placing my hand nervously on his back.

Justus greeted the Council with a bow.

"Bring forward the girl," the older male in the center demanded.

Truth be told, I was too nervous to look at them directly. They were introduced from left to right: Novis, Sasha, Samuel, Hannah, and Merc.

Novis was a young man no older than twenty-five (at least in physical appearance), lean with short, black hair, wide thin lips, and boyish features. Sasha was quite beautiful—young, long, blond hair and a bit of hollowness to her. Samuel was much older than the others, looking grandfatherly with a closely shaven grey beard and eyes that were such a pale liquid-blue they were iridescent in the moonlight. And while physically he was the eldest, I had the distinct feeling he was not the one in charge.

Hannah was all business with her tidy hair pulled up in a classy style, tucked neatly with small pins that sparkled like diamonds. Her lips were painted a deep ruby red, which made her thick wolfish brows stand out even more. Lastly, Merc, who looked like menace incarnate. Long, stringy blond hair fell over his shoulders and he towered in height as equally as muscle. As intimidating as he looked, I was more terrified of the lack of compassion in those eyes, which were penetrating. No sign of mercy, love, or an ounce of anything but disgust for me. Justus picked up on it and curved his hand around my wrist.

"Council, greetings."

Heads nodded.

"My name is Justus De Gradi. I have called upon the Council to present a newly created Mage."

"Where is her Creator?" Sasha interrupted. "You are not listed in our books as a Creator, so where did you find this little girl?"

Who the hell was she calling little girl? I inched forward but he jerked me back in place.

"Her power has come to us in a most unusual way." I could tell he was trying to word himself carefully and hold his tongue. "There are unique circumstances to her transition. Her maker has denied her with his unwillingness to step forward and stake his claim openly. This Learner is abandoned, so I am requesting her care be placed in my Ghuardianship, officially."

I felt the swell of the night around me and nervously shuffled my feet over the grass. I didn't understand these customs, and I sure didn't understand these people, so I couldn't imagine how they felt about me. But eyes fell on me with disdain and I wondered if I deserved such harsh judgment.

"Who is your maker?" Hannah's eyes pointed at me like a spear.

I shot a sideways glance at Justus for direction; was I supposed to tell the truth or dance around it like he had? Unfortunately, I couldn't read eyes.

"Are you impaired in some way?"

I snapped my head around and gave her an ugly stare.

The young man with the punk-rock hair leaned forward to look at Miss Bobby Pins. "Maybe she refuses to answer your question, Hannah." He was grinning as if amused by my behavior.

"I'll answer your question."

I swallowed hard and Justus released his grip on my wrist. "I don't know who my maker is."

Muscles—the guy on the right that looked like he could snap a light pole—blurted out, "Do tell us, are you an immaculate conception?" I felt a blast of cold that came from his stare. I couldn't figure out why he hated me so much, but I felt it. It was as palpable as the frosty wind on my skin.

"He never told me his name." Justus had given me no warning or preparation of any kind as to how I should answer these kinds of questions, or how much I should divulge. I would rightfully kick his ass for it.

Justus spoke again. "Council, I have tapped into her light enough to assess that she will be a strong addition. But as it is raw and she is without any guidance, I request permission to be her acting Ghuardian. I will teach her our laws; she will be learned properly. I will bring her to the Council to measure her potential when it is time."

"You are withholding," Hannah said. She was curious, observant, and a little annoyed judging by the frown lines. "Justus De Gradi, you have made the decision to risk the consequence of concealing truth from the Council with half-truths. You will prepare yourself for judgment, as no lie can remain buried forever."

Justus acknowledged her with a nod.

"Step forward, Learner."

The Learner stepped forward, and she was about to pee her pants.

Without looking away, Hannah said, "Novis, test her."

Novis was suddenly in my face before I could blink. He placed his thumb on my forehead the same way Justus had at the hotel in Memphis. No permission was asked, no explanation was given. A surge built within me, humming in my ears, and there was a sense of energy shifting, building, and pacing like a panther. I held my breath as my fingertips began tingling. There was an indescribable need to release something—like holding in a sneeze.

"Strong, indeed," he whispered.

Confused, I stepped back, breaking our contact, and looked at Justus in panic.

"That is enough, Novis," Hannah said.

He took his position beside Sasha, mouth slightly open and looking at me quizzically before he gave a short nod.

"What did you find?"

"She is strong. As she is yet undeveloped, I'm not able to fully measure. There is a shadow I cannot get around that is blocking her light." He paused, turning toward Hannah with slanted brows. "There is something I am not able to reach. But even with that being said, she is potential."

Good to know that I *was* potential, not that I had it. Suddenly I was not a person who had abilities, I was now the ability itself.

"Very well," Hannah said with a bored aristocratic tone. "Justus, you will need to teach her to level down. She can't even control a surge of power from measuring. We require an evaluation six months from now. I advise you to begin tonight, as she will be useless for days if you do not help her to release." They turned and disappeared into the woods, but not before I caught Merc arguing with one of them.

I dropped to my knees. Ripples of lightning shot through my skin and it was beginning to hurt. A metallic taste on my tongue and a sense of panic raced through me.

"Why did he do that; why can't I make it stop?" I was out of breath, struggling to control the monster living within me.

"Learner, look at me." Justus knelt down on one knee. "Give me your hands. Our power can be pulled, or pushed, or exchanged. But when it is not level within you—like when Novis pulled your strongest energy to the surface—you must learn to push it back down or it will consume you. Since you do not retain this skill, you must release the overflow."

"But what was he measuring?"

"Novis was pulling your power out so he could taste it; it's a method we use to determine how strong a Mage is. Anytime that your power is increased it becomes a danger to you if you do not control it. It is the most basic thing we learn as a Mage."

Leaning on my knees, I fell against Justus and he held me upright, pulling my hands to his chest. In his eyes were small flashes of light, like fireflies. I stared at his thighs and up to his neck, trying to find a focal point.

"Release."

I scrambled backwards. "What if I don't?" I argued. I couldn't help but think of that look he had at the hotel after I did just that.

"Then you will sleep for a long while and be weakened. I will not raise a Learner to be a weakling."

"What if I just release it into the ground?" I planted my hands on the dirt and he gripped them hard.

"Learner! Do not wield your power as a child. A Mage should never put himself in a situation where they are weak, let alone unconscious."

His large hands clasped mine firmly and I let the wave take over and gave it free rein. It pulsed like light through my skin and shot out through my hands into Justus, who fell slightly back this time.

I got up and ran back to the car. Hell yeah, he scared me. When I put my energy into him, I didn't know exactly what he was feeling. I thought about juicers and how addictive the energy was. Whenever I saw that look on his face, I knew it to be true.

A few minutes later, he returned to the car and settled in the seat. I was shivering relentlessly. Releasing excess power stole the heat from my blood, but I felt better, like I had purged something out of me.

"Let's get something straight—I am here to help you. Continue to challenge me and you are only a detriment to yourself," Justus said. "There's a world out there you don't understand, one you're going to soon find out about. Your biggest concern as a human might have been what flavor of coffee to buy, but in the world of Breed it is a completely different dynamic. There are first-generation enemies from eons ago; it can be a dangerous world if you are not prepared for it."

Justus looked beat, and not just from the drive. He rubbed an eye with his fist and yawned. "Look, I'm tired and I don't feel like talking for the rest of the drive. It won't be much longer, take a nap or something."

If Justus had a formula, it would be one-percent sensitivity and ninety-nine percent jackass.

But I wasn't going to pick that battle to fight, I was exhausted. There was too much I didn't know. I knew about vampires, wizards, trolls, fairies, and all other sorts of fantasy creatures, but no one ever mentioned a group of people who could harness and manipulate pure energy. Then again, he said human definitions were wrong.

CHAPTER 15

I AWOKE IN A CLOUD OF creamy white sheets in an oversized bed. There was a sense of relief when I turned over and saw that I was alone; at least I knew it wasn't that kind of night. The first thing that caught my attention was a candle flickering against a stone wall. Candles were mounted all around, but no lamps.

My toes lifted when they touched the cold floor, and I shuffled over to the wooden door. It was like something out of a medieval castle, with a long handle that clicked open revealing a dimly lit hallway. A gust of air cooled my legs as I peered around the corner. *Who the hell is this guy, Bela Lugosi?*

I tiptoed down the windowless hallway and past three closed doors. At the end was a giant archway that opened up to an enormous room with high ceilings and an impressive stone fireplace. No windows in here either, which made me think we were underground. While everything looked medieval, the furniture was comprised of modern black leather and oversized chairs. The same stone flooring and walls as the bedroom ran throughout, and the ambiance of the room was warm and rich with a soft amber glow illuminating the walls from a row of hurricane lamps. A soft, misshapen brown rug lay before the fireplace, whose hearth glowed with fading embers.

A steady bright light caught my eye, coming from a stairwell on my left that spiraled out of view. Next to the stairs was a heavy iron door like I had never seen before. I drifted down the steps and when I reached the bottom I raised an eyebrow or two.

The floor was a highly polished marble in uneven shades of grey and beige that stretched across a large open room with tan walls. Anchored across the ceiling were several long light panels. One side of the room sported all your basic workout paraphernalia such as punching bags, weights, and knives.

Knives? My eyes wandered over the vast collection of various weapons mounted on the wall. As I ran my finger along a sharp blade, I jumped.

"This is where you will train six hours every morning. In here I'll teach you the basics of channeling, but it's clearly your physical training that needs the most attention."

I spun around and put my hands on my hips. A fifteen-minute walk home from the train was one thing, but six hours of Justus as my personal trainer? "So this is your torture chamber, is it?"

Ignoring my comment he continued, "You'll be strength building and working on flexibility, but you will also learn to defend yourself. That is the rule."

"Defend myself or fight?"

He lifted his upper lip, clearly irritated by the notion. "Women do not fight, but I will teach you to defend against your enemies, Learner."

"Who are my enemies?"

"Everyone. Many Breed are highly respectful to women, but a Mage is your own worst enemy."

"Women don't fight back in your world—isn't that a little Middle Ages?"

"Haven't you ever heard of 'the best offense is a good defense?'"

"I think you have that the other way around. Was the quarterback ever chased with an axe?" I glared at the pointed blades on the wall. "Why can't I just zap them with a ball of light?" I wiggled my fingers only because I knew my mockery annoyed him.

Justus moved toward the punching bag and held it with his hand. "You should never put your power into another Mage. All that does is juice him up." He lightly pushed at the bag. "You'll be learning to manipulate energy."

I didn't even see him move—one minute Justus was by the punching bag and the next he was two inches in front of me. I jumped back and gasped.

"In time you will learn that you can harness it and move with it. An experienced Mage would be armed. A Learner cannot mortally damage a Mage of a higher rank, but you can slow them down enough to get away if you are clever." He turned his back to me and walked back over to the punching bag. "You can borrow light."

"This is a little confusing. I move things? If energy is in everything then why don't I just smash him with a couple of trees?"

Justus bent over with his hands on his knees, laughing in that rich voice. My eyes studied the tattoo wrapped around his arm, which was striking in his tight muscle shirt. I could see every angle of it, all the way up to his shoulder.

"No, Learner, you cannot move things. You can only borrow from the sun or the light of other living beings. However..."

"Borrow?" I let the word roll off my tongue.

"Much to learn. First, we'll start with testing your flexibility and stamina." Justus peeled off his tank top, allowing me an admiring view of his frame before he turned away. I briefly wondered what he meant by testing my flexibility and a smile played across my face as I stared at the defined muscles on his back. *Can't blame a girl for thinking it.*

"I'll shower up while you dress."

I so did not need that mental image floating in my head.

He strode to the bench against the far wall and I caught a glimpse of another tattoo on his back before he snatched up a small pile of fabric and turned back around. There was a gleam in his eye and a one-sided smile rose up his cheek. "This will be your training attire."

I unfolded the bundle as he made his way up the stairs. "I'll be back in fifteen. Be ready."

In my hand was a pair of what looked like Lycra bicycle shorts, only they covered even less than my underwear. The top was sleeveless and tight enough to accentuate every curve of my chest, which was a little curvier than it used to be.

"Hey, wait a minute!" I yelled in protest up the stairs.

My blood boiled as I heard a chuckle coming from topside.

Three hours later.

I learned a new word: pain. Justus had a tedious routine that involved sit-ups, pull-ups, and weight resistance. Basically, my muscles turned to putty as I staggered across the room falling on the mat; my thighs were screaming.

Justus hovered, ordering me to do more, more, more. I mentally ordered him to *die, die, die.*

The skimpy clothing did allow me to move more freely—but I still wasn't nimble. My Ghuardian assured that would come in time, yet why he got to wear sweats and a tank top simply irked me. That hardly seemed fair, although I hated to admit that it *was* motivational for a short while to have him as my focal point; Justus was built like a brick shithouse. His physique was stupendous to look at, but the minute he opened his mouth the thrill was gone.

Finally, I reached my limit as my muscles were trembling and I could no longer continue.

"I'm done; I can't do anymore," I panted on the mat.

My cheeks burned, my legs throbbed, and my hair was nothing but a sweaty mop halfway attached to my face.

"Are you telling me, Learner, that you have no more energy?" he asked, rubbing the bristles of hair across his scalp. *Justus was a man in love with a razor.*

Beads of sweat rolled down my temple into my hair. I glared.

"That's exactly what I'm telling you. In fact, I'm not leaving this mat for the rest of the day. I'm going to live here and build a little castle." I groaned, covering my face. "So you can just go about your business and leave me alone."

"Learner, this is your first lesson."

"What, that you can make my ass cry out in pain? Bravo. Anyone ever tell you that you'd make an excellent drill instructor? The Army is always hiring, you know."

He bent over, hands on his knees with a straight back.

"Lesson number one: there *is* no such thing as tired. What you will learn is that while your body may ache from your residual human limitations, the body of a Mage can replenish. You are a conduit; you channel energy. You can will it in, push it out, and manipulate it. There are limitations, however."

He stood up, and I winced as a shooting pain ran up my thigh. "When it comes to healing and restoring energy, you can only take that light from a Mage or sunlight. While you can take light from a human, it might require too much and could hurt or even kill them. And *never* take from another Breed."

"How do you take it from a Mage?"

"They have to lend it or be incapacitated enough that you can steal it. The latter isn't likely, as a strong Mage would have their shields up."

"So what happens if you don't take anything? Wouldn't you die if you had a stab wound or something?"

"Presuming you are nowhere near sunlight, your body would just heal slowly. Each Mage has a core light; you won't die from wounds inflicted, but you would suffer immensely. Should your head come away from your shoulders, then that is another matter."

"If I'm in the sun, I can just lie there and heal?"

"No. That is a dangerous process which must be carefully taught. One small drop of sunlight has more energy than most people realize. Once you acquire the skill, you will learn to harness that energy and extract it properly. But remember that borrowing is just that—borrowing. It will eventually remove itself, but if you take more than you need, it will take more from you."

My forearm weakly wiped away beads of sweat rolling down my temple and all the little synapses in my brain were firing off. If what he said was true, what else did that mean?

"Do we age? Will my hair grow longer, can I gain weight infinitely?"

Justus snorted. "You should not make light of this, but you will not age. We are one of the few Breeds who truly never age once we are made. Your body will remain in a… suspended state from the time you are made. So no, you will not gain weight, nor obtain any grey hairs."

That was a nice thought—no more guilt about taking out a carton of ice cream. "Why all the training if we can just heal in the sun?"

"Something to remember, Learner—most challenges against a Mage are at night because of that very fact. An experienced Mage who is capable in fighting need not worry as much as an inexperienced Learner, which is why they are so closely guarded by their maker."

"You're telling me that I can do sit-ups infinitely?" I began to laugh and rolled over. Every thought revolted. I sighed into the mat.

"That's exactly what I mean, Learner. As long as you have sunshine or a willing Mage, you are quite capable. Stand up."

"Sorry, my legs are going to have to turn down your offer."

Justus bent over me with determined speed and locked his hands over mine. "We'll just do it this way, then."

"NO!" I shouted, pulling my arms away as a sudden burst of energy sent me fleeing from him. "I'll get up."

I didn't need to be bullied, but when I looked at him, there was a severe look in his expression. It slivered those eyes, straightened the brow, and turned his mouth into a thin line. There was an awkward pause.

"Is that what your maker did?"

I didn't think I had it in me, every muscle screamed in protest, but I pushed myself up and met him face-to-face. "I don't want to talk about it, just don't do that again, okay?"

Justus gave a single nod and laced his fingers with mine as we stared at each other. My hands were swallowed by the sheer size of his.

"This is borrowing, Learner. I'm giving you some of my light."

"Hallelujah," I sang. "Heal me, brother."

"I'll do the willing, but we will switch our training later so you can learn how to draw from a Mage whose shields are down. If you dabble your inexperienced hand in the sun, you're likely to light yourself up like a Christmas tree. At least this way I can assess your ability to measure."

Blue threads formed between our hands and I felt sharp tingles like when your arm falls asleep and is waking up. This was the first time I would experience someone else's light and I was a little nervous. If I had to describe the feeling, it's as if your fingertips are drinking in energy. It moves throughout your body like a living organism with such speed and urgency that it's incredible.

"Your body is a glass with a line in the middle," he said. "When it begins to reach that line, you need to know when to stop. Never go past the line and fill the cup. Focus, you'll sense when that limit is reached. I can feel your light so I'm going to pull away when it's there, so pay attention. There will be a distinct fullness. That's it..."

The ache of hours of physical training melted away and I felt so revitalized that I could have sprinted out the door and run for miles.

Within a few seconds, my lips were numb and there was a fullness in my chest.

Too much.

I pulled back and the connection stopped.

"Very good, Learner."

"That's amazing!" I gasped. I walked around, flexing my hands open and closed. "I feel like I could…" I turned and gave him a sharp look.

I felt like I could kick his ass, that's what.

He must have read it in my eyes and stepped back.

"Easy, Learner. With power comes responsibility. Learn to redirect that energy, and keep in mind I could mop up this room with you in five seconds. Skills, Peaches—I got 'em. I can pin you against that wall in three ticks of a heartbeat. Now push it down," he said with irritation.

A minute later I felt less like a streak of lightning and more like myself. Not a single muscle ached.

"*Holy* shit. I'm a rechargeable battery!"

I was something more than I was yesterday. An old knowledge that settled in my bones was awakening, melding to my marrow, and becoming the very essence of who I was.

"You can see why it's addicting and we have a problem with juicers. The energy will allow you to heal or recharge, but once it leaves, you will be temporarily weakened. The more you have to take in—for example, if you had a severe injury—the worse off you'll be later. Your body will lose that energy and require sleep. So it would be better to let your body heal itself naturally for most injuries. Our healing is quicker than a human's."

"Got it."

"Feel like you could do five hundred sit-ups?"

"Tell you what—I'll let you know when I get to six hundred." I sat on the mat with an ear-to-ear grin. This was my new life, my new body, and I was excited to learn more about what I could do. Suddenly my life was brimming with a newfound hope and a future, whereas before it felt aimless and bleak.

He tilted his chin. "That's my girl."

"I'm not your girl.

CHAPTER 16

Six hours later, I took a long, hot, blissful shower. Today's attire would be casual—jeans and a green shirt with my laceless sneakers. I entered a dining room just off of the main hall and nearly choked with laughter.

There was a heaping pile of ribs with Justus parked in front of them. What had me absolutely tickled was not the ungodly amount of meat that was spread before him, but Justus wearing his napkin tucked in his shirt like an adult bib. He was ready to chow down with those hungry eyes already feasting. I slid into my chair and snatched a few ribs and rolls for my plate.

"Homemade?"

His fingers were laced as he hid a smile. "I don't cook. That's what you're here for."

"I'm not your slave."

"No, Learner, that you are most definitely not," he mumbled.

The moment I tucked a piece of bread in my cheek, Justus dug in. His whole body seemed to ripple at the joining of meat to his lips and I watched in awe a man who had the table manners of a troglodyte. His teeth gnawed into a rib, smearing a streak of sauce across his cheek as his entire body sighed in satisfaction.

My mind floated back to my ex, Brandon, who once ran a finger full of tomato sauce over one of my favorite tablecloths because he was mad at me, trying to provoke a fight. He challenged me with the look in his eye and all I could do was sit there and watch. He liked instigating things.

"Something bothers you."

I shook out of my past and flicked my eyes up to his. I could tell he was considering whether or not to pursue the comment.

"I can't cook, so you're out of luck," I lied. I buttered my roll with a dull knife and took another bite.

"That's all right; I prefer my women barefoot and pregnant."

I knew that was intended to be a joke, but it struck a nerve.

Justus looked up and his smile lowered. "What is that look, did I offend you?"

I tapped my knife on the table and just spit it out, something that had been bothering me for a couple of weeks since I missed my period. "I might be pregnant."

My panic turned into a wave of anger when he began to laugh uncontrollably. I grabbed a plastic container and threw it as hard as I could at Justus. He ducked as it smashed against the wall, sending a thick splatter of yellow potato salad sliding down like a horrendous display of artwork.

He sighed in disgust. "You will control yourself, Learner."

"That is not a funny joke."

"You are not with child."

He smirked and reached around, scooping up a finger full of the potato salad that still clung to the wall and put it in his mouth.

"What makes you so certain?"

"A Mage cannot have children. Females do not menstruate. I'd actually prefer not to discuss this topic over my meal," he said with a mouthful.

"Are you sure; what if I was before?"

He considered that a moment. "Were you?"

"No, but the man who attacked me, I uh… I don't know what happened after—"

"You are not pregnant. Males are not…"

He ended the topic, gnawing on a bone and I watched a dribble of sauce run down the edge of his hand.

Thank God. It was something I could hardly discuss with Adam, but when my period never came, I was scared and hoped that maybe stress was causing it.

"So, Justus…"

"Ghuardian."

"What?"

"That's what you call me, Learner. You cannot address me by my name while you are under my Ghuardianship."

"Yes, master," I said sarcastically.

He licked the sauce from his thumb, tongue slowly curling around the knuckle. "Master. Now, I kind of like that—has a ring to it."

"You are so obnoxious. Why don't you have any clocks or windows?" My eyes scanned the room. "Or *electricity*?" I chewed on some baked beans and washed them down with a can of soda, watching the shadows dance across the table from the candles. The only time I had ever eaten by candlelight was when the power went out after a tornado hit a few years back, knocking out the power lines.

"I prefer candlelight, it soothes the mind. And you will not have need for clocks."

"Elaborate?"

"You can sense time as accurately as an atomic clock in most circumstances."

"Does my body know when it's daylight savings?"

Ignoring me, he continued. "What time is it now? Don't guess... *feel*."

I set down my rib and licked my fingers as I tried to feel. But I didn't know what I was feeling *for*.

So, I guessed.

"Two thirty?"

"You're guessing." He reached over the table and grabbed a roll. "Soon it will come natural to you."

As we sat quietly, I noticed Justus had changed into a tight black shirt. I wondered if he bought it a size small intentionally to attract women, or if the fabric had simply shrunk in fear of him. Did he work for a living? Clearly, he did well for himself. Hell, just look at that car.

When my eyes bumped into his, I noticed he was staring at me... staring at him. I dropped my eyes to my plate and picked a few pieces of meat free from the bone. I could still feel him looking and he had even stopped eating—so the silence was a banging drum.

"Do you live here alone?"

"No one comes here."

I arched a brow. "So, no girlfriend?"

"I have no need for ties to another. This is my home and I enjoy the peace."

If that were true then why exactly was I here?

"What are we doing the rest of the day?"

I relaxed when he commenced eating.

"You will study. Much to learn."

There was little conversation as we were still getting used to one another's company. At one point, he nodded back at the crime scene on the wall and said, "You're going to clean that."

"Funny, I thought you might save me the trouble and lick it up." He cocked an eyebrow and I couldn't read his face.

I remembered the swarm of women with him at the bar, never a minute alone this guy had when he went out. But he seemed oddly uncomfortable with my presence in his home, not very chatty unless he was trying to educate me. How could a man of such prowess be so solitary? It was also worth noting that any time I contradicted him it drew a strong reaction. So as a result, there were long stretches of silence as we ate.

I also noticed Justus had a strange way of speaking. There was a layer beneath his tone that hinted he once had an accent of some kind. It was thick, every word meaningful and not rushed, and for the most part he didn't swear.

"Have you ever done this before? I mean, have you ever been a Ghuardian?"

Justus pulled his napkin free, carefully wiping his large hands on it. "No."

"Well, I just hope you know what you're doing."

I stood up and began clearing the table. I moved around to take his plate and ran my thumb along his cheek, scooping up that streak of sauce that had been annoying me the entire dinner.

"Missed a spot."

Before my thumb even finished pulling away, Justus took my wrist in his hand and swiftly rose from his chair.

He stood awkwardly, looking at the sauce on my hand before he let go. "Don't touch me. Go clean up and we'll meet in there."

I shrugged, wondering if I broke some cardinal rule of touching the Ghuardian.

I would later find out that Justus, much to my surprise, wasn't a very touchy-feely guy. Despite the fact that the first time we met he was being handled by every female within a fifty-foot radius, he didn't know how to handle personal affections.

"This is where we study; we have a history and you need to know not only where you came from, but also our laws." Justus paced in front of his bookshelf with his arms crossed.

I stepped over to the fireplace and ran my finger along the wooden shelf mounted above it, which held a large series of thick books. My god, did he expect me to read all of those? *The hell I will.*

I loved to read, but some of those monstrosities looked like they could be used as a weapon.

"Ouch!"

The wood plank used in the shelving was not polished down and a splinter—just the tiniest little sliver—went into my finger. I squeezed the tip painfully as it turned red and a small droplet of blood appeared. When my thumb brushed over it I hissed through my teeth. The splinter was still in there.

"Here, let me see," Justus said with disdain. "Hold very still." His focus was concentrated and he held my hand, using the very tips of his fingers to feel where it was. I winced again and he reached into his pocket, pulling out one of those handy little knife survival things that has everything from a screwdriver to a set of jumper cables. With a tiny set of tweezers, the little spear that impaled my finger was plucked free. "There."

"How can something so small hurt that much?"

"Because size doesn't matter?" He gave a sideways smirk and leaned up against the stone wall.

With a heavy groan, I plopped down on the leather chair. "All right, Ghuardian, teach me."

If I didn't know better I would have sworn I saw flecks of light dance in his eyes.

I studied for hours. We started out with basic 101 Mage history. We didn't work magic or sorcery, not exactly. Our kind had been around for centuries, and while nobody knew their beginnings, they remained secretive among humans in the latter centuries. Humans that discovered their abilities grew jealous, while others fabricated false rumors. Humans sought out to find Mage and other Breed and staged executions in manners that would guarantee their death. Often anyone suspected of alchemy or witchery was arrested. Justus confirmed we weren't the only preternatural beings, but this was a later lesson. Yes, save all the good stuff for last.

Each Mage has common abilities. Flashing involves riding the energy and moving at high rates of speed for short distances. We can also sense time and direction; we are able to heal; and flaring—well I couldn't quite grasp that.

"The only way I can explain it, Learner, is think of it like heavy cologne."

"You're comparing our aura to stinky cologne?" The air was chilly and I held my hands over my arms.

"In public places, your shield naturally goes up as a defense mechanism to protect your light by concealing it. But to conceal entirely in a human dwelling or establishment is a threatening gesture. We must make our presence known by occasionally leaking out our energy. The idea is that if you conceal while another does not, he is vulnerable and you are the threat because your motives become questionable. To avoid confrontation, we flare—allowing our bodies to release energy every so often to announce our presence. It's like shooting off a flare or waving a flag. If you pick up on another Mage, it is customary to seek them out and give introductions."

Justus slid down in his leather chair with his legs spread open and pulled the zipper of his hoodie down a few inches. The fireplace only had one log burning, but there was a comfortable heat that was beginning to build in the room. "It is not necessary in places where Breed congregate."

"So that's all we can do?"

He half smiled. "Not quite. Each Mage is born into their light with special abilities. Some have one, some have several."

"Such as what?" I leaned back on the sofa, noticing how ultra-soft it was for leather, and pulled a pillow underneath my arm. I later found a furniture catalog in a drawer with that exact sofa—and the price was listed at fifty thousand.

"Jumpers can ride the channel, like flashing, except against gravity. The distance of jumpers is longer, and is not unlike the concept of teleportation. Thermals, well… they have a gift with temperature. There are also different types of Mentalists: those who can send thoughts, those who can only receive them when called upon, and those who can do both. Then there are Creators, who are very rare and given special exceptions within the Mageri, as it is within their power to retain our lineage."

He leaned over and took a sip of water, setting the glass back down on the end table. "You can see why some are feared; there are a number of abilities out there, probably more than we even know of. Some gifts you can conceal, and it is within your right to do so. Only the Council and Mageri are required to know your gifts. There are some we know little about simply because most of us prefer not to elaborate to anyone but the Mageri—it could be a weakness for others to know your limitations."

"So, what can I do?" I asked.

"Annoy?"

I gave him a hurt look.

Justus pulled the tip of his hoodie over his eye and lowered his voice. "It remains to be seen; sometimes it takes years to uncover abilities."

"Maybe I can't do anything."

His blue eyes flashed up to mine. "Learner, we are all gifted."

I was given a book to read and found it thoroughly interesting and yet simultaneously boring. I felt like I was in school all over again and I hated studying. After lying on the sofa and finishing up three quarters of a volume on Mage wars (ugh, you really don't want to know), I glanced up at the bookshelf teeming with books and deflated. Justus was totally in his element being the instructor, whether it was tutoring my mind or my body. And neither in a way that felt good.

I closed my eyes and thought of what it must have been like back in the 15th century to be one of us. There were no advances in science and technology, and fear begat hatred. To be hunted down, stripped of your rights, accused of things you could not prove in a court of law to be innocent of. You could not disappear in a city like you can in today's world. No wonder they had come together to form their own social structure separate from humans.

Justus mentioned healing but it hadn't quite sunk in that I was now immortal. My life was renewable as it was constantly absorbing energy and rejuvenating back to its original state. I had a core light within me that couldn't be snuffed out so easily. I couldn't starve to death or even be beaten to death as long as that core light existed within me. Oh, we can die, the younger ones are especially more susceptible to death because we are not as strong and able to fight back. Who knew, and all this time I thought vampires had dibs on that.

I took a long nap and when I awoke, I drifted into the dining room and found a plate of leftovers with a note.

Learner, I am out for a while.
Be ready at 6 a.m., sharp.
Eat. Try to keep it off the wall this time.

I wadded up the note and tossed it at the kitchen door. Lifting the tin, I stared at the ribs, warm and freshly glazed. Dinner was always a social occasion with Adam; we never went to our corners or ate alone. There were really nice conversations between us and I missed having the companionship. I bet Justus had plenty of company; I was imagining him racing up to the nearest bar in his sporty little 'size doesn't matter' car.

I get to be locked up in a dungeon doing sit-ups all day while he's out getting his freak on. Is this the life I signed up for?

After wandering around the house and snooping through drawers, I went into my room, flipped on my music player, and listened to a favorite song. The house was so quiet the noise was a welcome relief and I danced, rolling my hips while I went through my bag. I didn't see any signs of air-conditioning, but he had ventilation going on somehow. It was cooler than I'd prefer, and if the fireplace was the only source of warmth, winter was going to be unpleasant.

I flung a shirt to a chaise lounge and backed up to the beat of the song. I used to think going to the club with Sunny was getting played out, but now I would trade anything to go out for a night of dancing and fun. I swung my hips and as I strutted across the floor, I swiveled right into Justus.

My face heated with surprise and I pulled the earbuds out. "What are you doing in here?"

His hands fell on my shoulders to steady me and I clutched his chest to keep from falling. I dropped my hands, but his lingered, and he moved them slowly down my arm. It was the first time I really felt him, not physically but something else. The energy was something extrasensory, nothing sexual or dangerous about it. Just an imprint that was unique to him much in the same way that someone has a smell, or the sound of their voice.

"What is that I feel?" I leaned in closer.

"That's me, Learner. You feel me."

Justus was pulsing on my skin like a heartbeat through his hands. "How come I didn't feel this before?"

His breath and voice softened and his eyes glazed as they lowered to my neck. "Your shields are down and you are open to it, and because I'm letting you. You need to recognize your Ghuardian's light."

It dawned on me that I was standing there in my panties, so I pushed him away. He stepped forward and as our bodies grew closer, the heat took away the chill. Hell, it obliterated it. He shut his eyes as if concentrating and let out a heavy sigh.

"Why do you not yield to me?"

"Are you trying to seduce the Learner? Because that was not in the brochure." I folded my arms, but I knew better. His tone wasn't a man beckoning a lover to bed but one of frustration for not having an answer to something else.

"That's not how I meant it."

"Maybe your trick doesn't work on others like us."

He laughed. "Oh, but it does."

"What did you come in here for; I thought you were out?"

"I brought you these. You need suitable attire. I'll leave them here. Your plate is on this table and I want you to eat. Goodnight."

He stepped out the door and I looked down and saw several large bags. Bending over, I lifted the edge of one bag so I could peer inside. It was filled with dresses, shoes, blouses, and baubles.

Justus had spent the evening shopping for me.

CHAPTER 17

4 MONTHS LATER.

Justus straddled me with a blade, cutting into my neck. "Better, Learner. Again."

I lifted my head and pulled up to my feet, legs slightly spread apart, one hand was behind my back, and the other was palm down. I waited for the anticipation of movement; he moved and I vaulted over him, landing on the other side. When his body spun around, we stared off again. I watched closely for subtle hints to pick up a sense of potential direction. Justus was teaching me about what the eyes tell, the position of the hands and feet, and even the lean of the body.

The training sessions had become my favorite time of the day. I was very pleased to find that I actually had skills, or at least potential. We did not have extraordinary strength, but we could utilize our abilities in a fight to gain the upper hand, making strength irrelevant… to a degree.

The only problem was that he wasn't teaching me how to *fight*.

Justus was teaching me self-defense until I learned to master it. It became pretty clear I was living with a caveman who believed that men were the protectors and women had no business learning how to fight. He taught me some basic moves but he treated me differently.

I learned how to feel out the other person—to find out what made them tick—look for repeated patterns in their fighting in order to gain the element of surprise. He often compared sparring to a mental battle, making sure to teach me to always keep my wits about me and look for signs of weakness in the other. And it was a challenge each and every day to find some way to stomp his ass to the ground. While I knew I would never best him, it didn't stop me from giving it my all.

His leg swiftly moved beneath mine and I lost my balance momentarily before I spun away and propelled myself to his left. In a flash, I moved back to face him—he wouldn't have expected that because that was not my usual move. Justus would have expected me to fake him out by going to his right. But I had caught him off guard and thrust my open palm to his chest.

It was a fluid motion; in the four months of training I had learned how to become a current. Justus said I needed to get over my inertia, to accept the fact that I could move with the current of kinetic energy by flashing. It should only last a period of seconds or it would otherwise drain you. Basically, I could move like a ninja on speed. It's not like I could zip on over to Canada and back in an hour, it didn't work that way because your energy would be spent.

But I could at the very least cross the street faster than any known pedestrian.

Of course there were rules; there were *always* rules. I was not to use (or abuse) my abilities carelessly. With cameras everywhere, it was a risk and Breed did not expose themselves to humans. Justus said it was easier when they had insiders who worked for law enforcement who always kept their ears open and would destroy any evidence of Breed. But now with all the new technology of cameras in cell phones, anything could be recorded and uploaded to the internet. So they also had to branch off with serious computer geeks who knew how to hack into a site and take down these videos or spread a rumor that they were doctored if they had already gone viral.

Videos and photos could be easily manipulated, so most people didn't believe what they saw anyhow, but it was still a conscious effort every Breed made to ensure that they were not outed. I wasn't surprised to find the government knew about us, but even they were not stupid enough to expose the Breed.

The fighting did not come so naturally. I was still learning defense, but I tried to mimic some of his hand-to-hand combat techniques.

Whenever I did, it pissed him off.

"Why do you keep fighting me?" he yelled, snatching my wrist.

"Because that is the point! I don't understand what you're trying to teach me, if I am not able to get away I need to learn how to fight back and win."

Justus was irritated, mostly because he knew I was right.

"You do not have to be the strongest or most skilled fighter to win. You tap into your source and ride it, trust it, then you have the advantage."

I wiped some blood from my lip. "Win. You say this, but you're not teaching me *how* to win, you're only teaching me how to dodge a punch. Why don't you teach me how to use one of those," I asked, nudging my head to his blade.

He sheathed it and placed it back on the wall, wiping sweat from his brow with his forearm.

"Because you cannot learn to use a blade until you properly learn to dance with one. Once you understand how it moves, how it is used, you can disarm your enemy."

"Care to dance?"

Justus whirled around and shredded me apart with those eyes.

"Do not continue provoking me, Learner. Remember your place."

Our sessions had gotten physical, and while we threw punches and drew blood, part of my learning was the acceptance of my immortality and ultimately, the acceptance of pain. Some of the bruises and scrapes I just had to suck up. I didn't like the idea of borrowing from Justus all the time and God knows I never saw the light of day. I was stubborn, admittedly.

What I did know about our weapons was that a few wielded special power; some metals were forged long ago with a kind of magic. They are called stunners, and once plunged into the body of a Mage, will paralyze them for as long as it remains.

I pushed back the pain and dropped to my knees. I had cracked a rib during the last sparring session and it was starting to flare up. If Adam knew about our little death sessions in the basement, that would have been it. If he knew I spent my days getting knocked around, spitting out blood, and being chewed out by Justus, I'm certain he would have killed him.

At least, that's how I imagined it. So much time had passed that it seemed like a lifetime ago since I had seen Adam. I often wondered if he had forgotten about me.

"Allow me." I presumed he felt guilty for some of the injuries he inflicted.

One thing I noticed was that my threshold for pain was higher—I wasn't sure if it was enduring the repeated sensation of pain and building a tolerance or if it was something more.

The room felt stuffy and the overhead lights were irritating my eyes. I could feel his light moving within me before it dissipated.

Pulling my ponytail tight, I took a few more shallow breaths. Justus was in his standard workout attire: black pants, tank top, and barefoot. In our sparring I found out his tribal tattoo on his arm wasn't the only one he had. Beneath his shirt was a hollow sun with what looked more like lightning bolts than flames coming out centered on his back.

My legs jumped when a deafening buzz reverberated off the walls.

"What's that?" I asked, staring upward.

He leapt to his feet and stared at the ceiling, a deep line forward on his brow. "Company." And by the look on his face, he wasn't expecting them. "Stay here, Learner." His tone was edged with concern.

Justus disappeared up the stairs. I felt a little uneasy when a few moments later there were footsteps moving around up there and muffled voices. No one had ever come to visit. Curious, I went up the stairs as quiet as a cat, eavesdropping.

"Just stopping in to give a shout. I'm done with England, for good. Couldn't exactly give you a ring, now could I—seeing as you haven't entered the modern era. I heard you were here so I came to see my old friend. What happened to your face, mate?"

I noticed the accent was mottled, mostly English that faded in and out. When he said the word "here" it sounded more like "heh".

"I thought you went home for good this time? It's been a long while."

"Well, Justus, that didn't work out as well as I thought, a bit of a mistake really. I've been back for a few years. The last time I rang you weren't here, so I got the sense that you were on the move again."

His voice was not as deep as Justus's and a little more melodic, but he put personality in his conversation, which made me believe he would be a really fun person to talk with… whoever he was.

"The Council is now up to five. Merc is one of them."

"Merc?" he exclaimed. "Sodding idiot was on probation; you're pulling my leg."

"I'm not; the dynamic has changed."

"Times are changing."

"That they are, my friend. That they are."

I stepped into the entrance and both heads turned.

"*Bloody hell*," the guest cursed as he moved his eyes to Justus. "Haven't we been the busy little bee?"

I looked over the man Justus was standing next to and he ran his hand invitingly down his chest as he appraised my attire.

He stood a hair shorter than Justus; his body type was leaner and he looked more like he should be fronting a rock band. Black leather jacket draped over his shoulders, graffiti T-shirt, and a silver chain that ran along the belt loop of his black pants. His brown tousled hair hung to his shoulders with that "just got out of bed" style. There was a sweet richness to his eyes, which were a light caramel and complemented his cheekbones and light skin coloring. And his mouth... a mouth that was full, kissable, and meant to be all over a woman's body. A mouth that began to curve into a wicked grin as his eyes locked with mine, revealing a pronounced dimple on his left cheek, which immediately made me blush and study the floor.

"Gonna introduce me, mate?" He folded his arms and elbowed Justus.

Justus took a position at my side. "Learner, this is Simon Hunt, an old friend of mine. Simon, behave."

"Justus, I would have never imagined you would finally take in a woman. Well done."

"No, it's not like that," I interjected. "He's my Ghuardian."

Simon dropped his arms and his jaw unhinged. I could see all the questions bubbling in his eyes. "You don't say." His mouth curled up again, showing off his dimple. "We've got a lot of catching up to do, Justus. I want every bleeding detail."

Simon strode toward me with a swagger that couldn't be taught. His hand reached for mine, and when I went to shake it, he bent over and pressed a kiss to it. There was a glimmer of amusement in his expression as he briefly looked at Justus. He seemed absolutely...

"Enchanted," Simon greeted me as he straightened his back. A dark look flashed across his face before it was replaced with a smile. "Your Ghuardian has no manners, love. Here, allow me." When he reached up to touch my face, there was a slap of skin as Justus caught his wrist.

"That'll be enough, Simon." He cleared his throat before adding, "She's already taken in more than she should."

"Of *course*." He winked.

"Will you be staying for dinner? I have to shower, but I'd like to come back and join you two if you don't mind."

"If you don't mind," he added, "I'd very much like to join *you*." Meaning—in the shower.

Justus leaned forward as if he meant to do something about the comment and Simon lifted his hands defensively. Simon was the fresh air that I craved; I was brimming with excitement that a visitor was in the house.

Strolling into the living room, Simon called out, "You know, now that I give it a bit of thought…" He fell on the sofa, arms wide across the back. "I believe I *will* be needing a place to put my feet up. Justus?"

Justus shook his head, displeased, and joined Simon on the couch. "Stay as long as you like, friend; my home is always open to you. I want to hear all about your travels. Learner, go clean up. Dinner will be at six. Be prompt."

I did as ordered and quickly sprinted down the hall into my room.

What I immediately liked about Simon was that while he looked like a bad boy, he acted like a total gentleman. Didn't really speak like one, but he wasn't vulgar about it, nor did he peruse my body with sexual need in those eyes. Not that I would have had a problem with that. He was a contradiction of himself and it fed my curiosity as to which one he really was. Oh my god, was I getting high school butterflies? You bet.

After my shower, I dried my hair and braided it back, threw on a little mineral powder to cover the bruise on my face, and applied lip gloss before rummaging through my clothes. I opened the closet and pulled out the black trousers and white shirt that Justus had bought me. I slid the trousers on and was satisfied with how well they fit— snug around my hips and the shirt was classy but simple. It made me curious how Justus knew my size when even I didn't. I gave myself a once-over in the mirror. My green eyes popped behind my black lashes and dark hair, accentuated by the light coloring of my skin, which had a honey tint. While my fingers were long and delicate, my nails were a mess. I had to keep them short due to the fighting, so I never bothered with a manicure—not that I ever had before—but now I was flicking at my cuticles with a little embarrassment.

I realized I was stalling. On the way to the dining room, I brushed my hands over my slacks and heard voices, laughter, and the sound of clinking glasses filling the space of a once-silent house.

"Hi," I greeted, clearing my throat.

No, it wasn't the grand entrance I imagined in my head. Someone forgot to cue the band and give me a witty line.

Simon's hand went down in slow motion, setting the wine on the table as he said, "Well, render me speechless."

Both chairs slid back and the men rose to their feet. Justus could have been catching flies as he looked at the outfit he had bought me that I never wore, and his cheeks were blotchy.

"Allow me," Simon said. "Someone has to be the gentleman here. It's not every day we're in the presence of a female Mage." Simon cupped my elbow and escorted me to my chair. Leaning around, his breath tickled my neck. "Hello, gorgeous."

"Wow," was all I could manage to say.

There were actually dishes and crystal glasses on the table. Candles flickered at the center and each plate had a serving of carrots and roasted potatoes next to a sumptuous rib eye steak. There was a beautiful salad and a plate of spring onions with radishes. My mouth immediately watered.

Simon's jacket was tossed casually over the back of his chair on my right, giving me an appreciative look at his physique. While he did not match Justus in size, he was hard and toned. His profile was very striking and made me look more than once.

He rested his elbows and forearms on the table, looking proudly at the setting. These two men didn't look like the type to forge a fast friendship, I thought curiously, looking at Simon's torn black shirt and leather wrist cuff. For someone who sported so much leather it was oddly contrasted against skin which didn't have a single tattoo or piercing that I could see.

My face scrunched at Justus. "You didn't cook this, did you?"

Simon leaned over and poured red wine into my glass. "That man may be able to dress for the occasion, but he could not cook to save his own life. Of course you know that by now." He gave a wink and took his chair. "I, on the other hand, am not without certain skills which I have refined to an art form. I find that the meal is a prelude to the pleasures of the bedroom. It sets the tone. If I can make a woman moan at the table, then I've already got her eating out of my hand. And... I do believe it's time you had a *proper* meal."

The statement was left out there hanging, making me wonder about the latter part. He took a napkin and sharply shook it out, placing it over his lap. "Is everything to your liking?"

That was a fully loaded question if I ever heard one.

"Umm, yeah. My eyes are having sex with this table as we speak."

Justus choked on his wine and I quickly covered my mouth with my hand. The silence was pierced by Simon's contagious laugh. He was a man who enjoyed a good one, too, as he let it go long and strong until the awkward moment was removed and I found myself smiling at him. I reached for a slice of fresh, warm bread in the cloth-lined basket and spread a blanket of butter across the top.

"I haven't had a home-cooked meal in ages. I'm going to devour everything—this looks amazing."

"As do you; don't you agree, Justus?"

Justus returned his stare with a contemptuous one of his own. I took a lingering sip of my wine and discovered what I had been ordering in restaurants was pure swill compared to this. Simon continued to ask for Justus's opinion of me, and I gathered he was testing the waters to see if Justus had any interest in me.

Little did he know that wasn't the case. As sumptuous-looking as he was, we had a very teacher-student relationship going on and our personalities clashed in a way that burned out any physical desire that bloomed.

"How did you get the steak cooked up so fast? Microwave?"

"I never arrive unannounced without something big and juicy in hand."

Oh dear Lord.

"So you two are old friends," I said, changing the subject. "Where are you from, Simon? I'm going to guess England, so if I'm wrong, dinner is on me next time."

"Define... on." Simon gave a wolfish grin and refilled his wine glass with a heavy *glug, glug.*

"Simon," Justus warned, plunging his fork into a potato that met its demise between his powerful jaws.

After taking a long, thoughtful sip from his crystal glass, Simon crossed his knife over the steak. "Well then, on those conditions I must confess that I am from Spain."

"While you're confessing, Simon, maybe you should mention that you only lived there, so that does not count."

After two or three chews of his meat, Justus continued with a mouthful. "He's from England. We've been friends for a turn of a century, give or take." Justus held his fork like a man still trying to stab his meal to death. "After I saved his ass."

"*Saved me?*" Simon seemed appalled by the very notion as his pitch rose. "I would have bested that Mage."

"You certainly bested his wife," Justus murmured.

"Yes, and he wasn't all too pleased with that, now was he?" Simon was very animated with his arms when he spoke, even if he held a glass in his hand. "I learned my lesson, mate. What a mouth on that one, right? And despite what you believe, I did *not* shag her knowing that she was bonded to him."

"Didn't see the mark, hmmm?" Justus replied. "You've been saying that for decades."

"Justus, my eyes were not in that postcode, my friend." He chuckled.

"What mark?" I took a long sip of wine as I studied the way they looked at each other.

Justus picked up a carrot with his fingers and popped it in his mouth. "Some choose to permanently stay together. It's not common... there aren't—" He paused.

"Aren't what?" I asked.

"Very many female Mage, is what he means to say," Simon blurted. "Those who hook up for the long haul get a bonding mark. Most Breed don't really believe in rings, we go for something more permanent." He snorted. "Can't be taken off as easily."

I liked Simon; he was honest and answered my questions. I felt like I could get information from him that Justus wasn't always willing to discuss. Everything was always for a later lesson.

"How long will Simon be staying with us?"

Simon was the one who replied. "That remains up to your.... Ghuardian." He thoroughly seemed to enjoy playing with that title as the tip of his tongue ran along the prongs of the fork. I heard a low growl across the table and Justus drank his wine to the bottom.

"Learner, what does he do all day with you, knock you around?"

I rolled my eyes. "Mostly; after that he reads me bedtime stories about Mage law."

"Oh, bloody hell." Simon gave an infectious laugh and winked. "Torture, indeed. All work and no play? Surely he lets you out."

"Never."

Justus was avoiding my stare. Simon laced his fingers together and obscured his mouth. Something played across his face I wasn't able to read.

"Justus, a Ghuardian needn't shelter the Learner. In fact," he said pointedly, "they absolutely must get out there and interact with the humans. She must learn how to handle that kind of energy and interact with her own kind, as well. You don't do her any service by keeping her locked up in here," he said, waving his fork. "You can train her all you want in that dungeon of yours, but if you don't expose her to the simple things she needs to learn to control, then she'll always be vulnerable."

Silence swept through the room and I set my fork down on the plate. That singular noise snapped the tension.

"It's decided." Simon gleamed. "Tomorrow, we go to the club."

Justus didn't look too thrilled, more defeated than anything. "Fine."

Simon rolled his tongue across the inside of his bottom lip, tasting victory. *Scratch "no piercing."*

"How did you two meet?" Simon asked.

"In a bar."

"Ah, a pub. Should have guessed." He chuckled softly.

"I was trying to enjoy my glass of tea while he was trying to get me to wear it." That conjured a smile on Justus's face as he took a bite of food.

"I see you still have a way with the ladies, Justus. But I have to give you a four-point-five in technique."

"It took some convincing, but I finally agreed to let him be my Ghuardian, and here I am."

"Yes, here you are," Simon said, raising his glass with a smile. I raised mine and our glasses clinked together. I couldn't remember the last time I had a social dinner with good conversation. Being holed up for months with Mr. Partypooper was beginning to eat at my fragile state of mind.

After dinner, I cleared the table to let the boys catch up. Simon watched the way Justus and I interacted with keen interest. It pleased him anytime I disagreed or made a sarcastic remark. He gave an expression like he had never seen anyone stand up to Justus.

I set a glass in the dish rack and reached for a plate when I jumped, startled by someone standing beside me.

"Simon is right. You must learn control in the outside world," he said, rubbing his tattoo. "We will talk about conditions to this; you'll require close protection."

"I'm sure I'll be fine, you'll be near, right?"

I ran a dish under the hot water, scraping the plate and wondering why it took a visit from his friend to make him figure that out.

"Here, allow me," he said. "You should take care not to ruin your new outfit." Justus took the plate but paused. I caught something in that look—it was warm and gentle. "You look nice; I should have told you before. This look is becoming on you." Color rose on his cheeks when I didn't respond right away, but I guess I was waiting for a punch line and was taken off guard by his sincerity.

"Are you paying me a compliment? That must have been some strong wine—I know how you hate the way I normally dress."

"You do not embarrass me."

Steam rose from the hot water and I reached over him to grab the plate and began to dry it with a cloth.

"You smell nice," he started to say under his breath before the door swung open and Simon waltzed in like a hurricane holding the empty wine bottle.

"We got any more of these, mate?" He waved the bottle and set it down on the stretch of cabinet.

"Had I known you were visiting, I would have made sure the wine was at the ready. Let me find something vile," Justus barked as he strode out the doorway.

Simon sidled up and put his elbows on the sink, leaning back.

"One hundred dollars says he leaves the bar with a girl on each arm."

"Whatever." I coughed. "He hasn't gone out in months and frankly the way he talks to women is infuriating. Plus, he would never do that in front of me; I think he'd be too embarrassed of my making fun of him," I whispered.

"Chicken?" He started to cluck.

"Nooo." I tossed the dishtowel at him and he flinched. "I don't have any money."

"Well then," he considered, "I shall take a kiss as my reward."

"Shall you? And if I win, I get the money?" The prospect of having a little pocket cash perked me right up. A girl could always use a little mascara, a few books, maybe some decent chocolate.

He dropped his head back, staring at the ceiling thoughtfully. I spied a mark on the back of his neck where his hair swept back. I leaned back for a better look when he snapped around to face me. Simon leaned in as if telling a secret and his arm lightly touched mine, making my hairs stand on end.

"You shall be… justly rewarded. But of course I'm good for the money! A word of advice, love? Put on your sweetest gloss. That man always has his cake… and eats it, too." He laughed.

The door swung wide and Justus came in, carrying a bottle in each hand, looking between them as if he couldn't decide.

"See what I mean?"

Pushing off of the counter, Simon plucked a bottle of vintage from his left hand and strode out the door.

CHAPTER 18

C LUB HIGH JINX SWELLED WITH human energy. I pushed through warm bodies pungent with the smell of sweat, perfume, and desire. The dance floor was energetic, and I could feel the pulse as if I were in a room of live wires. It was surreal to be among humans and know that I was no longer one of them.

Simon sported a leather coat and a tattered dark shirt, but tonight his jeans were replaced by tight leather pants. I had never actually seen a man wearing leather pants and I didn't have a single complaint. They were snug with a prominent zipper that ran up the front. I poked fun that all he was missing was a leash, given he was wearing a leather collar. His reply was more of a question of who would be holding the leash.

Justus, quite oppositely, had an ensemble that was sophisticated and put together. Given we were going to a club where nearly everyone was half-naked, I found this amusing. I felt a little like I was walking in with an angel on one arm and a devil on the other.

I wore a pair of knee-high black boots with a pleated skirt and a vibrant green, button-up top that matched my eyes perfectly. My black hair cascaded over my shoulders in soft, dark waves and a few wispy strands flew about my face.

"Can you feel that?" Simon shouted in my ear. "A human club is the best place to learn control."

We moved to a table that was off to the side with high stools, and I ordered something on the drink menu called an Absolut Pleasure, named after the vodka.

Simon continued once the waitress left. "You see, just being in a public place isn't going to provoke the same reaction as a club. The vibes here are more intense; energy levels are through the roof because of their emotional state."

He watched two women snake their way to the dance floor. They began to sway and move with the music, trying to tease the men around them by grinding on each other. I rolled my eyes but before I turned away, I noticed that something caught their attention, as it did many of the women. They began looking around as if they smelled something delicious in the air but couldn't place what it was or where it was coming from.

A cookie named Justus.

"Is this intense enough for you?" he asked, turning back to me.

"Well, I certainly see it must be for you," I replied.

The waitress returned with the chilled beers. "Yours will be out in a minute, honey." I sighed; why did waitresses always have to call you honey and sweetie? It was particularly worse when they were younger than you and barely of drinking age.

She batted her lashes at Justus and rolled that tongue across those pink lips. *Here we go.*

"Soooo… what do you do for a living?" I asked Simon.

The answer I got was a short laugh as he leaned over the table. "You haven't told her of the Mageri positions, have you?" Simon shrugged out of his jacket and threw it over the back of the chair.

I looked up at Justus.

"Later, Learner. School is out tonight, so have some fun." His hand ran over his tatted bicep in a slow, methodical manner, which signaled the ladies at the nearby table to come over and admire it.

"Hey, nice tat," one of them purred as her finger crawled over his arm, inching up his sleeve. Justus perked up like a flower in the sunshine coming to life, reminding me of the man I first met in that Memphis bar. He literally ate up the attention while his eyes licked every square inch of that woman. He was a cat named Ego being stroked, and I stewed at the women as if they were the ones that caused it. I didn't like it when Justus behaved that way; I preferred his stoic seriousness far more than the smug sex panther.

The platinum-blond waitress quickly swung back around with my drink and placed it on a napkin. She possessively leaned toward Justus as the nearness to his charm began to work its magic. If Love Potion #9 had an extract, it would be Justus. I mentally snickered at the thought.

"Can I get you something stronger; is everything to your satisfaction?"

It was like a PBS special on *Wild Kingdom.*

I reached down and bottomed out my drink. Within a minute or two, I felt the alcohol tingling in my body like a warm suggestion.

A redhead curled herself around Justus, running her fingers out of sight when I heard her muttering something about him being a very bad boy. His eyebrows danced in an *is that so?* expression.

Simon draped his arm on the back of my chair and turned his head as if he were looking behind me. "Pony up."

I smelled defeat—I was just refusing to admit it this early on. "The night is still young."

"And so are they," he noted as the girls were feeding on the nectar of the god that was Justus. Simon was gloating, clearly pleased that he was going to win his bet.

"Okay, boys, you two be good—I'm dancing." Inhibitions be damned, I was feelin' the flow after having been cooped up in that house for way too long. I didn't know these people, so what did it matter if I went out there and had a good time?

"Watch my purse." I slammed it in front of Mr. Leather Pants so it was clear he was not invited. Sore loser?

You bet.

Besides, I wanted to go out there and do a little fishing. I hadn't really test-driven this body.

The thrumming beat was driving the dancers wild as a current of energy was literally melting off them in a fine mist that engulfed me. The lights flickered and I worked my hips intentionally slower than the beat. I was delighted to see a few glances fall my way. I ran my hands through my hair and just let myself go as the swell of bodies moved like an ocean tide.

Just four feet away, bedroom eyes were poring all over me. A hot guy with short, spiked hair moved up without saying a word and began to dance. He lifted my arm to his shoulder, inviting me to join him, and with every move of our hips to the beat, he inched closer and closer. He had beautifully tanned skin already glowing with sweat. Steady hands smoothed down my side until they met with the bare skin above my waistline.

The feel of his skin was sinful. I didn't know who he was, and I didn't care.

I had been missing out on something all those months—and that was physical contact. The only contact I had received was fists, elbows, and heels knocking me down on a mat. Justus never hugged or touched me unless he was healing me; he was very peculiar about that. I wasn't a person who necessarily craved touch, but when you've been deprived of it for so long the first time simply ignites you in the most unexpected way.

"I'm Paul," he yelled out.

His fingers noticed my belly button was exposed as they brushed over my skin, sending a shiver through my body.

"You're fucking hot," he mouthed. His bottom lip was swollen from biting on it and his eyes were hooded. The man was already having mental sex with me.

He inched closer until our bodies joined, and pleasurable warmth spread through me as I looked into his eyes. His fingers clawed at my hips and I felt the raw need in them. Whatever his intentions were, he was priming me up, and I began to have flashes of this man stripping me down and running his tongue all over my body.

When his lips grazed my neck, I exhaled suddenly. The music felt good, he felt good, and those hands continued to move and explore the contours of my body. Energy was culminating within me and my arms dropped to my sides as my hair spilled across my face.

Paul stopped moving, took my wrist, and urged me forward. "Let's go somewhere private."

"Sod off, you manky bastard. She's taken."

I raised my head as the contact broke. It was then that I looked up and locked on Simon's softened eyes. The look behind them was amused and intrigued. He smelled good—like cinnamon—and I wanted to bury my nose in his hair.

"Careful, love, you're charged. Rein it back in, you need to level down," he whispered into my ear, pulling me close.

Only, I had no idea what the hell he was saying, nor did I really care. I only knew it was further arousing me.

"Why don't you help me level down," I said in a husky voice.

Simon managed a groan.

"You're a very bad girl, Learner."

Simon's hips moved with mine and we fell into a comfortable rhythm as I imagined his moves off the dance floor and in the bedroom.

Such sultry, sexual moves. He was the kind of guy you could imagine taking his time, savoring every moment and not hurried at all with his seduction. I spied a hole at the side of his shirt and pushed my hand inside of it, feeling the searing heat of his skin. His eyes melted down my body, torturing me with their secrets.

When he held me at arm's length with a scowl, I broke away and scanned the crowd, looking for the other guy. Simon had no interest in finishing this dance and was no better than Justus at merely teaching me lessons. I spun around and began to walk away when he grabbed my arms and pulled me back against him. The room churned around us as we stood like statues. I felt every inch of his body against my back. Arms snaked around my waist and across my chest, caging me in.

"Pull back; we can't do this here, love. Level down before you give them a free light show, will you?"

I turned to face him and snapped out of it. I was losing control, the sexual energy in the room leaked out and filled me like a drug and I was allowing it to take control of me and pull my energy. If I didn't level it out, the night would end early with me passed out. A deep breath later, I was myself.

I smirked. "You're a good dancer."

"You aren't too shabby yourself." Simon gave me a twirl and we returned to the table.

I couldn't assess the look on Justus. While he had two girls pawing on him, he appeared to be oblivious to everything except me and Simon walking off that dance floor.

Several hours and drinks later, flirtatious dancing had escalated into more serious matters for some couples. Seduction was a heavy perfume penetrating the club. Once you stripped away civilized behavior, humans were no less primitive than animals when it came down to it.

Justus was in a more private area of the room, led away by the women who became greedy, wanting him all to themselves. Simon kept me company the entire evening with interesting stories and plenty of laughs; our moment on the dance floor was likely nothing more than misdirected energy.

I popped the last mozzarella stick in my mouth, savoring that delicious deep-fried goodness that always tastes better when you've been drinking. I licked the tip of my finger, watching a woman run her fingers through the silky strands of her straight black hair, a visual request that Justus could not ignore.

"Women haven't a prayer, you know." Simon leaned forward and knocked back another shot of tequila. He grimaced and the glass tapped on the smooth tabletop that was littered with empty glasses, straws, cherry stems, and crumbs.

"For what?" I asked.

"Your Ghuardian over there," he shouted over the music before leaning in closer. "He's a Charmer, that one. That's why they're drawn to him."

"Like a bee charmer?" I threw my head back, laughing.

"You could definitely say that, love. It's one of his gifts, one a Mage cannot easily hide and not many have. He releases a certain kind of vibe that is seductive and irresistible, a magnet that draws in sexual energy. He can't turn it off, either."

"You're telling me he's a sex magnet?"

I laughed so loud it drew attention from a nearby table. "That explains a whole lot. Okay, so if that's true, then how come the men aren't all over him too?" I thought my question was justified—since when does energy discriminate?

Simon smirked, running his thumb over his bottom lip. "I don't know his magic, of course that isn't to say that he hasn't had the occasional bloke or two wander over, depends on which team they're batting for, I suppose," he said winking. "Chemistry, protons, electrons, voodoo…" He shrugged.

I tucked my chin neatly in my palm. "Well, I'm immune. Even

when we first met I was the only girl there that wasn't having an illicit mental affair with him." My grin widened. "I think that really pissed him off too. He's got a certain lure about him, he's handsome, but I guess I'm not feeling whatever vibe he's sending out."

There was a sexual frenzy unraveling near Justus. One of the girls was stroking his stomach as if she might get a wish. Meanwhile, he continued talking like he was telling the most interesting story.

"Yes, that is quite the curiosity. I've noticed that about you two," Simon said to himself as he circled his finger around the rim of a short glass. "You realize that's why he doesn't know how to behave properly with you? He's a cad because he can't trust women; they're too drawn to him sexually for him to know if it's genuine. That bloke has a wall around him with a moat, and yet there he is, talking up a storm as if they even cared what came out of his mouth. I feel a bit sorry for him."

"So that's why he acts like a manwhore?"

Simon laughed into his glass, spitting out some of his drink. "I'll tell him you said so."

"Please do."

"What I mean is, it's not unlike being rich; most women like you for your money, but how do you really know when they like *you*? His charm is his curse; he's never had a real friendship with a woman, so he doesn't know how to treat them. He's got his hands full with you, that one—I bet you have him shaking in his boots." He looked thoughtfully in Justus's direction and began to mutter to himself, "Maybe this will do him some good, having a female Learner immune to those charms of his."

"Maybe it only works on his type, which I am not." I pointed my head at the newly formed harem of big-breasted vixens before I rolled my eyes back.

"You're everyone's type. You've got a charm of your own," he said, letting his voice slide to a seductive purr.

"You don't know me very well then."

"Let's remedy that, shall we?"

The dimple in his cheek winked as he gave a playful grin.

Suddenly, the lights went dark and a blue laser flashed. I started to buzz and needed to remove myself from this predicament before I ended up electrocuting half the city, watching Simon's pierced tongue run over his teeth. Too much alcohol would only lead to regretted mistakes.

"I'll be back." I popped up out of my chair and tried to focus on the path to the bathroom. It was packed tight with only seven stalls, so there was a bit of a wait in line. Girls stood in front of the mirror in their tightest skirts and Band-Aid tops, leaning forward to plump up their lips and apply more perfume. Nothing like a nasal assault in a sweaty club to get the guys going. Eventually, I made it to the finish line and squirmed through a sea of silicone to head back.

I pushed against the crowd in the hall that had grown exponentially in just the past few hours. I awkwardly bumped into a couple making out and they hardly noticed.

Shit.

Simon and Justus were nowhere to be found. I scanned the crowd with my blurred vision and decided they must have headed out to the car.

My boots stomped erratically on the cement as I emerged and nearly stumbled down the steps. The frigid air splashed against my feverish skin and felt delicious. I thought about the dance with Simon and a tingle of energy rippled through me.

"Stop it, Zoë. Getting all worked up over nothing." My shoes scraped the gravel noisily as I fumbled with my tangled hair.

"You got a light?"

I followed the sound of the voice—sizing up a brawny man leaning against a car who could have been a bouncer for the club, probably on his smoke break. His hands were tucked beneath his biceps, which were completely covered all the way down with tattoos like he was wearing an ink shirt.

"Sorry, I don't smoke."

I kept moving and scoped the lot for the car. My eyes were useless at this point; squinting was only allowing me to get a closer look of my eyelashes.

"So you don't have a light, huh?"

"No." *Jesus, was he deaf?*

A gust of wind swirled my hair around and when I looked up, I was suddenly facing the man. He was intimidating, unmoving, and watching me in a way that made my skin crawl.

He yanked my arm when I tried to step around him.

"I didn't ask if you smoked, I asked if you have a light. And my guess is... you do."

Justus had taught me that we were not permitted to use any of our gifts around humans. I twisted my arm, breaking his hold, and stepped to the side. Just as quickly as I could move, he corralled me against a car with his humongous arms spread wide and low. He flashed a grin, lips pressed tightly together.

"Look, my friends are right behind me and they're big guys," I lied. Well, Justus was sizeable, but Simon didn't have a prayer against this guy. "They'd be pretty pissed to find someone out here manhandling me, so let me go." It was as if he didn't hear me, as if he were appraising me. "I'm warning you, I can scream loud and if you don't step off right now—"

"Shut the fuck up, bitch, you talk too much."

Adrenaline knocked at the door and asked if it could come in, so I let it.

I swept under the open gap but he snatched a handful of my hair and jerked me back. I was able to knock his legs enough to throw off his balance and when he lost his grip, I backed away slowly, eyes fixed on him. I learned to never turn my attention from the enemy, even when retreating.

"You're a new one." His tongue came out of his mouth, making an obscene gesture. "I can't wait to taste you, Learner."

He knew what I was.

He was a Mage, and I was in deep shit. My heart hammered against my chest as my eyes darted around for help. No one was near, no one who could help. Was I ready to fight a Mage?

"That's right, I know what you are." He studied me a moment. "You *are* new."

When his right foot inched forward, I flashed to the side.

"It's fucking rare to come across an unclaimed female, a definite two-for-one. I don't know whether I want to juice you or fuck you first. Maybe both, but your ass is mine." His laughter was chilling. "What's the matter, you scared? Can't play with the big boys?" His eyes lowered straight to my skirt and his tongue traced the corner of his mouth as he stepped toward me. I took a step back and thought about making a run for it. "That's okay, I'll be real fucking gentle, seeing how it's your first—"

I didn't hear anything in that second. One minute I was looking at this junkyard dog about to tear me up and the next all I saw were two bodies blocking my view.

Justus and Simon became a shield standing before me. Simon gripped my forearm as if I might fall off the earth.

"I would advise against moving another inch, juicer," Simon warned.

"You have concealed from us," Justus accused. "Introductions are no longer needed."

"Something tells me that neither one of you is her maker, which makes her…" He pointed. "… fair game."

Fingers were just a hair tighter on my arm.

"I am her Ghuardian, so be watchful of your threats!" Justus roared.

I heard a low chuckle. "Everyone knows a Ghuardian doesn't have the same rights to a Learner. You know as well as I do I can take her if I want. Guess what? I fucking want, and what I want… I take."

Simon replied with exquisite restraint. "Why don't you walk away while you still have your balls intact?" Simon had a tongue on him and I wasn't sure if he was trying to threaten or provoke.

Boots scraped on hard cement, but I couldn't see anything.

"Back. That. Shit. Up. You fucked with the wrong Mage!" the juicer shouted.

The reaction was explosive.

Justus flashed and his vacant spot was filled with Simon moving to the side to guard me. The man with tats spun around in a blur as he lunged at Justus just a few feet ahead.

I heard the occasional bone-crunching punches before Justus perched himself on top of a car. The juicer lunged with a growl to grab his ankle. Justus spun completely horizontal before vanishing.

He didn't just flash, Justus literally vanished!

In a few quick motions, I lost sight of the both of them. Simon's hand slid down my arm and I looked at him nervously. His head cocked to the left as if he heard something and he flashed away.

In the blink of an eye, I saw that Justus had been thrown against a car and his head was slammed violently against the door until he fell limp.

My heart froze, stricken with fear, as blood ran down his face and soaked his shirt.

"Ghuardian!" I screamed.

Simon reared up from behind and punched the man in the side, below the ribs.

Their bodies moved so heartstoppingly fast that the occasional stillness of movement was eerie. The slicing sound of a knife made me think of my training with Justus, and here I was standing like a deer in the headlights.

"Hey!" I yelled, walking toward the tattooed man, who held the knife in his right hand. If I could distract him long enough for Simon to heal Justus, we would have a chance. I couldn't risk doing the healing because I had never given my light and I could do more damage than good.

Simon's gaze was punishment enough. "I have this, love," he said in a low, angry voice through clenched teeth.

Fuck him and his male bravado.

I brushed my hair aside, letting him know he could shove that bravado right up his ass.

"Isn't it me you want?" I asked, coaxing the juicer with a crooked finger.

Distracted eyes traveled down to my legs before turning his focus back on Simon with the blade aimed at his heart.

"If I tell him to back off, he will. He has no claim on me. I go where I want."

"Then tell him to back off."

"Simon, this isn't your fight. Take Justus home. You're over your head on this one—it's not worth it." Simon's mouth opened and snapped back shut.

Simon you idiot, swallow that pride and go heal Justus.

"The thing is—you've got to catch me, if you can." I gave a lazy smile and flashed back several feet. The dare incited the hunter out of him and he gave chase.

While I wouldn't entirely recommend flashing while you're drunk, in my relaxed state of mind I had to admit I wasn't overly thinking my moves. My thoughts were fluid—feeling, and reacting.

He moved and I moved, and the dance began. There were moments I thought he would catch me, but I had enough defense tactics to slip free. I never continually flashed in any of my training sessions; Justus wanted me to learn maneuvers and not rely on my abilities. I was beginning to realize why as it was draining my energy. Still, we continued for what seemed like minutes as I continued to slip out of his grasp.

Suddenly a high-pitched laugh broke my attention. I couldn't help but wonder if the boys were sitting on the sidelines watching the whole thing with a bag of popcorn. I stewed on that thought and stopped to look.

Big mistake.

In a tenth of a second I was caught, and the juicer pulled me hard against his chest, squeezing the breath out of my lungs.

"Gotcha."

I struggled, but his arms were cement, and my feet lost sense of the ground as he lifted me up. Without fear, I looked him in the eye. I had one option, so I flung my neck back and slammed my head into his face.

My temple exploded in pain.

The sound he made was animalistic as blood poured from his nose. His arms relaxed and all hell broke loose.

From out of nowhere Justus appeared, pulling me off and ramming him so hard they both fell to the ground.

"Get her out of here!" Justus shouted.

CHAPTER 19

I HAD TO SWALLOW DOWN NAUSEA as throwing up in Justus's luxurious kitten could quite possibly result in the first sign of the apocalypse. That car was the closest thing to a pet he had.

"What just happened back there?" Touching my temple I felt the tight, swollen stretch of heated skin.

"Justus picked up on a vibe. Never go off like that; you should never be alone that long."

"So you picked up a Mage, but why all the panic that you would ditch me like that?"

"What the bloody hell have you two been studying these past months, philosophy?" He flipped the heater to a higher temperature, eyeing my fingers. "He wasn't flaring, but Justus sensed a weak energy leak. The juicers are a constant threat. Most of them are searching for weak Learners to collect for personal use or to be sold on the black market."

"I didn't feel anything."

"Love, you can barely feel yourself," he said with playful undertones.

"Ugh," was the only reply I could give.

"It's serious stuff. We put out our hello sign; suffice it to say he never put out his. I went to find you, but you weren't there." The engine purred as we neared the turnoff.

Simon gave me his full attention. "Are you hurt?" The steering wheel felt the pain of his grip as he whispered under his breath, "Limey bastard. I hope he throttles him good." He gave a sideways glance and reached out with his hand and touched my head, taking away my pain with a bit of light. "Better?"

"Miles," I replied.

When we pulled up to the entrance, I opened my door and fell onto the ground. I was exhausted from the flashing and still mildly drunk. Staring up at the sky, my view was eclipsed by a shadow as I focused my eyes. I saw leather pants that went right up to the heavens.

No wait, that was Simon.

"You're so pretty." I smiled.

He put his hands on his hips. "Funny, I was going to say the same thing about you."

"Sure, sure." I waved an arm and rolled over to push myself up. I felt as heavy as a ton of lead.

He curled his arms around my waist and tugged me gently to my feet. "Upsy daisy. You handled yourself well—fast."

"Not fast enough."

"You're also pissed. That was impressive, Learner. Someone as young as you? I'd love to see what you can do sober."

"I could have taken that guy, you know," I mumbled as he carried me more than I walked.

"Of course, love. That's a pretty thick head you've got."

"So I hear."

My eyes lifted from the uneven ground at the dark woods. The air had an icy, wet flavor to it that hinted another snow was coming. It didn't snow much where I was from, but the scent of snow left quite an impression.

"Why is he such a jerk?"

"Responsibility? He's not used to it. He's never been a Ghuardian, nor had to live with a woman. Justus is in a pressure cooker because he's a perfectionist. You are a reflection of him; I suppose he thinks if he's not hard enough on you then he'll have failed."

A twig snapped beneath our feet.

"I take it his maker was not a woman." I laughed sleepily.

"And where is yours?"

His voice softened a bit, suggesting he knew there was more to my story. Maybe he knew it, maybe he didn't. But whatever the truth was, I kept silent.

We approached the entrance and he lifted a hatch in the ground that looked like it had grass, leaves, and dirt glued on top of it. I stared down the dark hole.

"How did he get all his furniture down there?" I gave a quizzical stare and put my hand on my hip.

"You should see what he can do with a ship and a glass bottle."

I drew in a sharp inhale and sneezed. "Great, now I'm sick."

Simon laughed lightly. "That's one thing you won't have to worry about again. Mage do not get sick unless you count the occasional indigestion. That, unfortunately, we can do nothing about."

"You mean I can't catch a cold?" I rubbed at my nose.

"Our bodies do not respond to nor carry disease or viruses. I guess Justus taught you about our healing but failed to mention that part."

Another sneeze escaped. "So then why am I sneezing?" I felt a rub of worry, wondering if maybe certain things didn't apply to me.

Simon merely snatched my nose between his fingers and mused, "Because it tickles, love."

My boot gripped the thin metal rungs and I nervously lowered myself down the hatch.

"Get a good grip now, careful."

I went one step at a time with a blind foot reaching for the next narrow step; without a light it was impossible to see.

"Does Justus own this land?"

"Not entirely." His voice echoed in the room below. "Technically most of us don't own our own land. It's owned by the Mageri who controls our properties. It's a convenience, really. They manage all the goodies like taxes and securing the adjacent land from companies building a department store or gas station."

My heel slipped and I lost my grip, scrambling for the rungs as I fell back.

I freefell into the darkness and when I hit the ground—landing directly on my foot—I screamed. My body instinctively curled up and I held my leg, growling in pain.

There was an audible stomp and Simon knelt at my side. His hand lightly brushed over my face as if he were assessing my injuries based on my expression alone.

I guess it told him enough.

"Take my neck." He pulled my arm over his shoulder and lifted me into his arms. "Let's get you inside and take a look."

"Can't he get a freaking elevator?" I yelled out, biting down on his leather jacket as hard as I could. I kept my teeth clamped firmly until we made it to the bedroom where he laid me down on the bed—the one I never slept in—the bed I had nicknamed Goliath because of its monstrosity. The sheets never had to be changed because they were untouched. I preferred the red sofa chair against the wall.

Pain radiated up my leg with every beat of my heart.

"I need to remove your boot." He stretched his fingers nervously. "It's on tight; it'll hurt," he warned.

"Just do it," I breathed, throwing a pillow over my face. With a quick tug, he jerked it free and I screamed.

Slowly, my knee-high stocking was peeled off and my entire body shuddered. A tolerance to pain was something that I had been working on, but I was always prepared for it during our sessions. Here, I was not.

I slid the pillow away to watch, and the candles put out a dim glow in the room. I doubted under the circumstances he was looking up my skirt, but I felt a hint of embarrassment nevertheless.

Simon held my ankle gently in his hands while the slow rise of power transferred from his fingers to my leg. His eyes remained fixed and concentrated. The healing was not really painful, just a sensation of heat and blissful numbness.

I sighed—hell, I think I groaned—in relief. "Was it broken?"

"Doesn't matter now," he said.

Once residual waves of pain subsided, it occurred to me that Simon wasn't pulling back. The sensation changed to something completely unfamiliar as his energy spread up my thighs and a gasp escaped my lips.

Desire heated me unexpectedly—as if everything I felt at the dance club was magnified times twenty.

Confused by my reaction, I looked down at Simon, expecting he would be laughing at me. Instead, my gaze was met with one of attraction and a flush of heat licked across my chest.

"The male on the dance floor tonight..." he said, stroking my ankle tenderly. My brows joined together in a display of confusion, only I wasn't as confused by his comment so much as his thumb sliding up my leg.

"You can't do that with humans."

He climbed on the bed, blanketing my legs, hands on either side, prowling up my body with the gaze of a predator. Simon's eyes pulsed with light and I fell into their trance.

"Do what?" I whispered.

Leather pants stroked the outside of my legs. His hands seductively flirted with my hips, my breast, and my arm until he slowly opened my fingers.

Simon straddled me, bent forward. His palms rubbed against mine and the motion was so frictional that I held my breath. This was not like any other energy exchange I had experienced.

"Touch," he answered

Jesus, I had forgotten the question.

"You're a Mage now; you can only touch your own kind when you're charged up that way."

"Wait," I said in a scared voice. Simon silently turned his head to the side, continuing to rub our palms. Whatever I felt was instinctive; I wasn't supposed to restrain this. It wasn't light Simon was coaxing out of me... it was sexual energy.

"No waiting," he said in slow breaths. "Only doing."

I took the weight of Simon's body and felt him everywhere. His muscles tightened when I slid my hand beneath the leather coat and stroked the skin under his shirt. With a slight shake of his shoulders and a quick motion, the coat hit the floor.

I always hated obstacles.

My eyes made love with the shape of his lips, the way they parted. Simon had the sexiest mouth I had ever seen on a man and I wanted to kiss him.

But those lips disappeared when he nestled into my neck and began kissing his way up my jaw.

Need prickled throughout my body and I turned my head so he could continue on the other side. My receptiveness further aroused him, evident from the sudden grinding motion against my thigh.

"You feel so good," I whispered.

Hair scented with male spices tumbled onto my cheeks, but Simon had a subtle smell of cinnamon.

He enveloped me with his body and touched my hand tenderly as his energy began pouring into me like liquid lightning.

"Oh, God!" I exclaimed, feeling as if I might fall over the edge.

I felt *everything*—his raw desire coursing through me with such penetration that I was writhing beneath him.

"I've never done this before." It sounded so juvenile, but this transference was so distinctly intimate that it scared me.

My body felt as though we were already in the act of sex and neither one of us had removed our clothes. I knew this had to be something normal, and yet Justus had failed to explain any of it to me.

Was I doing it all wrong?

"What haven't you done?"

I squeezed his hand and Simon went cold. The connection stopped.

I opened my eyes with regret for having confessed such a thing and saw something in his eyes—judgment? apprehension?—I wasn't sure.

"I thought you'd been with him this way."

He must have known we weren't together in the other way—the way he was going if he slid a few more inches lower.

My fingers ran over his shoulder, which was heated and sticky. I liked the feel of him, the smell.

I shook my head and Simon was searching for a decision on where this was heading. I was feeling the flickering flames start to recede and I was afraid he would stop.

"Is this something you can do with just anyone?" I asked.

"Binding doesn't have to mean sex, but if I find out that you're going around doing this with other Mage, I'm going to hunt down those men and tie them to a flagpole, do you understand? This is not something you should give so freely; it's as intimate as sex itself." He sighed. "I didn't know it was your first time. I don't think I should be the one… it's too intense and—"

"Simon?"

He stilled at hearing his name. Inner conflict flashed across his face, so I reached around and locked my hand across the back of his upper thigh and pulled him hard enough that his hips sank into mine. Hot, tight leather pressed so sweetly against me and my thumb traced the line of his lower lip.

"You owe me on that bet, Simon. But you can keep your money—I want a kiss."

The inner conflict abruptly ended when I had his mouth on mine.

Simon kissed with such fervor that every part of me stirred and I felt myself moving all over. Our tongues twined so slow and deeply—coaxing all kinds of suggestions about what needed to happen in the lower half—that a primal moan rumbled through his chest.

If that man worked his sex half as good as his tongue, I was in for a hell of a night.

In my past I had never been an aggressive lover; my ex didn't like it. He thought a submissive woman was a loyal one. Simon was inviting me to take some control, so when our hands locked together I gripped him firmly by the hair with my other hand as he poured is energy into me.

Finally, I no longer held back. I reciprocated.

The moment my energy was returned, his teeth nipped my bottom lip and his head jerked back.

"Shit!" he cursed.

We were finally fluid. Connected. The energy swelled between us in waves. It was perhaps the most erotic thing I've ever experienced to that point.

"Christ, Learner, you're different," he breathed. "This is not like anything—"

I closed my fingers around his, arching my hips upward. He let out a moan and I felt every inch of his want pressing against me.

And oh god, how he *wanted*.

"You are…" He continued to kiss along my neck before he met my eyes and watched them with trepidation. "…a Unique."

I licked my lips and that drew his hungry eyes back to my mouth.

"Let me show you, love." He cupped his hands over mine and focused heavily on my eyes. "We call this binding."

Simon rolled through me like a psychic massage in every facet of my being. I twisted beneath him and felt his clever hands slide under my skirt, tugging at my panties until they were off. This time I wore the thin lacy kind, special night out and all. No intention that by the end of the night hands other than mine would be removing them.

I was out of breath, still charged from the exchange, when Simon moved down the bed and kissed my leg with long, slow licks. I trembled as his pierced tongue stroked along my inner thigh.

Clothes never felt more confining.

His fingers playfully slipped beneath my shirt and made small circles over my bra. Simon was releasing small increments of his light when he touched me that way, making me even more sensitive to his touch.

I stroked his arm, encouraging him to do more—I wanted his hands all over me.

"Don't stop," I begged.

"Now, why would I stop? I'm barely getting warmed up." Simon chuckled.

The deep shadow of his dimple formed when he looked up at me—god, how I adored that small feature over anything else. Charming, sexual, and mischievous all managed to wrap itself up in that little indentation. Every person has that one thing about them, so small that it defines them. For Simon—that was it.

He sat up and scooped me into his arms, sliding me over his lap. I straddled him and spread soft kisses across his eyes and rocked my hips forward. His chin lowered to the opening of my blouse and he pressed a long kiss.

"You taste as sweet as you look," he said, tongue tracing lower until it found that annoying fabric of my bra.

Simon could have torn my clothes off in five seconds and I would have been game, but he took slow seduction to a whole new level. We were drunk with spirits and energy, and the rest of the world melted away.

My fingers curled around the leather collar on his neck and pulled away the latch, sliding it free and tossing it aside on the bed.

I never imagined myself with someone like him; Simon was

unlike anyone I had ever met. It felt decadent, as if I were indulging in a sinful chocolate that I knew was bad for me.

My lips, my tongue, and my teeth staked their claim on his shoulder—and he hissed as his fingers bit into my skin desperately.

I was actually affected by his desire for me. It was a game to see who could arouse the other more, and who could show the most restraint. I caught this in his gazes—his smirks—when he did something that stimulated me and how I behaved. It was competitive, and my will was collapsing.

I just wanted to pass Go and collect my two hundred dollars. Simon wanted to take his time shopping for property.

His fingers unfastened the buttons of my blouse. "Darling, I fear I might tear this if it stays on any longer."

When my breathing became erratic with the sound of each button snapping free, my hips glided up and stroked the length of his sex through those tight leathers.

"What about these?"

Simon's eyes rolled back and I had a "gotcha" moment. Point to me.

He opened my shirt and let his hands float over my skin, but refused to touch it. Damn him, he was still playing the game. I followed my basic instincts and arched my spine and threw my head back.

"Christ, love, you're killing me," he groaned. I sat up and winked; I could be just as good at this game.

His hands moved beneath my skirt in the back, rubbing.

I never quite gave much thought to nuzzling, but when his mouth pressed against my neck and he moved his chin to do just that, it tickled something very primal in me that I couldn't resist. It was as if another part of me was alive and yet suppressed, trying to get noticed.

Instinctively, I rubbed my body against his like a cat marking its territory. It roused a startled look on his face and Simon threw back his head. "Why did you just do that?"

"Doesn't feel good?" I did it again and his voice cracked as our eyes drank each other in.

"I like, I like. It just reminded me of something. Never mind."

"You like to take your time," I said observantly.

He wiggled an eyebrow. "I never did like fast food."

His velvety touch found the tender spot where my legs joined my body and began rubbing in suggestive motions. Some circles were wider than others—sliding that finger into dangerous territory and reminding me that there was nothing between us except his leather pants and fifty tons of willpower.

If his willpower didn't give soon I was going to shred those leathers.

"Simon," I panted, "I want more."

Any restraint he had was eaten up by carnal desire. Simon suddenly switched gears and went into reverse as I was lifted up and thrust back onto the bed with him on top.

His hips rocked into mine, pressing urgently, while his tongue made long stroking promises in a deep, hard kiss. It wasn't until my fingers wandered to the waistline of his leather pants and laced the edges of his skin underneath that my question of boxers or briefs was answered.

Simon went commando.

He cupped my face in his hands and pressed our cheeks together as he whispered to himself, "*I want your name.*"

He was frustrated as the only name I went by was Learner.

"Simon, tonight I'd be happy if you'd just call me lover."

He rolled over, pulling me on top of him, lifting my skirt...

And then a door slammed.

Simon tossed me over like a hot potato and flashed into the hall. The sudden rush of air sent all the candles to tremble in terror. I jumped to my feet in stunned disbelief and began brushing my skirt down. My shirt was wide open and I had enough time to pull it together. I cringed as the heavy footsteps approached my open door.

Justus loomed in the doorway with a cold stare that could have obliterated mountains, turned diamonds into ash, and shattered statues.

And I stood like one.

There was a tic in his jaw as he made a mental note of my disheveled hair and crumpled outfit. Crossing my arms, I attempted to be casual.

"I was just getting ready for bed."

I just didn't mention with whom.

That might explain the fact I had only one boot on and my shirt was unbuttoned, but when his eyes roamed across the room and I saw what they locked on, it wouldn't explain why my panties were lying at the end of the bed.

Nor Simon's leather coat lying on the floor, for that matter.

Simon came up behind Justus. "I hope you mopped up that parking lot with his arse. Bastard had it coming."

Justus pivoted to face Simon, turning his back to me. I glanced at the sheets, which were now in disarray. Sheets that were always neatly tucked and straight since the day I moved in now looked like a horse had trampled across the bed.

"You. Kitchen. Now."

Simon peered over Justus's shoulder apologetically. Justus was not my father and we were not teenagers. Simon was a man of at least a hundred years and as I stood there I couldn't get over the fact that he wouldn't stand up to Justus—maybe shut the damn door in his face—and tell him to take a walk.

I closed my eyes for a moment in embarrassment. When I opened them again, Simon was gone. My Ghuardian could not look at me; he got that blank look that I wasn't able to read. I noticed that his nice shirt had spatters of blood on it, and regretfully I wondered what happened to that nice grey suit jacket.

I was looking at the panties and he was looking at the leather collar on the bed.

"Go to sleep, Learner. We skip training tomorrow."

CHAPTER 20

THE NEXT MORNING I STAYED in my room. I hardly ever drink but when I do, I have neither self-control nor foresight enough to appreciate just how hellacious I will feel the next morning. Overall, I didn't feel too bad, but my stomach was still turning somersaults. Part of that had to do with the way the night had ended.

It was afternoon before I decided to face the music like the mature adult I was supposed to be, but it was difficult considering how I'd been treated. Don't get me wrong, I like Justus, he's a very strong individual with the manners of an orangutan. But my father, he was not.

I'd spent too much wasted time overanalyzing the events of the previous night and quite frankly, I'd had enough of this silly bullshit. Perhaps a night with Simon would have been an inevitable regret, but I would have liked the choice.

Of course, I never slept with anyone on the first date so part of me was glad it was interrupted—the same part that made it easier to be pissed off at Justus.

The fact that Simon had tucked in his tail and run didn't help matters at all. I could have been mad at him for taking advantage of a situation—but in his defense, he was equally as drunk.

But he *must* have known the effect that binding would have on me, that it would remove all choice. Once Simon poured himself into me, there was no going back. I never imagined anything could feel so intense. In fact, hours later I could still feel his light. I hated that, because I didn't know if what I felt for him was real or conjured up by our exchange.

I scooped his leather jacket from the floor and straightened the sleeves when something caught my eye. Turning the shoulder, I saw teeth imprints in the material. The evil part of me wanted to laugh, but all I felt was embarrassment; it would be a constant reminder of this night. I threw the jacket over the back of the leather sofa in the main room and paused, noting the silence.

"We're in here, Learner," Justus called out from the dining room.

I never had to announce my presence around Justus; he had a way of sensing my energy even when my shields were up.

They were both sitting at the table wearing poker faces; Simon's hand wrapped around a short crystal glass, memorizing every angle. I had the feeling they had been there all night from the looks of the table scattered with six fast-food bags—some empty—and wrappers all over the place. It looked like a war room and they were eating their way to a strategy.

I reached for a bag and sat down with one foot up on the chair as I pulled out a sack of room-temperature fries. I wasn't sure what to think, I half expected that Justus would have kicked Simon out. Maybe they were sharing stories, maybe Simon was telling him all about how I was in bed. My eyes narrowed, but he never looked up from his glass.

"I've told Simon about how you were made."

I brushed the salt from my fingers and leaned back, interlocking my fingers over my knee. I didn't like my personal business being discussed as table conversation.

"Since when is my business everyone's business?"

I redirected my focus to a painting behind Justus. It was a maiden in a stream. A man held the sun in his right hand and reached for her with his left. Her hair was soft waves while his was wild, more like licking flames of fire. I often looked at the painting while we ate, wondering what the artist was really trying to depict. The woman wasn't even looking at the man, who was completely enraptured by her. What the hell was a guy like Justus doing with such a thought-provoking painting?

"Last night after you two left, I got a call from the Council."

I looked between them. "And?"

"Your Creator has come forward. He is requesting our presence tonight."

The blood moved away from every extremity in my body, including my head, and for a moment, I thought I was going to have a close introduction to the floor. I leaned forward and came close to losing the fry I just ate.

"What does he want?"

Justus was stoic and looked at me with dead eyes. "To claim you."

"I don't want him anywhere near me," I said as I shook my head. "You're my Ghuardian, can't you do anything?"

"I have no authority over your Creator. He's coming to collect you, and you will go with him."

"Just like that?" My anger snared like a drum as I leaned across the table and pointed my finger angrily on the wood.

"Adam would *never* have allowed this—*I trusted you!* Did you even try to keep me, or was this the release you were looking for?"

He flinched as though he had been slapped, but it didn't matter. I bolted out of my chair and ran to my room. Justus and Simon filled the doorway as I was shoving clothes into my bag.

"I'm leaving."

"He'll find you, Learner. You can't run from this."

"The hell I can't! Maybe I'll find someone else to take me in who actually wants me!" I screamed as I hovered over my bag, frozen like a statue, arms straight down and fingers wide open. I was charging up and I knew if I didn't find a way to level it down I was going to regret it.

"Justus, you have to try with the Council, they don't know the circumstances. You can plead your case before he makes his claim," Simon urged.

"With Merc on the Council, there's no way this will be unanimous."

"Look at her—you can't do it! She's not ready; he'll use her. Look how he brought her into our Breed, if that isn't proof enough for you. He's not going to release her."

"Eventually, he will give her independence."

"No, Justus, he won't. Ever."

"All Creators tire of the care they must give and grant freedom." Their voices were argumentative and growing in volume.

"He'll keep her, Justus."

"What makes you so sure?"

I sat against the wall, curling my arms over my knees.

"Do I really need to answer that?" Simon folded his arms and looked at him directly. A heavy silence fell before he continued. "I'm quite certain in all these months you have tapped her energy. You know she is a Unique."

In that moment, I realized Justus hadn't really known for certain everything that transpired between me and Simon last night, but now he knew that we had exchanged. He looked at me, disheartened, but I didn't care. My knuckles were white, my lips dry, and worst of all, as much as I wanted Adam to come take me away from all of this, I knew it would only put him in danger.

Justus suddenly raged out with a fury like I had never seen. "I am powerless, Simon, this is law. I cannot stop him!"

The air crackled as he faced the wall. Simon moved to my side, cupping my hands in his. I felt a calming sensation pouring into me, and Justus knelt beside him.

"Don't make me go," I pleaded. "I'll die; I can't go with him."

Justus and Simon exchanged a look and nodded.

Everything went black.

I was sitting on a large, polished black rock by a crystal blue river. Tall pine trees bent to the whisper of the wind. A few yellow butterflies flitted about. I heard the splashing of the water as it ran over the rocks and the sunlight shimmered on its surface. It felt peaceful, and yet... not real.

"It's *not* real."

Justus stood by the edge of the water with Simon at his side.

"How did you hear what I was thinking?"

"This is not the real world. This is the link between the waking world and the subconscious. It is the in-between we sometimes call the Grey Veil."

"How did we get here?"

He stepped up and found a spot on the edge of the flat rock, running his fingers in the water. "Not all Mage have the ability to do this and I don't have time to explain. I needed to show you how to get here. Anyone you have shared your power with can join you here, provided they are shown." He gave a slighted look at Simon who spun around and started pulling at the pinecones that spiraled from the branches above.

"But I don't know how we got here."

"You do, Learner, you felt the pull. You can do it alone, we just had to show you the first time, but you never forget the feeling and how to summon it. It's like sitting on the edge of a slide right before you slip down and give yourself to gravity."

I laughed unexpectedly as I wondered how Justus knew what a slide felt like. This was a man from probably the middle ages and I couldn't imagine him at the top of a slide.

A strand of coppery hair blew around my neck into the sunlight. I snatched it, looking carefully.

"Always liked the gingers." Simon winked.

"Sometimes how you see yourself is reflected here. But I can see you are still conflicted." He tugged at my hair to bring to my attention it had darkened to an almost black shade. "You continue to drift between both reflections of yourself."

Justus set a plan for us to meet nightly so I could provide him details about my maker. He hoped to find a loophole to get me out of his custody. Even if I was to go with my Creator, Justus would remain my Ghuardian as he is afforded a certain amount of rights by the Mageri.

But not enough. Not nearly enough.

CHAPTER 21

MY HANDS REMAINED TUCKED IN the pockets of my jacket so I could feel the dagger hidden in the lining. Justus didn't know about it and I sure wasn't going to tell him. I lifted the knife from his wall when he was showering and found a way to conceal it in the lining. I might not be able to kill my Creator—but I wasn't going down without a fight.

The engine clicked off with a turn of the key; it was the same spot as before, when I first met the Council. I recognized the broken-down stone wall off to the right.

"Let's just get this over with." I was angry and pushed myself out of the car, storming past Simon.

I was pissed off because I felt betrayed by someone I thought cared about me. I was never really sure how he felt, but Justus had to have had some kind of loyalty to me because he offered himself as my Ghuardian. Didn't that mean something?

The Council stood in a semicircle, but my eyes were glued to the shadow before them. His long black hair fell across his shoulders. Two hands grabbed each of my forearms. Never did I feel more like a reluctant bride being forced down the aisle.

The elder of the Council waved his hand to motion us forward; Justus and Simon complied, pulling me along. My Creator suddenly spun around in a fluid motion as if he were turned on by a switch.

"Progeny," he said delightfully.

It was as if I were looking into my own eyes, even our hair was nearly the same color. Then he smiled.

"Murderer!" I yelled, lunging forward but restrained by those annoying hands.

He gave me a look of *isn't that a shame*, turning his mouth down as Merc spoke up.

"What is this accusation she brings?"

"This, Council," he said, wagging his finger, "is why I did not immediately claim her. I was not confident that she was... stable." He tapped his forehead for emphasis. "I have come to find that since her transition, she developed a mental block due to my miscalculation. The Learner has no memory of the consensual act." He flicked his hand as if he were talking of a child.

"Liar," I hissed.

Justus squeezed my arm, stopping some of the blood flow. "Council, if you would permit."

"You may speak," Hannah said.

"We believe this man has committed a crime, although our laws do not define it, nevertheless it is unjustifiable. She was taken on death and I do not feel the Mageri would advocate this."

There was a muttering.

"Let us not forget the meaning of why we are present, Council. I, Samil, am hereby claiming my rights to this Learner, to teach her the ways of our heritage, to fortify her with my experience until she is fluent and—"

"Enough, Samil."

The woman, who looked like she could have been any upper-Manhattan attorney, waved for silence. "Speak out of turn once more and I will personally see that the pillory makes a comeback."

My shoes crunched on the frost-covered grass, fingers twisting together like ancient roots, and I remembered the dagger. Sliding my right hand discreetly into my coat, the cold feel of the handle motivated me.

My Creator waved his arm in my direction. "Council, she has been altered. I demand compensation." He turned his gaze to meet mine. "And they have armed her."

As he spoke the last word I knew they would seize my weapon.

I flashed at him and plunged the dagger into air. Samil flashed and when I turned to strike again, I was thrown to the ground.

Novis, the young man with the spiked hair, removed the dagger from my hand with blinding speed. He kept me pinned with a forearm across my neck as Samil brushed his hands along his coat, looking insulted. God, his pompous attitude angered me even more and I struggled against Novis in vain.

"Look at her eyes," Novis said.

Silence fell.

What they were looking at was something that happened under extreme conditions, the pinpoint pupils of my eyes turned a metallic color that was more noticeable when it was dark and they were expanded.

"What have you made, Samil? She is not like us." Novis placed his thumb on my forehead in the same manner he had done once before. He was testing me—summoning the power within me. Was he measuring? Well he could measure my fist up his ass if he didn't get himself up off of me.

I pulled back.

A sweet rush of perfumed energy whirled within my being—ancient energy—before the contact was broken. Novis gasped and rose to his feet. He stepped back in line with a peculiar expression that he quickly erased. Merc brushed back his blond hair and lifted a meaty arm to point his finger straight at me.

"She has broken the laws in front of the Council, Novis. She has attempted to take the life of her Creator." It wasn't just an observation—Merc was placing an accusation against me.

Simon approached quickly with his head lowered.

"Council, I implore you that I would offer my services, what you would ask, if she be spared her life and continue to be kept under Ghuardianship. Her maker forced her into being without a choice. She has not yet been named within the Mageri. Can a law be broken of a society you have not yet fully entered? Please do not punish ignorance."

I glared at him and I could tell he saw me out of his peripheral. I flicked my eyes back to the Council and noticed they lightly touched fingers while facial expressions changed, as if they were communicating. Another moment passed and Hannah finally spoke up.

"We have come to a decision. Simon, as you so offered your services, we will collect for our leniency. However, we cannot deny her maker his rights. For her life, we will require one service from you upon our choosing." Simon bowed his head with respect.

"Learner," she continued. "Rise to your feet."

I did so, without grace or speed, but with my dignity intact.

"Show us the mark of your maker."

Scratch dignity.

Justus nudged at me to do as commanded, but I never told him *where* my mark was. Brushing the dirt from my hands, I looked at her directly.

"I have a mark; you don't need to see it." I licked my lips and gulped.

"It is but required that you present the mark of your Creator so that we may act as a witness; it must be properly documented in our books that you are his progeny."

"I'm shy," I bit out through clenched teeth

Her eyes narrowed at my disobedience, but she wasn't backing down. Justus shoved at my shoulder and his eyes were unwavering.

I began to unbutton my jeans when Novis spoke up.

"*Hannah.*"

She rolled her eyes and waved her hand. "Fine. Learner, come with me."

She led me to a private area in the woods and what I showed her was sufficient. When we rejoined the group, they were all standing in silence.

"I have seen the mark, she is Samil's progeny. Samil, you will now present the Learner to us. Speak her name, for once it is heard she will no longer be an outsider among the Mageri."

Samil stepped forward as a victor in a battle—his long, wild hair obscuring his face.

"But first, Samil, you will know that we have made a decision to your fate as well. These are unusual circumstances, which we have not seen, and not all the facts appear to be disclosed. We will release her to your charge. However, in seven days there will be an open challenge that will entitle any other to stake their claim on this Learner. As she was not given the choice to be Mage, we will allow fate to decide." Hannah paused and her thick brows nearly met, giving the appearance of a goddess who could strike fear with a mere glance.

"Should there be a challenger, your gifts will be leveraged to give equal footing. The victor shall acquire the rights to this Learner and the power of the other Mage. Samil, should no one challenge you, then she will remain your charge. Upon your death, if she has not been released from your custody, then she will go to her Ghuardian. We will not retract his status."

"What happens to the loser?" I asked, hesitating, as I was told not to speak out of turn. Of course, I already fucked that up the moment I stepped on the field.

Her eyes flew back to Justus, annoyed by my questioning. "We do not challenge to the death, Learner. The winner will not borrow, but take the power of the other. The defeated will be tasked with rebuilding their life source and that will require a number of years to regain the same level of power. It is a fitting elevation for the victor."

There it was, a chance that my enemy could be weakened. A chance that I could be free of him. All of it depended on one small detail—someone would have to fight for me.

But who? It was between Justus and Simon. Simon didn't know me well enough and Justus, he already was so willing to pass me over. Even now he said nothing.

"May I ask another question?" Justus yanked my arm and I pulled out of his grasp, folding my arms.

"You may," Hannah answered.

"If no one challenges him… may I?"

My embarrassment turned to heated anger when the response was laughter. Hannah rolled her eyes and I saw smiles play across all their faces.

Novis clasped his hands in front of him and gave a nod to Justus before answering my question. "I like your tenacity, Learner. You will make a fine Mage one day. To answer your question: no. You are neither skilled nor strong enough. I'm sure you still value your life. No Creator would want claim over a Learner who challenged them. Someone must fight for you. Fear not—perhaps chivalry is not dead. We shall see."

The seconds were excruciating as no one said a word. Justus stood motionless and guilt played across his face as his eyes memorized the tips of his shoes. I had been expecting for someone right at that moment to give their intentions, perhaps in a moment of nobility to yell out something along the lines of, "I will fight for her!" But this was not an epic movie, and Justus said nothing.

No one did.

Except...

"Come." Samil's fingers curled around my elbow painfully as he pulled me forward.

"I am Samil, Creator of forty-three Learners. I stand before you on this night to present to the Council my progeny, a new member to our sacred lineage. I claim this Learner as her maker, and hereby name her..." He flicked a glance at my eyes. "Silver."

I hated him immediately.

Novis raised his chin as he replied. "That is an acceptable, and may I say, appropriate choice. Embrace your name, Silver; it is now your identity. Samil, we accept your claim to Silver as a fledgling Mage, you will take her into your home and respectfully teach her the ways of our kind."

Hannah adjusted a pin in her hair as she studied Samil. "These *are* strange circumstances." She sighed. "Samil, it is custom for the progeny to leave from this spot with their maker; however as she also has Ghuardianship, you will allow her one half hour to retrieve her things and pay respect to her Ghuardian. Seven days from now, we will assemble here. If you do not show, she will be removed from your care. That is all."

The Council turned and we stood in silence, listening to the sound of the grass rustle below their feet as they disappeared from sight.

"One half hour. Not a fraction more." Samil pointed a finger at Justus and stalked into the shadows as if he were nothing more than an apparition.

"Silver. It's not such a bad name, love. Silver metal has the highest electrical conductivity, you know, from any other element... and thermal conductivity."

Justus glared at Simon, who shrugged. "Just sayin'."

I felt empty. Abandoned. If I had stayed with Adam, none of this would be happening.

"So, I'm Silver Merrick."

"No."

"I'm not taking his last name, am I?"

Justus folded his arms, prepared to give me perhaps my last lesson.

"In the beginning it was custom for the Creator to give his progeny a new name as a Mage. Maybe they thought it would help them let go of their old life, or maybe it was an ego thing. But it's a tradition we still carry. Some kept their former human name while others did not. If the ancient had a surname or a second name— which almost all did—the progeny would take on that name like a female does when she marries. The name De Gradi is of my maker and he was of Italian descent. The only exception to this rule is if a Mage discovers their rare gift makes them a Creator, also. Then they are allowed to retain their own surname and pass it on to their progeny—it creates a lineage. There are not many ancients left and most of them no longer create fledglings."

Justus ran his hand across his head, rubbing it back and forth.

"So what is my last name? And so help me, if you tell me it's Ware, I'll dropkick you where you stand."

"You have none. You are only Silver. His people did not have surnames. Their first name was followed by the name of their father, so it would have been something like 'Samil, son of…"

"A bitch," I finished.

The wind gently rustled through the trees and I shivered from the icy air.

Simon approached and brushed his fingers through my hair, tucking away the one strand that was unwilling to join the rest. He studied my face and cradled my neck with his hands.

"You are stronger than you give yourself credit for." He kissed me lightly on the mouth and walked away.

"What the hell were you thinking, pulling a stunt like that with the dagger? I specifically told you how to conduct yourself. You must play by their rules, have you learned nothing I have taught you?"

My eyes were moist and Justus pulled me to his chest and held me tight.

He held me as he had never done before—with warmth and feeling. Large hands ran down my back and his baritone voice soothed, "Shhhh. I didn't mean to make you cry."

"I'm not crying, I'm scared."

"Remember, the Grey Veil."

I nodded into his chest.

"Silver... *Silver*," he whispered, adjusting to the sound of my name. "He may have named you, but I want you to own that name, do you understand?"

"I have seven days, I'll figure out something."

He pulled me at arm's length and I watched that thick jaw harden to marble.

"I'll work on the Council—don't get any ideas." He slipped a silver and jade dragon pendant over my neck. "Don't take it off. It is forged with hidden energy, should you need it. You'll have one chance to use it."

One chance was all I needed.

CHAPTER 22

"I WOULD LIKE TO SEE YOU just try it you fucking piss-poor excuse for a Mage! Come on then, swing away. I'll give you the first shot, but after that you better flash your arse off, you limey bastard."

"So it is you who will challenge me?" Deep laughter broke away from Samil. "Well then, I wager that it will not last very long. What a shame, your power wouldn't be enough to charge my phone as green as you are."

Through the trees they came into view—Simon and Samil were standing ten feet or so apart between the cars.

"Right here, right fucking now. All mouth and no trousers."

"Shame you won't see her curse your name during her beatings," Samil said in a thick accent.

Simon bared his teeth and charged with a fury that could only be rivaled by Justus, who flashed over and slammed him up against the car. The passenger window shattered from impact.

Samil casually strolled back to his SUV, brushing his shoulders with his hand.

"Enough, Simon!" Justus pressed a forearm into his neck. "You risk further punishment from the Council—do not provoke him."

Simon defiantly shook free of the fists that held him down and kicked his shoe into the dirt, sending up a flurry of rocks. "It's not right!"

Samil stood by the driver's side door as Justus tossed my bag in the back. He eased me in the back seat, making it clear he didn't want me sitting beside my maker any more than I did. If sitting on the roof were an option, I might have happily taken that.

The door slammed shut and I wrinkled my nose at the smell; it was like rancid pine cones and cheap vinyl. The interior light slowly dimmed and my breath fogged up the window as I leaned my face against the cold glass.

"I suppose you've tasted her. Extraordinary, isn't she? Can't say I've had the full pleasure, but no one makes them quite like I do. All good things come to those who wait, isn't that right?"

Cobalt eyes drifted down to watch me, softened and full of words I knew he would never speak out loud. He cared. Despite the fact we butted heads and spent six hours a day trying to kill each other, the man cared for me. Why did I ever doubt?

Because he was letting me go, that's why.

"Fear not, Ghuardian." The word rolled off Samil's tongue like a curse. "She's in capable hands now."

His laugh was unexpected and poisonous. My fingers clawed into the armrest of the door as I shut my eyes and pushed down all the sorrow and anger that was rising up within me. I refused to let my emotions take over. I was no longer Zoë; I was no longer a Mage. I was now a person I did not recognize. I was Silver, I was his, and I was nothing more than property.

A light tapping noise snapped me back to reality. Justus touched the window with his fingertips and I reached up, running mine along the glass. *Please don't leave me.*

His arms lifted over the car and he leaned over so I could no longer see his face.

My body came three inches off the seat when heavy fists slammed down on the roof of the car. If my heart was asleep before, it was now wide awake, on its fourth cup of coffee, and chilling out in my throat.

"One finger harms her, Samil, and I will bury you."

"Tsk Tsk. Careful, Mage," Samil replied with edged humor. "What would the Council think of such threats?"

"It's not a threat. It's my word of honor."

My seatbelt was pulled off and Samil dragged me across a gravel driveway. The rocks were white and sharp at the edges, as my hands could attest to.

"Home, sweet home, little girl."

I cringed as my bag landed on the arm I used to shield my face. Samil straddled me, bending over with his hair spilling down like dirty rain.

"Last time we met like this, I believe you looked a little... different." He spun a lock of my black hair between his fingers. "Took time to find you, but when I picked up on your energy, it was unmistakable. You can't run from me, Silver. You belong to me and I will always find you."

He stood up before I had a chance for my thumbs and his eyeballs to make their introductions.

"Get up," he snarled.

I tightened my lips and shot profanities through my eyes.

He backhanded me.

I spat a mouthful of blood on his big black boot and redirected my anger. "Thought you could use a shoe shine."

They say the first hit is never the last. They're right. Whoever *they* are, they know.

"It's going to be so satisfying to break you."

Except what he didn't know was that I had *been there* and *done that*. I was a survivor and would never be broken by anyone.

The white paint was so pristine on the three-story house that it was almost as if it were freshly painted. It was surrounded by a well-manicured lawn, illuminated fountains, and rose bushes all along the outside walls. There was a lot of money and pretentiousness put into this place. The porch was adorned with two life-size bronze sculptures of snarling lions and I thought if I stared into their jeweled eyes too long they might spring to life and gobble me up. I had never been in a house that fancy and always wondered about the people who inhabited them.

Now I knew.

Sailing across a smooth polished floor, I hit the end of a banister with my shoulder.

I looked up and against his hellboy appearance of the long black trench coat and matching heart, was a stark contrast of—for lack of better words—baroque. Gaudy mirrors with brass frames hung on maroon walls. The furniture was crushed red fabric with gold trim, black chandeliers hung from the high ceilings, the windows were arched, and an oddly constructed staircase curved up three levels of the house.

I laughed uncontrollably. "You look like a piece of shit in a porcelain toilet."

"Maybe you should clean that toilet with your mouth," he said.

Halfway down the stairs that led to the basement, Samil shoved me the rest of the way. I landed on my bag, which broke the fall.

"Welcome home, Silver. I think you'll find your quarters quite accommodating. Let us go over the rules, shall we?"

His heavy boots stomped down the wooden steps, making a hollow noise in the empty room as he spoke. "You will not disturb me when I am upstairs. Save your screams, no one can hear you out there and those who come to visit me won't care. Test me, little girl. I just dare you."

"You only have me for seven days."

One foot retreated before it forcefully kicked me in the side. I groaned with my face flat against the cold concrete floor, coughing in pain.

"Rule number two: every time you smart off to me, I will beat you until you have no more fight."

Big deal. I had a feeling this asshole was going to do it regardless.

I looked at my new home. The basement only had two lights, which didn't offer much. There were boxes by the stairs and the floor was as concrete as the walls. A pile of dirty blankets in the corner told me this was my bed, and I wondered if I was the only one who had ever slept there. Samil's arms were folded tight and he seared me with his cold, sharp eyes. I wiped the blood from my mouth on the back of my hand.

"Beg me to heal you," he demanded.

Samil had a strange accent; his tongue rolled thick and made the pronunciations very rich and dark as if it might be Eastern European. But, like Simon, it was perhaps not his true accent. If these men were hundreds of years old or more, then living in different places would influence their speech. It could have been Egyptian, given I had never traveled anywhere or met anyone to truly know the difference.

"Go to hell."

He sneered and shook his hands over his coat. "You first. It's only going to get worse, little girl. I have all the patience in the world. I'm going to enjoy making you beg. Make no mistake about it, you will beg. They all do… eventually."

"Beg for you to take a shower; I always thought your B.O. was just an urban legend."

His eyes narrowed to razor-thin slivers, but to my astonishment, he turned and went up the stairs, sliding a series of locks into place. I had a feeling that wasn't a get-out-of-jail-free card—it was a rain check.

I flipped on the switch and stared at a concrete wall in the bathroom. There was no mirror and I guessed that it was removed because it could have been used as a weapon. I felt the residual pain on my arm and thigh and knew it would not be long before they bruised, but I healed faster than humans did so I wasn't overly concerned.

My bed of blankets stank of mold and I turned my mouth in disgust. I shook out of my coat and slipped a sweatshirt on that Adam had given me. My body shook with a violent chill as I placed the coat over my bag and used it for a pillow.

When I woke, my thigh was screaming.

"So much trouble, you. And worth it all remains to be seen." He bent down and grabbed a fistful of my hair. "Ready to beg, Silver?" He laughed. "Oh, how I bet you love your new name. Did you ever watch *The Lone Ranger?*"

I jerked my head back and scrambled up against the wall, knees pressed against my chest, as he crouched in front of me. Bastard kicked me in my sleep.

"Why did you do it, why me? There are a million people who would want immortality, why force it on someone who *didn't* want it?"

Samil's words rolled from his tongue like molasses. "I am compensated well for my deeds, and I take great pleasure from the

Learners I have made." He huffed out a short laugh. "It's a formula, girl, one which I intend to keep secret. Why you? Well I can't take full credit… but you should thank me. How dare you turn up your nose at what I have given you. Your life has more worth than it once did… humans are nothing but cattle. Tell you what—I'll let you have one shot at me. You only get one, so make it count."

I heard a loud snap as I realized my hand had flown across his cheek. I didn't even stop to wonder if he were serious about giving me a free hit or just baiting me.

"We have all the time in the world to play." With that, he landed his knuckles on my face and I blacked out against the concrete wall. The bastard lied.

"Ow."

I opened my eyes, groggy and with the worst kind of headache. Pulling my neck up was not without its agony, either.

I sighed when I saw all the contents of my bag tossed over the floor as if a tornado had blown through. I picked up tiny bits of plastic near the wall that had once belonged to my cell phone.

At the foot of the stairs there was a tray with a silver lid. When I lifted it, an empty china plate stared up at me.

Hearing a latch to the door unlocking, I ran back to the blankets and threw them over my head. I struggled to steady my quickened breath as the door opened. A swish of liquid from a glass bottle sounded, along with stumbling feet. Was he drunk? Would be nice if he left me the bottle—I could use it more than he could.

"No," he mumbled. "She's not like the others and that's why we're negotiating. I've been more than generous, offering my previous Learners for a fair price, but this one is special."

Panic went full throttle when I heard a second set of footsteps.

"So this is she?" a strange voice spoke. It was sharp, clear, and sent a chill up my spine. "Scant little thing, and you want to negotiate for a pile of rags?"

"Are we good on the temporary agreement or not?"

"You forget yourself; it was one of mine who spotted her, careful how you speak with me."

"Fuck you, because without me you wouldn't have these toys. You *f-forget* that without a maker, without what I alone can do like no other…" Samil's words trailed off, followed by the sound of him drinking from a bottle.

"While you are her maker, do not forget who I am. You are in my debt, and I will decide when the debt is no longer owed. Show some gratitude."

There was an audible grunt. "What makes me think this debt will ever be square?"

"Your previous endeavors were less than acceptable, this one better be worth it," the man said. "Do tell me why you beat her— it would appear you are damaging the merchandise."

"That pile of crazy is dangerous. If she's not broken, she'll grow wild." Another swig of alcohol. "Have your sample and we can negotiate upstairs. This one I'm not giving so freely as the others; she was a pain in the ass to get. I've made her official with the Mageri and—"

"You *what?*" he shouted.

"That's right," Samil said in a satisfied tone. "So don't get any ideas, because they have watch on her now. I have to think long-term and guarantee my claim on her."

His heavy gait trampled up the steps until I heard the door slam. And lock.

My heart thundered as the stranger loomed above me.

One word kept echoing in my head: *sample.*

"Silver, is it? No need to play dead, child. I know you are awake." He ripped the blanket off me and frowned.

He was not a big man; he wore round glasses, a neat grey suit, and dusty brown hair crowned his head. He looked like he could've been a banker who worked a very boring job. A slender, pointed toothpick rolled across his tongue to one side of his mouth and he slipped out of his jacket, lightly dusting it with his hand. Behind the reflection of his glasses was only a physical resemblance of a human, but no humanity existed in that stare.

"Now you don't look like much trouble—Samil always did exaggerate."

Slowly the spectacles were removed from his face and he neatly polished one lens at a time with a white cloth he removed from his pocket. When he finished, he folded the arms of the glasses together and slipped them into his coat, giving it a casual shake as he flung it around the bottom knob of the staircase railing. He rolled up his crisp white sleeves, and I began to back up and crawl away.

"Easy, girl."

That's all it took to set me off, talking to me as if I were an animal. I scrambled to get on my feet when his arm yanked my ankle. The breath crushed out of me when he came down over my back and flattened me against the floor. He wasn't very big, or strong, and yet he was dripping with power.

Hot breath that stank of garlic slithered across the back of my neck and I turned my head as if I had been burned.

"Keep it up, I like it rough. I didn't have any intention of using you this way—but if you keep tempting me, I just might reconsider."

"What were you going to do?" I growled through my teeth.

"Were?"

He flipped me onto my back and straddled my sides so there was no going anywhere. My fists balled to hit him, but he pinned me down and my fingers were pried open.

"Let me go," I yelled. "I don't know what you want from me!"

My fingers tightened into a fist so impenetrable that his efforts to pry them open were in vain. He looked at me with calmness and made no effort to fight with me. He lifted my arms by the wrists and repeatedly slammed the back of my hands against the hard concrete floor.

Over and over. Until my knuckles bled.

When I could no longer endure the pain, I let out an angry scream and opened them.

"Now I see what Samil means, you keep this up with me and I will not show the kindness he has. I am far more experienced in punishment." His lips peeled away from his teeth in a snarl. "Let me see what you have for me."

When his thin cold hands touched mine, I cried out from the pain. The toothpick suddenly fell from his mouth and rolled onto my chest. I shuddered.

With everything happening, all I could think of was how I wanted that vile thing off me.

The Mage sat in a stupor after stealing my light, but eventually he lifted the jacket from the banister and left the room. The clock upstairs chimed once an I pushed myself through consciousness until I was standing by the rock at the Grey Veil.

Justus was on one knee, deep in thought as I arrived; I wondered how long he had been there. His dress was very different than what I had ever seen him in. Instead of a tight-fitting shirt, he wore a loose brown tunic, as if he stepped out of a Robin Hood movie.

"Silver." Justus touched the tip of my shoe with his finger and rose to his feet as I turned away.

"Does he feed you? How has he cared for you?" his voice asked demandingly.

I tucked my hands beneath my arms and tried to concentrate on willing away the marks, but I seemed to have no control over my appearance. "Did you come up with a plan?"

"I want you to tell me everything that goes on. Where he lives, who visits him, what he's told you."

"He's stinking rich, Justus. You'd never know it to look at him. Where do you guys get that kind of money?" I felt him against my back.

"What else?"

I sighed quietly. "Well, he's had one visitor, someone he knows and does business with but I don't know his name. I don't really have any information, Justus; it's only been one night."

"Silver, you need to give me the details. Simon is doing a background check on Samil, but so far, he's come up clean. You must cooperate."

"I am," I said flatly.

"Do you want to remain with him permanently?"

"Is that a threat or a wish?"

My energy was gone, evident in my voice, my heavy eyelids,

and the lack of movement. It had taken everything to even get here without passing out. "I don't want to talk about it right now, okay? I just want to sit here and forget—"

"I don't have time for your silly nonsense," he scolded, taking hold of my arm. When I pulled away, he suddenly went very, very still.

"Look at me."

I turned around with slow precision to face him, and his eyes pierced with light as they fell over my cut lip and broken hands, which he held delicately in his own.

"It doesn't hurt here." I pulled away and my arms fell to my side. "I'm just tired, not broken—got it?"

Justus turned his back to me as he looked into the thick of trees. "Don't say anything to agitate him. Comply with whatever he wants. He is the worst kind of coward, Silver. No man of worth would inflict such injuries on an innocent."

"That's not what you have been teaching me."

"To hell what I taught you!" he yelled. "Should he beat you—then appear to weaken before him. If he senses your strength he will beat you harder."

"I'm not doing anything you wouldn't do yourself, hypocrite. You're telling me not to fight back. I'm sorry, but that's not in my DNA. You warned me early on this kind of thing happens, and now I understand why you've worked so hard to train me."

"The Council will know of your treatment."

"The Council doesn't give a shit. You told me yourself the Creator gets extra privileges because of what they are. Why is that? Does the Mageri think they'll go on strike and quit creating more, ending our line? Someone needs to change the rules. Anyhow, it wasn't him that did this. Well, not all of it."

With that revelation, Justus spun around and outrage spread across his features; his eyes blazed like a raging fire and every muscle in his body tightened.

I stepped back.

"Who beat you?" A muscled twitched in his face.

"Never mind."

Justus stepped forward. "I'm going to ask you again—who beat you?"

I held my tongue as I thought about what it could mean to tell him. I loved seeing the fire in his eyes—that protectiveness warmed me in a way that words could not. But I wasn't about to give him more information. I was afraid he might do something stupid and get himself in trouble with the Council.

"What are you keeping from me?"

"Comply? Do whatever he asks? Just get me the hell out of here!"

"Silver, I am your Ghuardian and I am bound by the laws of the Council. But I swear as your Ghuardian, these men will die." His body moved up to mine and his head lowered to meet my gaze. "I want to know who put their fist on you."

"Are you saying that it's acceptable that my maker does it, but now that someone else is in the picture—"

"That's not what I meant."

I sighed. "I know. But I don't want you acting irrationally—I need you sane. I can't live with your death on my conscience. I know you're a man of honor; you follow the laws and have taken the Ghuardianship far more seriously than I did as your Learner. Walk away from this. I am not—"

My words cut off when his hands cradled my neck.

His devotion to defend me ran deep. What he felt for me as a man was questionable, but what he felt for me as a Ghuardian was undeniable. If there was ever any doubt of where I stood with Justus, it was answered in just four words.

"You belong with me."

CHAPTER 23

A FTER FIVE LONG DAYS, ONE thing I could count on was routine.

Samil was usually drunk when he wandered down to punch me around like I was some no good stray dog. Each time he asked me to beg to be healed, I gave him the finger. There was an advantage in knowing how to push his buttons. I was not fed, and my body slowly began to weaken. While his intent was to break me, I knew there was something more underneath it all. Resentment, and it had a lot to do with my nightly visitor.

Every night around the same time, the small man with the spectacles came in and stole my light. The first two nights I struggled and fought back. I learned the hard way that he followed through on his promises; being repeatedly slapped in the same spot carried more pain than a full beating. Chinese water torture taken to a whole new level.

His taste for me was becoming an addiction and the arguments between him and Samil increased in frequency. Samil never stole my light and I could see he wanted to, but there must have been some agreement.

The visitor was angry about Samil weakening me; apparently, it had an effect on the quality of my light. Samil claimed his right as my Creator to inflict whatever punishment he saw fit.

My body was frail and I reminded myself that I was a Mage and all of this was only temporary. *What I wouldn't give to be back on the sofa with a box of crackers and a book of Mage law.*

I could only guess the reason my healing was slowed to a non-existent state was because of how much energy was being juiced from me.

After the first night with Justus, I quit my visits to the Grey Veil. My deteriorating condition would only fuel his anger. He had warned me so many times about these types of people and how a Mage was my own worst enemy—I just never imagined. My perception was changed, now, and going forward I would be stronger for it. And smarter.

Almost all of the boxes in the basement had been cleared out after I tried impaling Samil on his own damn pen. That was the night I got my first broken rib. It was worth it; to draw blood from him brought me great pleasure. It was morbid, but I swelled with pride and looked forward to each confrontation—fighting back was empowering, even if it didn't end in my favor.

Part of my demoralization was the removal of all my personal items, including the dirty pile of blankets that kept me warm. The only clothing allowed was my bra and a pair of shorts and I slept barefoot on the cold cement floor. Samil wanted to strip my dignity thread by thread.

Quite honestly, I was running out of threads.

There was a gash in my forehead from the hairline to the eyebrow. My shoulders were riddled with bruises, I had a cut from his ring on my collarbone, and just to sum it up—I was a mess. All things considered in my weakened state, I felt tougher—hardened. I never gave the satisfaction of crying, which was a silent victory for me.

The visitor's beatings, on the other hand, were another matter. He found a sensitive spot on my side and slapped it repeatedly with full force… minutes went by and beads of sweat formed on my brow as I writhed in agony. On the second night, I was prepared to fight; I wasn't prepared to get punished in the same manner in the exact same spot, which was still raw. The pain was so severe I actually bit into my own arm to feel pain elsewhere.

The door creaked and I remained motionless. Something was off—Samil didn't give his usual introduction of "ready to beg?" He was also sober.

"Get up," he ordered. "We're leaving."

"Where?" I didn't just have butterflies in my stomach, I had pterodactyls.

A rope unraveled from his hands and I staggered to my feet. I tried to get by him, but he slammed me to the floor and bound my hands behind my back.

Then we were in an SUV and I was reminded that it was winter as I was shaking from the cold.

A key popped in the ignition and the vehicle roared to life. "If he cannot meet my demands, then I will not negotiate. He has no right to take what is *mine*."

The car rumbled down the road, throwing me off balance from my seat. I could still smell the embers from a fire burning, mingling with the scent of pine that was leaking from the vile car deodorizer dangling from his mirror. Despite the impending danger, it felt good to be free again. Nothing good ever came of being tied up with rope and thrown in an SUV driving through the dark woods, so I thought of what to say to him.

"I thought I *was* yours?"

His fingers bore into the steering wheel, and he made a hard right turn. Samil's temper flared and whether he was talking to me or himself, I wasn't sure.

"He was only to taste, but he has grown greedy and now expects me to turn you over. Why he wants you, I do not understand. I have made none that have transformed their appearance as you have, but I do not see anything special about you. He wants you *more* than the others and yet offers me less? Now he threatens to take without pay."

I swallowed hard, bouncing on the seat when we hit a pothole. His speed was erratic and my weak heart was struggling to race.

"He doesn't seem stronger than you." My voice remained cautious as I did not want to provoke him even further.

"You know nothing of his power," he snapped. "He plays with fire." His lips curled back. "But two can play at that game."

"Where are you taking me? Look, I'm no trouble."

"You are more trouble than you know. I do not give so freely to my enemy."

"Enemy? I thought you were business partners."

"Friends close, enemies closer."

"You're my Creator; I thought that gave you the trump card. Where are we going?" I felt nauseous and scared—I wanted Justus.

I couldn't jump out of a moving car with my wrists bound. Samil ran a hand through his stringy hair, flipping it away from his face.

Justus was right. It took little practice to move myself into the Grey Veil and I found that I could do it with ease, even in the car. I was alone, and I screamed. I screamed so loud it echoed off the distant mountains.

I fell to the ground in panic. "Please hear me, please come. I'm in trouble, I need you. Justus... Simon... *someone*."

Hands fell on my shoulders. "Silver, what is it? What's wrong?"

"Simon?"

"Tell me what is happening!" he demanded.

Simon looked different. He was dressed in white pants and tall boots with a long coat. He looked like a British soldier from one of those old paintings I remembered from history class. His hair was tied back into a ponytail and I wondered if that's who he was before he was turned.

He saw the damage done, all of the marks of abuse, and his eyes became daggers seeking a target.

"Fucking *animal*."

"Simon, he's driving me somewhere, I think he's going to kill me. My hands are tied, I can't get away."

Simon fell to his knees in front of me.

"Silver, you must listen to me. The pendant, do you still have it?"

"Yes. It's hidden in my bra, but I still have it."

"Good girl. When the time is right, you need to pull from it. The pendant will give you enough energy that you might be able to fight him off, but use it to run."

"Can you find me?" Simon scooted closer and held me in his arms, brushing back my hair with his hand.

"Yes love, but it will take time to pinpoint your exact location. Go back and look around for a sign or marker so we know where to look. If we are within proximity, we will be able to pick up your energy if you do not conceal. But hell, Justus will be able to sense you regardless."

I drifted back to the vehicle and watched mile markers fly by, hoping for something that I could give to Simon. Two miles passed with my head pressed against the window. A sign blinked in the distance and fast approached as I squinted to read it. Just as soon as

I returned, I blurted out the mile marker and the name on the sign before I was suddenly yanked back out.

"Nifty little trick he taught you, isn't it? I never did understand the use of that gift, now I see its value," Samil said.

Nausea loomed and something salty and metallic was on my tongue. I blinked and felt a warm stream of blood running down my head across my face. Samil had smacked my head against the dash to wake me and reopened a cut. I moaned, trying to wipe the blood from my eyes with my knee but I only smeared it. A fit of anger surged and I spit on his arm.

"Do that again. I dare you."

"Same goes to you," I threatened.

We hit a hard turn and I lost my balance, falling onto his lap. Revolted, I tried pulling myself away, which was not easy to do with my hands bound behind me.

"Remain where you are!" He held my head against his lap, curling his fingers tightly in my hair. "This could be enjoyable." He laughed darkly.

I bit his leg.

He stopped laughing.

Samil howled and I sat up against the door. While he cursed in another language, I noticed that my pendant had broken free and was lying on the seat between us. It was only a few inches away.

I didn't have time to waste because if he spotted it he might toss it out, or it might slip from reach. The chain moved a little more, sliding into the crevice of the seat, and panic washed over me.

Without thinking, I put my back to him, swung my legs up and thrust my bare feet at the window. On the second kick, I grasped the necklace tightly in my fist and the window shattered, spraying a shower of glass. A blast of cold air rushed in and I pulled myself up. Had I just bent over to grab the necklace, he would have suspected something. So as stupid as it might have been, a distraction had to be created. Samil peeled off of the road and threw the car into park.

"This place will have to do," he muttered as he stepped out and circled around.

I pressed the necklace in my hand and focused, pulling out the power. I'd never done anything like this before but there it was—a heat stirring in my fingers. With an audible snap, the energy was unlocked from the metal and flowing in my veins like a drug. My door yanked open and I was shoved to the ground.

"You know, Silver," he said with his knee pressed into my back, untying the rope, "it is my sincere regret that I have to do this."

"I'm sure it is." I grunted, spitting out a mouthful of dirt. Another tug and the rope loosened.

"Sometimes fate has a sense of humor. You are too much of a liability." He turned me over to my back and straddled me as he locked my wrists over my head. "I think I should like to have a taste before we end this."

"Why go through all this trouble creating me, just to haul me off and dump me in the middle of nowhere? You're a lunatic!"

"Maybe so, little girl."

"Too weak to kick his ass?"

His hand went around my throat and he bared his canines, lips peeling back angrily, and those green eyes looked as if they were on fire.

"You are too stupid to waste time explaining what you'll never comprehend with that puny little peanut brain of yours that is freshly human."

His thumb ran down my neck and I seized the moment, shoving my fingers into his eyes and blinding him.

I stumbled over my bare feet as I watched him shaking and moaning in pain. While you should never put your power into another Mage, I did discover that pushing it directly into the eyes causes temporary blindness. A split second was all I needed to decide what to do next: run like hell.

The icy wind burned against my skin and my lungs were on fire from the frostbitten air. My bloody feet ran on patches of snow and twigs, moving on a current of newfound energy. I felt his presence gaining on me. There was an open patch of sky as I emptied into a clearing. Samil was standing at the tree line and I knew I could no longer outrun him—it was time to face my maker.

The faint light of the moon illuminated a fog around me; my

breath stirred heat in the crisp air. I thought about my sessions with Justus and knew I had to listen to everything he had taught me. There was no more running. I swallowed back all of my pain until I was numb to it.

"Come out and face me, you worthless piece of shit!" The hatred inside of me was bubbling like an inferno, fueling the spit and fight I had left in me. I was going to need every ounce of energy I could get.

"Strong words from a weakling."

"You can either keep running that mouth of yours or come out here and get your ass kicked," I called out. I needed to do this while I still retained the energy.

Samil edged out of the dark, his long stride more pronounced as he stepped into the moonlight. Black hair obscured his face, but through the strands I could see the power within his eyes. Eyes like mine. I hated that the power in me came from him, that no matter what—I would always have a part of him in me. He stalked toward me, amusement touching his lips. That was the moment I realized help would never come.

"You are a brazen one, I will give you that. Come on then, show me what you can do."

He crouched and sprang, flashing forward. I used my senses to detect his movement and flipped to the side, kicking my leg out, which knocked him off balance.

Score one for the weakling!

I changed position before he could check himself and flashed behind him, stomping his head. He reached for my ankle but I moved to his other side.

Our bodies became pure reaction, slicing through the air as we gave attack and defense, until we were nothing more than rhythm.

His face crunched when I kicked it with my bare foot. A glimmer caught my attention and I glanced down at a knife he kept strapped to his lower leg. My hand touched the handle and I hesitated.

It was long enough for him to knock me to the ground.

It was over.

Samil suffocated me with the weight of his body and I wondered if there was ever a time in his life he had reason, sanity, or compassion. Was this man ever truly human?

I struggled against his punishing grip, Samil's savage eyes bore into mine, and he roared with the knife at my throat. The knife sailed into the ground all the way to the hilt.

"I will take what is rightfully mine—I have waited long enough!"

From my open hands, he pulled every drop of light he could get until I was as fragile as a dandelion in the breeze. I cried so loud that any living thing that heard me would have wept, but my screams were absorbed by the cold night.

His green eyes blazed as he bathed in the rush of my power—the power he had not been privy to. I was taken back to the moment of my death, which was replaying itself.

"A Unique—*no wonder.*"

His body slid over mine in a declaration.

"Not yet, little girl; we're not done by a mile. Why the fuck didn't you tell me you were a Unique?"

His gaze lingered on the marks he left on my body as his eyes claimed ownership. Ownership I didn't want and would rather be dead than have to endure. He groaned, rubbing at my breast—he stank of maliciousness. I opened my mouth, but the only word that came out was *Justus.*

The hammering of my heart against my chest became a battle cry. Now it was up to the stars if they would allow such an atrocity. I looked at them pleadingly, begging them to fall down and smite us with their power, but they only blinked indifferently.

As they had once before.

With my free hand, I weakly hit him in the face, unleashing the last remaining ounce of fight I had left in me. I clawed, scratched, and snapped my teeth until he smacked my face so hard it sounded like a whip crack.

I thought about how I had always wanted to visit Italy, Greece, even Paris, and travel on a train cross-country. What was Adam doing at that exact moment? I missed Sunny and wanted to know if she'd ever find love. What did an apricot taste like? I wished I could pet Max one last time and kiss his nose. It's funny the things that run through your mind in the end.

"You are unlike anything I have ever made," he whispered, high from the power he was juicing himself up with. His throat cleared. "I will find a way to keep you from him and build my power source. The light is so… strong."

There was a brief moment it seemed as though the earth was shaking, but it was only me. I was sick with fear, cold, and overwhelming sorrow. I was ready to die in that moment, but not ready to live if it meant staying with Samil. His hand pushed painfully against my thigh. There was the metallic sound of a zipper and my legs struggled against the horror of it.

"Please don't do this," I cried.

"It's customary, don't take it personal." He laughed. "A female Mage holds no value but to service the male."

The moon gleamed off the patches of fresh snow, and in the distance, I imagined Justus standing there, armed to the teeth with daggers to save me. His stance was fierce, as a warrior. I watched the light in his eyes pierce the darkness until they found me. In a flash, the image of my Ghuardian disappeared.

Dreams are cruel.

"Are you ready to beg?"

Violence exploded above from an impact of muscle. There was a surge of power all around me like a halo… and a battle cry so primal it was deafening.

But it wasn't mine.

CHAPTER 24

"SILVER."

Something warm and inviting moved through me—the soft touch of consciousness. But I was swimming in the deep waters, only noticing a faint glimmer of light above.

"Silver," the voice called again. Was that my name?

Emptiness anchored me to the cold waters, pulling me down. I fought against it and surfaced through the hollows of my eyelids. When they opened, they heavily drank in the images that swirled and blurred before they closed again.

"That's it, come on. Wake up, love."

"Is she alive?" another one shouted from a distance.

Familiar voices.

Warmth penetrated through soft fabric against my cheek. Miles of arms wrapped around me. I smelled cinnamon, tasted blood, and felt the sharp sting of winter's breath on my skin. A deep inhale reminded me that I was alive, and I shook in violent upheavals from coughing. Slivers of pain welcomed themselves back into my body, so I closed my eyes... anchors away.

"There now, you're safe. Silver, open your eyes." The voice was worried and demanding. A finger pulled at my lid and I turned my head, moaning. "Open your eyes and come back to us. That's not a request, it's an order."

A hand combed through my bloodied hair, pulling it away from my face. Shivers rolled through me as the world fell into focus. As Simon came into focus.

"Justus!" he shouted, the sound vibrating against my ear. "She's awake."

My neck turned left slowly until I saw Justus kneeling on top of Samil with his hands gripped onto something directly over his chest. A knife. Samil moaned and Justus twisted the knife in violent movements, provoking another scream.

It wasn't a dream.

Simon knelt with me in his arms. "We'll fix you, I swear to it."

He carefully rose to his feet. Justus also rose, placing his foot on the handle of the dagger, and another long moan escaped Samil.

An icy breeze caressed my skin, as did the sudden awareness that I was mostly naked. I twisted uncomfortably.

"Justus, she needs to be cared for. I will take her," Simon urged.

The snow crunched underneath Simon's feet as we neared my Ghuardian. His face was cut, although the bleeding had stopped, and his sweater was stained with blood. I lowered my gaze, unable to look him in the eye. My body shivered and I pressed against Simon.

Justus caught Samil's eyes lingering on me and anger flared as he forcefully kicked him in the face, knocking Samil's head in the other direction.

"You do *not* look at her!" He pushed the knife in, as if it could possibly go in any farther.

Justus peeled off his thick sweater in one swift movement. Neither was dressed for the cold. Justus did, however, have time to strap on weaponry. His muscles flexed as he inched near enough that he could gently tuck his sweater over me and it was searing hot, a welcome warmth. A worried expression blotted with anger spread over his face and I closed my eyes. The richness of spice and smoke from the fabric filled my nose.

"I'll take care of her. You take care of *him*," Simon growled. "Call the Council and have him detained."

Justus looked at me with regard and once again, I averted my eyes.

In a low whisper he asked, "Why does she refuse to look at me?"

"You're a bloody fool. Do you treat her as a Mage with value? Do you talk *to* her, or *at* her? I know what it feels like to be treated as a dog; it doesn't take a beating to instill that. It merely takes a word. You have locked her away, taught her only to protect herself, not valuing her worth as a fighter. What hopes have you given her for a future other than victim? This is not the dark ages, Justus. Females now have a place." Simon turned when Justus gripped his arm.

"Do you not think I respect her? Remember, I chose to be her Ghuardian. She called my name… I heard it."

"And we can argue about this later. She is suffering."

The grip loosened and we quickly moved away. A moment later, I heard Samil's screams slice through the night, one I had longed to hear, and one that went on and on as Justus exacted his punishment.

My lips parted and a biting scent filled my nose, settling on my tongue like candy. A soft pillow cradled my head and my eyes drifted open.

A dim light illuminated the corner of the room from a small lamp with a red shade. Scattered across the bed were soft fur blankets over black sheets. There was a small writing table that held a stack of books that were precariously close to tipping over. The door ahead was slightly ajar.

Simon slept in an oversized chair near the bed with his hair obscuring his face. His breathing was heavy and I could see one part of his face that gave the most peaceful angelic expression. His jeans were dirty and wet at the bottom. As I leaned over even more, I saw his feet were dirty and bare.

The sheet was pulled aside and I looked down at my healed body. Each mark had been individually tended. I still felt exhausted; no amount of energy could possibly restore what I had lost.

I wore a long, white T-shirt and thick socks pulled up almost to the knees. I still had blood matted in my hair and caked beneath my fingernails. I started to push myself up when a hand reached out and settled me back down.

Simon's warm eyes scolded me. "Not so fast, you. Stay as you were, you need to rest."

"Where am I?" My voice came out broken and raspy, so I cleared my throat.

I watched Simon's face harden. His eyes were locked on my thigh where there were bruising fingerprints. One he had missed, as it was in such a personal area he must have avoided looking while he dressed me.

"Simon, just leave it. It doesn't matter anymore." I sighed.

Something dark unleashed behind the depths of his glowing eyes as he pulled in a long breath through his nose.

He did not wait for a response and touched my leg as his eyes never moved away from mine. Within a few moments, the bruises were gone. All evidence was erased.

Simon retracted his hand and his features softened. "This is my home I always keep open. It was the closest place we could bring you, and you're safe here. Nothing to worry about, I've got alarm systems that go out to the bloody street. I just want you to rest."

"You healed me?"

He nodded in the affirmative and reached for a glass of water, bracing my neck as I took a sip. I nearly lurched at the glass, not having realized until that moment the intensity of my thirst. It rushed into my empty stomach, cold and uninviting, and burned my dry throat. I stopped to allow it to settle. My stomach did not protest so I took more sips.

"He did not feed you?"

"Where is Justus?"

The glass tapped on the wood table and he turned away. "Calling the Council. What he did…"

"Is Samil dead?"

Simon let out a long, heavy sigh. "Not yet. It is against our laws to kill another Mage—justified or not—everything must go through the Council. Justus wants Samil's death, do not doubt it. He is very clever and we will find your justice. It is not against our law for a Creator to control or even use their Learner, we have to prove the intent was more."

"He wanted to kill me." My eyes went blank as my mind recalled those moments in the field. "I fought him, Simon. I knew I couldn't beat him, but I fought him with everything I had left."

"You fought as well as any Mage could be expected to in their first year of being. I'm impressed, and one day you will be a strong warrior." When Simon looked at me, I saw anger on his face. "Don't you ever doubt yourself; you must always do whatever it takes to survive."

"What is a Unique?"

He stared at me pensively. "It is Justus who should do this."

"I have a right to know what I am."

He turned away, placing both of his feet on the floor and leaned forward on his elbows.

"A Unique is a rarity of our kind. We know very little of them. Your power is different, taking it gives a feeling like no other. It does not make you stronger, but you have the potential to become a powerful Mage. I have only seen one Unique come to full potential in my lifetime. I don't know enough to tell you what you are, only another Unique could do that. Some consider your kind… dangerous. If your identity is discovered while you are still so young, you would be used as Samil had intended, or killed out of fear."

"So my power gives an extra kick, but why is that worth anything?"

"If another takes from you, their energy is fueled and some of it becomes part of them, and over time it could increase their power, if they are able to control you. A Unique is a coveted thing by the wrong people. That is why I only know of one; they either stay hidden in secret or they are taken and used."

"Samil made others like me. I don't know if they were Uniques, but he's trading his services for making others. I still don't understand why I was different; do you think being a Unique has something to do with why my appearance changed?"

"I can't be sure. We do not know what it is that makes a Unique; is it just a random assortment of light during your creation, or does some of your human genetics play a role?"

I leaned forward and placed my hand on the back of his neck, sweeping his soft hair to the side so I could get a more intimate view of the tattoo on his neck.

"What does this mean?" It was a series of four symbols I ran my finger over.

Simon flinched and stood up, shaking his hair free. He faced me directly and it became obvious how exhausted he was as he struggled to keep up the conversation. His voice was weak and without its usual melodic pitch.

"That is what my Creator gave me. A constant reminder that I also know what it is to have a maker who is corrupt. It's not a mark meant to be touched with such…" He shook his head and flattened his hair over the spot.

"What, tenderness?"

There it was. Simon and I were connected by that similarity, our lives ran more parallel than I had thought and now I knew why we connected.

Quiet hung over the room like a spell where the slightest disturbance would break it. There was movement behind the door ahead and just beyond the opening I saw the silhouette of Justus. He was standing outside, listening in, but not saying a word. I couldn't make out his face, only his profile. I wasn't ready to face him just yet and clearly he didn't want to see me. That hurt a little more than I expected.

"Do you need anything before I leave you to rest?"

"I could use a bath." I scraped my fingers through my hair in disgust.

Simon walked into the bedroom hall where I heard him drawing water. I glanced back at the door and Justus was no longer there.

"Here, love, lift up." He slid his arm beneath my legs and carried me. I rested my head against him and, as we neared the tub, I stole a moment to admire him. He wasn't just decent—he was a man of character.

"Don't worry, I'm not going to join you. I'm going to put you down in the water and you can remove your shirt when I leave. There are fresh towels here. Just go straight back to bed when you are done."

As he set me down, I felt the delicious water, so inviting, surrounding my body like a warm caress. Simon removed each sopping wet sock, one at a time, before he tossed them into a hamper.

"Do you need anything?"

I ignored him, dunking my head in the water and trying to remove the vile clumps of blood. I heard a cabinet open and close before a hand came across my forehead, gathering my hair up.

"Sit up. I'll wash your hair."

I didn't argue. Simon tenderly held my head as he wet my hair with a pitcher of water, lathering in his hands shampoo that smelled of vanilla and coconut. He gently worked it through my dirty scalp and I sighed in relief.

I tried to remember the last time I had been taken care of like this, and I couldn't.

A tickle ran down my forehead as suds threatened to infiltrate my eyes, but his finger swept across my brow, wiping them away. In the short time I had known Simon, he surprised me at every turn. There was a softer side to him that I could see he kept hidden very well behind the façade of a tough guy. While we had a brief interlude in the bedroom, we didn't connect to the degree that I deserved such tender affections.

"Lean your head back and keep your eyes shut." His left hand supported the nape of my neck and a warm stream of water touched the edge of my hairline; I breathed out a long, restful sigh. Simon repeated this several times until his hand ran across my hair and it squeaked.

'Okay, I'm going to leave you alone."

"Simon?"

"Yes?"

I paused, a thank you was in order, but what came out instead was, "I don't want your pity."

It was the truth. It wasn't until I became a Mage that I learned what it was to be cared for. Part of me still resisted it, but it was a nurturing that I never had. But having someone do it because they felt sorry for me—I just couldn't stand the idea of him looking at me as if I were a broken thing.

He placed his hand on my knee. "That is one thing you will never, ever have from me. You have the heart of a warrior, and someday you will have the strength of one."

I looked up and saw honesty in his eyes. I knew this was a man who had hidden pain of his own. "I know what it's like, but just remember, love—a scar will always mark you, but never let it define you." Simon gently touched my hand and left me alone to bathe.

I found the soap and scrubbed myself raw. I drained the tub and ran the water a second time. Once I felt clean enough, I stepped out of the bath and tugged at the chain until water gurgled down the drain. The towel soaked up water from my damp hair before it was tossed in the hamper. While there were no clothes for me to dress in, a thin black robe hung from a hook on the inside door. The fabric was silky and smelled clean as I settled back onto the bed.

It did not escape my attention the sheets had been changed from black to white, and there were extra blankets for me to cover up in. Darkness engulfed me, and just as I was on the brink of falling asleep—a voice called out. His voice.

"*Sillllverrrr… you belong to me.*"

I let out a wail, flying out of the bed and sliding across the tile of the bathroom. *Samil.*

With a sudden bang, the bedroom door kicked in and I scurried to the corner, hiding behind the edge of the counter. I tucked my knees against my chest and held my breath, listening to the ominous sound of footsteps bearing down on me.

"*Silver… are you ready to beg?*"

When his body moved within my view, I thrust out my foot, kicking him in the groin with no mercy. Immediately, he doubled over and I kicked him again in the chest, sending him to the other side of the room.

My legs sprang up and I snatched a razor from the edge of the sink and flew forward, ready to strike. I saw nothing but blinding rage—I was running in pure survival mode.

Someone slammed into me and knocked the razor free. We fell to the floor but before I hit the tile, he pivoted his body around so that he took the brunt of the fall. I lay across his chest with my arms pinned so tightly that I couldn't move a fraction. Guttural noises came from my throat as I writhed and kicked.

"Silver, *stop!*"

I thrashed violently, kicking my legs and flailing my head. While my attempts were genuine, the results were feeble.

"Let it go, Learner. Let it go." The voice fell to a whisper. "Silver, calm down—it's Justus."

I made an animalistic sound before I recognized the voice and stopped struggling. Lying at my feet was a body slumped against the wall with a mop of brown hair covering his face. One knee was bent up with a rip in the jeans and my eyes trailed down to the bare feet.

Simon. I hurt Simon.

I threw my head back in shame as my eyes shut tight; comprehension was beginning to sink in like a dagger. Tightness gripped my chest that had nothing to do with the man pinning me.

"Get him out of my head!" I cried.

My voice dissolved into tears. Whatever held me together was lost. My body shook with unrelenting sobs. I pulled against his solid arms, which held me firmly to him no matter how much I tried to tear them away.

"Stop it; let me go!"

It was like fighting against a wall.

His voice softened against my ear. "Shhh, I've got you, Silver, be still. Lean into me. I'm not going to let him take you again. Forgive me. I failed you as a Ghuardian."

In that moment of clarity, I realized that I did not deserve the respect these men gave me. I wept on his cheek, and the minute I realized what I was doing I jerked away and hid beneath my wet hair. Samil didn't go as far as he might have, but in the past week I felt violated, robbed of my dignity, stripped of my independence, and treated like an animal. I had tried to stay tough and imagine myself as a warrior—but part of me was still human.

"He ruined me."

"You are not ruined." His hand brushed my hair gently away from my tear-stained face as the other still held me. Warmth radiated from his body and my chest rocked with heavy sobs that I was powerless to stop.

Justus cradled my wet cheek. "You break me with those tears, Silver. Please don't cry."

I calmed, taking slow breaths until the remains of my despair had faded.

"As long as I'm with you, I will keep you safe."

"And how long will that be for?"

He did not hesitate, answering the moment I spoke the last word. "For the rest of my life."

Justus pushed himself up to sitting position and loosened his hold. I leaned against him, wiping my face.

"I will train you properly and you will learn to fight. You will have the future you deserve—an independent one. You will be strong enough to protect yourself one day and have a job within the Mageri. I did not prepare you as I should have; this is my fault."

He jaw flexed and I could see he was taking it personally. There was no need. I'd come to realize that my life was out of my hands, as were many of the decisions.

"This life wasn't my choice and I used that as my crutch, my out for not following your rules. But I am making a choice now." I shifted to face him so he could see my sincerity. "I choose to be a Mage; I'll listen to you from now on and will learn. This is my life, and I accept it." I sniffed and wiped my damp lashes.

His stare was prideful. "I've never given you kind words, Silver. It does not mean that I am without them when I think of you. You're sterling, that's what you are. Always remember that."

My eyes met his, accepting the compliment. Justus hadn't been taking care of himself. His hair was grown out some and one cut on his face had not completely healed. I lifted my fingers to the gash that ran along his cheek when he caught my wrist. Without a word, I twisted free of his grip and pressed my hand over his wound. As my light began to work itself and heal his cut, it was the first time Justus really looked at me. With my hand cupping the side of his fearless features, his eyes regarded me with admiration.

A low moan redirected my attention to Simon. His head was against the tile wall at a peculiar angle.

I crawled over. "Simon? Please wake up. I'm so sorry." His eyes fluttered as if he were on the brink, but couldn't quite pull out of it.

"Move; let me."

I backed up, sliding across the grey flooring as my robe picked up a little of the water that was left behind from my bath.

Justus leaned over Simon, holding his hands across his chest.

"Simon—*wake*," he commanded. I had a feeling there was some kind of energy thing going on that snapped him out of it.

Simon's eyebrows sank into his sockets and he bared his teeth—

hissing in pain before letting out a snarl. I jumped, having never seen a more visceral reaction.

Justus threw his hands around Simon's head, cradling it like a melon, and tiny threads of light, so fine they could have been cobwebs, drifted from his fingertips.

Within a few seconds, Simon started coughing. Justus pulled him up to a sitting position.

"You okay in there?" He knocked on Simon's head jokingly and I smiled a little.

Simon's face strained—the rope of muscle in his neck was taut and he grimaced. Suddenly, he reached for a fistful of shirt and pulled Justus so hard they were nose to nose.

"Don't take this the wrong way," Simon grunted through his clenched teeth, "but *fuck* my head, mate! Put your bleeding hands on my *balls!*"

I sat back, laughing, as Justus considered his request.

"I swear I'll never tell." I said, crossing my heart.

As Justus aided a friend in need, Simon's eyes flitted around, falling on me before amusement stirred in his face. "I probably deserved that."

My humor receded. "I didn't know it was you. I'm so—"

"Fearless."

I knew in that moment I had more than an acquaintance in him, and a Ghuardian in Justus. I had companions, men I would be able to count on.

Some men do stick around.

CHAPTER 25

I HAD A FULL NIGHT'S SLEEP in Simon's bed, smothered with soft blankets of fur. I decided not to ask why a grown man was sleeping on fur; yet nothing about this man was predictable.

Once during the night I woke up in the darkened room and someone was sitting beside me. I wasn't afraid but felt... comforted. He was holding my hand, and the light drifting within me was so faint I wasn't sure if I was awake or dreaming. A thumb ran across my forehead and I heard a word softly spoken.

"Sleep."

When I finally did wake, I emerged from the bed and snatched up an apple sitting expectantly on the bedside table. It was sweet and crunchy and my mouth watered with each bite. I couldn't finish it because my stomach was aching from the new sensation of food, so I backed off and set it down. Before wandering the house, I glanced at the books on the table. Simon didn't read adventure stories or even smut. I was completely surprised to find they were books on science, psychology, and history.

Down the short hall, Simon was resting on a chocolate-colored sofa in the living room with his head propped in his hand. A slice of sunlight crept through the edge of a curtain, adding highlights to his hair. The floor was covered with a large brown shag carpet; everything about the room was casual, inviting, and truly lived in. Simon's eyes lifted and he greeted me with a warm smile.

"Hey, gorgeous, you sleep well?"

I nodded, moving to the empty chair. "Probably too well."

Some of the sunlight touched my feet, and in the quiet of the room I noticed how distinctly alien daylight seemed. I never imagined I'd see anything but darkness again.

"No TV?"

"The telly is rubbish. It hasn't been the same since it was live."

"So what do you do to pass the time?"

"Love a good book. I'm also quite addicted to board games, but it's not always easy to find a good partner."

Board games? I thought Simon lived at the bar, had dance parties on the roof, and yet once again he surprised me with the fact that he was a complete geek.

"We'll have to play sometime."

His eyes lit up. "That would be *brilliant*. I'll hold you to that. I warn you though—I've played with some of the best."

"Well I play a mean hopscotch." I smiled.

Simon had a cup in his lap and leaned forward, handing it to me. "I just made it, only took a sip."

The sweet perfume of cocoa tickled my nose. Simon rose to his feet and crouched beside my chair, stroking my hair absently as he stared out of the window. It was something he liked to do as he had done it on more than one occasion; an affectionate gesture one might do to a child.

"What was it that frightened you last night?" he asked.

"I heard him, I heard Samil. It was like he was there in the room with me. That's not the first time it's happened."

Simon's voice dropped an octave. "Hmm, he's a Mentalist."

"I know a little about that. Can he hear my thoughts?"

"Does he say anything that would make you think he can?"

I thought for a moment and shook my head, as I couldn't be sure. "No, he just calls my name and says things."

He rubbed his smooth chin and I stared at a tiny little freckle on his lash line. "Justus has a plan."

"Which is what? I don't want him challenging Samil. Will the Council punish him?"

"I can't say for sure. There's a grey area when it comes to a Creator and his rights to his progeny." He stood up and stretched his back to a lean arch. "We need to go. I'm supposed to drive you back this morning; he should be there now."

"In a robe?"

"No, I believe he'll be dressed."

"Your humor is legendary."

Simon stood with his legs slightly apart, staring down his nose. He looked nice today. Just a simple pair of jeans, a clean dress shirt with rolled-up sleeves and a thin, button-down grey vest that wasn't buttoned. I never imagined Simon in this style, but I liked it. He looked like he had stepped out of a catalog.

"Stay right here."

I stood up and peeked out of the window, staring down fifteen stories. We were in a high-rise. "How did you get me up here without anyone noticing?"

He strode out of the room without answering, and my stomach gurgled again. I wasn't sure if it was hungry or having an argument with Granny Smith.

"Here you are."

I spun around to a long trench coat held before me.

"Thank you, sir." I slipped my arm into a sleeve. "What about shoes?" I stared down at my bare feet.

"Apologies, love. My feet are too big."

"It's winter out there, you know."

"I will personally carry you every step of the way; you will never feel a moment of cold."

"Well, I guess you've thought of everything." My hair fell over my face as I watched Simon fastening the buttons of my coat.

"Simon?"

"Hmm?"

"I just wanted to say thanks, and I'm sorry."

He finished and pivoted around, shaking his head in disapproval at my apology. Past the kitchen of modern conveniences, spice racks, and a true sense that it was used to its fullest potential was a hallway that led to the front door.

Simon opened a small closet and reached in, pulling out his leather coat. I knew something was amusing him while he zipped up the front. I poked my finger into that little dimple of his.

"What's so funny?"

"I rather like the souvenir, adds a nice touch to my image," he commented, tapping at the bite marks in the coat.

"What kind of image are you hoping to portray?"

"Irresistible?"

"Well, you don't have to try much at that," I said factually. Simon looked embarrassed and I grabbed his wrist. "Do me a favor, open the door again," I said, pointing to the closet.

I was unable to decipher the look he gave me before he obeyed my request.

"*Holy...* you weren't kidding!"

The inside of the closet was deep and lined with shelves on all three sides from ceiling to floor. I stared at shelves in amazement as each one held stacks of games and cards of every imaginable kind, many of which I did not recognize. This was no ordinary collection of games, this was an arsenal. Simon took geek to a fresh new level.

"Anytime you want to sink my battleship, love, give us a shout."

"Game on."

The mystery of how Justus got his furniture in his underground dwelling was finally revealed. Simon drove to a back entrance I didn't even know existed. In a very James Bond fashion, he clicked a button on his visor and we descended into the ground, via a lift discreetly disguised. It went down just far enough that the car rolled through a tunnel and ended up in an indoor garage.

My jaw dropped.

One had to appreciate how much money Justus, or the Mageri, had at their disposal. I wondered why Justus went to such great lengths in designing the secrecy of his home. What was he hiding from? After seeing where Simon and Samil lived, it was pretty obvious that living as a recluse wasn't a prerequisite of being a Mage.

Thank God.

"Impressive," I remarked.

"That's definitely what *she* said," he teased. I groaned at his poorly chosen comeback.

Even more impressive was the car collection. Fuck James Bond, he had nothing on Justus. The brightly lit garage was filled with toys:

a sleek black Porsche, a classic English car, Mercedes, most I couldn't identify. In addition to the expensive models were sporty ones and a few motorcycles, including a Ducati.

"Justus always had extravagant taste. He likes to collect."

"I see. Where does he get the money for all of this?"

"He's been a Mage for a long time. You tend to acquire money over the years, and he offers his services for compensation," he said, shutting his door. "We have positions within the Mageri. We do earn a respectable living."

Once inside, we walked down a long hallway and ended up in a room I didn't recognize. It was filled with bookshelves on one wall from floor to ceiling. Only these were not books for Mage schooling, but a private collection. Some were very old and there were a number of familiar titles.

Overhead, a beautiful chandelier that ran on electricity glowed, casting shadows on the wood floor. There were a few photographs and a detailed tapestry. To the right was a desk, but what drew my attention was a commanding sword mounted on the wall behind it.

It was a large oak desk. Nearing the edge, I ran my fingers along the wood and over the beautiful rich leather binding of a very weathered book. It was a deep red with a striking symbol adorning the cover. My fingers traced the grooves of a large round circle that reminded me of the one I saw on Justus's business card—only this one had stunning detail. On the bottom right corner was a thinly embossed single word: HALO.

"Silver…" Simon urged.

"What's HALO?"

"I can't say. Come away from there."

Something on the desk caught my attention. It was a picture frame, and the photograph displayed was me.

Me!

It was a candid photo that Adam had taken when we were in Memphis and I was sitting in tall grass. *Where the hell did he get that?*

"Let's go, he doesn't like anyone in here. I knew we should have taken the other passage."

Hands deep in my pockets, I walked through a door and stood

in the middle of Justus's bedroom. I had only been in there once. It was very basic and similar to my room. An oversized bed covered with a red silk coverlet, an old black wardrobe with a mirror fixed on the front, and a black sofa. The walls were empty except for the candles. The door through which we stepped in was an oversized mirror mounted on the wall; when it clicked shut it was simply a mirror again.

Secret passageways, who knew?

I handed my coat to Simon and almost made it into my bedroom when I stopped dead in my tracks.

Voices. Plural.

Simon gave an indifferent stare as I pushed past him into the open room. Justus lifted his chin to look at me. I saw the back of someone's head in the opposite chair and my heart dropped. I immediately knew who it was.

When he stood up to face me, I had already flown into his arms. I was pulled possessively to him and my feet came up off the ground.

"Adam," I whispered. His face pressed against mine and I inhaled deeply. "You came, I can't believe you're here."

He smelled so good, like the Adam I remembered. Rich, earthy, clean. I nuzzled into his neck instinctively and his chest vibrated with a low chuckle. "I missed you too, woman."

I felt like if I broke into a million tiny pieces, his embrace was the glue that would put me back together.

Adam set my feet on the ground and his eyes dropped to every visible inch of my body—which was mostly covered with the robe— before he shot a hard look at Justus.

"As I've stated before, she's been healed, we've seen to her needs." Justus stood up to face Adam and set down his glass of brandy.

"Have you? Seen to her needs?" Adam's eyes flared with anger. "What kind of life do you plan to provide for her?"

Even if he was yelling, I missed the sound of his voice.

"An honorable one, human. I think you know better than anyone that it is not the easy road that makes us capable of great things. It is the hard journey that leads to a greater destiny. You can never rise if you never have anything to rise *above*." Justus swelled with the pride of a man who had perhaps done many great things and fought hard for them.

"That's fucking poetic. Tell me, does it keep you warm at night when you curl up with those thoughts, knowing that your views are putting her life in danger?"

Adam edged toward Justus.

"Don't test my loyalties or my intentions," Justus said. "We've already gone over this."

"You know what I want?" Adam began moving more out of my grasp. "Peace of mind. I want you to be man enough and stand here and look me in the eye… and tell me that you have her best interest in mind. Because I will hold you to it, feel me?"

"Please stop," I pleaded.

Adam snapped his attention back and I pulled him close as his exotic scent spoiled me to splendor.

"You need a shave," I said, scratching his chin. He smirked all the way to his dark eyes.

"I'm afraid Adam has forgotten his manners, letting the lady stand barefoot on this cold floor. Silver, come warm yourself."

I looked suspiciously at Simon, who was seeking opportunity to pull me away from Adam. I found a comfortable spot near the fireplace on a brown rug. I ran my fingers through real animal fur, certain whatever it was it either cost a fortune or Justus hunted the damn animal himself. Probably while riding an elephant on an ostentatious safari.

Adam wrapped a thin blanket around my shoulders and collapsed in the leather chair behind me. Simon and Justus took the sofa, talking softly.

My chin lifted, following the height of the stone fireplace that went flush to the ceiling.

"How does nobody notice the smoke billowing out?"

"Filtering system, it doesn't come out from straight above," was the reply.

I looked at Adam. "Why are you here; did they call you?" By the way they interacted, it led me to believe he had been here for more than just a few hours.

He leaned forward with his elbows on his knees, one hand cupped in the other.

"Are you keeping something from me?"

When he looked to Justus, I knew.

Justus rose from his seat and stretched, popping a few bones in his neck. "There are fresh clothes in your bedroom so you can freshen up. We'll discuss our plans over breakfast, or lunch."

"Which would you like?" Adam smiled.

I gave an innocent shrug. "I don't care."

In my bedroom everything felt familiar, but nothing was the same. The blankets on the sofa were just as I had left them—soft and gently crumpled over the arm with my music player sitting on the cushion. The rest of the room was as neat as a pin. Across Goliath was a new pair of clothes laid out expectantly.

In the bathroom, a small bottle of peach-scented lotion was next to my toothbrush—an expensive brand I could never afford. In his own way, Justus missed me.

But there was something at the forefront of my thoughts—why was Adam here? Was my Ghuardian going to give me over to him? Maybe he'd had time to reconsider his commitment.

Justus sat alone at the table and I took the seat directly across from him. An empty white plate stared up at me beside a glass of juice, which was gone in about four swallows. Justus gave a side glance at the kitchen door as if he were waiting for something.

When the door swung open, I was delighted to see Adam with a skillet. He leaned over my shoulder and placed his world-famous omelet onto my plate. It smelled sumptuous. I brought my left hand around the other side of his neck and pulled his cheek to mine in gratitude.

"I think I like this side of you, you're more affectionate than before," he said.

"I'm just glad to see you."

"You smell like peaches, yum."

Justus cleared something in his throat and the chair legs made a disagreeable sound as they scraped across the floor. He eyeballed Adam, who briskly walked back into the kitchen.

"Did you rest well?"

I nodded, ignoring an ache that was crumpling me like a sheet of paper—hunger.

Adam returned, filling each plate with an omelet. Simon followed behind like a shadow, carrying a bowl of fresh cut strawberries and toasted bread with jam.

"Eat." Justus nodded at my plate, fingers laced, not touching his own food.

I licked my lips and pulled my glance away, as hard as it was. "I'll wait."

He swallowed his temper rubbed his face in frustration.

"Silver, please start before it gets cold. Don't wait for us," Simon sang out from the kitchen.

Justus lowered his chin and gave me *the look*. So I caved, pressing my fork into the omelet. It was warm, buttery, and bursting with flavors of tomato, cheese, diced vegetables, and salty meats. Each bite wasn't enough. Before I knew it, I was shoveling it in my mouth and swallowing faster than I could chew. My throat was out of practice and I had to dip my chin and struggle with each swallow.

Simon set a plate of sausages down and by the time everyone was seated I had managed to pack the entire omelet in my mouth like some kind of an animal.

Everyone stared.

Embarrassed, I looked down at my lap. It seemed like a lost cause to retain any sense of normalcy.

Adam leaned behind my chair, cupping his fingers beneath my chin to lift it.

"I don't want to see those pretty green eyes on the floor anymore, you hear? I'll go make more." He looked away. "Why don't one of you sorry bastards give her more juice?" Adam left the room and a second plate made its way insistently to me, as did Simon's drink.

"He didn't feed her," Simon mouthed to Justus.

"Are my abilities, gone? Did he take them from me?"

"No, Learner, you will always be able to restore because you still retain your core light."

I moved my empty plate away and began to work on his. Adam

returned with a second omelet twice as big as the first and I felt a wave of guilt. I sat there stuffing my face on Justus's plate as all his efforts went to waste. He didn't seem disappointed, just set the plate in the center of the table and threw a leg over his chair to take a seat.

Justus nibbled a sausage, licking his fingers as he stared at his plate. "Adam is going to be the challenger."

My heart skipped a beat. "No, he isn't. Don't even think about it. If that's what you've been sitting around scheming, then you can—"

"The decision is made," Adam interrupted, resting his arm on the table as he wrapped his fingers around a small coffee cup. "It was decided days ago, Silver."

I only quieted because it was the first time he called me Silver. Before I could catch my tongue, Justus lifted his voice.

"We've gone over every possible scenario, but we all agree on one thing."

"What's that?"

"Samil must die," Justus replied. "The rule is that the power between him and the challenger will be leveled out. If a human challenges him, the Council will have no choice but to remove his power temporarily. The law is no Mage shall kill another, but there is nothing in the law about humans. Adam would have the power to take him out because Samil will be reduced to human form."

"How do you temporarily remove his power?" My appetite began to shrink.

"A Mage can pull energy from another, but it's only temporary and it leaks. Each Mage is born with gifts. Merc so happens to have the ability to retain all power, including core light for a period of— we speculate—twenty-four hours. After that, it leaks. The Council will use him to hold Samil's power until after the challenge. In fact, I can easily see why it would have been one reason they brought him on the Council."

His thought wandered and Simon picked up where he left off.

"We don't trust Merc. We have a history with him. A Mage that can absorb all the power of another is dangerous. It's an uncalculated risk."

"So you want to remove all power from Samil to make him

mortal so Adam can challenge him to the death? They said they don't fight to the death because of the value of a Creator."

"But there is a loophole, Silver." Justus gave a cold stare. "He will be human. Adam would have full rights as a human to end his life for his own justice. A Mage is only Breed because of their light."

"What about the Council saying the winner takes the power?"

"If the power is infused to your core light, it becomes yours; that is how it would be returned to Samil. There is one on the Council who has such a gift."

"That's a pretty nifty gift. Sounds like between the members of the Council they could steal everyone's power if they wanted."

Simon laughed. "Assuming they worked together, but two of them avidly hate each other. Merc and the one who holds the ability to infuse power—Sasha. They were former lovers. So if it is not infused to anyone, it will be lost from Merc."

Someone rapped their knuckles on the table and I pushed my plate forward.

"You still didn't answer my question. He's human, he has no core light." I stared at Justus.

"Correct, he would not receive the power because it would kill him. The power is too strong to give even to a new Learner, which would be like giving a Lamborghini to a toddler. I haven't worked out what the Council will do, we can only speculate. Honestly, Silver, I don't give a fuck where that energy goes, pardon my language."

"He's not a fighter! It's too dangerous, Ghuardian, you're putting his life at risk!"

Simon muffled a laugh, almost choking on his omelet.

"Mind telling me what's so funny?"

Adam cleared his throat and tugged at his ear. "Silver, you know I was in the military. I was part of an elite force, one that no one knows exists except the right people—or maybe the wrong. The assignments we were given were risky and dangerous. I am well-trained in specialized hand-to-hand combat, among other things."

"*Among other things.*" I always thought that should be the title of a book that revealed the biggest secrets in history, because that small little phrase was the most enigmatic and dangerous of all.

"The man can bang out an omelet in three minutes, but he can also give a good beat down. Trust me, I fought him without using my energy. Bloke might have snapped my neck, but he hesitated. Guess he forgot that we heal." Simon chuckled, biting a strawberry all the way to the green, leafy top.

"Maybe it's because he's not a killer."

Adam ran his tongue across his front teeth beneath his lip, and there was something in that look that made it self-evident without any confession, that my statement was not entirely true.

"You know, I never asked where you got those panties from that you put on me the night you found me. Some things are best left unsaid." I stood up from the table and burned him with my stare. "But being some kind of military assassin? Not one of them. So anymore secrets that you guys want to tell me? Because apparently," I yelled, "I'm just on the need-to-know basis. No big deal, it's only my life you're gambling with… *his life.*"

I could feel the power surging within me as my shoes tapped down the hallway.

"Silver, wait." Adam beckoned from behind.

"I cannot believe that I wasn't part of this, Razor, and what are you thinking? I didn't want you involved and now if anything happens to you it's *my* fault!" I spun around. "Don't you get it? I can't take that chance—you don't know what the Council might do. You don't have a clue what our world is like."

"And you do?"

"Why are you doing this? There's got to be another way."

"Please, listen," he said, stepping forward.

My fingertips began buzzing with anger as I raised them up. "Back off, because I could hurt you. Go back to your life—it's safer, it's easier that way. I never wanted you to be dragged into this." I took a breath and leveled down.

His body leaned in and I stepped back until I bumped into the door.

"You'll join us tonight, no more secrets," Adam said. "I know you're pissed off, but I want to be the one. It's not a favor or an obligation that I'll enjoy breaking his neck. The way he hurt you…"

"You don't even know how he hurt me." I nearly choked. "You

haven't seen me until now, and I look okay, don't I? So why the fuss?"

"I saw what he did to you the night I found you, goddamn it! That waking nightmare, which I will live with for the rest of my life, is all the motivation I need to know that I want to be the one to put him in the ground. It was always my decision, there was no convincing. I was in from the beginning."

"Look, if you are on some kind of mission to make peace with the world because of some bad shit you did in your past, do not play martyr for me."

He pressed his hand against the wall over my head and leaned in. "I care about you, Silver; I don't want to see you hurt anymore. I'm not backing away from this and you can't make me. I know the risk and it's worth it."

Words that should have given me comfort but tore me apart instead.

"The risk is *your life*! It's not worth giving up because of some ideal you have of protecting me from the world. Doing this won't bring me happiness. I know you aren't that naïve."

"No, but you will be free of him, and that is a fucking start."

I lowered my head; there would be no talking him out of this. Adam lifted my chin and ran his thumb over my lip. "What did I tell you about looking down? There's something else."

My body tensed and I swallowed hard.

"I knew what you were when I saw your mark."

"What the hell do you mean by that?" I said, shoving him. I felt like my universe was unraveling—Adam was not the man I thought he was. He was a man of secrets and lies.

There was a pregnant pause.

"I've seen a mark like that before. Exactly like yours. The man who killed my sister—the men who jumped us were Mage, Silver. They were juicers. I've spent my whole life looking for him. I joined the military just so I could kill someone if I couldn't kill him. The Mage have been my enemy, even before I knew what they were. Until I met you, Silver—you changed that. You can't imagine how much I wanted to hate you."

I pushed at his chest, but he wasn't backing down, Adam

leaned in even closer. "Why didn't you tell me this before?" My voice softened.

"I didn't want you to know what you were."

"Because you wanted me to be normal, is that it? You wanted to hide what I was, go on pretending I was like you. How do you think that makes me feel? I'm sorry for what happened to your sister, but this is who I am." My eyebrows crushed together as something else came to mind. "If that makes me your enemy then there's nothing I can do about it, I can't deny what I am. Why did you help me?"

His head tilted. "Curiosity? You needed help and I couldn't turn away. I didn't know for sure what you were in the beginning. Not until the kiss, and by then I was gone, and you already had me in your pocket." He dropped his head so it was nearer to mine. "And you are *not* my enemy."

My fingers brushed over his cheek and his eyes softened. "I'll never be human. If one of Samil's progeny killed your sister, that light is in *me*. I know your intentions are good, but be honest with yourself. No matter how long we stay friends, that's always going to be racing in the back of your mind."

A sound in the hall turned my attention away. Simon had his arms folded and a tightened expression, clocking Adam. I didn't think he appreciated Adam's domineering posture over me although I was quite used to it—Adam was a leaner.

"And you are a wanker!" I yelled at Simon.

"Why am I the wanker?" He laughed. "Do you even know what a wanker is?"

"I don't like secrets," I said, staring between both of them. The truth of it was, Simon and Justus knew the dangers and I felt like they were using Adam as a pawn.

"If we're going to do this I want to know everything that's been going on—do not treat me like a child with my own life. I want you to keep training," I said, pressing my finger in Adam's chest, "and you can start by kicking Simon's ass."

"With pleasure," he smirked.

We both looked at Simon, who spun around on his heel and strode off, taunting Adam with, "Break a leg, my friend. Break. A. Leg."

CHAPTER 26

CCORDING TO JUSTUS, THE RED DOOR was a private, members-only club. He arranged to meet with his friend, Remi—someone he consulted with when he needed sound advice. I rode with Justus while Adam and Simon tailed behind; they had to wrap up their training, which had been going on all day.

I did find out where Justus had acquired the photo of me that was on his desk in the hidden room. Not because anyone admitted it, I just put two and two together. When Adam first arrived, he had a satchel with his newest photographs that he wanted to give me copies of. Adam was frustrated to find that particular photograph copy missing.

Simon admired the *original* photo (which I insisted Adam keep) and showed Justus, who seemed curiously disinterested as he raised his brandy glass and cleaned the bottom.

Justus had gone through Adam's things without his knowing and stolen that picture for himself. I don't know the reasoning, or why he couldn't just take a picture of me himself, but I didn't ask.

My hair was tied back with a few stray pieces hanging in my face. I chose a long black skirt with a modest slit, an amethyst-colored blouse, and a simple pair of flats. Justus purchased these expensive items, and he was extremely proud to see me in them, even though he didn't admit it.

There were customs I had to get used to, one of which included being escorted by my Ghuardian at all times when I went out in public. While it wasn't a concern I had now, I was fully aware that I would begin to feel the pinch at my privacy in the future.

We approached the side entrance of a large brick building lined with people hoping to get in.

Justus pulled a pair of mirrored sunglasses from his coat and slid them up the bridge of his nose. He leaned over and whispered, "Humans aren't usually allowed, but we have a pass for Adam."

"A pass for what?" I looked over the crowd again. "Is this a Mage club?"

His laugh was more of a growl. "No, Learner. This club welcomes all Breed. It's neutral ground. It's social, indeed, but many come here to do business or favor trade. You'll find that you fit right in here. These clubs are all over, but they are very exclusive—Breed only. This is what you've been missing out on, Silver."

Justus gave the bouncer a nod. The big meaty guy with the shiny bald head turned his mouth up in a crooked smile as he pulled open a large red door.

"Haven't seen you around, Mr. De Gradi—the ladies have missed you."

I snorted as we stepped through the door; my senses were getting hazy and I began to feel jittery all over. I stopped and grabbed Justus's hand. "I don't feel right."

He leaned down and whispered, "Give it a few minutes to adjust. You're feeling the energy of the Breed. It feels confusing the first time but you'll get used to it. Come on, we're down this way."

Justus secured his arm around my back and escorted me through the club. Women were turning their heads with extreme precision to follow Justus as he tunneled through the crowd. I didn't particularly think it was his winning smile that was pleasing the ladies—it was the charm he was throwing out like beads on Mardi Gras.

Some even called him by name, and I realized his talents must have been legendary.

I began to soak in my first glimpses of other Breed. One gentleman nodded and winked at me, flashing a brilliant gold glimmer behind his lashes. His features were so gentle and yet I had to look away as those golden eyes locked onto me, unblinking, as if I were prey. Two men lingered by an open doorway; their skin was phenomenally smooth and beautiful. The one with the long straight hair tipped his head in my direction and grinned, and I caught the gleam of a sharp tooth lowering.

"Are those…"

"Vampires. Yes, and don't stare. If he lowers a fang at you again, it's coming out of his mouth." His eyes glared back at the Vampire as if he had been giving him a warning, but they were too far apart for him to have heard.

"I feel like I fell down the rabbit hole."

"Just remember not to make human assumptions when you meet anyone, because it only shows ignorance."

"Like Mages being wizards?"

"Mage," he corrected. "Not Mages, not Magi, not Magaree. Different rules, different world, different word. And you don't see me carrying a wand, do you?"

"Well…"

"You've always got a counter for everything, don't you?"

I giggled and caught his eyes smiling at the corners behind the shades because of the way they crinkled at the side. It felt good to laugh again.

We stepped up to a private booth area. The oval tables were surrounded by lovely red seats, all of which had tall glass frames for privacy behind them. Each table was adorned with crackled glass votives, glimmering on the polished wood from the candlelight.

A very marvelous man in appearance stood up and bowed. "Justus, we must meet more often."

I noticed a few eyes near us fall on him fearfully. Nothing about him struck me as menacing. He had a tall, slender build and could have easily been my age, but his regal stature made him seem more mature. Soft brown hair fell to the square shoulders of his black coat. When his eyes lifted to greet us, I thought they were a pretty shade of hazel until he looked at me and the color shifted to a deep orange. But what *really* caught my attention was the frightening tattoo of a dragon, prominent on his neck. I could only make out part of the claws and head from his raised collar, but it was enough to see its sinister smile around the gnashing teeth.

I timidly clasped my hands together, which he noticed.

Justus bowed back. "Remi, it is good to see you again. Still keeping the mane, I see."

Remi lightly touched the ends of his hair and arched a brow.

"I would like to introduce you to Silver, my Learner."

Remi gave a slow nod without breaking eye contact and I returned the gesture.

"I wondered when I would receive an introduction, as I have heard much about you," Remi said. "It is with great pleasure." He stepped aside and made a sweeping gesture for us to join him. "Do sit." There was something odd about him I couldn't put my finger on. There was something very off, very detached behind his expression. It was as if he were going through the motions without feeling.

I took a spot at the edge of the booth as Justus and Remi moved to the curved bench on my left at the end.

"Room for more?" Simon and Adam finally graced us with their presence. Simon was also wearing sunglasses, but he looked more like a rock star incognito.

"Remi, you know Simon. This is Adam Razor." Justus made a small hand gesture to the new additions.

"Ah, so you are the one."

Adam nodded, taking the seat across from me and I eased over, giving Simon some room. I caught a faint whiff of his cologne but kept my focus on Remi, who hadn't looked away from me. I didn't like the intensity of his stare, so I squirmed in my chair and waited for Justus to speak.

Remi was a Gemini. It was very interesting to hear of other non-humans outside of the ones I'd read or seen movies about. There was a whole world that existed that I'd never even imagined. Some were immortal, while others led shorter life spans. Some were born into their Breed while others had to be made.

Gemini are a very old Breed of immortals who are only loyal to the very few that they trust. All Justus reiterated was that I should never provoke a Gemini. Ever.

Gemini learned to shut off emotions of anger, jealousy, and revenge, as they considered them a weakness. Particularly since they had a raging beast inside of them that, once provoked, would not rest until they killed their intended victim or otherwise. He did mention that most carried the gift of intuition, not the same as premonitions, but just an ability to assess a situation and understand the outcome. They were often employed as advisors.

Remi had also had a brief relationship a long time ago with Hannah, which made Justus think he might have some specific insight as to the decision the Council might come to.

Adam suddenly reached across the table and took my hand. "You're not well," he insisted.

"I'm fine, I can't get sick, remember?" I smiled weakly. "It's just the energy here."

I became more acclimated to the energy with each passing minute. I guess it takes a while to get your sea legs.

"May we begin?" Remi looked to Justus and I pulled away from Adam.

"Remi, I've asked you here to gain your intuition. You know Hannah, our intention, and Adam being the challenger. What I didn't explain—"

"Yes, that it is to the death of course. That intent is quite clear." Remi waved a hand as if he had already seen the elephant in the room before we even came in.

"You must know then the outcome is not certain, Adam is well-trained but Samil has centuries of technique. If Adam wins, we do not know what they'll do with Samil's power."

A waitress came to our table and set down four small glasses filled with a milky-green liquid. As the men began to slowly sip their drink, I dipped my nose in the glass, smelling something sickly sweet. I took a small taste and turned my nose as I set it on the table.

"Not to your liking?" Remi asked, watching my reaction with mild interest and a blank expression.

"No it's fine. Just reminds me of kryptonite." I caught a smile hovering at the corner of Adam's lips as he lifted his glass in a toast to our inside joke.

Remi tilted his head and his straight brown hair fell away from his face, allowing me to see his eyes more clearly. They were pronounced with a wonderfully rich orange hue and a well-defined black rim around the outer edge of the iris. I looked down at my drink; he was very charming in every gesture but something about him intimidated the hell out of me behind the façade of being calm and collected. It was not unlike having a conversation with a grenade.

"Justus, friend, what I can tell you of the outcome is this: there will be a decision made on Adam's fate. The Council will deny a proposal."

"Will Adam be the victor?"

"That I cannot tell you."

"So you *do* know."

"I may. We both know that fate is not without its sense of humor and its cruelty. To intervene with fate can bring consequences, if not change the path entirely. I must be selective in what I reveal. This is one situation where I cannot offer much."

"Fuck, mate... what *can* you tell us?" Simon blurted.

Justus cleared his throat and Simon protested. "I'm sorry, but what the hell was the purpose of coming here if we can't get a little edge on this? If I knew it would be a total waste of time I would have knocked boots with that sweet little blonde standing over by the—"

I hit Simon on the arm with the back of my hand and he slouched in his seat, glancing away.

Remi leaned back and his lashes softly kissed as he looked between all of us.

"All of your efforts for this Mage are not in vain. She will save many lives in the course of her life." His eyes washed over me with strange familiarity. "Silver, the Breed do not live an easy life. You must be strong for it, but never harden on the inside or you will lose your humanity. It would be a great loss."

The table quieted, it seemed as if everyone was afraid to interrupt that thoughtful piece of advice. But I needed a real drink.

"Excuse me, I'll be right back."

Elbowing Simon to move his ass, I hopped up out of my seat and noticed Remi was standing up as a gentleman might. I smiled, and Simon suddenly flew up out of his chair, followed by Adam.

"Too late now," I said, rolling my eyes as I walked off.

The wall behind the bar was shelved with liquor bottles illuminated by blue lighting inside the paneling. The bar top was a rich mahogany, and underneath there were soft lights that lit up the stools and floor. I tried to capture the bartender's attention with my eyes as he mixed a cocktail for an older lady in a black hat. I heard a woman laughing so loud it reverberated off the walls.

"Over here!" someone shouted.

"That one is itching to mark me. See how he looks at me?"

"You are a new one."

Ignoring the conversations around me, my fingers tapped on the wood as I admired the display of alcohol bottles.

"Learner, I'm talking to you. It is impolite to not look someone in the eye who is speaking to you."

Who the hell?

I turned to my right and my eyes raked over a man with a cool and steady gaze. His inky black eyes appreciated every inch of me, and he was taking the scenic route.

"Bartender, vodka and tonic?" I asked. He nodded and gestured he would be with me in a moment.

I realized the man next to me was a Vampire as I spied another glimpse of him in the mirror. Unlike the stories, he did cast a reflection. I recognized him from when we came in; he was the one with noticeably long, straight hair who showed me his fang.

The very edge of his pinky brushed against my hand as he cupped his glass, and I felt no sensation of energy as I would with anyone else, including humans. I was unnerved and looked down at his drink to see the contents were not thick and red in color, but amber.

"Shy?"

"No, I'm just not interested in conversation."

"Well, then… that makes two of us," he implied suggestively as his tongue traced the corner of his lush mouth.

He inched closer and I stepped to the left, bumping into a pudgy woman sitting on the stool. The bartender was busy stirring a tall glass and I leaned over impatiently.

"I can guarantee that you would not forget a night with me."

This guy wasn't flirting, he was propositioning.

"That's a little direct. I'm not sure what kind of women you usually pick up, but I'm not one of them, so you're just wasting your time."

"I am a direct man, and let me assure you that no time would be wasted with me. What we can do together goes beyond any binding you have felt. I can make you curl from your hair to your toes."

My fingernails impatiently tapped on the bar. My first impression of a Vampire and I wasn't impressed; if they were all egomaniacs I wasn't going to have any problem staying away from them. Good thing they cast a reflection because if I didn't know better, I'd guess the mirrored ceiling above his bed was providing him with daily affirmations.

I turned my back to him and watched a blonde fuss with her hair as a very handsome man stepped closer as if his intent was to cage her in the corner.

"I've never seen eyes quite your color, would you mind if I had another peek?"

The woman next to me was listening with bated breath and her painted brows rose as she was anxious to hear my answer.

"Tell me, what brings you to the Red Door, if not for coupling?"

There was something disturbing about his eyes—I wasn't sure if they were naturally black in color or if his pupils were fully dilated, but it gave me the creeps. I caught a whiff of perfume when the woman next to me leaned in.

"Someone told me the cheese fries are out of this world."

His eyebrows lowered, perplexed.

I was leaning over the bar when a blast of wind came up behind me. I jerked my head back and saw Simon holding the Vampire's wrist. It hovered over my arm as if he meant to touch my hand to gain my attention.

"The lady isn't interested." Simon growled, but his tone changed abruptly to non-threatening pleasantries. "Hands off, like a good vamp. Run along now. Plenty of lovely lasses to go around. Or did I mean... asses? Either way."

The man merely shrugged and gave me a long, teasing smile as Simon released his grip. He found a new victim—a woman sitting alone at a table twirling a long straw in a short glass. For a fraction of a second, Simon gave a hateful look at the Vampire before he turned away.

A tap on the wood made me jump when the bartender set my drink down. "Oh, thank you." I nodded at him. He winked and went to another customer.

I took a fast sip as Simon leaned in. "I seem to keep coming to your rescue. You should stay away from those blighters—nothing but trouble."

I reached around and tugged at his collar. "Sure you don't have a red cape in there?" I asked facetiously.

"Let's find out, shall we?" His dimple winked and I took a short sip from my glass.

"I'm a big girl, Simon. I can handle myself. I would have put him in his place." I bumped the corner of a table with my hip as we walked back to our booth, spilling some of the drink on my wrist. Simon concealed a laugh.

"Did you flash over there? Justus said we aren't supposed to do that," I said, remembering his warning about public display.

Simon slipped his hands into his jean pockets and gave me a crooked smile. "What happens in Red Door, stays in Red Door. Breed-only club, there are exceptions to the rule."

My glass slid over to my spot at the table as Remi once again was on his feet, waiting until I was settled. Once he took his seat, his conversation with Justus continued. That man would undoubtedly get some exercise if he had lunch with the ladies' auxiliary.

Adam was unusually quiet and his eyes roamed around the room, observing some of the patrons. When they stopped just over my shoulder, I turned in my seat to see what caught his eye. A shapely woman with short blond curls stood in front of a tall, lanky man. Her hands were placed directly on his chest beneath his shirt, where I could make out a soft red glow.

"What are they doing?" I whispered to Simon, who took a quick stretch to look.

"Well *that's* completely inappropriate. Those are Sensors, they lift your emotions. Eh, they also sense the ones left behind, which makes them particularly good trackers," he said, facing front again. "Of course their specialty is recall." He took another disapproving glimpse. "They really should be doing that in private quarters."

The vodka passed my lips as Justus and Remi were laughing in their own conversation.

"In English?" I insisted.

Simon threaded a finger through his hair to enable him to see me more clearly through those glasses.

"They retain emotions. Ever wished you could relive that one great orgasm? Oh no, don't give me that shocked look, Silver. They can pull any feeling from you that you experienced and allow you to live it all over again. For the right price, of course. Because they store those feelings, they also sell them to others. But most go to them as sex traders. It can be fairly intense."

"Ohhh," I said, my lips making a round O. "Well, guess it cuts down on STDs."

Adam spit out some of his green swill, shaking his head.

I touched my fingers on the tip of my cold glass and slid the vodka toward him. "Here, need something to wash it down?"

He took the glass and Remi followed me with his eyes. Nothing went past him unnoticed.

"Silver, there is something you want to ask me," he said. "Please speak."

All eyes at the table shifted gears and rolled in my direction. I adjusted my skirt apprehensively. "What about the second Mage?"

"What second Mage?" Adam ground through his teeth before Simon cut him off with a raised hand.

Remi's eyes admired his empty glass before he replied. "I'm afraid the benefactor is where your concern should be. Samil plays an important role; I would be curious to know if the other potentials are like you. But the benefactor, gentlemen, that is who you need to find. He is playing with darkness. Silver, you will never be safe now that he knows what you are. He is powerful and protected."

"Who is he?" Adam demanded.

I took the drink from him and gulped down a swallow, feeling the burn as I swallowed my nerve.

"There was a guy who came in and stole my light every night. I don't know his name. I only know what he looks like, maybe what his energy feels like." I gripped the glass so tightly that I wondered if I had the strength to shatter it. "With Samil, I always knew what to expect. But with him…" I bit my lip as my mind flashed back to the basement during his nightly sessions. "I don't want to talk about it."

My fingers pressed into the table, reaching for the keys Simon had been playing with a few inches away. I curled the tips inward and pulled back my hand; as I did the keys jingled and began to slide toward me. When I heard a gasp, my attention diverted.

"What?"

Remi gave a knowing smile while Justus blurted out, "That's impossible. Silver, we can manipulate energy from living objects, but a Mage cannot move them."

"Ever? I thought you said everyone has a gift?"

"Not this kind."

"Try the glass," Remi suggested.

I raised my hand, focusing on my glass, willing it to move, but nothing happened.

"You see," Remi confirmed, "she only has the ability with metal. Although I suspect there may be limitations you will need to test."

"That could come in handy," Simon muttered.

"He could do it too, you know. The other Mage, after…"

Justus's hand went over his mouth and the crease in his eyebrow deepened; he had a habit of rubbing his chin whenever he was thinking. "You think he can retain that ability, or will it fade?" His head turned to Remi and his inquisitive voice was low.

"The energy would increase one's power, but the gifts rarely transfer. The retention, of course, is temporary. However, I wonder—" His voice cut off as he pulled his glass closer. "Gentleman, let's be aware of our surroundings."

Justus and Simon gave a nod as they withdrew from the topic. I realized they never used the word *Unique* and were careful as to how much detail was discussed—prying ears, I suspected.

Remi looked to Simon and leaned in our direction. "A piece of advice I would give you—look to Novis. He is very clever. I always sensed a little rebellion in him."

Justus let his hand fall on Remi's shoulder. "You're a trusted friend." He gave it a hard squeeze; Remi raised his glass to him and knocked it back before the waitress brought another tray of kryptonite.

We whiled away the rest of the evening in friendly conversation. There was one moment where I fell away into my thoughts, feeling hollowed out. Laughter pealed around me and Simon's hand suddenly squeezed mine.

I tapped on Simon's frames. "So, what's with the mirrored glasses?"

"Vamps. Got to watch out for those ones, love. They'll steal your secrets."

"I thought they just controlled your mind."

"Oh, humans and their movies! They can *suggest* you to do things—those who are weak-willed will comply while others will if just a small part of them wants to. A weaker mind is more susceptible to suggestion. Vamps can get you to talk; their eyes pull it from you. Not the kind of thing you want, someone invading your mind."

"They read minds?"

"No, only make you speak your mind, whether you want to or not. Their gaze is like a truth serum."

"So why didn't you make the rest of us wear glasses?" I made a circular motion with my finger between myself and Adam.

"We didn't come here for social mingling, did we? Leave it to you to wander off for five minutes and run into a vamp."

"What would have been the worst that could happen, him getting me to confess my disapproval for his tacky wardrobe that was channeling 1892?"

"I was thinking more 1915, let's give him the benefit of the doubt." Adam snorted. His face relaxed into one of the sexiest smiles I'd seen. He had classic features that were ruggedly handsome as his hand ran across his forehead. I liked the easygoing side of Adam.

Simon shifted in his seat and dropped his left arm behind me with the other on the table. "Vampires by nature can uncover secrets. All secrets have a price, some which others are willing to pay for. Not a respectable way to earn a living; I much prefer those who guard." He pinched my chin and softly said, "I don't think I told you before, but you look very smart this evening." I smiled and fumbled with a strand of hair.

Adam made a deliberate journey, sliding down the seat until he was directly in front of me; there was a silent showdown for my attention happening right before my eyes. While I knew Simon and Adam respected each other, it was also clear they perceived the other as some kind of a threat. And Simon never turned down a challenge… he was always in it to win it.

"Vampires trade information for money?" Adam asked.

"Humans trade for money. Other Breed, we're more… creative."

"So," I hinted playfully, "you didn't want him to plunder my secrets?"

Vying for my attention was sliding into dangerous territory. His mirrored gaze was lingering on me. Adam didn't look too comfortable with where our conversation was headed, but Simon was eating it up.

"Simon, I think he would have been sorely disappointed to have wasted his time with me. I'm afraid I don't have any good secrets worth giving up."

Simon's finger made a slow journey across my shoulder blades as his arm retreated back to his side. I shivered at his familiar touch. "Never underestimate the power of a good plunder."

He grinned and my body responded with nine million goose bumps standing at full attention.

"Well, what do we have here? If it isn't Justus De Gradi, in the living flesh," a voice interrupted.

My eyes rolled up to a hard-looking man somewhere in his forties. He had a silver tooth in the front and an almost albino appearance. Silence chirped around us and I glanced at Justus, who looked like he just saw a ghost. The man slapped Simon on the back with a gravelly smoker's laugh.

Simon's tone was leery. "Cedric. Been… well, not long enough."

The man laughed and Justus rose up from his chair.

"Let's make room; two of us were just leaving. Adam?" Justus looked over Adam to be sure he wasn't intoxicated. After the green swill and sip of vodka, Adam had been nursing on a glass of water all night.

"We'll catch you guys later. Remi, good to meet you." Adam leaned across the table with an outstretched hand and Remi deliberated a moment before he took it, suppressing a smile. Most

Breed did not shake hands—that was a human custom. I didn't know if Adam was aware or if he even cared.

Justus reached around and took his light jacket from the seat, draping it over my shoulders. "You'll need this. You really need to dress more appropriately for the weather." I slipped my arms into the brown sleeves, rolling up the cuffs so I could use my hands. The lining was warm like it had just come out of the dryer. One of these days I was going to ask Justus about that little trick.

Cedric appeared annoyed. "No, no, why don't they stay? No need to rush off so quickly. I'd especially like to chat with this one, is she new? Well of course she is. You can't keep the newbies all to yourself, Justus; that just wouldn't be gentlemanly."

I looked at Adam in time to see a small, black device being slipped in his pocket by Justus.

"Sit, Cedric. Tell us what prison let you loose this time." Simon's mouth curled to one side of his face as he sat back, defeated, looking like a man whose plans were ruined.

"Since when do they allow humans in here?" Cedric complained.

Justus put his arm around Adam, moving us away. "Keep her safe, we'll return later."

"She's always safe with me," Adam damn near snarled.

CHAPTER 27

"**Y**OU'RE KIDDING ME." I WAS three seconds away from calling a taxi as I stood there staring at a large black motorcycle. "Adam, I can't ride on one of those things." I was on a motorcycle once in my life. Back in high school, an old boyfriend saved up enough money and bought a bike. One night, he asked me to go for a ride with him. All my romantic notions about motorcycles were cast aside when he took perilous turns through the city streets at such high speeds that his intent was merely to scare me to death. I screamed for him to stop, but his silent laugh was drowned out by the motor. We broke up after that. Can't say the bike was the reason, but it sure didn't help his case.

"Well, you're going to... so hop on," he said, patting the seat.

"You drove all the way across how many states—on that? What about the Rover?"

"Broke down a month ago."

"Why does that not surprise me? Did it finally spit up a camel?"

Adam proudly placed his hand on the bars. "I like it, it suits me."

He was right, it really did. Despite my hesitation, I could imagine that Adam looked very mysterious and dashing on that bike.

I ran my finger along the seat. "Jesus, Raze, you sure you know how to ride one of these? Ever had a passenger?" Immortal or not, I was scared shitless. The idea of flipping over and tumbling down fifty feet of concrete sent shivers down my spine.

He handed me the helmet and threw his leg over the seat, mounting the bike.

"Trust me, you're in capable hands. Once you get this baby between your legs, you'll wonder why you ever doubted me."

"I bet you say that to all the girls," I mumbled, wrapping my arms reluctantly around him.

"Not that tight." He chuckled. "I have to be able to steer this thing, woman. Just hold my waist and let me do the rest."

Something told me he said *that* to all the girls too.

Adam was right—I was more than fine. Wind in my hair, the freedom I felt as we raced down the dark road, the roar of the motor, and most of all the feel of holding Adam and trusting him with my life.

I did. I trusted Adam with my life, and it wasn't something I took for granted. There was always an instant bond with us, a playful ease and a comfort like I hadn't felt with Justus or even Simon.

Twenty minutes later, we were home and I was so tired I could barely keep my eyes open. I changed into my sleep shorts and tank top, grabbed a bottle of vitamin water and crashed out on my sofa bed. When I woke up four hours later, I shuffled my feet into the living room with a mess of hair in my face.

"Wake up," I grumbled, tossing a pillow at Adam. He was splayed out on the sofa, still wearing his jacket, one leg on the floor and the other slung over the armrest. Poor bastard, he actually drank the green swill to the bottom, which was probably to blame. That might explain my sudden exhaustion too, even though I only had a sip. He groaned sleepily as I made my way down to the training room.

"What's up?" Adam asked, drifting down the stairs. He was palming his eye with one hand and fighting a yawn.

"You say you can fight; well I want to see it. Show me what you can do."

Without a word, Adam pulled out of his jacket and it dropped to the floor. "What do you want to see?"

A loaded question.

"I can demonstrate fight technique with weapons or hand-to-hand." He eyed the knives on the wall.

"Let's start with hand-to-hand," I said, walking to the center of the mat. "Justus hasn't really let me handle any knives outside of chopping up carrots."

He backed up a step. "Let's? I'm not fighting you—I said I'll demonstrate."

"Yes, you are." I folded my arms and narrowed my eyes. "You

need to respect what I am now, Adam. I've been training here for months with the master Bruce Lee himself—plus I have that nifty healing ability. So show me what you got. I promise I'll go easy on you."

His tone changed and his arms flew up. "Hold up, Justus fought you?" I could see the anger building and he paced toward me and paused for an answer. "You're telling me that you two were down here—"

"I won't use my abilities," I promised, crossing my heart and using my most innocent voice. "The pinner is the winner."

Adam stepped to the mat and eyeballed me. "Silver, I can't do this with you."

Faster than he could blink, I flashed over to the stairway and blocked it. "You're not leaving this room until you pin me."

Adam's eyes went wide as that was the first time he had ever seen me move like a Mage. At least, I'm pretty sure that's why he was looking at me the way he was.

His lower jaw punched out, he kicked off his shoes one at a time and threw them by the stairs. The socks were peeled off next and that left him standing barefoot in his jeans and white shirt as he flexed his muscles. Toned muscles that were losing their summer tan, but not their glorious shape. My knees almost buckled. *Damn him.*

Without warning, Adam reached for my ankle, trying to throw off my balance. My hand went to his shoulder and I flipped myself over his back, kicking him in the ass. He hopped, nearly falling to the ground, but caught himself and turned around.

"Nice move."

My toes pressed down as I stifled a smirk. Yeah, I was feeling a little badass showing off my moves with Adam. "I'm not without skills," I bragged.

Without warning, he came at me and nearly locked his grip around my wrist before I twisted around and moved behind him, elbowing him in the back. I was getting pissed because I could tell he was going easy on me.

"Quit pussyfooting around and hit me, Adam. I can take it, I'm a big girl. I want to see how you'll fight Samil."

"Woman, if you keep provoking me I'm going to pin you down and never let you up."

"Ooo, is that a threat or a promise? Or maybe it's just a wish."

He stalked forward, crossed his arms over his stomach, and stripped out of his shirt, tossing it to the side. Adam was intentionally distracting me by flexing his pecs; I knew this because of the smile that stretched across his face when I was stupid enough to look at them. He had been working out.

"Did he teach you to rattle your opponent with that mouth, or does that just come naturally?" he asked. I smirked, because I guess that was just my God-given talent.

When he threw a fist out, I blocked it with my arm—we went through several maneuvers with our bodies moving like a dance. I swept my leg forward to lock around his and throw off his balance, but he sidestepped over it.

I came at him doing a mix of martial arts moves, and he countered every strike until I slapped him in the face to throw him off.

Justus said the best way to win the advantage is the element of surprise and finding your enemies weak points psychologically.

It worked.

Adam was so stunned he almost looked ashamed. I seized the opportunity and leapt around him, kicking the back of his knees.

He started to fall but caught himself and swung his leg around, causing me to do a limbo move to avoid contact. I crouched, ready to spring up and knee him. But as I lunged forward, he pivoted around and inadvertently struck me in the face with his elbow. I saw tiny little stars for just a minute.

I was too close to him, so I went for his throat, not hitting too hard, remembering that he could not heal as we could. It momentarily stopped him as he gasped for air.

I took that chance to move away, but he unexpectedly turned and grabbed the back of my neck, tripping me up with his feet and slamming me against the mat. His body fell over mine, pinning me hard as we were face to face.

"Winner," he gloated.

We were both panting and laughing. I didn't even last five

minutes with him. My ego might have been bruised, but it put me at ease and stripped away some of the worry that I had been carrying over the challenge. His grip relaxed behind my neck as he touched my cheek where his elbow had struck, cursing under his breath.

Our chests moved together in one motion and I'd never felt more aware of his body against mine, feeling the weight of him. Feeling his life as our hearts slammed against one another.

Through my slightly raised shirt, I could feel his abs stroking against my stomach… this was too much intimacy for me to be in with Adam.

"Why are you challenging him?"

He delicately stroked my neck with the back of his knuckles. "I never fought for the right reasons."

"They can come up with another plan; it doesn't have to be this way. I can't lose my best friend."

"Is that all we are?"

"It's what I feel in my heart, don't you?" I felt a heartbeat quicken against my chest.

His fingers traced up my arm and found their way to my hand. I closed my fingers into a tight fist. "I can't touch you, Adam, not when I'm like *this*."

Whether it was hearing his name or the suggestion that I was charged up, Adam lost all control and gave me what was lacking the day we parted—passion. His mouth crushed over mine, devouring me with every stroke.

His tongue swept over my lips, requesting entrance, and when it was granted a fire sparked. A fire I knew shouldn't be there, one I wanted to extinguish… but I was curious. Adam truly was the perfect man, and maybe I was foolish to not give it a chance. I wanted to feel what it could be like to be with him, but internally I was so conflicted.

His hand slid down to the bare skin of my waist, fingers pushing beneath my tank top. I gasped and he moaned simultaneously.

Bracing on one elbow, Adam's lips never gave me the chance to have second thoughts. I was burning up all over and when I nipped at his lower lip, Adam groaned so deeply I imagined the noises he would make in the bedroom.

"Adam," I whispered, "This isn't right. We shouldn't…"

His warm lips brushed over my neck as he pulled my tank top up on one side. When his mouth came over my breast and pulled in the first teasing suck, his tongue swirled and I began to have second thoughts about my second thoughts.

Whiskers scraped against my skin, sending the most basic need to my very core. I concentrated on controlling my energy, but it was distractingly difficult. All I knew was that I had to keep my hands safely away from him, and not touching was torture.

Adam slowly melted down my body and I watched with anticipation as he bit down on the hem of my tank top. Eyes locked on mine, he dragged his body upward, lifting my shirt completely and running his chest across my body. Pleasure hit me like heavyweight boxer and I was almost knocked out in the first round.

Something triggered within me when he rubbed against my body; it was a feeling so primal that it felt natural. I almost growled in response and rubbed my cheek against his as I leaned up from the floor. There was no sense of amusement on his face. Seeing this side of Adam was electric—feeding every insatiable curiosity I had suppressed.

"Adam, wait—I'm serious, we can't do this."

He settled on top of me once more.

"Woman… let me love you," he breathed.

His slow, deep kiss sent me over the edge as he moved against me. I wanted desperately to touch him, to feel him, but was too afraid of what I could do. My body hummed like a generator, my fingers tingled, and I concentrated to keep it locked down.

All notions of stopping disintegrated when his hand moved down my shorts. His tongue stroked mine in the same rhythm that he stroked me with his other hand—slow, and deliberate. God, what if this was Adam's last night on earth—could I deny him this?

I gasped and cried out, writhing beneath him, and he responded by slowing the rhythm. When his lips broke away, his expression quickly changed.

He was looking at my eyes.

"Don't look." I slammed them shut and turned my head.

When I was charged up, my pupils widened and took on an appearance that looked like liquid silver rimmed with the green of my eyes. There was no explanation to this reaction, but Justus guessed it might have to do with the fact I was a Unique.

"Silver, look at me."

As he studied them, his breath began to slow. "Keep those on me, you hear?"

Adam's mouth fell to my shoulder where his teeth scraped over my skin and then I heard a zipper.

That was the moment that I disconnected.

I wanted Adam, but that sound took me to a place I didn't want to be. I struggled beneath his weight and my legs stiffened at the feel of hands tugging at my shorts. A cry pealed out of me like an animal screaming.

"What's wrong?" he nearly shouted, cupping my cheek.

I lost sense of my vision and my legs began to thrash, kicking wildly as my arms came down, hitting him everywhere I could. Hot tears streamed down my face and my body shook uncontrollably with energy I needed to release, but I was still in there somewhere and I knew I couldn't hurt Adam.

Kicking myself backwards, I met up with the wall and pulled my knees to my chest with my hands out protectively… threateningly.

He reached for me and I screamed.

Adam cursed and rose to his feet. I felt a lick of embarrassment for him seeing me that way. I was pissed off as hell that I couldn't have any normalcy in my life because of Samil. He seemed to creep up in my mind when he was least welcomed.

"I'm going to kill that sonofabitch!"

He hurled a bottle of water that was resting on a bench and it smashed against the wall, sending a spray of water to the floor.

An army of footsteps stormed into the room. Justus flashed at Adam, it didn't take much to figure out what happened with Adam's zipper down and my disheveled tank top.

He didn't put up a fight; Adam took those punches as if he deserved them before he threw a hard uppercut and knocked Justus off him.

"Why didn't you tell me what he did?" Adam roared so ferociously the vein in his neck bulged.

Simon flashed ahead and knocked Adam to the floor with a hard blow, pinning him while Justus stood dazed.

It was Simon who replied in anger.

"Could you not keep your hands to yourself? It's not even been a *day*!" Simon got right in Adam's face as he hissed through his teeth, "What did you think you were doing, human? You cannot be with one of us. You had no right to impose yourself on her! She is in no position to make these kinds of decisions so soon after the attack. What the *fuck* did you think you were doing?"

Simon's forearm pressed into Adam's neck so hard that Adam turned to the side, facing away. I heard short quick breaths and focused my attention on Justus, who crouched in front of me.

"Silver..." Justus curled his fingers around mine, which were shaking. There was no judgment or blame in his eyes. He lifted his brows in a nonverbal request for me to release my power. It nearly knocked him over, but he took a deep breath and steadied himself.

When emotions were high and there was an exchange of energy, you could taste the emotions from the other Mage like a flavor.

Justus was sampling fear and shame.

My body shook from the cold loss of energy. Justus leaned in and scooped me up in his arms. He hesitated for a moment, letting out a sigh of relief before he finally rose up.

"I'm *sorry*," I breathed.

"Shhh." He quieted me as we moved up the stairs. He cut Adam a punishing glare.

Simon was now sitting up, but Adam was motionless on his back with his arm shielding his eyes.

"It wasn't his fault—don't hurt him."

"Shhh." There was intentional warmth that was penetrating through his skin to mine until my shivers began to cease. The bedroom was dark and he placed me on the sofa, tucking a blanket around me. I ran my finger along the soft fabric and enjoyed the coolness of my pillowcase. Justus knelt on the floor beside me—left arm above my head on the armrest and the other one on the cushion. His warmth surrounded me and I realized that Adam wasn't home for me anymore—it was Justus.

"Give yourself time."

"I don't want him to die; he's my friend," I whispered. "He could *die*."

"And he's willing to; would you take that honor from him?"

I curled on my side to face him. By the wall was the faint flickering of a candle nearly spent. My fingers wrapped around his right hand and I pulled it to me as a child would hold a teddy bear or security blanket. He jerked a little, not expecting my gentle touch, but I held it fast between my hands and closed my eyes.

"I'll never understand why you have done so much for me."

While I had noticed how large his hands were, I had never really felt them—they were rough and strong, hands that could love just as easily as they could kill. I rubbed my long finger across his thumb and he settled on the floor.

"Remi called the other Mage the benefactor. What did he mean?"

"Whatever Samil is doing, he is not the one running the show. A benefactor would be one who is funding him. If he is collecting others who are made differently, we don't know the reason behind it or what he may be planning. There's always someone out there conspiring, Silver… someone up to no good. The more money they have, the more dangerous they become."

"I want Samil dead. I would fight him if I could." My heart quickened. "Please don't let me go back, it's the other one I'm afraid of. His beatings were brutal; I never felt pain like that before. He stole my light—they had some kind of a deal between them where he wanted me for himself."

Beneath my fingers, Justus's hand tightened into a massive fist and I felt the burn of his anger.

"He's stronger than he looks— dangerous—and in some kind of position of power, even Samil was afraid of him. I'm scared of what he could do."

A hand rested against my temple and his thumb slid down between my brows tenderly.

"Worry not, Silver. I am your Ghuardian and that means that I am your protector. I will never let him have you as long as I have watch on you. Sleep."

Drifting between the waking world and darkness, I heard voices in the distance.

"Is she okay?"

"Leave us."

A door closed.

Gentle fingers brushed through my hair, and continued to do so until I was out.

Adam was leaning in the fridge when I entered the kitchen, so I had a bullseye view of his ass. This was one of the few places in the house that ran electricity because of the appliances. Although I never quite understood the point since most days of the week Justus brought home burgers or barbeque. It was going to be my mission to have it running through the entire house except his bedroom by the time I was done with him. I suspected he just liked to get away from modern conveniences.

Then again, he had a sports car collection and a top-of-the-line garage.

The man confused me to no end.

"Hey." I sighed. "About last night."

"Don't say it; don't you tell me you're sorry," he said, waving a hand in the air. I spun around and fumbled with a package of gourmet coffee on the counter. "Well, I am."

"Silver, I was way out of line. I had no right. Not after what you just went through. I didn't know, but I should have kept my distance."

"Just forget it. It's past."

He leaned over the counter and combed his fingers through his hair. I wondered what he was thinking, if he regretted starting that up with me or if he only regretted that we didn't finish.

"Just try to forgive me, if you can."

"It's not your fault; we just got out of control. Must have been that kryptonite—I only had a sip and it knocked me out." I fished a bean out of the package and retrieved a cup from the cabinet.

Adam straightened his back and chewed on his bottom lip.

"You've had a hell of a year. I guess you have plenty more years coming, so I want to make sure they're easy on you, feel me?"

"Nothing is easy. But I want to learn how to fight. I think it's time I learned how to kick some ass for a change. I may never be on the same level as Justus because I'm not as physically strong, but I don't want to go through life not being able to take care of myself, you know?"

I placed my elbows on the counter and dropped the bean in the empty glass. It clattered, rolling around the bottom.

"Give me that," Adam scolded, taking the package over to the coffee grinder.

"I can't be serious with anyone right now; I'm not ready for that. I don't know if I ever was—I'm not a relationship girl."

My back was still to him and I rubbed my wrist with my thumb. What I really meant was that it was him specifically. Adam wanted to get far more serious than I would have been willing to go, and it wouldn't be fair to lead him on. He *was* a relationship guy, and I just wasn't there yet. I also had no intention of ruining the friendship we had.

"I know. But I'll still be here for you." Before I could say anything, he added, "And there isn't a damn thing you can do about it. It is what it is, woman."

"You take good care of me."

He came up from behind and crossed his arm around my shoulders, kissing me on the head.

"Someday, Adam, you're going to find someone who deserves you."

CHAPTER 28

"WHAT IF HE DOESN'T SHOW?" I looked out the car window nervously, a random urge to fly into the road and run like hell was suppressed.

"Silver, you try my patience." Justus stretched his oversized legs in the back of Simon's car.

"But what if he doesn't? They said that if he doesn't show then..."

The leather in his jacket creaked and I knew as much as he wanted to yell at me, he was biting his tongue given that I might break down crying.

"The Mageri have custody of him. We turned him in."

"Oh."

That was the other out—if Samil didn't show then I would be removed from his custody.

I tucked my hands under my legs to calm myself. Adam was in the front talking to Simon, but all I could hear were the tires rolling along the pavement before we took a turn and ended up on a dirt road.

The engine roared off and the lights went black.

Simon and Adam exited the car, leaving their doors open.

Justus had a hard look on his face as he leaned in. "Listen to me when I tell you that you will not interfere with anything that goes on tonight. There could be consequences. Just keep your mouth shut, no matter what happens."

"Is that supposed to be your best motivational speech? Because if it is, it sucks."

I cleared my throat and watched my Ghuardian run his palms down his thighs as if he were rubbing off his anger.

"I'll make sure this works out in your best interest, Learner."

"And his. If anything happens to Adam, I'll never forgive

you for dragging him into this." I got out and slammed the door for punctuation.

My combat boots crunched through the underbrush as we neared the clearing. You should dress for battle when appropriate and I sure as hell had no plans to dress for a funeral.

Through the trees, the figures of the Council became visible. My breath caught and my feet stopped working.

Samil was not facing the Council but facing us. The blistering menace of his gaze penetrated the darkness and seared my skin.

He lowered his head with a malevolent smile.

"*Ready to beg?*" I heard him ask in my mind.

"I'll never beg for you," I gritted through my teeth.

Adam turned and gave me a cold stare. Vengeance consumed him like a holocaust to which there was no salvation without the spilling of blood.

I wanted to rush into his arms because of that protective gaze and let him know how important he was to me. I wanted to tell him to turn back; I wanted to see him ride off in the distance on that big bike of his.

"Stay close," he said.

He positioned himself in front to block any view Samil had of me and took my hand from behind, leading me forward. Adam locked me against him tight as a safe, and when I tried to move away, his arm corralled me back in.

"Council," Justus greeted.

"This is a most unusual set of circumstances," the older man, Samuel, said with a curious tone.

It was a rule that no conversations would begin on the matter until all parties were present. That meant the Council detained Samil on trust without explanation of the circumstances.

"Explain to us, Samil, why your Learner is not in your care and we have you in our custody?"

His thin lips peeled back. "I was attacked without provocation by the Mage you see before you and *my* progeny was stolen from me. They cannot take what is rightfully mine, I demand justice!"

My forehead fell on Adam's back in anger. I stared at my boots and began to kick one of them as a riled-up mare might.

"With the challenge already set, what would be their intention if they know this would bring consequence?" Novis asked.

"I think it's because they know they cannot defeat me and wanted to use her as much as they could. They covet her. They tried to kill me; do our laws not protect a Mage whose life is threatened?"

"Your life was in no danger, Samil. Otherwise one of the parties present would be dead and we would not be standing here," Hannah interrupted.

I'd had enough. I tried to move around Adam when his arm reached to push me back. Shoving at it, I stepped out in the open.

"Justus, did you attack Samil and remove the Learner from his custody?" This time it was Sasha who spoke in her bright voice.

"I did. Ask me why," Justus replied.

"Of course," she laughed. "Do tell."

I could have slapped her.

"In her Creator's care, she was beaten, nearly raped, had her power prostituted out. That Mage stole her light with intent to end it. If we did not feel her life was truly in danger, we would not have interfered."

Which was a lie. If he knew a fraction of what was going on in that basement he would have come in, guns blazing.

Samil waved his arms. "Lies. Why would I want to kill my progeny? After all that it takes to create a Learner, what he says is ludicrous."

By his reply, he did not deny the other accusations, and it was noted on the faces of the Council.

"As you know, Justus, it is not our place to interfere with the relations of a Learner and their maker," Hannah began. I heard a low growl, but wasn't sure where it came from. "But I am interested in one small detail, Samil. You lent out your progeny for others to use? You are aware that we have laws against light stealing if it was against her will."

"She is mine!"

"That remains to be seen," Novis interrupted. "Learner, come closer."

I looked up at the young man as Justus and Simon parted

like the Red Sea. Closing the distance, I found myself side by side with Samil.

Novis watched me with eyes that sparkled in the dim light that emanated from Hannah as it illuminated the space around her.

A drop of rain splashed across my nose and I wiped it away.

"Silver, was his intention to end your life?"

"Yes." But that was not the whole truth. I could tell Merc sensed this by the way his body swayed in protest.

"Would you care to elaborate?"

"Only if I can ask a question."

I liked Novis. There was nothing condescending in his voice or expression when he spoke to me. He almost looked like Simon did when I would smart off to Justus. Of course, I knew it wasn't appropriate with the Council, but something told me that deep down he really did like my outspokenness.

"You may."

"Mage have been around for a long time, and on many levels are superior to humans only in that they have the advantage of time and power. You have more time to learn, to grow, to educate yourself. But in the short time I've been a Mage I can't help but wonder, why haven't we evolved?"

He didn't appear to know how to answer. A few of them looked between each other and I shook my head and went on with the story.

"Yes, he took me in that field to kill me. It wasn't until after he stole my light that he changed his mind and planned to keep me for himself—to use me. The only thing that man ever wanted to teach me was how to beg for mercy."

"You motherfuck—"

"Silence!" Hannah barked at Justus. I was so shocked I turned to look at him because Justus never swore like that around me. Maybe once, but it scared the life out of me.

That admission had released Samil from any charges he might have faced with the Council. This was no human court of law where attempted murder would hold up. Either you murdered someone or you didn't. What you intended to do held no importance.

Samuel mumbled impatiently, "Let's get on with this."

"Samil," Hannah began, "the Council presented an open challenge in which the rights to this Learner could be sought after by any challenger due to the circumstance of her creation. As defined, the power will be leveled down to the weakest, making fair the fight. Is there any here who would challenge Samil for this Mage? Speak up, or this Learner will be returned to her Creator."

"I challenge him."

Adam stepped forward and allowed the Council to appraise him.

Sasha snapped her head around and glared at Hannah. "He is not Mage," she nearly whined in her high voice, sounding like a teenager.

"No, I am not a Mage. My name is Adam Razor and I am challenging Samil to fight as a human. I want justice for what he did to her as a human and I will leave with nothing less."

"Well played," Samil bit through his teeth at my Ghuardian.

The Council recognized their gaping loophole that would allow a human to fight Samil. They set forth the rules and were bound by them.

"As a human, it is within my rights to challenge him to the death."

Adam removed a dagger from the inside of his jacket and snapped his wrist, sending the blade slicing through the air until it plunged into the earth. He bowed his head and silenced himself. Simon had coached him well.

But my focus was not on Adam.

I stared at the handle of the dagger and my throat was dry, my palms sweaty, and my heart raced like a hummingbird. That was never part of the plan. If Justus thought I was going to sit back and allow this to happen, he had another think coming. While I was pretty clear on the "to the death" rule, the weapon added a whole new element of danger to the equation that I was not prepared for.

I spun my head around and charged him with an accusatory glare. "A dagger? When the hell were you going to tell me? This is not going to happen," I hissed. But he already snatched an arm around me and clamped his hand over my mouth.

I struggled, kicking him in the shin. But his hand was firmly pressed and I wasn't even able to part my lips enough to bite his palm. So instead, I stomped on his toe with my heavy boot.

He growled in my ear, "Feel better?"

I smiled in the palm of his hand. Actually, given the circumstances, I kind of did.

"The Council accepts," Samuel said. "Merc?"

The large blond man took a slow stroll to Samil with eyes as ravenous as a lion.

"Samil, give me your hands."

"How do I know you'll give it all back," Samil hissed.

"Our word is law." Hannah looked annoyed at the accusation as her fingers began to tighten one of her hairpins that had come loose. "Do let us know if you wish to strike an accusation against the Council. We'll make a note of it."

As the transference of power began, the light became a strong aura that nearly burned my eyes with a white flash. The air crackled and I jumped when I heard a snapping sound like the crack of a whip. Samil doubled over and Merc stood up—his body was literally vibrating. Merc's eyes rolled to the back of his head and as he faced the night sky, he released a slow, satisfied breath.

Tiny droplets of water awakened the forest from its slumber. The trees stretched their arms and bowed to us. Merc pivoted around and stepped back into place. "It's done."

My wide eyes went to Samil, standing before me as a mortal. *I could kill him myself.*

"Silver," Justus whispered harshly in my ear. I didn't even notice that he was restraining me with his left arm wrapped around my waist. I had at some point lunged.

"Let go of me," I mumbled through his fingers, shaking my head wildly as he pulled me tight to his chest. I let out a long exhale through my nose as a dragon might, giving him all the warning he needed with my gaze. His eyes dropped to meet mine.

"Do nothing," he stressed in my ear before his hold released.

"Then let it begin," Hannah said.

She motioned the Council to move back and they formed a wide semicircle. Hannah sent out energy in the form of light to illuminate the clearing. That was her gift, or at least one of them.

Adam's feet took a vengeful journey toward Samil. He was

dressed in black pants similar to what Justus wore in training and a long-sleeve black shirt with his combat boots. Samil also wore all black, so between them they looked like shadows, only Samil's coloring was much paler, making him easy to identify.

Samil spat on the grass. "You have no idea what you just asked for, human."

"You look like a scrapper to me, without all that power."

"I've got hundreds of years on you. Don't waste your breath with such feeble remarks. I could disembowel you faster than you can say amen."

"Big words for a big pussy."

Samil threw off his coat in a single movement. "All this for a whore."

Adam moved so fast he could have been a Mage. His arm swung out, but not quickly enough.

Samil leaned back and struck out with his palm—Adam dodged it with ease.

Watching him from afar, I could appreciate his skills and truly see him as the fighter he was.

They cut a circle in the grass as they sized up one another… both eyeing the dagger a mere fifteen feet away. It was a game of who could get to it first; it was a game of keep-away.

When Samil rushed forward, the physical contact started. Adam ducked out of the way and struck Samil in the stomach with a hard blow. As Samil bent over, Adam knocked him hard in the jaw the way a street fighter would. I wanted to cheer and shout, but I didn't dare distract Adam.

My arms were hurting when I realized that I was being restrained. I glimpsed at Simon, who was very much into the fight as if he wanted to join. He was dripping with pride when Adam moved the way he taught him.

Samil cracked a hard fist against Adam's temple and blood sprayed out from the gash caused by the ring he wore. Some of it got on Sasha, who looked horrified as she tried to wipe her robe clean. The second strike went straight for the throat—fingers extended—and Adam staggered back, almost falling.

Samil went for the dagger. Adam snapped his leg out and made contact with Samil's ribs hard enough that both men fell to the ground.

The fog thickened with the steady rain and thunder crashed overhead, sending me straight to my knees. I had a metallic taste in my mouth and although I was always a little afraid of lightning before, I sure as hell wasn't warming up to it now.

Justus caught my arm and pulled me up, never taking his eyes from the fight. "What's wrong with you?"

"I'm okay—it's nothing."

Adam looked like a predator with arms spread wide and his body bent forward. Samil stayed low to the ground and I couldn't predict what would happen next. Saying I was on pins and needles would be an understatement—it was more like daggers and spears.

"Watch his hand," I heard Simon whisper in a quick voice.

I looked up and at first didn't notice anything, but then my eyes shifted to Samil. His hand was in the mud, raking up as much earth as he could in a slow drag. I surged forward with all my strength and was tugged back. "Learner, you cannot interfere!"

Samil swept his leg, knocking Adam off balance. Adam took some hard blows to the head, including one that rammed mud into his eyes. He bared his teeth and grimaced as Samil took the palm of his hand and shoved it in hard.

Not for long, because Adam hit him so hard in the jaw that I thought it cracked as Samil groaned and leaned back, holding his face.

Once again they were fighting, Adam blocking the attacks with complete concentration.

Blind.

His eyes squeezed shut and he grimaced in pain. Samil tossed a rock in the opposite direction, hoping to throw him off and gain the advantage by confusing him. In a blur of movement, they were in hand-to-hand combat once more.

My respect for Adam went through the roof as he was every bit as good fighting blind as he was seeing. Each chance he got, another fingerful of mud was scraped from his eyes. This went on for five minutes... ten minutes... I stopped counting.

Adam's hand came up fast and hit Samil under the chin, knocking him back. Before Samil even hit the ground, Adam took his wet shirt and rubbed his face until his vision was clear again, leaving a smudge of mud across his cheeks.

Once Samil hit the ground, he rolled and knocked Adam down, leaping on him. Each man held the throat of the other—Adam was on his back.

"What use could you have for a Mage? Humans and their stupid notions of nobility—I hope she is at least fucking you for this."

Adam's face tightened. "*Who* is he? What is the name of the other Mage!"

Angry hands squeezed Samil's throat with choking force.

"*Rot*, human," Samil spat.

I knew he got what he was looking for... a way into Adam's mind, a way to break down his defenses. He found the crack in the foundation and was exposing its weakness.

I pulled free from Justus and stood very still. The rain was chilling me to the bone, plastering strands of hair to my face. My teeth chattered uncontrollably, but I was hardly even aware that I was cold.

Samil growled through his clenched jaw, "You haven't had her, have you? What a pity."

Those jeweled eyes deliberately rose to mine and venom poured from my stare as a laugh escaped him.

"She tastes every bit as sweet as she looks." His tone was calculating as his gaze crawled up my body like a plague. He was slowly inching his way in, looking for Adam's breaking point.

"You sonofabitch!" Adam shouted.

In a swift move, Adam threw off Samil, who stood up and retaliated by kicking Adam in the ribs. I winced when I heard a bone snap.

His pain was my doing.

I wiped the rain from my brow with my trembling hand.

Samil strolled over to the dagger as if he were already the victor. He gave a nod to the Council as he pulled the handle and unsheathed the blade from the muddy earth.

Bright red blood poured from his nose and forehead. Most of the Council looked on with bored interest.

Bastards.

Samil stalked in my direction with Adam between us, holding the knife at eye level to be sure he had my utmost attention as the tip of the blade waved at me. "You should have begged."

A surge went through me when I threw my arm out and the knife suddenly plucked free from his hand flew into mine.

Sharp end in, of course. In those moments, I knew it was just a regular knife, not a Stunner.

I might have made a sound, maybe shouted, but it was all a blur. I didn't even bother to remove it as I pulled back my arm, aimed, and sent it flying back at my enemy.

Samil's expression went to shock as it penetrated his leg. I had never thrown a knife that distance, but I had to give myself credit where credit was due. At least I hit my intended target and not a tree.

I knew I had broken the rules, not that those particular rules were ever verbally said in front of me by the Council. Nevertheless, I was prepared.

But not quite prepared for what I saw next.

Samil pulled the knife from his leg and sailed down on Adam, planting it firmly into his chest. He never once took his eyes off me.

Adam's mouth opened wide in horror as the knife sank in to the hilt.

"No!" I screamed. It was as if the world were moving in slow motion. "You can't do this to him; I won't let you!"

Adam turned his chin so that I saw him more clearly. I saw him more clearly than I ever had since the day we met. A man who gave me everything and asked for nothing. That's when I lost all feeling and my knees gave in, sending me to the wet mud.

"Little girl, this is the price of disobedience!" Samil took a few steps in my direction. "Look at your human now—did you think you could win?" He laughed. "He is but a weak speck of nothing. Now you will live with that speck on your conscience for the rest of your days."

My hand smeared across my face as I wiped away strands of

wet hair from my cheek. I would never go back to him. I had a few remaining moments to decide what I needed to do. I felt hopeless and lost to a fate I did not choose.

Samil's eyes went wide and his mouth opened in silent surprise. He lifted his arms and his knees buckled, sending him to a hard fall. When he fell to his knees, it was Adam who stood behind him, holding the knife.

The knife he pulled from his own chest. The knife he used to cut the throat of my maker.

My Creator collapsed, trying in vain to stop the blood from pouring out of his jugular as he crawled on the muddy earth.

Adam did something unexpected when he grabbed Samil by the hair and straightened his head to face me, opening his wound even more. He bent over and the words that came from his mouth were filled with vengeance.

"Look at her! I want her face to be the last one you ever see." His voice weakened, becoming raspy and thick with blood. "You lose."

Samil was on his way to meeting his maker and I hoped he was as big a sonofabitch as Samil was. His eyes glazed over, becoming dull, his skin paled even more than it already was, and Samil took one final gasp before hundreds of years of wasted living fell facedown in the mud and died.

Adam stood the victor. But he didn't stand for long.

CHAPTER 29

I NEVER REALIZED HOW FRAGILE LIFE was until it shattered before me. Hope dissolved, satisfaction decomposed, and nothing remained but hollow victory.

Samil was dead.

The rain tapered off and a pool of blood mixed with the wet earth. There was complete stillness among the Council.

"Adam," I cried, running to his side. There was no hug, no kiss of victory, not even tears. My only concern was his injury. I knew that Mage could heal each other, but I did not know if our magic worked on humans.

Adam pressed his palm where the knife had gone in to stop the flow of blood. His life was escaping him with each beat of his heart. My hands went to cover the opening in his chest.

"It's okay, I hardly feel a thing." His ragged voice chuckled. "S'not so bad." He lightly touched my lip with his thumb and tenderness filled his smoky brown eyes.

"You're going to be fine; you just need a doctor." I sobbed. Composure was no longer something I could hold—it was as heavy as a glacier and all my emotional walls tore down. He smoothed away my wet hair and fell to his knees.

"Adam!"

My arms cradled his head as I looked to Justus. "Help him!" My frustration spiked as Justus and Simon stood motionless, eyeing the Council. Adam's breathing sputtered out, a mixture of air and blood.

Turning to the Council, I begged. "Please help him..." My eyes streamed with hot, salty tears that ran into my mouth and I could taste the pain. I looked down again. "Adam, hang on—do you hear me?"

Hannah sighed impatiently. "Mage, let your mortal die, it is his time."

"Yes," Merc said. "Do not let the wailing of a woman be the last thing he hears."

I shut them out, because if I allowed myself to entertain the idea of truly hearing their words I would have literally snapped out of my skin.

That beautiful masculine face cupped in my hands was the only thing that anchored me.

"You shaved," I said, stroking his jaw, attempting a smile as tears spilled.

He smiled and looked up. "You're always telling me and I never listened. I clean up pretty good, huh?"

Adam leaned on me when I brought my lips to his head and cried through my whisper, "Please hold on; it's not supposed to end like this."

My grip on him became possessive as I stood there with the first man who ever truly cared for me, bleeding out his life all over me.

"Silver," he said softly against my jacket. His face peered up and I wiped away the mud on his cheek with my thumb. "You're free now. It was worth it."

All tension released in the lines of his brow; it was a look of relief, a look of someone who had reached the end of a long journey.

I wanted to yell at him, to tell him that I would have taken it all back if it meant that he would live. But I knew that would take away his honor, and if he was going to die in front of me, I wanted him to have that, if nothing else.

"The human has won the challenge." Hannah moved forward with the rest of the Council closing in to surround us. "He fought remarkably well."

"Can he be healed?" I shouted, more than asked.

"I'm afraid our healing powers do not transfer to humans, it would kill him, to be certain."

Adam slipped through my arms and fell to the ground. Every breath was a struggle but his eyes were alert as he watched. He was drowning in his own blood, and I had to sit and watch while the Council toiled over their formalities of conversation.

"Does the victor gain nothing?" I boiled in anger.

"We cannot transfer Samil's energy to him."

"He was willing to die for my honor, no strings attached. Adam had nothing to gain from this; he wasn't trying to acquire power, or even me. He is a man of worth!"

My voice cracked as I screeched out the last bit. I shut my eyes as my mouth broadened in pain, a pain I could no longer shovel away with a hardened face. Random drops of water fell into the puddles, the wind blew, and a small rabbit poked his head out from the tall grass.

"I would like to know, Learner, how it is you moved that blade." Merc stood with folded arms and a thought flashed in my head of driving that knife into him.

"*What are you?*" he whispered in my head.

Tension filled the air, sending tiny needles over my entire body. I could almost feel Samil's power rolling through Merc, and he was reveling every moment of it, for as long as he had it. I don't think he was even aware that he put his thoughts in my head, something only Samil could do. I only hoped he and Sasha hadn't conspired, I couldn't help but distrust political figures and wouldn't put it past them to work together to become all-powerful. Frankly, what was to stop them?

"Council, if you would—"

"Silence, Justus. I was not speaking to you." Merc's shoulders went back in a show of authority. "So tell us, Learner… are you a hybrid?"

What kind of question was that? Who gave a shit?

I heard Adam draw in a gasp and all focus shifted.

"There must be something you can do!"

"No, Learner. That is the price for taking the life of a Mage."

"But he is *not* a Mage, it is not his law, and none were broken! His death should not be a punishment. If you removed the core light from Samil, then he was human and not Mage. They fought as humans."

"And they shall die as humans," Merc stated with little feeling. "We have lost one of our own tonight—a Creator. That is not a loss to be taken lightly."

"Fuck your loss," I snarled.

"Novis," an English accent spoke with genuine respect. My head cocked around to see Simon focused on the youngest member of the Council. "Do you not find Adam to be a… worthy warrior?"

His question was pointed, and there was subtext that I couldn't see.

Novis raked his sparkling eyes over Adam, quiet in his thoughts. He brought his smooth hand up to his chin pensively; his eyes had such a reflective quality it reminded me of moonlight on a river. He took a couple of steps and turned to address his peers.

"We set a challenge and a door was left open by not defining our rules more explicitly. That aside, a winner prevails and we are not able to fulfill our obligations to reward him. I have considered all that has been discussed, and what I have witnessed. I see a great potential in the human; how rare it is to challenge to the death for principle and honor without seeking any personal gain."

Novis looked over Adam with admiration. How young he seemed. His eyes were free-spirited but wise. I couldn't imagine how old he was. Twenty years? Two thousand years? Did it matter?

"His loyalties are strong, as are his skills. It has been a long time since I have witnessed a worthy battle and one against a man with years of acquired technique under his belt."

There was a pause as Novis nodded his head. "It is my decision, as a Creator, that I would offer him the life of a Mage, should he choose it. While we have lost one of our own this night, perhaps a renewed life will be a fair trade."

"He cannot do this!" Merc raged.

While Novis was dwarfed by Merc's overwhelming physique, he faced him directly.

"You have no say in this Merc, and you know it. This is my decision alone to make."

"Novis, you are a fucking fool if you do this. It is irresponsible to bring in a new Mage without knowing his character."

Sasha snorted and shuffled her feet.

Samuel waved a hand. "It is within his right. He may be Council, Merc, but remember that a Creator retains certain rights and thus—we cannot interfere. As for his character, I think we have seen enough of it tonight to know it is not in question."

I let out a shocked breath that one of the Council members was also a Creator.

But Adam, a Mage? This was not the ending I had imagined. They were asking Adam to choose between life and death, and life also meant death, the death of his former life. My head was spinning. The offer that Adam was receiving was to become the same thing that killed his sister—his enemy.

Novis approached Adam and knelt before him. Adam propped himself up, short on time but long on bravery. Novis crouched to look at him more directly.

"Human, I give you a choice. If you are willing to accept a gift I have to offer you, then you will be granted the life of a Mage. As such, you would be a Learner under my custody and therefore obedient to my teachings and rules. There are no exceptions to this. You will only be independent upon my approval, and that time will only be of my choosing. Until then, you remain in my care. We have laws, a way of life that will become your way of life. This will mean your former life will be no more. You will sever your attachments and relations to others as you will not be able to expose them to our world."

Novis watched Adam for reaction but the only movement was the blood that ran between his fingers.

I felt sick.

Whatever he chose would be of my doing. Whatever regrets he had—I would be to blame. Justus and Simon watched with bated breath. Simon shot a satisfied glance at Merc, who looked ready to snap.

"Your time grows short, human. This gift is a great honor, not to be taken lightly or with haste." He laced his fingers together and tilted his head. "Breed life is a difficult one, far beyond anything you have experienced. I see potential in you, rarely seen in that of your kind. A Creator chooses wisely—there is nobility within you I find most appealing. It is evident there is a military background, which has shaped you with skills, obedience, and leadership."

While Adam didn't reply, he gave a single nod.

"This is a choice selection. However, consider that your life as you know it will no longer be—you will be crossing the Rubicon. If you lose consciousness or die, it ends. As you are willing to die before us for honor alone, I see you as a man who would not take his choices lightly. Think a moment, and let me know how you decide."

Adam motioned me over and I crawled to wrap my arms around him. His lips pressed to my ear, whispering words so softly they were only meant for me.

"Of my own free will I do this, Zoë."

Zoë. He said my human name, a person I was no more. Those would be the words to forever haunt me. Part of me knew what he meant, that he wanted to give me peace of mind not to blame myself that he chose this life because of me. And yet, there was something else in the undertone that stilled me.

No one could ever know what a difficult choice this truly was for Adam. He was choosing to be something that literally smashed his life apart when the other half of him was murdered.

Someday I would ask him about this, and the meaning behind his words.

Adam offered me peace. It broke my heart, every last bit of it.

"You'll make a fine Mage, Adam," I whispered.

Then I walked away.

"I accept," he sounded clearly.

"Then it shall be done. You will be formally introduced to the Council in due time."

Novis sat down on his knees and commanded Adam to lift his palms.

It is a rare thing to be witness to the creation of another Mage, and I was seeing it with new eyes. Novis joined their fingers and poured his power into Adam until he fell back. Adam was winded, but his breathing had improved. It was a familiar process I remembered all too well.

Marinating, Samil called it. I suspected the transference was a calculated exchange of energy prior to the actual insertion of core light. There were two more exchanges before it was done.

It ended with a loud crack that ripped through the night, through my being—the sound of the first spark. One that sent chills up my spine, and Justus placed a calming hand on my shoulder.

It was done. As it was meant to be—willingly.

Their hands remained clasped, fingers intertwined; it was a moment between Creator and progeny that was quite beautiful. Adam was rich with the new power, saturated in it.

A delicate smile crept across the face of Novis as he gazed down into his progeny's soft eyes.

Adam's eyes resembled his Creator's—sparkling light.

Novis rejoined his position beside the Council with Adam following obediently behind—healed. While Adam did not die this night, the part of him that I loved so much did. The Adam I loved: barefoot on his rickety porch feeding the birds, the photographer… the human. My Adam.

Adam leaned in behind Novis and whispered quietly. Novis was brimming with pride as he stood beside his progeny, listening. A pride I had never seen, nor felt, upon my own making.

Novis spoke. "As Silver is now without her Creator, her care will transfer over to her Ghuardian until such time as he chooses to release her."

Justus placed his hand across my back but did not speak. I felt like I owed Novis. Whether I liked it or not, he saved the life of someone I held close to my heart.

"The Council will order her back to measure her abilities. Justus, we hope that you will nurture her talents to draw out any special gifts she may have. All Mage must be documented in our books within the first year with any discovered abilities. Should any new arise after the fact, we will require you to provide that information to us. This also includes the display we saw this evening. If there is anything you have not revealed, you will do so at such time. To conceal from the Council in the official record keeping will result in severe consequences." He shifted his gaze to the Council.

Hannah gestured toward the body in the field. "We will have a ceremony. Collect his remains, Merc."

Merc threw the body over his shoulders and followed behind the other members. When they reached the edge of the clearing, Adam looked over his shoulder and a smiled curved up his cheek.

And then he was gone.

Justus snatched my hand and I knew I was in for another scolding. As my Ghuardian, it was his duty to learn me, train me, and reprimand me. But I jerked free and ran a few long strides before falling on my hands. I choked, coughed, thought I was going to be sick, but I just stared down at the mud. Adam's blood was all over me.

"I didn't want that for him. Why Simon... why?"

"Because it was the only way he could live, and I know you would have regretted it more if we had not given him that choice. We had discussed this as a possibility, Silver. It came as no surprise this evening. You mistake our lives for a punishment, and that can be blamed on your maker. It is a blessed life we live."

I rubbed my nose on my sleeve, disgusted with my pitiful display. I stood up, took a calming breath, and walked to the car. I was covered in mud and rainwater, so it was a relief that we took Simon's car, which was an old, black, two-door GTO. I would need to be wrung out like a wet sponge before I got in one of Justus's cars, if not strapped to the hood.

Oh, and I'm sure he would have liked that too, given the way I defied his orders this evening.

I jumped in the back behind the passenger seat and cursed as I melted into a comfortable position. Simon and Justus got in and the engine revved up.

"We're cracking open your oldest bottles and we're all going to get pissed! The bastard is dead; I cannot bloody well believe it!"

He slammed his fist on the wheel and screamed out a victorious cry as the car flew into reverse. "He moved well, didn't he? Just like I taught him. Cept' for that little bit in the end where he got himself killed, but overall I think he put on a damn good show."

Justus, on the other hand, was a little more reserved on the enthusiasm. "I want to go to his house to collect her things later; we might find clues to the identity of the other Mage. I want to know who he is and what he's up to."

"Agreed," Simon nodded. "But I have one rule tonight and that is we're not discussing anything depressing. This is going to be a night of celebration, so unpop that cork from your arse and put on your party dress, you morose bastard."

Simon cocked his head excitedly and winked at me.

"Simon, turn the heat up will you?"

My jacket was made for warmth but not for rain—it was more of a sweatshirt, which was now soaking wet. Water and mud covered my legs and ran down into my shoes. I felt the squishing as I wiggled my toes and my feet were starting to itch.

Screw this.

"Ghuardian, roll down your window. Please."

He minced me with his look but complied. The icy air blasted across my wet body and, not able to stand it any longer, I peeled my jacket off and tossed it out the window. Next came the boots—one at a time. The second one bounced off a tree and hit the side of the car.

"What the bloody hell, Silver?" Simon gave me a curious glance. "You realize someone is going to find those and think there was a murder." He paused and laughed like a hyena. "On second thought..."

"Silver, I bought those," Justus said. I knew he was disappointed that his thoughtful gestures were now draped across a bush. He liked buying my clothes; it was the one way he knew how to show his affection for me.

"If you want 'em, go get 'em. They're covered in blood and I don't want any bloody thing on me that reminds me of this night. No pun intended, Simon," I added as I caught his humored eye in the rearview mirror.

"Are you done or will you be stripping off more?" Justus asked.

"Please say yes," Simon murmured.

Without my response, his window rolled up with a squeak.

I was numb. Not just emotionally, but my skin was so wet and clammy that I rubbed my arms fiercely to generate warmth. They were still slick with water and when I looked closer in the interior light I saw dark streaks. Blood.

I dropped my forehead against the seat in front of me, teeth chattering. "Heater?"

Had I known it was going to rain I might have dressed for it, or maybe not. For some reason my lack of planning when it came to attire really provoked Justus, and I enjoyed my petty torments.

I groaned in misery as the vent was blowing cool air over my already frozen body.

"Will I see Adam again?"

"Yes. Novis is a respectable chap. We do not imprison our Learners, do we Justus?"

"How did you know Novis would do it?"

Simon replied with a little cockiness, "It's what I would do if I were him. Novis is intelligent, and I knew that while he hadn't made a progeny in a very long time, he wouldn't pass up this opportunity. He's one of the few who is very selective and it was strategically a good move on his part. Someone with Adam's background can be an asset—the Breed tend to be very closed off in many ways. You know Justus," he trailed off, "we also need to have a night out. Maybe a welcome to the Mage party and invite Adam and Novis—good opportunity to sharpen our connections."

"Hey, I didn't get a party."

Simon purred, "Now, love, what do you call that night on the dance floor?"

"Scandalous?"

I loved the sound of his laugh and I closed my eyes to let it warm me. When I heard a deep creak of leather I sat up and flinched. Justus was turned completely around in his seat, staring at me.

"What?"

"I smell blood."

"Well it's a good thing I don't have my monthly—"

His seatbelt clicked open and Justus crawled through the tight space between the seats, looking ridiculous. He was way too tall to be moving around in such a confined space. Those athletic legs got tangled up in the front as he fell against the seat. One foot kicked Simon in the face and I hid my laugh.

"Bloody hell! A man is trying to drive here. Hard to keep the passengers alive when one of them is crawling around in the car like a moose. Could've run off the road and slammed into a tree and then what? Yeah, lying in a field for days trying to heal while animals gnaw on us, that's what..." He rambled on.

"Let me see," Justus insisted.

He turned my hand palm up and blood pooled from the gash. I shrugged; I was immortal after all, so I yanked it back and closed my fingers.

"You bleed."

"I'll bandage it when we get home. I promise I won't bleed all over your studly car, Simon. I just need to get warm and I'll be all right." My limbs stiffened as I stretched them.

Simon glanced around. "Don't worry, love, won't be the first drop of blood spilled in here. Justus, why don't you tell her about the time you thought you could jump on a moving truck?" He snorted and turned the wheel as the car hit the main road.

"Why are you so stubborn," Justus asked, pulling out of the jacket he tossed in the front seat. He also was rain soaked; small droplets clung to him in various places around his neck and lashes.

"I take after my Ghuardian." I grinned.

Justus reached over and brushed back my wet hair, coaxing me gently to lie across his lap.

My Ghuardian draped his arm over me and I felt his warmth move across my body as if he were the sun warming cold waters on a hot summer day. I thought of the tattoo on his back and it made perfect sense.

He was the sun... my sun. He was the center of my new life and I basked in his light and protection. My eyelids sank heavily and his hand rested over mine.

Despite what I had told him—my hand was healed by his magic. Justus made me whole again.

CPSIA information can be obtained
at www.ICGtesting.com
Printed in the USA
LVOW12s1025060217
523337LV00001B/13/P